KISSING THE COUNTESS

Without a word, Alexander dropped the cue and put his arms around Victoria. He lowered his head, his mouth covering hers in a kiss that drugged her senses and made the world fade away.

Victoria savored the sensation of his mouth slashing across hers. She pressed into the kiss, losing herself in it, surrendering her whole being.

His tongue caressed the crease between her lips, seeking and finding entrance to her mouth. Alexander groaned when she touched her tongue to his. Tentatively at first and then growing bolder, Victoria pushed her tongue past his lips to explore his mouth, mimicking his every move.

Leaving her lips behind, Alexander sprinkled kisses across her temples, her eyelids, her throat. He dropped his hands from the small of her back to her buttocks and held her against him.

Victoria moaned, feeling his hardness pressed against her. She entwined her arms around his neck and melted into him . . .

Books by Patricia Grasso

TO TAME A DUKE

TO TEMPT AN ANGEL

TO CHARM A PRINCE

TO CATCH A COUNTESS

Published by Zebra Books

TO CATCH A COUNTESS

PATRICIA GRASSO

ZEBRA BOOKS
KENSINGTON PUBLISHING CORP.
http://www.kensingtonbooks.com

ZEBRA BOOKS are published by

Kensington Publishing Corp.
850 Third Avenue
New York, NY 10022

Copyright © 2004 Patricia Grasso

All Kensington titles, imprints and distributed lines are available at special quantity discounts for bulk purchases for sales promotion, premiums, fund-raising, educational or institutional use.

Special book excerpts or customized printings can also be created to fit specific needs. For details, write or phone the office of the Kensington Special Sales Manager: Kensington Publishing Corp., 850 Third Avenue, New York, NY 10022. Attn. Special Sales Department. Phone: 1-800-221-2647.

Zebra and the Z logo Reg. U.S. Pat. & TM Off.

First Printing: June 2004
10 9 8 7 6 5 4 3 2 1

Printed in the United States of America

CHAPTER 1

England, 1814

"Teach me how to flirt."

Eighteen-year-old Victoria Douglas gazed out her bedchamber window at her uncle's, the Duke of Inverary's, country estate. Hearing her sisters' laughter, Victoria smiled and walked across the chamber to where they sat on the chaise near the summer-dark hearth.

Twenty-year-old Angelica was marking an *L* on the soles of the left feet of Victoria's new shoes. Nineteen-year-old Samantha was browsing through the morning *Times*.

Victoria knew her sisters were teasing her. "What is so amusing about my wanting to learn to flirt?"

"Why do you want to learn to flirt?" Angelica asked, without looking up from her task.

"Aunt Roxie had one of her otherworldly visions," Victoria told them. When her sisters looked up at her, she rolled her blue eyes heavenward. "Apparently, I am destined to marry an earl and a prince, not necessarily two different men, though. I want to be ready to charm him."

"Why do you need to charm him if you are already destined to marry?" Samantha asked.

Victoria became serious. "I need to overcome handicaps like my red hair."

"Your hair matches your personality," Samantha told her.

"I wish I had your black hair or Angel's blondeness. Men adore blondes," Victoria said.

"Count your blessings," Samantha said. "You could be bald."

"Did you know I always wanted Samantha's or your hair color?" Angelica asked, picking up another shoe to mark with an *L*.

Samantha laughed. "I always wanted to look like either of you."

"I suppose no one is ever satisfied with what they've been given," Victoria said with a smile. Her smile drooped, and when she spoke again, her voice mirrored the desperation she felt. "I can't tell left from right. I'll never read the *Times* because I can't read, write, or cipher. If I knew how to flirt, I could find a gentleman and marry him before he realizes I'm stupid."

When her sisters stared at her in surprise, Victoria felt a hot blush rising on her cheeks. She couldn't imagine why her frustration surprised them. They had known her problem for years, but knowing and understanding were different things. Her sisters could never understand her frustration because they *could* read, write, and cipher.

"You are *not* stupid," Angelica told her.

"Something prevents you from learning," Samantha added.

Victoria forced herself to smile but was unable

to mask the pain in her voice. "That something is commonly referred to as *stupidity.*"

When both sisters opened their mouths to argue, Victoria held her hand up. "Most people are stupid because no one bothered to teach them," she said. "I cannot learn in spite of being taught. My *p*'s look like *q*'s and my *b*'s look like *d*'s, not to mention my sixes and nines getting confused." Her voice rising with her emotion, she cried, "You see a dog bark, but I see a bog dark."

"Everyone has a weakness," Samantha told her. "I limp from that carriage accident."

"I would switch my stupidity for your limp any day of the week," Victoria replied.

"You have so many talents," Samantha argued. "You play the flute beautifully, and your *joie de vivre* is contagious."

"What is that?" Victoria asked.

"Joie de vivre is joy of life," Angelica answered, and then shifted her gaze to the pile of shoes still needing to be marked with an *L.* "How many new pairs of shoes do you have?"

"His Grace and Aunt Roxie bought me an extensive new wardrobe, complete with shoes and other accessories," Victoria told them, wandering back to the window. "A trousseau without a husband. They're hoping I'll soon meet a suitable gentleman and marry."

Victoria stared out the window. Her brothers-in-law, the Marquess of Argyll and Russian Prince Rudolf, were practicing golf on the large expanse of lawn behind the rear gardens.

"Your husbands are golfing," Victoria called over her shoulder.

"Is Rudolf swinging those clubs near the children?" Samantha asked.

"No."

"What about Robert?" Angelica asked.

"Sweeting and Honey have taken the children closer to the house," Victoria answered, and then turned around to smile at them. "Both of you gave birth to twins within a year. Do you think I'll have twins, too?"

"Having a husband would help," Angelica replied, marking the last shoe with an *L*.

"Rudolf's brothers will be arriving tomorrow," Victoria said.

"Aunt Roxie invited Alexander Emerson for the weekend," Samantha said, without looking up from the *Times*.

Victoria grimaced. "Alexander Emerson is so boring."

"Why do you say that?" Angelica asked.

"He is always so serious," Victoria answered. "Rudolf's brothers are much more fun."

Samantha looked up from the paper. "Are you developing a fondness for Prince Stepan?"

Victoria noted her sister's concerned expression but had no idea what it meant. She glanced at Angelica who wore the same concerned expression.

"Stepan and I are friends," Victoria told them. "Like cousins."

"We'll teach you to flirt, and you can practice on Alexander Emerson this weekend," Angelica said.

"That's an outstanding idea," Samantha agreed, glancing at Victoria. "If someone as serious as Alex succumbs to your flirting, then you'll have no problem with any gentleman."

"Alexander Emerson is a tad elderly, don't you think?" Victoria asked.

"Twenty-nine years is hardly at his last prayers," Angelica replied.

"The Earl of Winchester is considered quite a catch," Samantha told her.

"Alex's title and wealth have more than a few mamas pushing their daughters in his path," Angelica added.

Victoria had never thought about Alexander in that way, but her sisters' words had her seeing the earl in a new light. "I'll bet all those mamas would be green if they knew the Earl of Winchester was spending the weekend in the country where there was an available young lady, albeit a stupid redhead."

"If you flirt with Alexander," Angelica warned, "you can never admit you're only practicing."

Samantha nodded. "Men have sensitive feelings about things like that."

Victoria gave them a mischievous smile. "As the weekend progresses, you can tell me if what I'm doing is correct."

"That's a good idea," Angelica said.

"Well, sisters, I'm ready to begin," Victoria said. "Tell me what to do."

"Stare at Alex intensely," Angelica told her. "When he catches you looking, hold his gaze for a second or two longer. Then drop your gaze shyly and blush."

Victoria burst out laughing. "Alexander isn't going to believe I'm shy."

"Stand *very* close to him when you are speaking," Samantha said. "Look at him with adoration in your eyes."

"How do I do that?" Victoria asked, puzzled.

"Imagine that he has conquered the world and placed it at your feet," Samantha told her.

Victoria couldn't suppress her bubble of laughter. She couldn't imagine Alexander Emerson or any other man placing the world at her feet. She wasn't exactly Cleopatra.

"Let him hold your hand," Angelica said.

"Let him kiss you if he wants," Samantha added.

"Not too much, though, or he'll think you're fast," Angelica added.

"How much is too much?" Victoria asked, completely confused. She had never even kissed a man. How could she possibly know these things?

"You'll know," her sisters said simultaneously, and then looked at each other and laughed.

"Do *not* let him touch you anywhere private, or you'll be ruined," Samantha warned.

"Alexander must be very smart," Victoria said, her confidence waning. "What should I say to him?"

"Engage in light-hearted conversation," Angelica said. "If he says something naughty, say something naughty back."

"Ask him a question or his advice," Samantha suggested.

"Advice about what?" Victoria exclaimed, knowing she was destined to fail. "Maybe I should ask him how to flirt."

"Why, Tory, that is a brilliant idea," Angelica said with a smile. "If Alex is teaching you how to flirt, he won't be aware that you're attracted to him."

"I'm *not* attracted to him," Victoria said.

"If you are a good listener, men think you are a good conversationalist," Samantha told her. "Men have high opinions of themselves and love to share their wisdom with inferior creatures like us."

"Read me something from the *Times*," Victoria said. "I'll ask him about it."

"Napoleon was exiled to Elba a few weeks ago," Angelica said. "I heard Robert and Rudolf discussing it."

"Here's something," Samantha said. "The apprentice law was repealed."

"What is that?" Victoria asked.

"I don't know," Samantha said with a shrug. "You'll need to ask Alex."

A smile spread slowly across Victoria's face, and her blue eyes gleamed with excitement. "He'll think I'm smart enough to read the newspaper," she said.

"Alex has already arrived," Samantha told her. "He's in a business meeting with His Grace."

Victoria grabbed her flute case and headed for the door. "I'm going to walk to the stream and concentrate on what I'm supposed to do."

Leaving her chamber, Victoria walked to the end of the corridor. Like an old friend, insecurity caught her at the top of the stairs. She hurried back to her chamber. Her sisters looked up at her entrance.

"Do you think my white gown looks presentable?" Victoria asked. "I mean, in case I meet Alexander in the corridor."

"You look pretty," Angelica assured her.

Victoria looked at Samantha for confirmation. When she nodded in agreement, Victoria smiled with relief and left the chamber.

While Victoria was learning to flirt, Alexander Emerson sat one floor down in the Duke of Inverary's study. With them was the Duchess of Inverary, Victoria's aunt.

Tall and well-built and blond, Alexander Emerson sat in one of the chairs in front of the duke's desk and stretched his long legs out. He cast a sidelong glance at the duchess, who sat in the chair beside his, and then fixed his hazel gaze on the duke.

"I've had a letter from Australia," Alexander said, referring to his exiled sister and father.

"Oh?" Duke Magnus said.

"Venetia has married a Harry Gibbs, one of the

richest men in Australia, or so she claims," Alexander told him. "Venetia and her husband are planning a trip to England."

"The deal was that she and your father—"

"Charles Emerson is not my father," Alexander interrupted. "He made that perfectly clear."

Duke Magnus inclined his head and continued, "Venetia and Charles agreed to live in Australia in order to escape prosecution for attempting to murder you, Robert, and Angelica. Their jealous greed hurt all of us, especially you."

"*We* forced them to do that to avoid a scandal," Alexander reminded the older man. "What do you propose we do? From her letter, I assume Venetia and her husband are en route to England."

"Is Charles accompanying them?" Duke Magnus asked.

Alexander shrugged. "Venetia didn't mention him."

"I think we should do nothing," Duke Magnus said. "Let them come to England, and I'll keep my agents watching them."

"Will they be here for the wedding?" the duchess asked, looking worried.

Alexander slanted a glance in her direction. "I don't know."

"Your marriage to Victoria could be fortuitous," the duke said. "As a newlywed, you won't want them staying with you. They will be forced to stay in a hotel or rent their own house."

"Have your investigators discovered any information about my natural father's identity?" Alexander asked, trying to keep his tone casual.

"I'm afraid not," Duke Magnus answered. "I'm sorry."

"Your betrothal announcement appears in today's *Times,*" Lady Roxanne said, changing the subject.

"Your Grace, I told you I wanted to tell Victoria," Alexander said, a tinge of irritation in his voice.

"And you will," the duchess replied. "That's the reason I planned this weekend."

Alexander began to argue, "When Victoria reads the—"

"There is no chance of that happening," Lady Roxanne interrupted, and then laughed. "Victoria never reads the newspaper. The invitations are going out on Monday so you will have three days to break the news to her." The duchess paused for a breath of air and then gushed, "Just imagine, my sweet Victoria will be the Countess of Winchester in less than a month and, a year from now, could be a mother."

"I would never call Victoria sweet," the duke said dryly.

Alexander shifted his hazel gaze to the duke. The duchess had told him that his intended could be difficult at times, but he would never believe that her uncle would have difficulties with her. After all, the chit was barely eighteen. How difficult could she be? Well, her behavior would calm when she married and delivered their first child.

"Victoria has a slight rebellious streak," the duchess was saying.

"Slight? She'll fight the betrothal if she believes we are pushing you on her," Duke Magnus said.

"I suggest you charm her," Lady Roxanne said.

"What if she fights it?" Alexander asked.

"No matter what, Victoria is going down that aisle on the twenty-fourth of June," Duke Magnus said.

"Dear Alex, Victoria needs you desperately. She's had little discipline in her young life and needs a strong man to curb her wilder impulses," the duchess told him. "Because of her father's decline in fortune, Victoria was only five when they moved from the Grosvenor Square mansion to the cottage on Primrose Hill. Her mother died the following year, and her father soon became sick with drink."

And the fault lies with Charles Emerson, Alexander thought, for swindling a fortune out of the Earl of Melrose. That was one reason he had agreed to the duchess's offer of marriage to her youngest niece. It was the least he could do to atone for Charles Emerson's crimes against the Douglas family.

"Beginning today, you are in charge of Victoria," Duke Magnus said. "Do whatever you think best. We won't interfere."

Alexander inclined his head. His betrothed was going to learn who would be the boss in their household. She had better get over her difficult behavior quickly.

Duke Magnus cleared his throat. "Roxanne and I have had a long discussion," he told the younger man. "We agree that once you—ah—bed her, she won't fight and will remain steadfast. We are suggesting you bed her as soon as possible."

Alexander sat up straight. Unable to credit what he was hearing, he looked from the duke to the duchess and then back to the duke.

"Are you giving me permission to bed her *before* the wedding?" Alexander asked, surprised.

"We are *encouraging* you to do it," Duke Magnus said, and then chuckled. "Can you seduce her in a weekend?"

What an unexpected turn of events, Alexander thought. Most guardians fought to protect their ward's virtue.

"Well?" the duke asked.

A lazy smile spread across Alexander's face. "I can certainly try, Your Grace."

"Sneak into her room if you must," the duchess said. "Sunday morning would be a good time if you aren't leaving too early for Winchester. Victoria never attends Sunday service."

Alexander raised his brows at the duchess. "She refuses to attend church services?"

"Victoria never actually refuses to do anything," Lady Roxanne told him. "She agrees to whatever you want and then does what she wants. At times, I feel that I'm trying to catch a butterfly."

"The chit has a repertoire of four maladies, a different complaint for each week of the month," Duke Magnus said, unable to suppress a smile. "The first week Victoria suffers from the headache, and the following week she's felled by a stomachache."

"Victoria rouses herself the third week but suffers a dizzy spell before we leave," Lady Roxanne said. "The final week of the month, she has menstrual cramps."

Alexander burst out laughing. His betrothed sounded highly entertaining. "Where are we in the cycle?" he asked.

"Victoria is due for a headache this week," the duchess answered.

"Except for weddings and christenings, I've never seen Victoria in church," Duke Magnus said, a grudging smile on his face. When Alexander laughed again, the duke warned, "I wouldn't laugh yet. You're the one who needs to tame her."

"Victoria has some slight trouble with her eyes," Lady Roxanne continued. She glanced toward the windows, adding, "It isn't a major difficulty, merely an inconvenience."

The duchess is lying, Alexander thought, wondering what she found so threatening she would lie. He wasn't about to cry off at this late date.

"What exactly is her trouble?" Alexander asked.

"Victoria has a slight reading problem," the duchess told him. "She doesn't see some letters clearly."

"That's it?" he asked.

The duchess nodded. "Yes."

"Victoria doesn't need perfect vision for what I have planned for her," Alexander said, giving the duchess a lazy smile.

Duke Magnus sent his wife a concerned look. "What do you intend for her?"

"Her wifely duties and caring for our children will keep Victoria busy," Alexander answered.

"Keep her in line by keeping her belly filled with a baby?" Duke Magnus chuckled, his expression clearing. "How about a shot of whiskey?"

Lady Roxanne rose from her chair and wandered across the study to the window overlooking the rear gardens. "There goes Victoria now," she said.

Rising from his chair, Alexander crossed the study to see her. With flute case in hand, a slender young woman, with a mane of fiery curls cascading to her waist, started to cross the lawn nearest to the house. She was immediately surrounded by her nephews and nieces.

Alexander smiled, enchanted. His future countess set her flute case down and formed a circle with the children. They held hands and, dancing to the left, sang, "Ring-a-ring o' roses, a pocket full of posies. A-tishoo! A-tishoo! We all fall down!"

Victoria and the children fell down on the grass when the last word slipped from their lips. Then they started to laugh.

"I'm glad she likes children," Alexander said.

"Victoria adores her nieces and nephews," Lady

Roxanne said. "I'm positive she will be an excellent mother."

Alexander watched Victoria stand and grab her flute case. Waving at the children, she started to walk away but crashed into a hedge. The children laughed uproariously.

Her next stop was her brothers-in-law who were practicing golf swings. Prince Rudolf called something out to her, and Victoria laughed. Then she headed in the direction of the woodland.

"Where is she going?" Alexander asked, delighted by what he had witnessed.

"Victoria likes to wade in the stream in the woodland," Lady Roxanne answered. "I've told her dozens of times that ladies do not wade, but she refuses to obey."

"If you will excuse me," Alexander said, turning away from the window, "I would like to speak with her."

"When will you tell her about the betrothal?" Lady Roxanne asked.

"I'll tell her when the moment is right."

Alexander left the duke's study and walked downstairs. He hadn't seen any evidence of Victoria being headstrong. In fact, she appeared as if she would obey his every command without hesitation. Apparently, the duke and the duchess didn't know how to handle an energetic young lady.

Outside, Alexander waved to the children and started to cross the wide expanse of lawn. He paused to speak with his future brothers-in-law, still practicing their golf strokes.

"Welcome to the family," called Robert Campbell, the Marquess of Argyll, the duke's son.

"Does everyone know why I'm here?" Alexander asked.

Prince Rudolf flashed him a wicked smile. "Everyone except the bride knows."

"I will take care of that before leaving Sunday morning," Alexander told him. He looked at the marquess, saying, "I think your father may be getting senile."

Robert smiled. "Why do you say that?"

"His Grace gave me permission to deflower Victoria this weekend," Alexander told them. "In fact, he encouraged it."

His future brothers-in-law laughed at that.

"My father may be expecting a bit of hesitation on the lady's part," Robert replied. "Once she's ruined, so to speak, Victoria will have no choice but to marry you."

"Where is this stream?" Alexander asked.

"Walk down the path behind the gazebo," Prince Rudolf told him. "Then follow the sound of flute song."

Humming a sprightly tune, Victoria peeled her shoes and stockings off when she reached the stream. She grabbed her flute, hitched her skirt up to her knees, and sat down on a rock at the edge of the stream.

Victoria dangled her feet in the cool water and sighed in pleasure at the warm, early June afternoon. She lifted the flute to her lips and began to play the tune she had been humming. The melody was a jaunty air, the sounds of springtime songbirds and chuckling brooks lending the song a bewitching charm.

"Hello, Victoria."

Startled by a man's voice, Victoria whirled around so fast she nearly fell off the rock but managed to steady herself. Alexander Emerson leaned against a tree a few feet from where she sat.

"Hello, Alexander," Victoria said in a soft voice. Oh, Lord, she sounded breathless like one of those female pinheads who fawned over the bachelors at society functions.

"I heard your siren's song and came in search of a wood nymph," Alexander said.

Victoria didn't answer. She'd fixed her blue-eyed gaze on his physical attributes. Now that she intended to flirt with him, he seemed different, as if she was noticing him for the first time.

With his blond good looks, Alexander had pleasing features—hazel eyes, full lips, straight nose. His broad shoulders accentuated his tapered waist, and those tan breeches fit his well-muscled thighs like a second skin.

"Do you like what you see?" Alexander asked, a smile lurking in his voice.

Victoria snapped her gaze to his and blushed with embarrassment. She was certainly making a mess of this flirting business.

"I apologize for staring," Victoria said with a sheepish smile. "I was supposed to stare intensely and then pretend shyness by dropping my gaze."

"Why?" he asked, wearing a puzzled smile.

Since she'd mucked up the whole flirting business, Victoria decided to make a joke of it. "Do you want to hold my hand?" she asked baldly, instead of answering his question.

Alexander looked surprised. "Do you want me to hold your hand?"

Victoria ignored his question. "Could you possibly tell me how much kissing is too much kissing?" she asked.

Alexander burst out laughing. "What are you talking about?"

"My sisters were teaching me to flirt," Victoria told him. "Those were some of the rules."

"I didn't know there were rules for flirting," Alexander said.

Victoria brightened at that. "*You* don't know how to flirt, either?"

Alexander shouted with laughter. Victoria didn't know if she should be insulted or not.

"I've had some flirting experience," he told her. "Why were your sisters teaching you to flirt?"

Victoria blushed. "I wanted to flirt with you this weekend."

Something flickered in his expressive hazel eyes. Victoria felt as if his gaze on her had warmed by several degrees.

"Did you wish to flirt with me specifically?" Alexander asked. "Or would any gentleman do?"

Victoria stared at him, her face crimson with embarrassment. An unexpected excitement leaped to life in the pit of her stomach.

"I wanted to flirt with you specifically," she told him.

"Come closer," Alexander said. "I'll flirt with you."

Victoria felt suddenly nervous. She flicked her tongue out to wet her lips and then asked, "Couldn't we flirt from a distance?"

"Come here," Alexander said, his gaze fixed on hers.

Victoria heard the quiet authority in his voice and, for the first time in her life, obeyed an order without arguing. Holding the skirt of her gown, she stood and waded out of the stream. She returned her flute to its case and walked the few feet that separated them.

And then she wished she hadn't. Alexander was so much taller that she needed to tilt her head back to look into his eyes. She felt intimidated and nervous.

"Please don't tell my aunt I've been wading in the stream," Victoria said.

"Wading is forbidden?" The hint of a smile appeared on his lips.

"Young ladies of good breeding do *not* wade," Victoria drawled in a perfect imitation of her aunt.

Alexander laughed, amusement lighting his eyes. "Your secret is safe with me . . . for a price."

"I don't own any money," Victoria told his chest.

"I don't want money." Reaching out, Alexander gently forced her to look up at him. "I want a kiss."

Victoria's heart slammed into her chest, and the excitement in the pit of her stomach fanned into a flame. She felt every nerve in her body tingling and dropped her gaze from his hazel eyes to his lips.

"I—I don't know how," she admitted.

Alexander cocked a brow at her. "Has no young man stolen a kiss?"

"His Grace and my brothers-in-law won't let any young man near me except for Rudolf's brothers," Victoria said, shaking her head. "Viktor, Mikhail, and Stepan are more like family than eligible bachelors."

"Would you like to learn to kiss?" Alexander asked.

The flame in her stomach grew, warming by several degrees. Unfortunately, her self-consciousness grew apace with the flame.

"I don't think so," Victoria refused. "I am tempted but would hate to see all of my brothers-in-law's protection go to waste. I'm sure you understand my dilemma and won't be offended."

With a smile playing on his lips, Alexander dropped his gaze to her mouth. Leisurely, his gaze drifted from her mouth to her breasts, lingering for a long moment, and then traveled down her body to her waist.

When Alexander raised his hazel gaze to hers, his eyes held a possessive gleam. Victoria felt an invisible connection between them.

"I don't think a gentleman should look at a lady like that," she told him, frightened by the intensity in his gaze.

"How was I looking at you?"

"You looked like a hungry wolf contemplating a juicy morsel you intended to gobble," she answered, a note of disapproval in her voice.

Alexander smiled. "If you aren't afraid of the big bad wolf, step closer so I can collect my kiss," he challenged her. "I promise not to gobble."

With her blue gaze fixed on his, Victoria took tiny steps forward until she stood inches from him. She caught his scent of bay and felt the heat emanating from his powerful body.

Alexander drew her closer. One of his hands held the back of her head while the other pulled her against his muscular frame.

"Are you afraid?" he asked, his lips hovering above hers.

"Very worried," she answered, making him smile.

Alexander lowered his head, his lips touching hers in a gentle first kiss. Trembling on the inside, Victoria stood statue-stiff. She didn't know what to do except close her eyes.

"Relax," Alexander breathed against her lips.

His lips were warm, soft but firm. Undemanding. She began to relax and enjoy feeling them pressed to hers.

The tenor of his kiss changed. He slid his hand

from the back of her head to her neck, and his fingers caressed her delicate nape.

When she sighed at the sensation, Alexander began moving his lips on hers, encouraging her to move her lips with him, to follow his lead. Victoria felt his strength, sensed his power held in tight control. A melting sensation in her lower regions caught her by surprise, and suddenly she wanted more, so much more.

Tentatively at first, gaining confidence with each passing second, Victoria moved her lips on his and returned his kiss in kind. Their kiss was long and languorous. He exuded power and skill and mastery over her senses with each movement, and she had no choice but follow wherever he would lead her.

Victoria shivered with the heat. He captured her whole being even as his lips had captured hers.

The world faded away, and his lips became the center of her universe. Still, she yearned for more.

Staking his claim, Alexander sensed her surrender and brushed her lips with the tip of his tongue. In answer, Victoria inched her hands up his chest to hook around his neck. She pressed into the deepening kiss, her supple body touching his from breast to thigh.

Victoria parted her lips, inviting him to give her more, and Alexander slipped his tongue inside to explore her sweetness. Heat flowed through her veins, and she clung to him, offering herself, enjoying his possession.

And then it was over.

Lifting his lips from hers, Alexander smiled at her dazed expression. He wrapped his arms around her, keeping her pressed against his body as she floated back to earth.

Victoria rested her head against him, her cheek

resting on his chest. She felt safe and protected in his arms, a feeling she hadn't experienced since the age of five when she still had been able to bask in the warmth of her parents' love.

Victoria smiled to herself. This man had given her the most intense experience of her life, yet she sensed no danger, only an unspoken promise of protection. Somehow, she knew no other man would make her feel this way, no other man's kiss would affect her in the same manner.

"Tory," Alexander murmured.

Victoria looked up, and he stared at her face. Embarrassment washed over her, coloring her cheeks. She felt vulnerable, as if she had revealed too much of herself, and dropped her gaze to his chest.

"You have just done it correctly," Alexander told her.

"What have I done?" she asked, confused.

"You stared at me intensely and dropped your gaze shyly," Alexander answered, making her smile. "That blush is a nice touch, too." Then he asked, "How do you feel now that you have experienced your first kiss?"

"I tingle in places I never knew existed," she answered, drawing a shaky breath. "Is that normal?"

"Yes."

"Do you tingle?"

"You'll never know how much."

Victoria became aware of the hardness at his groin, pressing against her belly through her light muslin dress. "I don't think we should stand this close," she said, making no move to separate.

Alexander silently refused to release her. "Do you like opera?"

"Well, I love the intermission," she hedged, making him smile.

"Would you like to accompany me to the opera next week?"

"Do you mean the two of us alone?"

He nodded.

"I don't think His Grace will allow that," Victoria told him.

Alexander looked down at her upturned face. "His Grace will make an exception for me."

"In that case, would you consider taking me to Covent Garden at night?" Victoria asked, her smile mischievous.

"That isn't a good place for a young lady," he told her.

"I'll be safe with you," she replied. "If not, how about Vauxhall?"

Alexander laughed. "Victoria, you are pressing your luck."

"If you don't want to take me," Victoria said, giving him a flirtatious smile, "Prince Stepan will be happy to accompany me."

"Is that so?" Alexander smiled at her practicing her wiles on him.

Victoria nodded. "Prince Stepan has already taken me to Drury Lane," she told him. "I sneaked out of the house one night."

Alexander lost his humor. "Your reputation could have been ruined."

"I'm joking," she lied, uneasy with his apparent mood change.

Alexander seemed to relax. "Tell me why you wanted to flirt with me specifically," he said, changing the subject. "Did anyone encourage you?"

"My sisters said you would make an excellent husband," she answered.

"What do you think?" Alexander asked, running a hand up and down her back.

"I thought I was having fun until I saw you and

my body began acting strangely," Victoria answered honestly. Then she changed the subject, asking, "Are you very smart?"

Alexander gave her a puzzled look. "Smart enough, I suppose."

"I admire intelligence," she told him, gazing into his hazel eyes. "I bet you read lots of books."

"I thought young ladies admired titles, wealth, and good looks," Alexander teased her.

"Titles, wealth, and good looks are easily lost," Victoria said. "Intelligence is something a man can keep forever."

"Your philosophy impresses me," he said.

Victoria smiled, preening at his praise. She had no idea what *philosophy* meant, but if he was impressed, then she was proud of it. After all, she possessed very few talents to make her proud.

"Let's return to the house," Alexander said, releasing her.

Victoria didn't especially want to return to the house. She wanted to be alone with him. She also didn't want to be put in the position of looking for the *L* on the bottom of her shoes.

"Walking barefoot in the grass tickles my feet," Victoria said. "I'll carry my shoes."

Alexander lifted the flute case off the ground. With her in the lead, they started down the path. Victoria stopped short before they left the woodland and turned to face him.

"I want another kiss," Victoria told him.

"I'll kiss you tonight," Alexander said.

"Why don't you want to kiss me?"

"I want to kiss you," he answered, "but if I do, I will embarrass myself."

"No one is watching," she said. "I don't understand."

"I will explain it tonight," Alexander promised. "Will you trust me in this?"

Victoria nodded, relieved that he wasn't rejecting her.

Alexander put his arm around her shoulder, and together, they continued down the path. Emerging near the gazebo, Victoria noted her brothers-in-law still practicing their golf.

"I want to speak to Prince Rudolf," Alexander told her. "I'll see you later."

Ignoring her brothers-in-law in an attempt to avoid their teasing, Victoria continued walking toward the house. And then she heard Prince Rudolf, calling, "Tory, have you been kissing Alex?"

Embarrassed, Victoria quickened her pace. That only made her brothers-in-law laugh.

CHAPTER 2

Intense and sophisticated, Victoria decided, amending her earlier opinion of Alexander Emerson. *Definitely not boring and old.*

Since returning to the house that afternoon, Victoria had closeted herself in her bedchamber and daydreamed about Alexander Emerson. She replayed the scene of his inspiring kiss over and over again in her mind. Nearing dinnertime, her excitement grew to a feverish pitch until she burned with anticipation.

Victoria primped in front of the cheval mirror for more than an hour. She had chosen a silk gown in the palest shade of yellow, its color complimenting her fiery curls, cascading almost to her waist. The gown's squared neckline hinted at cleavage instead of exposing it, and she wore matching slippers on her feet.

"How do I look?" Victoria asked her sisters when they slipped into her chamber.

"Like a pretty buttercup," Angelica said.

"Actually, you look more like a pagan princess

with that mane of fire hanging loose," Samantha said.

"How did your flirting work?" Angelica asked.

"Alex kissed me," Victoria answered, a blush staining her cheeks. "I liked it when he put his tongue in my mouth. Would any man affect me like that?"

"Only Alex would have such a profound effect," Samantha said.

"I wanted to let him touch me," Victoria admitted in a whisper.

"Since he did give you your first kiss and your attention seems fixed on him," Angelica said, "letting him touch your breasts would be permissible."

"That would still be within the bounds of propriety," Samantha agreed.

Victoria gave her sisters a doubtful look. "This morning you said my reputation would be ruined if I let him touch me," she reminded them.

"Only in general terms," Angelica said, waving her hand in dismissal.

"Rudolf touched me before we married," Samantha said.

"Rudolf made you pregnant before you married," Victoria replied. She looked at her oldest sister, adding, "Robert made you pregnant before you married, too. I don't think you are the best people to advise me."

"Don't be so prudish," Angelica said.

"A little groping never hurt anyone," Samantha added. "If God didn't want men and women to touch, He would never have given us skin or hands."

"Did Alexander say anything to you?" Angelica asked.

"He invited me to the opera next week," Victoria

answered. "I doubt His Grace will give me permission, though. How should I behave toward him at dinner?"

Before her sisters could reply, a knock sounded on the door. Then it opened to reveal their aunt.

"Hello, my darlings," Aunt Roxie called, walking into the chamber. Her smile slipped when she turned her gaze on Victoria. "Tory, His Grace wants to speak with you in his study. Now."

Victoria felt an inkling of fear. Apparently, the duke had caught her in some infraction of his rules, but she could not recall what she had done.

Descending one flight of stairs, Victoria walked the length of the corridor to her uncle's study. She paused outside the door and wondered what she had done this time. It seemed she never did anything right, and her uncle's scrutiny had grown since her sisters married and now were considered their husbands' concerns.

There was no mistaking the look in her aunt's eyes that said she was in trouble. She hoped His Grace wouldn't reprimand her in front of Alexander. That would be too humiliating to endure.

Summoning her courage, Victoria knocked on the door. Almost instantly, she heard the duke's voice.

"Enter," he growled.

Victoria hesitated when she heard the anger in his voice, thinking whatever she had done must be terrible. Should she enter or make a run for it? If she bolted, her uncle would catch up with her at the dinner table, and then Alexander would witness her humiliation.

Striving for an innocent look, Victoria wet her lips and pasted a smile on her face. She opened the door, stepped inside, and stopped short. His

Grace stood behind his desk; Prince Rudolf and Alexander stood nearby.

Relief surged through Victoria at this unexpected reprieve. The duke was in the midst of a business meeting.

"I'm sorry for interrupting," Victoria said, her smile sunny, starting to close the door. "I'll come back later."

"Come in, Victoria," Duke Magnus called, gesturing to her. "Sit down."

"I don't mind waiting." Victoria started to close the door again.

"I said to sit down here," Duke Magnus ordered, sounding irritated. "Close the door behind you."

Victoria glanced at Alexander and Rudolf. Their expressions were grim. Had Alexander told His Grace that she let him put his tongue in her mouth? Was her brother-in-law there as a witness to confirm they had been alone in the woodland?

In that instant, Victoria knew she should have bolted. She glanced at the door and wondered how far she could get before one of them caught her.

"Close the door and sit down," Alexander ordered in a voice that brooked no disobedience.

Victoria took more time than necessary to close the door. She decided to brazen out the oncoming conflict. And deny, deny, deny.

After crossing the study like a woman going to meet the executioner, Victoria sat in the chair in front of the duke's desk and wasted several moments arranging the skirt of her gown to buy herself time to gather her wits for battle. Looking up, she faltered at the duke's expression of disapproval.

Long moments passed. Victoria began to squirm as the three men stared at her.

"Have you gone out in the evening without my permission or knowledge?" Duke Magnus spoke finally.

Victoria put a finger across her lips in a gesture of trying to remember. Then she raised enormous blue eyes to him and lied, "I can't recall going out without your permission or knowledge."

Duke Magnus banged his fist on his desk. "I will not countenance your lies."

"Oh, yes, I remember now," Victoria said, pretending innocence. "I did go out once."

"One time only?" Duke Magnus echoed. "Where did you go and with whom?"

Victoria leveled an accusing glare on Alexander. He had betrayed her trust.

"I am waiting for your answer," the duke said, his stern voice filled with irritation.

"Prince Stepan took me to Drury Lane," she blurted out.

Victoria heard her brother-in-law cursing in Russian, but she refused to look at him. She fixed her gaze on the duke, saying, "Becoming upset never helps, Your Grace."

"You arrogant little witch, do not speak to me in that condescending tone," Duke Magnus shouted, frightening her. "I ought to take you across my knee and give you the spanking of your life." Pausing, he flicked a glance at the earl and said, "I will, however, leave that satisfying task to a younger man."

Victoria panicked and turned enormous blue eyes on Alexander Emerson. Was the earl going to spank her? Oh, God, how humiliating.

"How did you get out?" Duke Magnus asked. Then, "Victoria, I am speaking to you."

Victoria shifted her gaze from the earl to her uncle. "I climbed out the window and down the tree."

"Good God, you could have been killed," Duke Magnus said.

"I was in no danger," she cried. "I'm an excellent climber."

"I'll just bet you are," the duke replied, his disgust all too apparent. "Have Prince Stepan and you been intimate?"

Victoria dropped her mouth open in surprise. She couldn't imagine how the duke could even ask her such a question.

"Tell me if Stepan touched you," the duke demanded.

Victoria felt her face flaming with embarrassment. "Stepan wouldn't do that," she answered. "He's my friend." She sensed the three men relax but could not understand why they were so tense about one tiny escapade.

"Stepan is no friend of yours if he places your reputation, your virtue, and your life in jeopardy," Duke Magnus told her. "Why did you go there?"

"I was curious about those women," Victoria answered, her face flushing again when she realized how idiotic she sounded.

"Did you consider that your curiosity could cause you trouble?" the duke asked, his voice rising in anger. "Did you consider that no decent man would want to marry you? Did you consider that you would need to become one of those women if you ruined your reputation?"

Victoria didn't know whether his questions were rhetorical or not. She bent her head in a gesture of submissive remorse.

Duke Magnus banged his fist on the desk again, startling her. "Damn it," he shouted. "Answer me when I speak to you."

Victoria trembled with fear. She had never seen the duke so angry. "I did not consider any of those things," she said in a voice no louder than a whisper. "I was wrong to do what I did."

"Do you have even one ounce of common sense?" Duke Magnus asked.

"I apologize for my foolishness," Victoria said, hoping her words would placate him. "My behavior was inexcusable."

"Your behavior would scandalize your parents if they were alive to see it," he told her.

Victoria felt her heart wrenching at the mention of her parents. She had known her mother for five years only, and for as long as she could remember, her father had been lost in drink. Unshed tears glistened in her eyes, and her bottom lip quivered with her effort to control her emotions.

"I'll speak to Stepan about his part in this escapade," Rudolf said, looking at the earl. "I guarantee it will never happen again."

Victoria felt confused. Why was Rudolf reassuring Alexander?

"Please don't say anything to Stepan," Victoria pleaded. "I threatened to find someone else if he refused to take me. He was only trying to protect me."

"Victoria, are you absolutely truthful when you say that nothing sexual has passed between Stepan and you?" Duke Magnus asked.

"I never even kissed a man until today," Victoria said, casting the earl a disgruntled look.

"Lord Emerson wants to speak with you privately," the duke told her. "Good God, Rudolf, I need a healthy swig of your vodka."

The two men started for the door, intending to leave her alone with the earl. Alexander stood with his arms folded across his chest and the grim expression on his face had not eased.

"Your Grace, I have other crimes to confess,"

Victoria called, not wanting to be left alone with the earl.

Duke Magnus turned around and stared at her. She flicked a glance at the prince, who appeared to be steeling himself for whatever she said.

"I went into the woods and waded in the stream today," Victoria confessed.

Duke Magnus looked at her as if she had turned purple. Prince Rudolf was fighting a smile.

Victoria wet her lips, and summoning self-righteous indignation, pointed at the earl. "That man is a rake," she cried. "The earl accosted me at the stream. He kissed me and pushed his tongue into my mouth. And—and I believe he is plotting to molest my body before this weekend is over. You should call him out for trifling with me."

Prince Rudolf burst out laughing. Duke Magnus seemed at a loss for words.

Victoria watched her uncle shift his gaze to the earl, who shook his head. "Don't believe his denial," she cried. "He's guilty."

"For once in your life, be quiet," Duke Magnus said in a long-suffering voice.

The duke left the study, muttering about how grateful he was never to have fathered any daughters. The prince followed him out, and the door clicked shut behind them.

"Excuse me, my lord," Victoria said, standing to leave.

"I want to speak with you."

"You betrayed my confidence."

"I was protecting you from yourself."

"Who appointed you my guardian?" Victoria countered, defiant.

Alexander perched on the edge of the duke's desk. "Come here, Tory," he said. "I want to explain myself."

Victoria was instantly suspicious. "Are you planning to molest me again?"

The earl's lips quirked into a smile, and his hazel eyes lit with amusement. "You look very pretty tonight," he said. "I love the riot of red curls against your alabaster skin." Then he amended himself, "That is, your alabaster skin with the rosy hue of a blush."

"Thank you." Victoria stepped closer until she was inches from him.

Alexander lifted her hand to his lips. The warmth in his hazel eyes was impossible to resist. He drew her closer until his thighs teased her yellow gown.

Victoria felt his closeness with every fiber of her being. She felt the heat from his body and inhaled his fresh bay scent. Her heart began to race with excitement.

"I wanted His Grace to impress upon you the danger in what you did," Alexander told her. "I knew you wouldn't necessarily listen to me. I like you very much, Tory, and admire your *joie de vivre.*"

"My joy of life?" Victoria echoed, feeling smart.

Alexander inclined his head. "Do you still want to accompany me to the opera?"

Victoria smiled ruefully. "His Grace doesn't trust me."

"His Grace trusts *me,*" Alexander replied, drawing her into his arms. He stared at her upturned face, his gaze drifting from her enormous blue eyes to her alabaster skin to her full lips. His mouth covered hers, and when she responded, he deepened the kiss until she allowed him entrance to her mouth.

Victoria made a little whimpering sound in her throat and leaned into the kiss. She loved the warmth of his mouth on hers, the power of his arms holding her close. And yet, she wanted more, something he hadn't offered her, something only he could give her.

"You are everything a man could want," Alexander whispered against her lips. "Am I forgiven?"

Cradled against his chest, Victoria raised her gaze to his, and a feline smile turned the corners of her lips up. "At the moment, I would forgive you anything."

"You are so wonderfully, artlessly innocent," Alexander said, hugging her close.

Victoria decided she was glad to be artlessly innocent, whatever that meant.

Everyone was already seated at the table when they walked into the dining room. Duke Magnus and Aunt Roxie sat at either end of the table. On the duke's left sat Rudolf, Samantha, and Robert. Angelica sat on her aunt's left, leaving the two empty seats for Alexander and Victoria. Her family watched them in silence as they slipped into the chairs.

Victoria glanced at her aunt, whose attention had fixed on Alexander. Almost imperceptively, the earl shook his head, and Victoria wondered what that meant. The same signal had passed between the earl and her uncle. She would ask Alex about it later when they retired to the drawing room.

Tinker, the duke's majordomo, stood at attention near the sideboard and supervised the footmen serving dinner. A delicate spring soup with vivid green vegetables arrived first. Next came baked Dover sole, asparagus with a tangy vinaigrette, and potatoes dressed with spiced cream and lemon juice.

Still smarting over her dressing-down by the duke,

Victoria remained silent and listened to the men discussing politics while her aunt and sisters threw in comments about the children. She had the suspicion that everyone at the table knew what had happened in the study, her sisters' furtive looks of sympathy tipping her off.

When a lull developed in the conversation, Victoria spoke up for the first time, addressing herself to Alexander. "I read that Napoleon was banished to Elbow," she said. "Do you think he's finished?"

Everyone at the table stopped eating and stared in obvious surprise at her. Even one of the footmen, in the act of clearing a plate, froze with his hand in mid-air.

"Where did they banish Napoleon?" Alexander asked her.

Hoping to sound sophisticated, Victoria drawled in a good imitation of her aunt, "Darling, Napoleon was banished to the Island of Elbow."

Coughing and choking erupted at the table. Victoria looked at Rudolf, who sat across from her. The prince had covered his mouth with his hand, and his shoulders shook with silent laughter. She shifted her gaze to her sister. Samantha was smiling at her plate.

Victoria glanced at Alexander. He wore a broad grin, too.

"Being banished is no joke," Victoria told them.

Everyone at the table burst into laughter. Confused, Victoria couldn't imagine what was funny.

Alexander placed his arm on the back of her chair, leaned close, and whispered, "Sweetheart, Napoleon was banished to the Island of Elba, not Elbow."

Victoria felt the blood rushing to her face. Too embarrassed to look at anyone, she set her fork down and stared at her plate.

Everyone except Victoria resumed eating. She had lost her appetite.

Hoping to redeem herself, Victoria waited for another lull in the conversation. "I read in the *Times* that the apprentices were peeled this week," she said.

Her brothers-in-law shouted with laughter. With smiles on their faces, everyone else stared at her.

"Tory, the Apprentice Law was repealed," Samantha corrected her.

"*Re*pealed?" Victoria echoed, glancing at the earl. When he nodded, she said, "I can't imagine why they would peel those poor boys twice."

Alexander shouted with laughter, joining her brothers-in-law's mirth. Those two sophisticated aristocrats were laughing so hard that tears streamed down their faces.

Victoria blushed again, realizing she'd made an error.

"Tory, are you a bluestocking?" Alexander asked, leaning close.

"No one wears blue stockings," Victoria answered in an appalled voice.

Everyone, including the duke and the duchess, burst into laughter. Even the servants wore smiles.

Victoria tossed her napkin down on the table. Too embarrassed to endure another moment, she leaped out of her chair and bolted from the dining room.

Alexander caught her in the corridor. He grabbed her wrist and gently but firmly prevented her flight.

"Let me go," she cried.

Alexander pulled her into his arms and kept her imprisoned against his body. Humiliated, she hid her face against his chest.

"I am sorry," he apologized. "I never intended to hurt your feelings."

"I don't like people laughing at me," Victoria told him. "It makes me feel stupid."

"You are inexperienced, not stupid," Alexander said, stroking her back in an effort to soothe her. "Anyone could have made those mistakes. I bet you read the newspaper without your spectacles."

Victoria looked up at him, her complexion a vibrant scarlet. "I did read the paper without my specs," she lied. "Thank you for trying to make me feel better."

"Come back to the table," Alexander said, guiding her toward the door. "I live alone, and dining with a real family is special. I won't enjoy myself if you leave."

Victoria returned to the table but refused to look at anyone lest she see laughter in their eyes. Fearing her stupidity would surface again, she refrained from joining the conversation.

Alexander relaxed back in his chair as dinner ended and rested his arm across hers. Victoria glanced at him, sensing his gesture possessive, staking a claim on her. She'd seen her brothers-in-law make the same gesture with her sisters.

"I have invited Victoria to attend the opera next week," Alexander said to the duke. "With your permission, of course."

Expecting a refusal, Victoria peeked at her uncle. The duke was smiling at the earl.

"I'm certain Victoria will enjoy herself," Duke Magnus said. He glanced at her, adding, "I am also certain she will appreciate a distinguished gentleman thinking so highly of her. Won't you, Tory?"

The duke sounded threatening, probably expecting her to refuse. He couldn't have been more wrong. She wanted to be with the earl. Preferably alone.

"I am very appreciative and looking forward to

the evening," Victoria said, smiling at the duke's surprised expression.

"Come along, my darlings," Aunt Roxie said to her nieces, rising from her chair. She looked at her husband, saying, "Don't delay too long. We're going to play famous people charades."

Duke Magnus smiled at his wife. "I can hardly wait, my dear."

Victoria cast Alexander a smiling glance and then followed her aunt and sisters out of the dining room. When the men joined them a short time later, Alexander walked straight to the settee and sat beside Victoria. Her heart began to pound faster with excitement, and that was before he rested his arm on the settee behind her.

The majordomo and two footmen walked into the room. They carried coffee and tea pots along with the accompanying cups, saucers, spoons, cream, and sugar.

"I'll have black tea," Victoria told the majordomo. She looked at Alexander and said, "Plain black tea is beneficial to the brain."

"You'll need to drink the whole pot if you want to improve your dinner table conversation," Prince Rudolf teased her. The prince laughed when she gave him a disgruntled look.

Angelica passed a white card to everyone. On the card was the name of a famous person.

"The youngest goes first," announced the oldest, Duke Magnus.

Victoria looked at the name on the card and felt her heart sinking to her stomach. How was she going to play charades if she couldn't read the name?

"You don't have your spectacles?" Alexander asked, leaning close.

Victoria shook her head. "Will you help me?"

she asked. "We can be a team. You read me the card and I'll act it out."

Alexander gave her a devastating smile and leaned close, his face nearly touching hers. Victoria felt hot and cold at the same time. She definitely wanted to be alone with the earl.

With his hand cupping the side of his mouth, Alexander touched his lips to her ear. Victoria felt a melting sensation in the pit of her stomach.

"King Louis," Alexander whispered, his warm breath sending a delicious shiver down her spine.

Victoria gave him a sidelong glance and nodded. When she rose from the settee, she saw her family watching their byplay.

Victoria felt the blush rising on her cheeks. She suffered the embarrassing feeling that her family knew she wanted to be alone with the earl.

After pausing a moment to think, Victoria grabbed a decorative pillow and, holding it in both hands, marched across the room to set it on a table. Then she lifted an invisible crown off the pillow and placed it on her head.

"King George," Angelica called.

Victoria shook her head and then mimicked digging a hole with a shovel. She made the digging movement six times. After tossing the invisible shovel away, she crouched down and pretended to open an invisible box. Using both hands, she pulled an invisible object out of the box and dragged it across the floor.

Samantha burst out laughing, drawing everyone's attention. "King Louis . . . poor, poor Mister Lewis," she said.

Everyone except Rudolf and Alexander burst into laughter. Even the duke smiled.

"Who is Mister Lewis?" Prince Rudolf asked.

"When we lived in the old cottage," Samantha began, "before His Grace sent for us—"

"It was right after Angelica met Robert," Victoria interjected, taking her seat beside Alexander.

Samantha nodded and then continued, "One day Tory persuaded me that we could make fast money."

"Mister Lewis lived in our hamlet on the far side of Primrose Hill," Victoria said, turning to Alexander. "He liked us and was always very helpful."

"Tory believed if Mister Lewis helped us in life, he would want to help us in death," Samantha explained. She looked at her younger sister, and both dissolved into giggles.

"Wearing garlic necklaces to keep evil spirits away," Angelica finished for them, "my sisters went to the graveyard the night of Mister Lewis's funeral and dug the poor man up."

"Samantha and I wasted several hours dragging Mister Lewis to the cottage," Victoria added.

"Why did you dig him up?" Alexander asked.

"We wanted to sell him to the anatomical school," Samantha answered.

Prince Rudolf shouted with laughter. After a moment of stunned silence, the earl joined in his laughter.

"Angelica and I put Mister Lewis back in his grave," Robert said.

Alexander became serious. "You would never have needed to resort to that if my father—I mean, Charles Emerson—hadn't swindled your father."

"Whatever he did is not your fault," Victoria said, taking his hand in hers. "Living in the cottage wasn't as bad as you think. In some ways, it was better than the life I lead now."

Alexander gave her a skeptical look. "In what way was your life better?"

Leaning closer, Victoria pressed her lips against his ear and whispered, "I didn't have His Grace yelling at me for my bad behavior."

Unexpectedly, Alexander turned his head and planted a quick kiss on her lips. With a high blush staining her cheeks, Victoria didn't know what to do. If they had been alone, she would have kissed him.

"I told you he was planning to molest me," Victoria told the duke.

Her brothers-in-law burst into laughter. Alexander gently grasped the back of her neck and forced her to turn toward him.

"You are incorrigible," he said, and planted another kiss on her lips.

When her sisters and brothers-in-law left the drawing room to say good night to their children, Alexander turned to Victoria and asked, "Would you care to learn to play billiards?"

Her eyes sparkled with excitement. "Yes."

While a footman lit extra lanterns in the gameroom, Alexander readied the rectangular billiards table. He set the colored balls, positioned the cue ball, and then smoothed the tip of the cue with chalk.

"Will there be anything else, my lord?" the footman asked before leaving.

"No, thank you." Alexander poured himself a brandy and then asked, "Would you care for a brandy, my dear?"

Victoria laughed and shook her head.

"Taste it," he coaxed.

Victoria wanted to tell him that she didn't like spirits. After all, she had learned a hard lesson from her father's dependency on alcohol in order to blot the pain from his heart. She knew if she said that, he would blame himself again for what his father had done.

Taking a tiny sip, Victoria grimaced at the taste. A burning sensation traveled from her mouth to the pit of her stomach.

"That tastes horrible," she said, and coughed.

Alexander grinned at her pained expression, set the glass on the table, and reached for the cue. "Watch what I do," he said, and then paused. "Are you right- or left-handed?"

"I'm right-handed," Victoria answered, holding her left hand up.

"Which is it?"

Victoria held out her left hand, saying, "My right hand, the same one I use for my fork."

"This is a billiard cue," Alexander explained, holding the stick up. "The player hits the cue ball with the cue, hoping the cue ball will hit his colored ball and send it into one of the pockets. He continues play as long as the ball goes into the pocket. Do you understand?"

Victoria looked at him blankly. She couldn't remember a word he had said. Too many verbal directions confused her. She needed to see the game in play.

"Could you explain as we go along?" Victoria asked. "Hit a few balls to demonstrate how it's done."

Alexander nodded. He lifted the cue, leaned down close to the billiard table, and studied the balls.

"I'm trying to hit the red ball into the pocket," he told her.

Laying his cue on the table as a directional, Alexander leaned down and held the shaft in his right hand. After positioning the butt through his left hand to steady it, he hit the cue ball which, in turn, hit the red ball into the pocket.

Victoria clapped for him. "Do it again."

Alexander moved around the table, and Victoria followed. He leaned down, judging the shot.

Victoria studied him instead of the billiards. She started with his light blond hair, his pleasantly chiseled features in profile, and saw, in her mind's eyes, his expressive hazel eyes. Sliding her gaze down to his shoulders, Victoria admired the way his broad shoulders and chest tapered into his waist and lean hips. Her gaze drifted lower to his groin, and she recalled feeling his hardness pressed against her when they kissed at the stream.

As he readied the shot, Victoria glanced at his hands with their long fingers. She wondered what it would feel like to have his hands caressing her body, his strength pressing her down, his powerful legs spreading her thighs. *His hardness filling her softness.*

A shudder of desire shot through her. Victoria trembled, and an involuntary whimper escaped her lips.

"Is anything wrong?" Alexander asked, giving her a puzzled look.

Victoria shook her head, a high blush coloring her alabaster complexion.

"What kind of man do you want to marry?" Alexander asked, glancing sidelong at her while chalking the tip of the cue. "Titled, wealthy, and handsome?"

"The man I marry must be smart, patient, and understanding," Victoria told him.

"Admirable qualities, to be sure," Alexander remarked. "Why do you prefer those qualities?"

"I admire smart people," Victoria said, and then

gave him a rueful smile. "My husband will need
the other two to survive marriage to me."

Alexander smiled at that.

"What do you want in a wife?"

"I'm becoming increasingly partial to red hair,"
he answered, making her blush. He tipped his
head toward the billiard table, asking, "Would you
care to try?"

"Will you help me?"

"I was hoping you'd ask."

With both hands, Alexander grasped her delicate shoulders and positioned her at the table.
After bending her body forward, he stood behind
her and moulded his body to hers.

Victoria felt faint from his touch. She inhaled
his fresh bay scent and felt his heat seeping
through the thin layers of clothing separating his
flesh from hers.

"Take my shaft in your right hand," Alexander
said in a husky voice. "No, your *other* right hand.
Good girl."

His arms went around her, holding her hands
on the cue. "Put your left hand on the table to
steady the shaft as it thrusts forward," he said, with
laughter tingeing his voice. "Take aim and hit the
cue ball."

Victoria watched the cue ball roll across the
table and strike a colored ball, which dropped into
a pocket. "I did it," she said.

"We'll want to hit that ball over there," Alexander
said, his body still moulded to hers.

Victoria turned within the circle of his arms, her
breasts pressing against him. "If I ask you a question, will you give me an honest answer?"

"That depends on the question," Alexander
said, tracing a line down her cheek with one finger.

"Do you have a mistress?"

His lips quirked into a smile. "No."

Relief shot through her, but she wasn't finished yet. "Have you ever had a mistress?"

He stared down at her for a long moment as if deciding whether to answer her question or not. "Yes," he admitted.

"When you marry," she asked, "will you get another mistress?"

"Do you think I should?" he teased her.

"No." Victoria dropped her gaze to his lips. "Will you kiss me like you did at the stream?"

Without a word, Alexander dropped the cue and put his arms around her. He lowered his head, his mouth covering hers in a kiss that drugged her senses and made the world fade away.

Victoria savored the sensation of his mouth on hers. She pressed into the kiss, losing herself in it, surrendering her whole being.

His tongue caressed the crease between her lips, seeking and finding entrance to her mouth. Alexander groaned when she touched her tongue to his. Tentatively at first and then growing bolder, Victoria pushed her tongue past his lips to explore his mouth, mimicking his every move.

Leaving her lips behind, Alexander sprinkled kisses across her temples, her eyelids, her throat. He dropped his hands from the small of her back to her buttocks and held her against him.

Victoria moaned, feeling his hardness pressed against her. She entwined her arms around his neck and melted into him. Her knees buckled when he cupped her buttocks and ground his hardness against her.

Alexander kept her from falling and lifted her onto the edge of the billiard table, almost level with his groin. He pushed the skirt of her gown up and stood between her thighs, rubbing his hardness against her softness.

Wild with passion, Victoria clung to him. His lips burned a path down her throat, and his hands caressed her breasts through the silken material of her gown.

"Yes," Victoria gasped in a whisper. And then she felt cool air on her breasts, felt her gown sliding down to her waist, exposing her to his heated gaze, his masterful hands.

Moaning with pleasure, Victoria arched her body, urging him on, reveling in his caresses. When he slid his thumb across her nipples, molten desire throbbed between her thighs.

Alexander tormented her with these new, incredibly exciting sensations. His fingers glided across the sensitive tips of her nipples, squeezing and rolling them into aroused beads.

"Exquisite nipples," he said thickly. His lips replaced his fingers—licking, nipping, sucking while his long, skillful fingers teased the other.

"Alex," she moaned, clasping his head to her breast. She had never known pleasure like this existed. She wanted more and more, knowing there was something else, something more pleasurable awaiting her.

Victoria froze, the sound of a door opening penetrating her sensually-dazed brain. Then she heard her brothers-in-law's voices behind her.

Robert started to speak, "We thought we'd play billiards with—"

"Excuse us for intruding," Rudolf finished.

Alexander straightened and put his arms around her protectively. Embarrassed, Victoria hid her face against his chest and waited for her brothers-in-law to leave.

"Give us a moment or two," Alexander said

hoarsely. He looked down at her stricken expression, saying, "Victoria was about to retire for the night."

"What must they think of me?" she whispered, hearing the door click shut.

Alexander drew her gown up to cover her breasts. With one finger he lifted her chin and said, "Look at me, Tory." When she did, he told her, "Your brothers-in-law do not think badly of you. I want you to go to bed now. Tomorrow, we need to have a serious discussion."

Worriedly, Victoria searched his hazel eyes. "A discussion with His Grace about my behavior?"

Alexander planted a chaste kiss on her lips. "No, Victoria, we will discuss us."

CHAPTER 3

She would never leave her bedchamber again!

Victoria decided that when she awakened late the following morning. In the unlikely event that she would change her mind, Victoria dressed in a blue gown and wandered across the chamber to gaze out the window at a cloudy, warm day. She hoped a maid would come by. Starving herself was not on her agenda.

The thought of walking downstairs to face Alexander and her brothers-in-law filled her with shame, staining her cheeks with a rosy hue. She could not face the earl after the liberties she had allowed him, nor could she face Rudolf and Robert because they had witnessed her wanton behavior.

What would she have done if the lovemaking had gone further? Victoria asked herself. What if her brothers-in-law had walked into the game room and seen even more?

Her gaze fixed on the woodland behind the gazebo. She saw nothing but Alexander in her mind's eye and replayed their amorous encounter, sending a melting sensation coursing through her body.

Again, Victoria felt her softness pressed against his hard, unyielding frame. His wonderfully talented mouth claimed hers, scorched her skin, and marked her as his.

Victoria closed her eyes, almost feeling the incredible sensation of his lips and tongue on her nipples. She hadn't known such pleasure existed, and there was more she yearned to experience.

Giving herself a mental shake, Victoria wondered if she suffered from some unnatural defect as well as her inability to read, write, and cipher. No matter what she did, she could never please her uncle. Only yesterday, His Grace had given her a humiliating dressing-down for alleged immoral behavior. What would the duke do if he knew what she had actually done with Alexander?

By one o'clock, Victoria despaired that any maid would bring her food, and she was hungry. The idea of sneaking down the servants' stairs to the kitchen popped into her mind.

Victoria crossed her chamber to the door and listened. No sounds emanated from the corridor. She opened the door and then gave a startled cry, as did her sisters, who had been just about to knock.

Stepping aside, Victoria held the door open for them. Angelica and Samantha slipped inside the chamber.

"Why haven't you come down yet?" Angelica asked.

"Alex is concerned," Samantha said. "He asked us to look for you."

Victoria sighed. "I don't want to see the earl."

"You were getting along so well last night," Samantha said.

"I'm embarrassed to see him," Victoria admitted, a blush staining her cheeks. "Alex and I went to the game room, and when your husbands arrived to play billiards, I was naked to the waist. Alex was kissing my breasts."

"Rudolf was more embarrassed than you," Samantha said.

"So was Robert," Angelica added.

"They told you?" Victoria moaned.

"Seeing Robert embarrassed *me* after the first time we—you know," Angelica said.

"I felt the same way," Samantha agreed. "Seeing Alex is the only cure for embarrassment. If you don't go downstairs, Alex will come upstairs to reassure you."

"Why would he do that?" Victoria asked.

"Perhaps Alex is falling in love with you," Angelica answered.

"How could a sophisticated man like Alex love someone as stupid as I am?" Victoria asked, unable to credit what her sister was saying.

"You aren't stupid," Samantha said.

"Even if you are stupid, Alex doesn't know it," Angelica said, hiding a smile. Then, "Don't get your back up. I'm only teasing."

"Do you want to face Alex in the drawing room or the bedchamber?" Samantha asked.

"Tell him I'll be down in a few minutes," Victoria said, surrendering to the inevitable.

Ten minutes later, Victoria paused outside the drawing room to smooth an imaginary wrinkle from her skirt. The thought of seeing Alexander tied her stomach in knots.

And then Victoria heard familiar voices coming from inside the drawing room. Rudolf's brothers,

Princes Viktor, Mikhail, and Stepan, had arrived. She was about to start forward when she heard the princes speaking to the earl.

"Congratulations, my lord, on your betrothal and impending marriage," Prince Viktor was saying.

"We read about your good fortune in yesterday's *Times,*" Prince Mikhail said.

"She will make a devoted wife and give you many strong sons," Prince Stepan added.

"Thank You, Your Highnesses," Alexander replied to their good wishes.

Victoria froze. Alexander was engaged and would soon marry?

Backing away from the door, Victoria leaned against the wall. Her heart sank to her stomach, and her head swam dizzyingly. Tears of hurt disappointment filled her eyes and rolled slowly down her cheeks, but she brushed them away. She wished she could crawl into a hole and die.

Alexander had flirted with her, kissed her, and touched her but had been betrothed to someone else the whole time. She felt tarnished and stupid. The earl had used her for a toy, a diversion for the weekend.

Victoria almost felt sorry for the lady. The poor woman would endure a lifetime of his unfaithfulness.

And then Victoria recalled what he had told her in the game room. The earl said that he had no mistress.

A tidal wave of anger surged through her. Alexander Emerson wanted to make her his mistress. He had nearly succeeded, too. If her brothers-inlaw had not interrupted, she could be a fallen woman.

Victoria decided to put the whole affair behind her. It could have been worse; she might have succumbed to his seduction. Her feelings were hurt, but her virtue was intact.

She would practice her flirting skills on Rudolph's three brothers. That should effectively tell the earl that he had no chance to make her his mistress. She needed to be careful never to be alone with him again.

After taking a deep breath, Victoria squared her shoulders and pasted a sunny smile onto her face. Then she walked into the drawing room.

Victoria saw Prince Stepan first. Ignoring the earl, she brushed past him and headed straight for the youngest prince.

"It's good to see you," Victoria greeted him.

"Best wishes," Stepan said, and lifted her hand to his lips.

"Best wishes to you, too," Victoria replied, confused by his words.

"Stepan, I want to speak with you," Rudolf called, from where he stood with his two other brothers.

"Luncheon will be served in the garden," Aunt Roxie announced.

Feeling a presence beside her, Victoria glanced to her right and saw Alexander. He didn't look especially happy.

"I want to speak privately," Alexander said. "Will you come with me to His Grace's study?"

"I will go nowhere with you," Victoria answered, anger coloring her complexion.

"Are you embarrassed about last night?"

"Please do not remind me of my folly," she replied, waving her hand in a gesture of dismissal.

Alexander narrowed his gaze on her. "I would like to speak with you about us," he said.

Victoria knew he was going to make her a proposal. "There is no 'us,'" she informed him. "Nor
will there ever be an 'us.'"

When she moved away, Alexander encircled her
shoulders with his arm and pulled her back to his
side. "We need to speak."

"I'm sorry to spoil your plans, my lord, but I am
a virtuous woman," Victoria told him. "Stay away
from me, or I'll scream." At that, she lifted her
nose into the air and walked out of the drawing
room.

Tables had been set up on the expanse of lawn
nearest the house. The children and their nannies, nearby at long tables, had already had their
luncheon. Tinker and his squadron of footmen
stood at attention, ready to serve.

Victoria intended to sit with the three Russian
princes and as far from Alexander as possible.
Prince Rudolf materialized beside her and, gently
but firmly, escorted her away from the table. "Is
something wrong?" he asked. "You know you can
confide in me."

"You know what is wrong," Victoria answered.
"You saw what Alexander was doing in the gameroom."

"That behavior is natural between a man and a
woman," Rudolf told her. "There is nothing to
be—"

"I heard your brothers congratulating him
about his betrothal," Victoria interrupted, her
voice an angry whisper. "Alex is trying to seduce
me into being his mistress after he's married to
someone else. What do you say to that?"

Rudolf stared at her in obvious surprise. Then
he threw back his head and shouted with laughter.
"Tory, you are more entertaining than a Drury

Lane actress," he said. "Alex does not want you for his mistress. You are not the mistress type."

"What is the mistress type?" she asked, insulted by his laughter.

"A man chooses an experienced woman for his mistress," Rudolf explained. "You are barely out of the schoolroom. Why would he want a virgin mistress?"

"You should ask him that question," Victoria said, and stalked off toward the table.

Victoria sat down with the three princes though they appeared not to want her near them, especially Stepan who seemed unaccountably uncomfortable when she slipped into the chair beside his. She pretended blindness but surreptitiously watched Alexander sitting at the far end of the table with her brothers-in-law.

Seeing the three of them put their heads together, Victoria knew they were discussing her. She could feel the earl's gaze on her. His disgruntled expression became a smile, which made her even more nervous, and then the three men exploded into laughter.

Victoria lost her appetite but looked over the luncheon fare and filled her plate anyway. She helped herself to a crisp salad with sharp creamy dressing and a spicy egg and anchovy sandwich.

"What has been happening in London?" Victoria asked Stepan, trying to banish the earl's presence by making conversation.

"The usual," the prince said without looking at her.

No help there. The prince's behavior verged on rudeness.

"Have you attended any balls?" Victoria asked Mikhail.

"I've been passing my evenings at White's," the prince answered.

"How do gentlemen pass their time at White's?" Victoria asked Viktor.

This prince, at least, smiled at her. "We drink and gamble."

"How interesting," she said. "Do the gentlemen ever discuss the ladies?"

Prince Viktor coughed. "I've never heard any gossip."

Victoria wanted to ask to whom Alexander was betrothed, but pride kept her silent. Suddenly, she realized why the princes were behaving strangely. Rudolf had warned them away; her own brother-in-law was conspiring with the earl.

Rising from her chair, Victoria gave the princes a reproving look. "Though I find your company charming, Your Highnesses, I promised to lunch with my nieces and nephews."

"Where are you going?" Duke Magnus called to her.

"I am going to sit with the children," Victoria answered. "The children have no ulterior motive for liking me."

"Roxanne, I want to know what is going on here," Victoria heard her uncle saying. She didn't hear her aunt's reply because, as she passed the far end of the table, Rudolf stopped her.

"We are playing croquet after lunch and need a fourth," Rudolf said. "Will you play with us?"

Victoria looked at him and then flicked a glance at Alexander. She was about to refuse when she realized the damage she could inflict with a mallet and croquet balls.

"I would love to play croquet," Victoria said, her smile bright.

She ate a pleasant lunch in the company of the

children and their nannies. No one avoided conversing with her, and no one tried to seduce her.

An hour later, after the footmen had set up the wickets and the pegs for croquet, Robert, her partner, and she stood with mallets in hand at the start line. Rudolf and Alexander had insisted the lady should go first.

"The first wicket is on your left," Robert told her.

"I do understand we go around clockwise," Victoria replied in an irritated voice.

Robert inclined his head. "I apologize for underestimating you."

Victoria set her red ball down on the start line. She held the top of the mallet with her left arm close to her body; her right hand grasped the shaft lower down.

Hearing the snickering of the three men, Victoria decided to ignore them. They were trying to break her concentration. She placed her left foot, bearing her weight, in advance of her body. Slowly, she drew the head of the mallet back and struck the ball, which rolled about halfway to the first wicket.

With a triumphant smile, Victoria turned to the men. Rudolf and Alexander were laughing; Robert wore a pained expression.

"You were supposed to hit the ball toward the first wicket," Robert told her.

"I did."

Robert shook his head. "Wicket one is to your left. You struck the ball to the right, wicket four."

"Victoria can't tell left from right," Alexander called, making her flush with embarrassment. "She had the same problem at the billiard table last night." His tone became suggestive when he added, "You remember the billiard table, Tory. I believe you were sitting on it."

Both Robert and Rudolf turned their backs, but Victoria could see their shoulders shaking with laughter. She suffered the sudden urge to hit the earl with the mallet but managed to control herself.

Victoria marched to her ball, picked it up, and crossed the lawn until she stood halfway between the start and wicket one. Then she set the ball down and walked to the sideline so the next player could start.

"You can't do that," Alexander told her. "You'll need to start over when it's your turn."

"I can do anything I want," Victoria said, whirling toward him. "Shooting the wrong way was an honest mistake."

Rudolf started next, and then came Robert. Both men shot their balls closer to the wicket than she had.

Alexander stepped up to the start line. He hit the ball expertly, and it rolled through wicket one.

"Nice shot," Rudolf called.

"That was great," Robert added, and then turned to Victoria. "Do you think you can hit the ball in the correct direction this time?"

With her anger rising to the boiling point, Victoria approached her ball. She positioned her body and drew the mallet back.

"You are holding the shaft incorrectly," Alexander called. "I would be happy to teach you the proper way to grasp a shaft, *Mistress* Victoria."

Rudolf and Robert shouted with laughter. Victoria felt her face growing hot. And then she noticed Rudolf's brothers and the duke walking toward them, apparently attracted by the men's laughter.

Victoria hit the ball. It rolled close to the first wicket but did not go through.

"What do you think, Tory?" Robert asked. "How many strokes will it take to get the ball through the wicket?"

Victoria ignored her unsympathetic partner. Both Rudolf and Robert hit their balls through the first wicket. Then, Alexander hit his ball through the second wicket on his first stroke.

While the men were admiring the expert shot, Victoria kicked her ball through the first wicket. She dreaded the oncoming ribald comments but supposed she deserved them. She had fallen from grace by allowing the earl to touch her but would never have expected him to be so cruel.

"Tory, it's your turn," Robert called.

"Wait a minute," Alexander said, marching back to the first wicket. "Your ball was on the other side of the wicket."

"You are mistaken," Victoria said, looking him straight in the eye.

Alexander towered over her. "I would never have expected you to cheat, *Mistress* Victoria." He walked away but managed to hit her with a parting insult. "Let her cheat," he called to the prince. "She's going to lose anyway." Then, in a louder voice, "I'm sorry we stuck you with her, Robert."

Victoria felt her complexion flaming with embarrassment and inwardly cursed her red hair. She hit the ball, which rolled near the second wicket.

Both Rudolf and Robert managed to get their balls through wicket two. Alexander shot next, his ball rolling only part way toward the third wicket.

"Perhaps your luck is changing, my lord," Victoria called, relieved that the earl was less than perfect.

Alexander did not respond. Instead, he turned his back on her as she stepped up to her ball.

Victoria didn't miss his insult. This one smarted as much as his comments.

At the last minute, Victoria changed direction and aimed for the earl. She hit the ball as hard as she could and watched it fly into the air and strike the earl's leg.

"I'm terribly sorry," Victoria called, when he whirled around. "You know I have a problem with directions."

Her apology didn't stop Alexander. He started toward her, marching purposefully across the grass, and there was no mistaking the fury etched across his features.

Victoria stood frozen as the earl closed the distance between them. She began to tremble when he reached the halfway point.

And then God sent her a reprieve. The clouds yawned, and a torrential deluge of water fell from the sky.

Everyone, including Victoria, ran toward the house. When she reached the door, she was still clutching the mallet and then she dropped it.

Once inside the house, Victoria kept running. Alexander caught up with her at the bottom of the foyer stairs. He seized her upper arm and whirled her around.

"If you ever do anything like that again," he warned, "I'll take you across my knee. Do you understand?"

Frightened, Victoria nodded. She didn't stop nodding until he walked away, muttering curses.

An hour later, Victoria had changed her gown and brushed her hair. She debated hiding in her chamber for the remainder of the weekend, but the earl's threat precluded that. She had shown fear and, in order to save face, needed to return downstairs to pretend that he hadn't frightened her.

Summoning her courage, Victoria forced herself to go to the drawing room where everyone would congregate after drying off. She paused to collect herself and then, hiding her trembling hands in the folds of her skirt, walked into the room.

Spying Alexander sitting with Rudolf and Samantha at a card table, Victoria walked in the opposite direction. She didn't bother to approach the prince's brothers but gave them a frosty glance as she passed them.

"Victoria, I want to speak to you," Duke Magnus called.

Her damned uncle.

Victoria had forgotten that he had seen her trying to injure the earl. Now His Grace would give her a dressing-down in front of everyone. Her whole life had been falling apart, one humiliating event after another, since speaking to the earl at the stream yesterday.

Victoria knew she couldn't prevent a tongue-lashing from the duke. She deserved it, too. Aiming the ball at the earl had been wrong, and she would have to apologize.

With her gaze on her uncle, Victoria crossed the room. The duke shifted his gaze to a point behind her. She glanced over her shoulder and caught the earl shaking his head at the duke. What did that mean?

"Never mind," Duke Magnus said, gesturing her away. "I'll speak with you later."

Victoria wasn't about to argue the point. She wasn't looking forward to a dressing-down in front of guests.

It would be best to apologize to the earl now, she decided. Waiting meant continued worry.

Turning around, Victoria caught Alexander watching her. When her gaze met his, he looked away and started speaking to her brother-in-law.

On shaking legs, Victoria crossed the drawing room and stood beside Alexander. She waited for him to acknowledge her presence, but he ignored her.

"My lord," Victoria said softly. When he looked at her, she flicked her tongue out to wet her lips gone dry from nervousness. "My lord, I apologize for trying to injure you. My behavior was inexcusable, and I hope you will forgive me."

His hazel gaze warmed to her, and the hint of a smile touched his lips. "Are you apologizing on orders from His Grace?"

"No, but His Grace would have ordered me to apologize if he had spoken to me," she answered honestly.

Alexander arched a brow at her. "Are you apologizing in order to prevent a dressing-down?"

"No, Alex, I am apologizing because I was wrong," Victoria answered, and then tipped her head in the duke's direction. "I'm certain His Grace will still spare a few minutes out of his busy schedule to give me a dressing-down."

Alexander smiled at her. Victoria felt a fluttering in the pit of her stomach.

"We wanted to play whist and needed a fourth," he said, gesturing to her sister and brother-in-law. "Will you play?"

The last thing Victoria wanted to do was play cards. Her inability to distinguish certain numbers would only cause trouble, but refusing the earl's invitation would appear rude.

"I would love to play cards," Victoria lied, "but I've misplaced my spectacles."

"You'll only be looking at a few numbers," Alexander said. "I'm certain you can muddle through."

Victoria acquiesced with a nod of her head and sat across the table from the earl. She glanced at her sister. Samantha wore a worried expression; she knew the danger in Victoria's trying to read numbers.

Alexander shuffled the cards, set them down for Samantha to cut, and then dealt them. He placed the last card, the trump card, face up on the table before him.

"Diamonds are trumps," he said.

Victoria picked her cards up and felt her stomach flip-flop in dismay. She had a fair number of sixes and nines, as well as red and black. The reds seemed to be the same shape, as did the blacks. How was she to know which red card was the trump suit?

Victoria wished she had refused the invitation. She glanced at Samantha whose eyes held a question.

Responding to her sister, Victoria gave an almost imperceptible shake of her head. She refused to tell the earl or anyone else about her problem and would muddle through the game as best she could. Never would she even consider admitting to her stupidity.

Rudolf, on her right, led the play by tossing a black ten on the table. Victoria stared at the black ten, a one and a zero. She could read that much, but had he tossed a spade or a club?

"Any day now, Tory," Alexander said with a smile in his voice.

Victoria gave him a sheepish smile. Avoiding the sixes and nines, she tossed a black queen down.

"Tory, are you certain you understand how to play whist?" Alexander asked, stopping the game.

She nodded. "I play with my sisters all the time."

"Do you mind if I check her hand?" Alexander asked Rudolf.

The prince didn't mind, but Victoria did. "Why do you want to see my cards?" she asked.

"Pass me your cards," the earl ordered without giving her a reason.

Victoria handed him her cards. Watching his expression, she knew she had blundered.

"Rudolf played a ten of spades," Alexander said, irritation tingeing his voice. "You played a queen of clubs, which you are going to lose because it isn't the lead suit. You could have played the knave of spades and won the trick."

"I'm sorry," Victoria apologized, feeling self-conscious.

Play resumed.

Samantha played the two of spades. Alexander followed her with the four of spades, giving the first trick to Rudolf and Samantha.

Next, Rudolf played a red eight. Praying to choose the correct suit, Victoria picked a nine and tossed it down. Samantha threw a red three and Alexander the red two.

When the prince reached to gather the cards, Victoria said, "I won that trick."

"Eight beats six," Rudolf told her.

"I played the nine," Victoria said.

"You played a six," Alexander told her, sounding more irritated than before. "Let me see your cards."

With her frustration growing, Victoria passed him her cards. Again, she knew from his expression that she had made an error.

"Why did you play the six when you are holding the ten?"

"I thought it was a nine."

"How could you possibly think that?" he asked. "Sixes and nines are completely different numbers."

"I'm sorry," Victoria apologized, her voice no louder than a whisper, her complexion a vibrant scarlet.

Rudolf started the third round with a red ten. Victoria knew she needed a red picture card to beat it. Was the knave the correct suit? "Play your card," the earl said.

Victoria worried her bottom lip with her small white teeth. Then she tossed the knave on the table.

"Good God, Victoria," Alexander exclaimed. "You can't play a trump unless you have nothing in the suit thrown. Are you trying to lose the game, or are you just stupid?"

The word *stupid* echoed in her mind. The earl had no idea how difficult life was for stupid people. Like her.

Fighting back tears, Victoria exploded in anger. "Don't call me that," she cried, her voice rising with her anger. "Find yourself another partner." In a fit of humiliated rage, she swept the cards off the table.

Everyone in the drawing room turned to watch the scene unfolding. Victoria wanted to bolt out the door. Her uncle would certainly give her a dressing-down now.

Alexander relaxed back in his chair and studied her. "Pick the cards up," he ordered.

"No," she refused, rising from her chair. The word fell like a gauntlet between them.

Samantha leaned down to get the cards, but the earl's voice stopped her, "Leave the cards on the floor." When she looked at her husband, Rudolf nodded at her to do as the earl said.

Victoria felt her anger growing. The earl had upset her to the point of losing control, and now he sat there looking as if he had not a care in the world.

"Pick the cards up," Alexander ordered, a sterner edge to his voice.

"You are not my lord or my guardian," Victoria informed him. Unable to keep her bitter disappointment from surfacing, she added, "If you want to be obeyed, give your betrothed orders, whoever the unfortunate lady is."

Victoria knew she sounded like a scorned lover and wished she could recall the words. She flicked a glance at their audience; their smiles surprised her.

"Apologize to the earl," Aunt Roxie told her.

"Let Alex handle her," Duke Magnus said to his wife. "He will be dealing with her fits for a long time and should start now."

Victoria stared at the duke, his words confusing her. And then she knew—her uncle was giving her to the earl for his mistress.

With her complexion paling, Victoria began to tremble. She turned a troubled expression on the earl.

"I should give my betrothed orders?" Alexander said, amusement lighting his gaze on her.

"That is your business," she answered.

"When I give these orders, should my betrothed obey them without question?"

Victoria shrugged.

"Does that mean yes or no?"

"That means I don't give a fig."

"I'll take that as a yes." Alexander rose from his chair and walked around the card table to tower over her. A warning note crept into his voice when he said, "If my betrothed does not obey my orders, I'll take her across my knee and spank her."

"Tell that to your betrothed, not me." Victoria lifted her nose into the air and moved to turn away.

Alexander snaked his hand out and grabbed her wrist. "Pick up the cards, my sweet betrothed," he ordered.

Victoria couldn't credit what she had heard. The earl was already engaged. He couldn't marry two women.

"Are you implying that *I* am your betrothed?" Victoria asked, staring into his hazel eyes.

"I am saying it, not implying," Alexander told her. "Pick the *damned* cards up."

Victoria stared at him blankly. She would know if she was betrothed, wouldn't she?

"You never asked me to marry you," she said.

"Your guardians proposed the match," he told her.

Shocked and hurt, Victoria stood there, frozen, as disturbing thoughts swirled around inside her. Her aunt and uncle had proposed the match. Alexander hadn't even wanted her.

"How long have we been betrothed?" Victoria asked in an aching whisper.

"I'm sorry," Alexander apologized, recognizing the pain in her eyes. He regretted telling her that her guardians had proposed the match.

"How long?" she repeated.

"Almost a year."

"A year?"

In the next instant, Victoria whirled away and marched across the drawing room to confront her guardians. "How could you?" she asked, her tone mirroring her anguish. "You promised me in marriage but never asked what I wanted. You didn't even bother to tell me."

"We thought it for the best," Aunt Roxie said.

"Stop the theatrics, Victoria," Duke Magnus ordered. "The match is good."

"I'm questioning your treatment of me, not the match," Victoria told him. She turned to her aunt, asking, "When is the wedding?"

"June the twenty-fourth," her aunt answered, obviously flustered. "The invitations will be sent next week."

"Were you planning to send *me* an invitation?" Victoria asked, her voice dripping sarcasm. "Is that how you planned to tell me?"

Without waiting for a reply, Victoria whirled away and advanced on the card table. "And my sisters," she said, her gaze on them. "When I think of your play-acting yesterday . . ." Then she mimicked them, "Practice your flirting on Alexander. Drop your gaze shyly. Look at him as if he had just placed the world at your feet."

This last statement earned muffled chuckles from her brothers-in-law, nor did they escape her tirade.

Victoria cast a murderous glare on Robert and then looked at Rudolf, accusing, "If my sisters knew, then you knew, too."

"I asked everyone to remain silent," Alexander said in a quiet voice. "I wanted to give you a chance to grow up."

"I despise you most of all," Victoria said, rounding on him. Without warning, she slapped him, eliciting shocked gasps from the gathering.

Catching her around the waist, Alexander lifted her off her feet. Surprise kept Victoria from reacting.

"Don't touch those cards," Alexander ordered, tucking her under his arm. He marched toward the doorway, calling over his shoulder, "My *sweet* betrothed will pick them up."

Victoria had never seen anyone as angry as Alexander Emerson. She didn't dare struggle, nor did she give him the satisfaction of crying for help that would not come.

"Open that door," Alexander growled at a footman when they reached the duke's study.

Hanging from beneath his arm, Victoria kept her head down and closed her eyes against the humiliation of being carried like a recalcitrant child. She couldn't imagine what he intended, but he seemed too angry to talk things through.

Marching into the duke's study, Alexander shifted her like a ragdoll in his arms. Sitting in a chair, he forced her across his lap, and she realized in growing horror what he was going to do.

Mortified almost beyond endurance, Victoria tensed but remained silent. He swore savagely and pushed her off his lap, though not ungently. The most humiliating experience of her eighteen years was over.

"I refuse to do that," the earl said, his voice laced with self-disgust.

Victoria sat on the floor where she had fallen. She kept her head bent and her gaze fixed on the carpet.

"Are you listening to me?" he asked.

Victoria nodded but remained silent. She refused to look at the triumph in his eyes. He was bigger than she; of course, he would win when strength was the deciding factor.

"We are going to walk back to the drawing room," Alexander told her. "You will pick the cards up and keep your mouth shut. If you fail to cooperate, I *will* spank you in front of the others. Do you understand?"

Again, Victoria nodded.

"We are making progress," Alexander said. "This pleases me." He stood then and placed his hand in front of her face, silently offering to help her up from the floor.

Victoria stared at his hand and raised her gaze to his. She saw no gloating in his expression.

And then Victoria did what he least expected. She placed her hand in his.

Everyone watched in silence when they returned to the drawing room. Victoria saw their surprised expressions at the change in her demeanor and then dropped her gaze.

Reaching the card table, Victoria knelt on the floor and collected the discarded cards. She didn't utter a word, nor did anyone speak to her.

Alexander stood nearby and watched her do his bidding. She had one bad moment when he said, "There's one over here you missed."

Victoria stiffened in angry embarrassment when one of her brothers-in-law muffled a chuckle. She remained silent, knowing she would be more humiliated if she argued.

"I'll be damned," Duke Magnus said, breaking the silence. "How did you manage that?"

"Victoria and I reached an agreement," Alexander told him. "I will give the orders in our family, and she will obey them. Isn't that correct, darling?"

Too embarrassed to look up, Victoria kept her gaze on the carpet but inclined her head in the affirmative. She stood, placed the cards on the table, and turned to leave.

Alexander put his arm around her and guided

her toward the doorway, saying, "Remain in your chamber until I send for you."

And then Alexander did what she least expected. He tilted her chin up and waited for her to meet his gaze. "I apologize for embarrassing you," he said.

"I forgive you," Victoria said, and walked out the door.

CHAPTER 4

"Congratulations on your accomplishment," Prince Stepan said.

Alexander slanted an amused glance at the youngest prince. "To what accomplishment do you refer?" he asked, lining up his next shot on the billiard table.

"Taming Lady Victoria, of course."

Alexander and the other men laughed at the prince. "I haven't tamed Victoria, merely won the first skirmish," he said. "She will do my bidding, but gentling her will take time." He couldn't predict how long that would take. The chit had hammered a croquet ball at him. Fortunately, she hadn't thought of using the mallet.

"Life with Tory will never bore you," Robert said.

"She'll make you fight for every gain," Rudolf agreed.

"Nothing worth having is easily won," Alexander said. With that fiery red hair and the passion he had glimpsed the previous evening, Victoria would be well worth the fight. "Struggling to win her obedience is one thing; being bowled over by her is quite another."

"What do you mean?" Prince Stepan asked.

"We know you escorted Victoria to Drury Lane," Alexander said.

"She threatened to ask someone else to take her," Stepan defended himself. "Another man might not have protected her."

"Stepan, did you ever consider that Tory did not know any other gentleman to take her there?" Rudolf asked his brother.

Prince Stepan flushed. "I never considered that."

If he had taken Victoria to Drury Lane, Alexander thought, he would be enjoying her body by now instead of fighting her. How could he have known the little virgin would be so passionate?

"Stepan, you had better stick with the debutantes being put in your way," Prince Viktor said, entering the conversation.

"Controlling a spirited woman might be beyond your capability," said Prince Mikhail.

Tinker, the duke's majordomo, walked into the gameroom. Alexander watched the man heading straight for him.

"Lord Emerson."

"Yes?"

"Lady Victoria demands to be released from prison," Tinker announced in a voice that brooked no refusal.

Alexander cocked a brow at the older man. He couldn't credit the retainer's insolence.

"Do not be offended," Rudolf said. "Tinker told me once to fetch my own coffee."

Tinker turned to the prince and looked down his nose at him. "As I recall, you deserved that set down for making Lady Samantha weep." The majordomo looked at the earl, saying, "This matter is entirely different. Lady Victoria instructed me to repeat her words *with emotion.* "

All the men laughed, including Alexander. Tinker's lips twitched with amusement.

"Gentlemen, place your bets," Alexander said, smiling. "Skirmish two is about to begin." He turned to the majordomo, saying, "Tell Lady Victoria my answer is *no.* "

"Yes, my lord."

"Who would you bet on if you were a gambling man?" Alexander asked.

Tinker gave the earl a long look and then reached into his trouser pocket. He produced a one pound note, asking, "Who is holding the bets?"

"I will hold all bets," Rudolf said, lifting the note out of the older man's hand.

Tinker glanced at the earl and then told the prince, "I'll wager one pound on Lady Victoria."

The men howled with laughter and began reaching for money. Alexander felt better when the other gentlemen wagered on him.

"I thank all of you for contributing to my retirement fund," Tinker drawled, leaving the gameroom.

Billiards play resumed.

The majordomo returned five minutes later, calling, "Lord Emerson?"

"Could you possibly wait until my shot is complete before you call my name," Alexander said.

"I'm terribly sorry," Tinker apologized, wearing an unrepentent expression. "Lady Victoria wants to know if you are planning to starve her into submission."

"That sounds like an interesting idea," Alexander replied, making the men smile. "Tell Lady Victoria she will be eating with the children until she grows up."

Watching the majordomo hurry away, Alexander decided that when Victoria's emotional maturity caught up with her body, she would be magnificent. And she would belong to him.

Tinker returned five minutes later. The men chuckled when he walked into the room. The majordomo headed across the room to Prince Rudolf instead of the earl.

"Your Highness, Lady Victoria has no money but wishes to place a one pound bet on the outcome of this conflict," Tinker told him. "In the unlikely event that she loses, her exceedingly wealthy fiancé will cover her loss."

"The hell I will," Alexander called out, laughing.

"Tell the lady we deal only in ready cash," Prince Rudolf instructed the majordomo.

"The lady will not be pleased," Tinker said.

Next, the majordomo approached the earl. Alexander was already smiling in anticipation of the message from his betrothed.

"Lady Victoria said it's customary for the bride and the groom to sit together at the wedding breakfast," Tinker said. "She wondered if you will be joining her at the children's table."

Alexander shouted with laughter, as did the other men. His betrothed was proving entertaining and sharp-witted.

"I may grant her a furlough for that one meal," he told the majordomo.

Instead of leaving the gameroom, Tinker turned to Robert and said, "Lady Victoria asked me to remind you that a marquess outranks an earl. Would you consider granting her permission to leave her chamber?"

"No."

"What a conniving little witch," Alexander said, laughing.

"A prince outranks a mere marquess and an earl," Tinker said to Rudolf. "Would you consider—?"

"Today is my day off," the prince interrupted. "I never do any considering on my day off."

"Your Highnesses?" Tinker asked, turning to Rudolf's younger brothers.

All three choked with laughter and ignored him.

"I will relay your messages," Tinker said, and left the room.

Play resumed. Alexander chalked the tip of his cue and lined up his shot.

"Lord Emerson," Tinker called, returning to the room.

"What is it this time?" Alexander asked, irritated at missing his shot.

"Lady Victoria requires your presence upstairs," Tinker told him. "She wants to apologize."

Alexander raised his brows at the majordomo and then smirked at his future brothers-in-law. "Tell her I'll come when I'm free," he said.

"Lady Victoria instructed me to tell you that she hasn't long to live," Tinker replied. "If you delay, she will have expired."

Alexander grinned. "What is her malady?"

"The lady is bored to death," Tinker answered, unable to suppress his smile.

"Tell her I'll mourn her passing," Alexander said.

The other men smiled when the majordomo left the room. Prince Rudolf and Robert Campbell, the only married men there, nodded their approval for the earl's response.

"Victoria wanting to apologize means you have

won," Prince Stepan said. "Why didn't you go upstairs to accept her apology?"

"If I did that, I would be doing her bidding," Alexander explained, slanting an amused glance at the youngest prince. "Winning means making her wait until I'm ready to listen. Then she is doing *my* bidding."

Prince Rudolf and Robert raised their glasses in a salute to the earl. Alexander inclined his head, accepting their praise.

Five minutes passed without the majordomo's return. The minutes stretched to ten, twenty, thirty. And then almost an hour.

Everyone smiled when Tinker walked into the gameroom and headed straight for the earl. "When you have a free moment and if it isn't too much trouble, would you please speak with Lady Victoria?" Tinker asked. "She is beside herself with remorse, desperate to apologize, and anxious to share the lessons she has learned from this experience."

"Lady Victoria is a pain in the arse," Alexander said.

"Shall I relay that message?" Tinker asked.

Alexander's lips twitched. "Please do."

Miss Victoria Douglas had to realize who was the master in their family. She was a fiery creature of passion; her response to his caresses the previous evening had told him that. A frightened virgin, she had placed herself in his hands, trusted him to keep her safe and pleasure her. Though she hadn't known they were to be married, some part of her had known she belonged to him. He had seen that in her eyes before he had kissed her into a daze at the stream.

"You delayed too long," Prince Rudolf told him.

Alexander looked at the prince, who stood near the window. "What do you mean?"

"Take a look." Prince Rudolf grinned and gestured toward the window.

Alexander crossed the room. With flute in hand, Victoria walked in the direction of the gazebo. A smile flirted with his lips when she skipped a few steps as if unable to contain her joy at being free of her prison.

Taking the glass of vodka the prince offered, Alexander gulped it down and grimaced at its strength. Then, in an irritated voice, he said, "I instructed the maid to let me know if Tory left her chamber."

Alexander marched across the room and yanked the door open to reveal Tinker who was just about to enter. "Damn it, Tinker, where's that maid I set to watch Lady Victoria?"

"Lady Victoria went out the window and climbed down the tree," Tinker answered.

"Does this mean Tory has won?" Prince Stepan asked, smiling.

Alexander turned to the youngest prince. There was no mistaking the murderous gleam in his gaze.

"I have a fondness for my brother," Prince Rudolf said. Then, "Stepan, you are making it more difficult for Tory to extricate herself."

Without a word to anyone, Alexander turned away. He was going to drag her inside and give her a spanking she would never forget.

Lady Roxanne appeared in the doorway and slipped her arm through his. "Do you want to sprain your hand with constant wife-spanking?" she asked in a low voice. "Or would you prefer to catch a countess for yourself?"

Alexander cocked a brow at her. "I'm listening."

"Escort Victoria to her chamber, and then go to your own chamber to start packing your bag," the duchess said, her smile feline. "I will tell Tory that you are releasing her from the betrothal. I guarantee she will go to your chamber to persuade you to stay."

"What if she doesn't?"

"I know Tory better than she knows herself," the duchess told him. "Her pride is hurt because you never courted her, and we kept silent for a year. A young naive girl like my niece yearns for a gallant knight to woo her into marriage. Victoria got a business deal."

"Does this mean I'll need to polish my armor until it shines?" Alexander asked with a wry smile.

"It would certainly help."

"I'll see what I can do."

Alexander left the house and sauntered across the grounds toward the gazebo. He could almost feel the watching gazes from the window of the gameroom.

Victoria spied the earl crossing the lawn toward her and returned the flute to its case. Alexander Emerson was handsome and well built, especially in those tight breeches he was wearing. She could hardly believe that he was the man who would be her husband, who would sleep beside her at night, who would father her children.

Victoria tried to gauge his mood. He didn't look especially angry, not as he had earlier.

"Should I lay across your lap or wait until you return me to my chamber?" she asked.

Alexander stared at her a moment, giving her a look she couldn't read, and then sat beside her. Putting his arm around her shoulders, he drew her against the side of his body.

"I want to hear about these lessons you've learned," Alexander said.

Victoria felt confused. She had expected him to give her a dressing-down.

"I apologize for escaping," she said.

"Your apology does not absolve you," he told her.

"I understand."

"About those lessons?"

"I need to control my temper," Victoria told him. "I also need to please you because, short of murder, my family will not interfere."

"You still need to learn patience, my lady," Alexander said, standing and holding his hand out to her as if asking her to dance.

Victoria looked from his hazel eyes to his offered hand. "Would you consider spanking me instead?"

"One does not learn patience from a spanking," Alexander said.

Victoria sighed and lifted her flute from the bench of the gazebo. "Since we are betrothed," she asked, "will you kiss me again like you did in the gameroom?"

"We will kiss when I am ready, not when you are," he answered.

Hand in hand, Alexander and Victoria walked across the wide expanse of lawn. Victoria stopped suddenly as they neared the house.

"I want to ask you a question," she said.

Alexander inclined his head and waited.

"Why do men give the orders and require women to obey?" she asked.

"Men are stronger and smarter," he answered.

That answer didn't sit well with Victoria. "Are you telling me that the weakest, stupidest man in the world is stronger and smarter than the strongest, smartest woman?"

Alexander grinned at her logic. "Men rule the world because we *think* instead of *feel* as women do," he answered. "We have all the money and enough wisdom to keep women pregnant so they can't compete against us."

"I wish I could live for one day in a world where women were the bosses," Victoria said.

"What would you do for that day?" Alexander asked, amusement lighting his eyes.

Victoria crooked her finger for him to lean close. "First, I would scold His Grace for his bad behavior," she whispered against his ear. "Then I would spank you and send you to your chamber without supper."

Alexander feigned fright. "Surely, you wouldn't deny me sustenance?"

"What's that?"

"Food."

Victoria flashed him an unconsciously flirtatious smile and said, "I would let you eat with the children."

Alexander laughed, enchanted by her irreverence. "You are incorrigible," he said, pointing a finger at the tip of her nose.

Unexpectedly, Victoria leaned close and grabbed his finger between her lips. Her gesture was blatantly sexual.

Alexander grabbed her upper arms and yanked her against his body. He lowered his head, his mouth claiming hers in a hungry kiss.

Victoria slid her hands up his chest and entwined her arms around his neck. She leaned heavily against him and returned his kiss in kind.

"Why were you ready now and not a few minutes ago?" Victoria asked, her lips still pressed to his.

"You little witch." Without warning, Alexander lifted her into his arms and tossed her over his shoulder like a sack of grain.

"My flute," she cried.

"I'll send someone out for it," he said.

Victoria giggled, feeling the blood rushing to her head. "My brains are going to leak out of my ears," she called.

"I'll send someone out for them," Alexander said, making her laugh.

"Don't you think you're carrying husbandly discipline a bit too far?" Victoria called.

"I'm enjoying this view of you," Alexander said, patting her upended bottom.

With Victoria giggling, Alexander carried her into the house. The four Russian princes and the marquess stood in the foyer to watch.

"I guess the earl won," Prince Stepan said.

"Don't fool yourself," Prince Rudolf said in a loud voice. "If Victoria is laughing, she won the skirmish."

Halfway up the stairs, Alexander grinned when he heard Victoria calling, "Don't listen to him. Rudolf wants you to spank me."

Reaching her bedchamber, Alexander set her down on her feet. "Do not go out the window again, or I'll chop the tree down," he told her. "You wouldn't want to cause the death of a perfectly healthy tree."

Victoria lay on her bed and concentrated on learning patience. She didn't believe she would be successful. If only she could learn to read. Readers could lose themselves in books for hours and hours. That would never happen for her; she was much too stupid to learn.

How would she ever keep her stupidity from Alexander? Living with him and keeping the secret would be impossible. She needed to try to learn to read again. This time she would bypass her sisters' and aunt's instruction and hire a tutor. With her mind made up, Victoria decided she would speak to Samantha's children's tutor, Phineas Philbin, once she returned to London.

Twenty minutes later, Aunt Roxie walked into her chamber. Her aunt looked upset, and Victoria wondered what she had done wrong this time.

"Well, Tory, you have gotten your wish," Aunt Roxie said, giving her a displeased look.

Victoria had no idea to what her aunt was referring. "What do you mean?"

"Lord Emerson is canceling the betrothal agreement," Aunt Roxie told her. "He doesn't want to force you into an unwanted marriage."

"I want to marry him," Victoria said, alarmed.

"Darling, Alexander is returning to London tonight," her aunt informed her. "He has gone to his chamber to pack his belongings."

"Tell him I am content," Victoria said.

"If you want to marry the earl, you need to persuade him that His Grace and I aren't forcing you into this," Aunt Roxie said.

With a worried expression, Victoria bolted off the bed and hurried across the chamber to the door. She did not see her aunt's smile of satisfaction.

Alexander couldn't change his mind about marrying her. That was unacceptable. Now that he'd touched her breasts, he was going to marry her. After all, she hadn't let him win these skirmishes between them for nothing.

"The earl's chamber is the last door on the right," Aunt Roxie called.

Victoria marched down the corridor, stopping when she reached the last door on the right. Her hands were shaking, and her heart was pumping furiously.

Eating crow galled her, but she wanted him.

Steeling herself for another humiliating experience, Victoria knocked on the door. When she heard him call out, she stepped inside and closed the door behind her.

"Yes, Victoria?" Alexander said, looking up from his packing, his hazel gaze fixed on hers.

Victoria wet her lips, dry from nervousness. She shifted her gaze to his bag, asking, "You're leaving?"

"That is quite perceptive of you," Alexander said, and resumed his packing.

"Why?"

"*Why?*"

Victoria leaned back against the solidness of the door for support. "Please don't leave."

"Why shouldn't I leave?" Alexander asked, giving her his full attention. "You aren't interested in marrying me."

"I never said I wouldn't honor our betrothal contract," she said.

"I have no wish to pass the next forty years spanking a wife," he told her.

"I will obey you in all matters," Victoria promised.

Alexander cocked a brow at her. His skepticism was amusingly apparent.

"Very well, I promise to obey you in *most* matters," she amended herself.

That brought a smile to his lips. "I don't want a wife who is merely honoring a contract," Alexander said. "I want a wife who will care about me."

"I *want* to marry you," Victoria said, a high blush staining her cheeks. "I do care about you."

Alexander stared at her for so long that Victoria feared he was going to reject her. Then his gaze softened, and he said, "Come here, Tory."

On shaking legs, Victoria crossed the chamber until she stood merely inches from him. She tilted her head back and gazed into his hazel eyes.

"We will be married for a long time," Alexander said, grasping her upper arms in a light grip. "Are you absolutely certain this is what you want?"

"This is what I want. Only—"

"Only what, Tory?"

"I wish you had courted me first and then asked me like other gentlemen do with their ladies," Victoria told him. "I don't understand why everyone but me knew we were betrothed."

Hearing the hurt confusion in her voice, Alexander pulled her close and put his arms around her. "*I* made the mistake," he admitted. "The others only honored my wishes. Will you forgive me?"

"Yes." Victoria tipped her head back, looked into his hazel eyes, and wished that he could love her. Too bad she was too stupid to love.

Pressing her head against the solidness of his chest, she told him, "I feel safe and protected with your arms around me. I can't remember ever feeling safe and protected."

"Look at me," Alexander said in a husky voice.

When she did, he dipped his head and his mouth covered hers in an endless, drugging kiss. She entwined her arms around his neck, pressed herself against the hard planes of his body, and returned his kiss in kind.

"You never felt safe and I never had a loving family," Alexander whispered, his lips hovering above hers. "Together, we will create our own family, and our children will always feel safe, protected, and loved."

"Yes, Alex," Victoria breathed against his lips.

His lips covered hers again. This time her lips parted in invitation, welcoming his tongue inside her mouth.

The world faded away for Victoria, her whole being focused on his lips, his tongue, his body pressed intimately against hers. His strength surrounded her, comforted her, aroused her. A soft whimpering sound escaped her throat as she surrendered to his kiss and yearned for more.

Alexander kissed her thoroughly, inciting her to meet his passion. He cupped her buttocks and lifted her off the floor to feel the rock hardness at his groin. Slowly, he lowered her to the floor and then slipped his hand between their bodies to caress her breasts, so soft beneath the bodice of her dress.

Victoria moaned at the contact. She wanted to feel his hands on her bare flesh.

Knowing what she needed, Alexander unfastened her gown, drawing it and her chemise down to her waist. Victoria felt the cool air caressing her breasts. And then his hands were on her bare flesh—cupping, kneading, caressing. When he flicked his thumb across the tips of her nipples, pleasure buckled her legs.

Alexander steadied her and placed her across his bed. Fully clothed, he stood there for long moments and gazed at her alabaster breasts with their pink-tipped peaks.

After removing his shirt, Alexander leaned over her, supporting himself on his elbows. He saw the blush creeping from her cheeks to her neck to the swell of her breasts.

"Never be embarrassed by what we do in our bed," Alexander told her. "A wife belongs to her husband."

"Like property?" Victoria whispered, her expression troubled.

Alexander shook his head. "A husband and wife belong to each other, no matter what troubles may come," he amended.

Alexander pressed a kiss on her lips and then

lay on the bed, rolling her on her side to face him. He dipped his head and captured a nipple between his lips, sucking upon it, flicking his tongue across its tip, while his fingers tormented her other breast.

Victoria burned with desire. She held his head and arched her back, thrusting her breasts forward for him. Instinctively, her hips began to move in rhythm with his sucking and fondling. She needed him closer and closer until she would be one with him.

Suddenly, Alexander released her and rose from the bed. He pulled her off the bed and smiled when she moaned in disappointed protest.

"We will have years to enjoy what we started here," Alexander told her, helping her dress. He escorted her across the chamber to the door, saying, "Thank you for agreeing to be my wife. I will come to your chamber thirty minutes before dinner to escort you downstairs. I have a surprise for you."

"I don't like surprises," Victoria told him, still dazed by his caresses.

That brought a smile to his lips. "I promise you will like this one."

Two hours later, Victoria stood in front of the cheval mirror in her bedchamber and eyed herself critically. Her gown had been created in celestial blue silk with a medium-high waist, a low-cut and rounded neckline, and short melon sleeves. She had woven her fiery mane into a simple knot at the nape of her neck, but several curly tendrils had escaped.

What surprise did Alexander have for her? Victoria wondered. She hated surprises. Being startled made her feel disoriented, panicked, and stupid.

The bedchamber door swung open. In the mirror, Victoria saw Alexander walk into her chamber. She noted that he hadn't bothered to knock, as if he had the right of ownership.

Without turning around, Victoria smiled at him in the mirror. Alexander placed his hands on her shoulders and nuzzled the nape of her neck, sending a delicious shiver down her spine.

Victoria sighed. She didn't want to go to dinner. She wanted to marry him now, this moment. She wanted to learn what other pleasure he could give her.

"You are beautiful," Alexander whispered against her ear. "Except . . ." She felt his hands at the nape of her neck, and then her hairknot came unfastened, sending curls of fire cascading to her waist. "I prefer your hair loose. You remind me of a pagan princess."

"Ladies always wear their hair up in the evening," Victoria told him, parroting her aunt's words.

Lifting her hair away from one side of her face, Alexander placed his warm lips to the side of her throat. "My passionate pagan," he murmured.

Victoria decided she would always wear her hair down unless pinning it up was absolutely necessary. She leaned back against his strength, savoring the feeling of his lips brushing her neck.

Through half-closed eyes, Victoria watched in the mirror as Alexander slid his hands under her arms to embrace her from behind. He cupped her breasts and glided his fingers across her nipples, which hardened beneath the silk.

A bolt of desire shot through her from her nipples to the sensitive spot between her thighs. Closing her eyes, she whimpered and leaned heavily against him.

"Open your eyes, Tory," Alexander whispered. "Watch me touching your breasts."

Victoria opened her eyes and saw him slide his hands inside the bodice of the low-cut gown. Alexander flicked his thumbs across the tips of her nipples and then, holding them between his thumb and forefinger, squeezed them gently and rolled the tips back and forth.

"Oh, God," Victoria moaned.

"After we're married, we'll stand naked in front of a mirror," Alexander said, his voice seductively husky. "You'll watch me do this and other things. You'll moan my name instead of God's."

His words made her legs buckle, but he held her steady. Turning her around in his arms, Alexander smiled at her dazed expression.

"Kiss me," Victoria breathed, sliding her arms up his chest to entwine his neck.

Alexander planted a kiss on her lips and then set her back from him. "We are expected downstairs," he told her. "If we don't arrive soon, everyone will wonder where we are."

"Let them wonder," Victoria said, gazing into his hazel eyes. "No one will fuss about our absence. We've been betrothed for a year already."

Alexander laughed in her face. "*I* have been betrothed for a year," he corrected her. "*You* have been betrothed for less than a day. Remember, you need to learn patience."

"Can't I learn patience tomorrow?"

"No, you owe apologies to everyone."

Victoria slanted an unhappy glance at him. She hated apologies almost as much as she hated surprises.

Everyone had gathered in the drawing room before going down to dinner. Nobody looked up at Alexander and Victoria when they entered.

"Are we invisible?" she whispered. "Or is this the cut direct?"

"They're afraid you'll suffer one of your fits if they greet you," Alexander said, close to her ear, steering her in the direction of her guardians.

"I do not suffer from fits," Victoria replied, insulted.

When they stood in front of her guardians, Victoria glanced at Alexander and then looked at her aunt and her uncle. "Sorry," she mumbled, embarrassed.

"Victoria." Alexander's voice held a warning note.

"I know you want what is best for me," Victoria told her guardians. "I am sorry for my bad behavior."

Aunt Roxie smiled and hugged her. "Darling, I understand what a shock your betrothal must have been."

"We only want you settled and happy," Duke Magnus said. "Alex is a fine man."

Victoria nodded. "It isn't your fault that I'm flawed. Besides, you were too old to deal with someone like me."

"That was a wonderful apology," Alexander said, covering her insulting *faux pas,* as smothered chuckles sounded from somewhere behind them.

"Darling, ladies wear their hair up in the evening," Aunt Roxie chided her, clearly unhappy about being described as old.

"Alex prefers my hair down," Victoria informed her, and lifted her nose into the air.

Ignoring her aunt's narrowing gaze, Victoria turned next to Angelica and Samantha. "Sisters, I am sorry for what I said and want you to know that I do love you," Victoria told them.

"Don't concern yourself with us," Angelica replied.

"We know you love us as much as we love you," Samantha added.

"You should have heard them," Victoria said, turning to Alex. "First, they told me not to kiss you too much, and later they told me that your touching my body would be perfectly acceptable." Raising her voice, she added, "My sisters were the worst possible women to ask for advice since both were pregnant when they married. Imagine, I'll be the only sister who doesn't actually *need* a husband."

Alexander suppressed a smile. He understood she was getting even without getting herself into trouble.

After casting her sisters a sweet smile, Victoria turned to her brothers-in-law. "I cannot believe how much you love to tease me," she said, her blue eyes sparkling with merriment. "I apologize for my angry words."

"I admire your pluck, Tory," Prince Rudolf said, lifting her hand to his lips.

"We apologize for embarrassing you," Robert added.

"I forgive you," Victoria said, starting to turn away. She paused, as if just remembering something, and added, "The next time you practice your golf, though, please don't swing those clubs so close to the children. You might injure one."

Victoria flicked a glance at her sisters. Both were glaring at their husbands.

"Troublemaker," Alexander whispered against her ear.

"Thank you for the praise," Victoria said, making him smile.

"You are doing a remarkable job training her," Prince Rudolf said, his gaze on Victoria.

"The prince is teasing you," Alexander said quickly.

"Yes, I know," Victoria said. "Simple things amuse simple people."

Prince Rudolf burst out laughing. "Very good, Tory. Do not let us upset you."

"Shall we go down to dinner?" Aunt Roxie asked.

"Not yet," Alexander said, drawing everyone's attention. He held his hand out to Victoria, saying, "Come, sit on the settee."

Victoria smiled in confusion but placed her hand in his, letting him escort her to the settee in front of the hearth. After settling herself, Victoria lifted her gaze to his. Warm hazel eyes held her gaze captive. Something was happening, but she couldn't imagine what.

With the hint of a smile flirting with his lips, Alexander stared down at her for a long moment. Then he schooled his features to a proper solemnity.

"Lady Victoria," Alexander said, surprising her by kneeling on one bended knee in front of her. "Will you do me the honor of becoming my wife and my countess?"

Victoria couldn't find her voice. She had never expected this from the earl. Could he possibly harbor tender feelings for her?

"Yes, my lord, I will marry you," Victoria answered, giving him a smile filled with sunshine.

Ignoring the applause from their audience, Alexander raised her hands to his lips. He turned them over and pressed a kiss on each of her palms. Then he reached into his pocket, produced a ring, and slipped it on the third finger of her left hand.

Victoria stared at her betrothal ring. More than nine carats, the ring had a diamond center and baguette diamond sides.

"The image of fire and ice appealed to me," Alexander told her. "You are the flame, and these diamonds are the ice. I promise to deck you in diamonds for the rest of your life."

Lifting her gaze from her betrothal ring to his hazel eyes, Victoria didn't know what to say. Instead, she leaned forward into his embrace and kissed him as if no one was watching.

CHAPTER 5

"Well done, my lord," Victoria heard her aunt say as Alexander lifted his lips from hers. "Shall we go down to dinner now?"

With her arms entwined around the earl's neck, Victoria didn't move. She had no wish to end their embrace, wanted to remain within the circle of his arms. Forever.

Victoria gazed into his hazel eyes. She certainly wasn't hungry. Except for him.

And then the moment passed.

Alexander stood and offered his hand as if he was asking her to dance. Giving him a shy smile, Victoria placed her hand in his and rose from the settee.

Ignoring the others, Alexander escorted her out of the drawing room. "I can tell from your expression that you like your betrothal ring," he said, leaning close.

"Your sentiment touches me," Victoria told him.

"You don't care for jewels?"

"Jewels can be lost or stolen," she answered. "Warm sentiments last forever."

At that, Alexander put his arm around her and pulled her against the side of his body. Then he dropped a kiss on the top of her head.

The Duke and Duchess of Inverary presided at either end of the dining table. Alexander and Victoria sat on the duke's right, followed by Prince Stepan, Angelica, and Prince Mikhail. On the opposite side of the table sat Prince Rudolf, Samantha, Prince Viktor, and Robert.

Tinker stood near the sideboard and supervised the footmen serving dinner. First came tomato soup, enriched with green herbs and a swirl of cream. Dandelion salad, dressed with crisp morsels of fried bacon and a sharp vinaigrette, followed the soup. The entrees consisted of moist chunks of finnan haddie, poached in milk and dotted with sweet butter, roasted fowl with lemon sauce, and roast beef accompanied by Yorkshire pudding and gravy made with horseradish. Various vegetables included potatoes *à la crème*, stuffed meadow mushrooms, asparagus with melted butter, and saffron pilaff.

Pretending interest in the conversations swirling around her, Victoria dropped her gaze to the betrothal ring, its diamonds sparkling at her from the third finger of her left hand. She could hardly believe that the handsome, sophisticated man beside her had slipped it on her finger and requested her hand in marriage. Tantalizing thoughts of lying naked with him in bed made her breathing shallow and her heartbeat quicken.

"Tory?"

Victoria lifted her gaze and focused on her brother-in-law. "I beg your pardon?"

"You are unusually quiet tonight," Prince Rudolf said, with a smile.

Feeling as though she'd been caught doing something she shouldn't, Victoria felt the heat of a blush staining her cheeks. She glanced at Alexander, who was watching her.

"A penny for your thoughts," Alexander said in a husky voice, as if he knew what she had been thinking.

How could she possibly answer that? Victoria wondered. She couldn't announce that she'd been thinking about making love with him.

"Tory?" Alexander said.

Her gaze fell on the roast beef with its horseradish gravy. "I was thinking of the mystery of horseradish gravy," Victoria lied.

"Horseradish gravy?" he echoed.

"I was wondering what the horses had to do with the radish," Victoria said, ignoring her brother-in-law's smothered chuckle. "I understand that radish is a vegetable, but the horses have got the better of me. Is it called horseradish because horses like to eat it?"

Flicking a quick glance at the others, Victoria realized everyone was staring at her with what appeared to be amazement in their expressions. She looked at the earl and knew she had blundered. Perhaps she should have admitted to impure thoughts.

"What an interesting idea," Alexander said smoothly. "I have an extensive library. After we're married, you can investigate the word's origin or the plant itself."

She couldn't even read the word, Victoria thought, much less discover its origin.

"Alex, you have spoken like a man avoiding an argument with his intended," Prince Rudolf said.

"Why would Alex and I argue about horseradish?" Victoria asked.

"Horses eating radish, Napoleon at Elbow, and peeling apprentices," Prince Rudolf teased her.

"Your dinner conversation is amusing but lacking in logical thought." He looked with feigned sympathy on the earl, adding, "Do not plan on much entertaining."

Again, Victoria felt the heat of a blush rising on her cheeks. Anger put it there instead of embarrassment.

Before she could think of a nasty reply, Alexander put his arm on the back of her chair. "I find your dinner conversation rather charming," he told her.

Victoria cast him a smile and began to eat, pointedly ignoring her brother-in-law until he said, "Tory, Alex needs to say that, or you will not marry him."

"Rudolf, stop teasing her," Samantha spoke up.

When Alexander reached for his wine goblet, Victoria shifted her gaze to his hands. She admired his elegantly long fingers and recalled how they had caressed her, tormented the tips of her nipples, pleasured her as she had never imagined being pleasured. The memory quickened her heartbeat, and she yearned to feel those hands sliding across her naked skin.

Shifting her gaze, Victoria stared at his lips as he spoke with her brother-in-law and the duke. Again, she felt those lips kissing, searing her breasts, sucking her nipples. A fire ignited in the pit of her stomach, and the spot between her thighs throbbed.

"Victoria?"

A woman's voice penetrated her brain.

"Victoria, did you hear me?" her aunt asked.

Embarrassed, Victoria looked at her aunt and whispered, "I beg your pardon?"

"You are behaving strangely tonight," Aunt Roxie remarked. "Are you ill?"

"Tory is dreaming about her wedding," Robert teased her.

"Is that wedding or wedding night?" Rudolf quipped, embarrassing her even more. "She does have that smitten expression, though." Then, "Samantha, why are you kicking my leg?"

"I never thought I'd see Tory hit by Cupid's arrow," Robert added.

Victoria glared at each brother-in-law in turn, but that only made them laugh. "With Englishmen like you on the watch, no wonder Napoleon has been so successful."

"I am Russian," Rudolf reminded her.

"And Napoleon very nearly swallowed your country," Victoria shot back.

"Was that before or after he moved to Elbow and peeled apprentices?" Rudolf asked with an infuriating smile.

Victoria tossed her napkin on the table and rose to leave. She could never win against her brothers-in-law.

"Sit down, Victoria," Alexander ordered in a quiet voice.

Victoria turned toward the earl, her gaze crashing into his. She could almost hear everyone suck in their breaths, waiting to see what she would do.

Without a word, Victoria sat down and placed the napkin on her lap. Catching her brother-in-law's eye, she speared the haddock as if she was using a dagger.

Rudolf burst out laughing. "Tory, this family would be excruciatingly boring without you."

"Thank you very much," she snapped.

Hearing the absurd discrepancy between her words and her tone, Victoria laughed, too. "Do you see how much I've suffered since my sisters married?" she asked, turning to the earl.

Alexander leaned close and pressed his lips to her ear. "I'm proud of your control in the face of extreme provocation."

His whispered praise made her smile. She looked at her brothers-in-law and said, "Do your worst. You don't bother me at all."

"That is no fun," Rudolf said, and the conversation turned to other matters.

Alexander stood when the ladies rose from the table. "If you will excuse me," he said to the men, "I would like to walk outside with Victoria."

Leaving the mansion, Alexander and Victoria stepped into a warm June night. Created for lovers, a full moon shone down on them, and thousands of stars glittered like diamonds in the setting of the black velvet sky.

Inhaling deeply of the garden's mingling scents, Victoria sighed as they crossed the lawns to the gazebo. Alexander stopped walking and pulled her into his arms. He dipped his head, his mouth capturing hers in a long, slow kiss.

"I've been wanting to do that all evening," Alexander said in a husky whisper.

"I wanted to kiss you, too," Victoria admitted, her tender feelings echoed in her slightly breathless voice.

"I love your smell," he said, crushing her against him.

"I smell?"

"You smell like vanilla and jasmine and pure woman," Alexander said.

Victoria gave him a blank look, innocent to his meaning. She smiled, then, taking his words as a compliment.

"We will be man and wife in less than four weeks," Alexander said. "Now I wish your family and I hadn't kept the betrothal a secret for so long. We could have been married months ago."

"Will we live at the Grosvenor Square mansion?" she asked.

Alexander nodded. "Among other places."

"I lived in your mansion when I was a child," Victoria said.

"Yes, I know." Guilt gripped him. How could he possibly forget what Charles Emerson had done to her father?

"What did you think when my aunt suggested a match between us?" Victoria asked, almost afraid of what he would say, but wanting to hear it.

A typical woman's question, Alexander thought with an inward smile. His little betrothed needed to dissect every nuance of emotion and motive.

"Well, I thought you were too young and—"

Victoria laughed, interupting him. "I thought you were elderly."

"Elderly?" Alexander echoed, surprised. "Twenty-nine hardly makes me ancient."

"Why did you say *yes* to the match?" she asked.

"I wanted to make amends for Charles Emerson's crimes against your family," he answered honestly.

Alexander knew his answer disappointed her, but professing his love would be lying. Real love— if there was such a thing—took time. After the twenty-fourth of June, they would enjoy all the time in the world.

"Is there something wrong, Tory?"

"During the year we've been betrothed, have you kept company with any women?" Victoria asked, fearing his answer.

Alexander cursed himself for not seeing this question coming. "You sound like a wife," he evaded with a smile.

"Kiss me again, please."

The impertinent minx closed her eyes, waiting for him to do her bidding. In her innocence, she had no idea how difficult being close to her was proving to him. And that was something he had not expected.

"Kissing you is torture," Alexander told her. "I want you in my bed."

"Sneak into my chamber after everyone goes to bed," Victoria invited him.

"You do have a wild streak . . . and very little common sense," Alexander said, softening his words with a smile. "If I visited your chamber, I wouldn't be satisfied with merely touching. I want you a virgin on the day we marry."

"Why?"

"I want no scandal attached to my firstborn," Alexander explained. "If he arrives too early, people will gossip."

Learning that he was some unidentified nobleman's bastard had felled him for months. He wanted no child of his to doubt his parentage or the legitimacy of his birth.

"What makes you think I'll—" Victoria broke off, too shy to continue.

"Getting with child takes only one coupling," Alexander told her.

Victoria sighed.

Alexander didn't know if she was disappointed or relieved. In spite of her passionate nature, Victoria Douglas was untouched, subject to a virgin's fear of the unknown.

Tinker opened the door when they returned to the mansion. "My lord, the other gentlemen have gone to the gameroom," the majordomo informed him.

"Thank you, Tinker." Alexander turned to Victoria, asking, "Will you ride with me to church to-morrow?"

"Well, I have the beginnings of a headache," she told him. "I may not attend church services."

"I want you to go directly to bed," Alexander said, thinking how predictable she was. "I'm certain you will feel better in the morning."

Victoria stood on tiptoe and, wrapping her arms around his neck, drew him toward her. After planting a kiss on his lips, she turned and walked up the stairs.

Alexander watched her climb the stairs. When she disappeared, he turned away, but the major-domo's voice stopped him.

"My lord, when may I expect to receive my winnings?" Tinker asked.

Alexander stared at him for a long moment. "*I* won."

Tinker raised his brows at him. "Without your permission, Lady Victoria escaped her chamber," the majordomo said, "and you rewarded her with a diamond ring. I believe the lady won."

Alexander grinned and inclined his head. "I believe you are correct," he said. "I will instruct Prince Rudolf to release the funds to you."

"True nobility is gracious in defeat," Tinker replied.

"Would you care to speculate on whether I'll get her to church?" Alexander challenged the man.

"I have a one-pound note that says you may get her to church but never to stay and pray," Tinker told him.

"I accept your challenge," Alexander said, and then walked away.

* * *

The next morning, Alexander stood outside Victoria's bedchamber door. Determined to outsmart her, he carried a tray containing a teacup and saucer, pot of tea, and a hot, buttered scone. He stepped inside the chamber, closed the door, and smiled at the lump in the bed hidden by the coverlet.

Alexander set the tray on the bedside table. "Awaken, sweetheart," he said.

"Go away," grumbled a muffled voice from beneath the coverlet.

This wasn't going to be as easy as he had thought, Alexander decided, and sat on the edge of the bed.

Alexander pulled the coverlet down, and his breath caught in his throat at her near naked body. Sheerer than gossamer, her nightgown hid none of her charms—softly rounded breasts with pink-tipped peaks, tiny waist, curvaceous hips.

Without opening her eyes, Victoria reached to pull the coverlet up. When he stayed her hand, she opened her fabulously blue eyes.

"Alex," Victoria breathed, his name on her lips like a sigh. "I was dreaming about you."

"How is your headache?" he asked.

Victoria stared at him blankly for a long moment. He could see her mind clear of sleep and appreciated her quick recovery from near blunder.

"I have a stomache ache and won't be able to—"

"Drinking tea will settle your stomach," Alexander said, pouring the tea into the cup. "The fresh air on the ride to church will revive you."

Victoria sat up, leaned against the headboard, and realized her state of undress. She blushed but made no move to cover herself.

Alexander passed her the teacup. Victoria took

a sip and smiled, not bothering to argue about church services.

And then Alexander recalled the duchess's words to him. *"Victoria never actually refuses to do anything. She agrees to whatever you want and then does what she wants."*

"I'm leaving for my estate in Winchester directly after church," Alexander said conversationally. "I'll return by Thursday to escort you to the opera."

"I'll miss you," Victoria said.

"Will you?"

"As your betrothed, missing you is my duty."

That made him smile. When she finished the tea and scone, Alexander lifted the tray off the bedside table. "I expect you dressed and downstairs in one hour," he told her, and then left the room.

An hour later, Alexander stood in the foyer with the others. Victoria hadn't made her appearance yet, and he was becoming irritated.

"She won't come down," Duke Magnus told him.

"I have never seen Tory at any church service," Rudolf remarked.

Alexander looked toward the stairway as if he could will her to appear. "Victoria will attend today's service even if I—here she is now."

Dressed in a high-waisted white gown embroidered with pink roses at the hem and neckline, Victoria walked down the stairs. She carried a pink parasol and a white bonnet with pink ribbons.

Alexander thought he had never seen anything so lovely. She was the essence of innocence, yet there was an air of sensuality surrounding her.

Everyone walked outside, their coaches in a line in the front courtyard. With Victoria holding his arm, Alexander glanced at Tinker and said, "I told you so."

"Many mishaps can happen between now and church services," the majordomo reminded him.

Victoria was silent on the way to the village. She despised going to church but knew she was trapped. It wasn't that she didn't believe in God and certainly wanted to worship Him. However, her inability to read the prayer book or hymns made her feel self-conscious and kept her away.

Reaching the village church, Alexander climbed out of the coach first and then helped Victoria down. The family was standing in front of the church and exchanging pleasantries with the vicar.

"Alex, I would like you to meet Vicar Small," the duchess introduced them. "Vicar, Lord Emerson is the Earl of Winchester and betrothed to my youngest niece, Victoria."

The two men shook hands. Victoria curtseyed to the vicar.

"I didn't realize there were *three* nieces," Vicar Small said to the duchess, eliciting smothered chuckles from the prince and the marquess. "Has she been away?"

"Victoria is a sickly child," the duchess explained.

"Well, miss, I am certainly glad you are feeling well today," Vicar Small said.

"The will of God has made me better," Victoria replied.

Vicar Small turned to lead the way into church. Victoria smiled sweetly at Alexander and slipped her arm through his.

"God's will had nothing to do with your presence," Prince Rudolf whispered, leaning close to them. "Alex's will prevailed."

The Duke and Duchess of Inverary led the way and marched down the aisle to the front of the church. They nodded to the villagers they knew, most of whom did business with the duke.

The duke and duchess sat in the first pew. Angelica and Robert, accompanied by six-year-old Colin, Robert's nephew by his deceased brother, and six-year-old Daisy, Robert's and Angelica's adopted daughter sat in the second pew. Their year-old twins were too young to attend services. Samantha and Rudolf claimed the third pew. Eleven-year-old Grant and nine-year-old Drake, their adopted sons, as well as Princess Zara, Rudolf's daughter by his first wife, sat with them. Their six-month-old twins were also too young to attend services.

Alexander and Victoria sat alone in the fourth pew. He passed her the prayer book as the vicar began the service. Opening to the first page, Victoria pretended to focus on the words.

Surprising her, Alexander lifted the book out of her hands. He turned it around and passed it back to her. She had been holding the book upside down.

Embarrassed, Victoria glanced at Alexander, who whispered, "Behave yourself."

"I forgot my spectacles," Victoria whispered in defense of herself.

First comes the prayer book and then comes the hymn book, Victoria thought, beginning to panic. If she stayed here, Alexander would realize she couldn't read. Would he cancel their wedding? More likely, he would marry her and hire a tutor for her. If she was unable to learn, Alexander would hold her in contempt for the rest of their lives. He would think she'd tricked him into marriage. She couldn't bear that he knew how stupid she was.

Her panic level rose. Victoria knew she needed a distraction. If she told him she felt dizzy, Alexander would know she was lying and keep her prisoner in the pew. But if she actually—

Victoria dropped the prayer book and grabbed his arm. "Alex, help—"

Relaxing every muscle in her body, Victoria fell into a swoon. She knew he would catch her before she hit the floor.

Victoria heard the exclamations of alarm as she went down. She almost smiled as Alexander caught her and lifted her into his arms.

"I'll help you," she heard Prince Rudolf say. A moment later, she was floating on air as Alexander carried her down the aisle.

Victoria struggled against a bubble of laughter when she heard the vicar saying, "Let us pray for the quick recovery of His Grace's niece." And then she felt the fresh air as Alexander stepped outside the church.

Moaning softly, Victoria let her eyes flutter open and gazed into his hazel eyes filled with concern. "I can stand," she protested weakly. "I'll be fine."

"I'm taking you home," Alexander said, setting her down on her feet but refusing to release her. "Hold her steady," he said to the prince. "I'll climb inside and you help her up to me."

When he turned his back, Victoria winked at Rudolf and mouthed the words, "Do not laugh."

"Help her up," Alexander said, lifting her into the coach and settling her beside him.

"I wouldn't worry," Rudolf told the earl. "With the congregation's prayers, Tory will soon recover."

When they reached the mansion, Alexander

climbed out first and then helped her down. Unexpectedly, he scooped her into his arms and carried her inside.

Tinker opened the door. "I told you so," the majordomo said.

Victoria feared he would realize her ploy. "Help me upstairs," she said when Alexander set her down.

Putting his arm around her, Alexander helped her to her chamber. Once inside, he closed the door and walked her to the bed.

Victoria decided she couldn't have planned this any better. The Lord did move in wondrous ways.

"Shall I bring you a pot of tea?" he asked.

"Will you help me undress first?" she asked.

Alexander inclined his head and sat beside her on the bed. When she turned her back on him, he unfastened her gown, starting with the top button, slowly making his way from her neck to her waist. Parting the two sides, he ran one finger up her delicate backbone.

Victoria sucked in her breath. A delicious chill shook her body, but where he touched burned.

Pushing the gown off her shoulders, Alexander lifted the heavy mane of fire off her neck. He touched her nape with his warm lips and blew lightly on her sensitive skin.

"I like to feel your lips on me," she whispered.

Alexander rose from the bed and offered his hand, saying, "Stand, please."

Without hesitation, Victoria placed her hand in his and stood, her blue gaze never leaving his. She watched in fascination as he slid the gown down her body until it pooled at her feet.

"Sit down," he ordered in a husky voice. When she obeyed, he lifted the gown off the floor and raised it to his face, saying, "Your scent lingers on it."

Alexander set the gown on a nearby chair and faced her. Victoria recognized the gleam in his eyes as he studied her from the top of her head to the tips of her toes. She wore only her chemise, garters, stockings, and shoes.

Holding her gaze captive, Alexander removed his jacket and placed it on top of her gown. Then he removed his waistcoat and cravat and unbuttoned the neck of his white shirt.

Victoria stared at him, her blue eyes enormous. She had the feeling she was about to get what she wanted. Only, the thought of it frightened her.

"Are you feeling better?" Alexander asked, placing the palm of his hand on her cheek.

"Much better." Victoria turned her face to kiss the palm of his hand and then rubbed her cheek against it like a young female cat claiming her valued territory.

Alexander knelt in front of her. He removed her right shoe, set it aside, and lifted her stockinged foot to kiss it.

Victoria felt a surging panic when he reached for her left foot. She closed her eyes against his seeing the *L* on the bottom of the shoe, but relaxed when he lifted her foot to his lips.

Opening her eyes, Victoria watched him slide his hands up her legs. Reaching the bottom edge of the chemise, he pushed the silk and lace garment up to reveal her thighs and then removed her lacy garter, slowly rolling her silk stocking down her leg.

Her breathing shallowed when he removed the stocking and kissed her foot again. He drew each of her toes into his mouth to suck gently upon it.

Alexander slid his hands up her other leg. Without rushing, he rolled the silk stocking down and then sucked her toes.

Victoria felt her stomach tightening into a knot of desire. She knew he was seducing her. Though she had no idea what changed his mind, she wanted him . . . wanted to savor the feelings he was creating . . . wanted whatever he could give her.

"Do you want to lie down?" Alexander asked, sitting beside her.

"Only with you," she whispered, her gaze captive to his.

Alexander encircled her shoulders with his arm and drew her against his hard, muscular body. At the same time, he cupped her chin and ran his thumb across her lips. When she leaned into his stroking, he lowered his head, and his lips replaced his thumb.

Victoria sighed at this contact. She pressed herself against him, offering herself. She was a woman of passion, though untouched and unawakened to the power of her own sensuality.

Alexander groaned. He wanted what she offered—her body, her heart, her soul.

Deepening the kiss, Alexander dropped the hand caressing her shoulder to the small of her back. Victoria entwined her arms around his neck and pressed herself against him, surrendering to his kiss, willing to follow where he would lead, yearning for his possession.

Alexander moved a hand to the back of her head to hold her steady while he kissed her hungrily. Victoria met his kiss with equal hunger, falling under his sensuous spell, melting into him. A primitive mating instinct pulsed through her awakening body, spurred her on, urged her to become one with him.

When he caressed the crease of her lips with his tongue, Victoria opened her mouth for him, letting him ravage her sweetness. Alexander pushed her back on the bed and lay on top of her.

For the first time in her young life, Victoria felt the weight of a man pressing her down. And she liked it. The world faded away, leaving only this man, her mate, the center of her universe.

Alexander slid his lips to her cheek, her eyelids, her temples. He tongued her ears, making her shiver with the sensations. His lips drifted slowly to her throat.

Then Alexander knelt, his legs on either side of hers. Holding her gaze captive, he slid the straps of her chemise off her shoulders, down her arms, until the lacy edge of the delicate bodice perched on the edge of her nipples.

Victoria reached up and drew the chemise down, baring her breasts for him. Alexander groaned, and cupping her breasts, he buried his face in the crevice between them, inhaling her enticing vanilla scent.

"I love your nipples," Alexander said, a hoarse edge to his voice.

With those words, Alexander sucked upon one pink-tipped peak and then the other. Victoria arched her back into his kiss, holding his head against her breast.

"Yes," she moaned, the spot between her thighs throbbing, the folds of her flesh wet with desire.

Alexander drew back and knelt again. With both hands, he peeled the chemise down and tossed it aside, baring her body to his smoldering gaze.

"You're sure?" he asked.

Victoria held her arms out in answer. She wanted him in her body, her heart, her soul.

Alexander stood to remove his shirt, his shoes, his trousers. He nearly laughed out loud when he noted his sweet betrothed kept her gaze above his waist. She suffered from a virgin's fear of the unknown.

"Don't be frightened," Alexander said, lying beside her, pulling her into his arms.

"I'm worried, not frightened," she whispered.

"Don't worry." He kissed her lingeringly, rekindling the fire, stealing her breath.

Moving over her, Alexander used his legs to spread her thighs. He pressed his weight on top of her, accustoming her to spread her legs for him.

"What worries you?" he asked, feeling her trembling.

"*It.*"

Alexander wanted to laugh in her face. Instead, he kissed her and said in a soothing voice, "I promise *it* is nothing to worry about. *It* is part of me, not a monster intent on hurting you. You trust me, don't you?"

Victoria opened her fabulously blue eyes. "Yes, Alex, I trust you."

Alexander knelt between her legs but made no move to enter her body. He lifted her hands and kissed them, then turned them over and kissed her palms.

Bending over her, Alexander kissed and licked her breasts. His tongue swirled around one alabaster globe, coming closer and closer to its center.

When he touched its pink tip with his tongue, it hardened and rose into arousal. Victoria whimpered, the pleasure almost too much to bear.

Alexander flicked his tongue back and forth, finally drawing her nipple between his lips—pulling, nipping, sucking. Releasing it, he blew on its wet tip.

Dazed with desire, Victoria pleaded, "Don't stop . . . please."

In answer, Alexander sucked hard upon one nipple while his thumb and forefinger teased her other nipple. He kissed a burning trail from her breasts to her stomach and then buried his face in the fiery red curls at the juncture of her thighs.

Inhaling her intoxicating scent, Alexander started to move lower but felt her stiffen. He reached for her sensitive nipples—squeezing their tips, rolling them between his fingers, making her squirm.

"I want to savor every inch of your body," Alexander said, his voice husky with need. "Don't deny me. Please, Tory."

Victoria moaned and spread her legs wider. There was no mistaking her invitation.

Alexander lowered his head and tongued the folds of flesh between her legs. She opened for him, surrendering her most intimate self, allowing him access to the center of her pleasure.

When he tongued her swollen nub, Victoria arched her body, pressing herself against him. She cried out as a tidal wave of pleasure surged through her.

After the last spasm shook her body, Alexander slid his hand down her body to the spot where his tongue had been. Lower his hand drifted, and then Victoria felt a burning sensation as he pushed one long finger inside her quivering body.

Deeper and deeper, Alexander pushed his finger until he reached her virgin's barrier. He caressed her wet, silken interior and then inserted a second finger.

Victoria felt vulnerable, helpless to his desire.

She never imagined this feeling of being filled. When he slipped his fingers out, though, she felt empty and moaned in disappointment.

"Another moment, Tory," Alexander soothed her, positioning himself between her thighs, sliding a pillow beneath her bottom to raise it. "Another moment and you will be mine. Completely. Forever. You want that, darling. Open your eyes and tell me you want me."

Victoria opened her eyes, glazed with desire. She could feel the wet head of his manhood poised to pierce.

"I want you," she said. "I want you deep in—"

Alexander thrust forward. She whimpered when he broke through her maidenhead and slid to the mouth of her womb.

Victoria felt vulnerable again, completely at his mercy, possessed. She hadn't known it would be like this, had never imagined in her maiden's day-dreaming—

Alexander moved, slowly at first, and then increased his tempo. Victoria caught his rhythm and moved with him. He thrust deeper and deeper, pulling back and then thrusting to the hilt, their groins touching.

"Alex," she cried, spasms shaking her body.

Alexander groaned and shuddered, his seed flooding her. Wrapping her arms around him, Victoria felt him giving himself to her and knew that, in this moment, he was as vulnerable as she. Love for him swelled in her heart.

Recovering first, Alexander rolled off her and pulled her with him. He wrapped her within the circle of his embrace.

"Alex?" she said, snuggling against him.

"I am *not* sorry we didn't wait," he told her, hearing the question in her voice.

"Will we do this on our wedding night?"

Alexander laughed out loud. "We can do this whenever you want," he promised.

"Today?"

"Well, sweetheart, I need a few minutes to regain my strength."

"Why did you want to wait?" she asked.

"Charles Emerson is not my father," Alexander told her, becoming serious. "I don't know who sired me. I suppose I am being overly sensitive about observing society's proprieties."

Victoria looked as confused as she felt. "I don't understand."

"I didn't want the gossipmongers fueled by your giving birth early," Alexander said. "Three weeks doesn't signify, though."

Silence reigned in the chamber for several minutes.

"Tory?"

"Yes?"

"If you ever need money, you have a bright future on stage at Drury Lane."

Victoria realized he knew her swoon had been feigned. "I don't know what you mean."

"You owe me one pound," he told her, ignoring her denial.

"For what?"

"Tinker and I wagered on your staying and praying at church," Alexander answered. "I lost."

"I don't own any money," Victoria said, looking up at him with a pert smile on her face.

"People do not own money," Alexander said. "I will need to take the proverbial pound of flesh."

"Proverbial pound—What is that?" she asked.

"I will accept payment with your delicious body," he told her.

Victoria gave him a flirtatious smile. "You won't get much for a pound," she said, making him laugh.

Faster than she could blink an eye, Alexander had rolled her onto her back and loomed over her. He dipped his head, his mouth claiming hers.

This time Alexander didn't need to coax her slowly. Victoria met him kiss for kiss, caress for caress, stroke for stroke.

The bedchamber door crashed open, startling them. Cuddling beneath the coverlet but still imbedded in feminine heat, Alexander turned his head and looked toward the door while Victoria peeked out from under him.

"I see that you do feel better," Aunt Roxie said, her smile feline. "As you were." At that, the duchess quit the chamber as quickly as she had entered.

Alexander looked down. Victoria's face was almost as red as her hair. "Don't worry," he said, planting a kiss on the corner of her lips. "Your aunt approves of me."

At that, Alexander ground himself into her. Within minutes, Victoria forgot that she even *had* an aunt.

Two hours later, Victoria stood with Alexander in the front courtyard. She glanced at her betrothal ring, sparkling in the sunshine, and then looked at him.

"I'll miss you," Victoria told him.

"Thank you, love." Alexander lifted her hands to his lips and then leaned close to kiss her. "Be ready for the opera, Thursday at seven."

Victoria stood in the courtyard and watched until his coach vanished from sight. She turned toward the mansion and stopped short. Her brothers-in-law stood there, their grins boding ill for her.

"Excuse me," Victoria said, lifting her nose into the air as she passed them.

"We know what Alex and you were doing," Rudolf teased her.

Victoria ignored him.

"Look, she's walking differently now," Robert said.

Victoria whirled around, her face crimson with embarrassment. "Aunt Roxie is a terrible gossip," she said.

Rudolf and Robert burst into laughter. Realizing she would never win, Victoria hurried inside but the sounds of their laughter echoed in her ears and chased her all the way to her chamber.

CHAPTER 6

"I am desperate to learn," Victoria pleaded.

Standing in the front room of the small house on Oxford Street near Soho Square, Victoria gazed hopefully at Phineas and Barnaby Philbin, who tutored her sisters' children. Slightly overweight, Phineas appeared to be in his early forties; slightly underweight, Barnaby appeared to be in his late thirties. Both men were short of stature with nondescript brown hair and eyes, but kindness shone in their expressions.

"If you can teach my nephews and nieces to read, you can teach me," Victoria said, desperation tingeing her voice.

"What is wrong, Lady Victoria?" Phineas asked.

"My letters and numbers misbehave," Victoria answered, making the two brothers smile. "My *b*'s look like *d*'s and the sixes look like nines."

"Would you be amenable to taking lessons with the children?" Barnaby asked.

"That would be too embarrassing," Victoria told him. "Besides, the Earl of Winchester and I will soon be married, and I will live in Grosvenor Square."

"Accept our best wishes," Phineas said. "The earl is a lucky man to have won your hand in marriage."

Victoria smiled, pleased with his compliment. "I thank you, sir."

"Shall we give you lessons at Grosvenor Square?" Barnaby asked.

"I prefer to take my lessons here," Victoria answered. "I want to improve before I tell the earl about my stupidity."

"Your having lessons here would be improper," Phineas told her.

"I can see no impropriety if both of us are present," Barnaby amended, seeing her disappointed expression.

Phineas nodded agreement with his brother. "Thursday afternoon is the only time during the week when we are free together."

"Thursday is perfect," Victoria said, with a relieved smile. "I will pay for the lessons even when I am required elsewhere on a Thursday."

"That is most generous, my lady," Barnaby replied.

Phineas walked to the desk near the window and reached for parchment and ink. He wrote a few words, sanded the paper, and turned around.

"Sit here, Lady Victoria, and read what I have written," he said. "We need to test your current ability."

Victoria sat at the desk where she could see by the light streaming through the window. She took the parchment and stared at it. Moving her lips silently, Victoria tried to sound out the words in her mind before she spoke. Then she set the parchment flat on the desk and leaned close. With one finger pointed at the words, Victoria read haltingly as if each syllable was a separate word.

"At nine in the morn-ing, the dark-ing bog saw in the bark dog."

When she finished, Victoria lifted her gaze to the two brothers. Hope and determination shone at them from the depths of her blue eyes.

Both men smiled and then turned their backs to stroll across the chamber to confer in private. Watching, Victoria willed them to accept her as a student. What would she do if they refused her? Where could she go? How could she explain her stupidity to Alexander? The Philbin brothers were her only hope.

Phineas and Barnaby spoke in low voices but seemed to be in the midst of a heated discussion. Victoria knew that was not a good sign. Abruptly, the brothers walked back to the desk.

"Lady Victoria, you are not stupid," Phineas told her.

"I'm not?" she echoed in surprise.

Barnaby shook his head. "You suffer from word blindness."

"What is that?"

"Certain letters and numbers become jumbled inside your mind," Phineas explained.

"I told you that a few minutes ago," Victoria said, wondering if they could be as stupid as she.

"Unfortunately, there is no cure for word blindness," Barnaby told her. "At least, we have never known anyone who has been cured."

Victoria closed her eyes against the disappointment, frustration, and anguish. Her bottom lip quivered, but she managed to swallow a sob of failure.

Victoria knew she couldn't marry Alexander now and would need to tell him about her hopeless condition. Alexander hadn't sought her out or wanted to marry her. Aunt Roxie had proposed the match, and Alexander had accepted in order to make amends for what Charles Emerson had done to her father. How could she marry a man who didn't love her and had no idea that he was trapping himself into a marriage with a stupid woman?

"My brother and I do know certain strategies that can help you read simple sentences," Phineas said.

Victoria brightened at that. "Can you teach me enough to read bedtime stories to my children and the *Times* gossip column?" she asked, making them smile.

"We can teach you how to live with this impediment," Barnaby told her. "You know, my lady, gentlemen like the earl want a wife who doesn't think too much. Society gentlemen want to know more than their ladies."

"All men want to think they know more than all women," Victoria corrected him. "Besides, there is no danger in my knowing more than the earl. Alexander is highly intelligent and the smartest man I have ever met."

"That a bride should feel such admiration for her husband is a good thing," Phineas said. Then he warned her, "Learning won't be easy for you."

"I promise to be the hardest-working student ever," Victoria exclaimed with enthusiasm. "Thank you so very much." She surprised the two bachelors by giving each a kiss on the cheek, making them blush. "Shall I come here Thursday afternoon?"

Both men nodded. "We will be waiting," Phineas said.

"Oh, I can hardly wait to learn," Victoria said,

turning toward the door. She paused before leaving and asked, "What did the parchment say? Was I close?"

Barnaby lifted the parchment off the desk and read: *"At six in the morning, the barking dog was in the dark bog."*

Victoria frowned. She hadn't even been close. "You read beautifully," she praised the tutor.

Barnaby inclined his head, accepting the compliment.

Victoria left the small house and turned right to walk to the end of Oxford Street. Unexpectedly, a hand grasped her arm, and she whirled around.

"Park Lane lies in the opposite direction," Barnaby told her.

"How stupid of me," Victoria said, an embarrassed blush staining her cheeks.

"People who suffer from word blindness get lost easily because of a faulty sense of direction."

"Do we have trouble judging left from right?" she asked.

"Yes, you do," he answered. "We'll see you next Thursday, my lady."

Victoria arrived home at tea time. Climbing the stairs to the second floor drawing room, she wondered if her aunt had noted her absence. Victoria wanted no one to know what she was doing until her reading improved. Then, if the Philbin brothers really did help her, she would give a reading recital for the whole family. That ridiculous thought brought a smile to her lips.

"Where have you been?" Aunt Roxie cried, rising from the settee when she walked into the room.

"I was visiting Samantha and forgot the time," Victoria lied.

"Come along," Aunt Roxie ordered, escorting her out of the drawing room and up the stairs to her bedchamber. "Alexander sent a note and will be here in a couple of hours. He wants you to wear blue, and I've selected the sapphire blue silk."

"He's telling me what to wear?" Victoria asked in irritated surprise.

"I'm certain he has a good reason for the request," her aunt said, gesturing across the chamber. "The bath is set up behind the screen. My maid will bring you tea and then dress your hair. Don't dally, Tory." Her aunt paused at the door, asking, "By the way, darling, have you been nauseated?"

"No. Why?"

"Never mind."

Wearing the sapphire blue silk gown, Victoria left her bedchamber two hours later and walked down the corridor to the stairs. The gown's bodice, cut low in front and back, sported short melon sleeves, and a sash tied in a big bow at her backwaist. The fashionably short skirt showed her ankles and feet encased in silk stockings and sandals.

Alexander turned when she walked into the drawing room and smiled, savoring the sight of her walking toward him. Her delight in seeing him gleamed from the depths of her blue eyes.

"Lady Victoria, you are the most beautiful woman I have ever seen," Alexander said, lifting her hand to his lips.

"My lord, you are a flatterer," Victoria replied, her lips turned up in a pleased smile.

"On the contrary, I enjoy the reputation of being an honest man." Alexander produced a midnight blue velvet-covered box, saying, "I requested that you wear blue because of my gift."

Opening the box, Alexander smiled at her surprised expression. A sapphire and diamond necklace set in platinum lay on a bed of midnight blue velvet. With it was a sapphire and diamond bracelet.

"This gift seems excessive," Victoria said, lifting her gaze to his.

"Darling, jewels are never excessive," Aunt Roxie drawled. "If covering you in jewels makes Alex happy, then accept them with a pretty smile and a thank-you."

"Turn around," Alexander said, lifting the necklace out of the box. When she obeyed, he fastened the necklace around her neck. Next came the bracelet.

"You had better curb your spending," Victoria warned him. "I have no wish to live in the poorhouse again."

Alexander laughed and planted a kiss on her lips. "Thank you for humoring me by accepting these gifts," he said.

"Thank you, Alex," Victoria said, planting a chaste kiss on his lips.

"I did promise to cover you in diamonds," Alexander said, slipping her hand through the crook of his arm.

"No pearls?" she teased.

"I will deck you in diamonds, place you in pearls, engulf you in emeralds, and soak you in sapphires," Alexander told her.

"Rubies?"

"I intend to roll you in rubies," he answered, his smile devastatingly wicked.

"How provocative," Victoria said, a blush staining her cheeks.

Escorting her to his waiting coach, Alexander wondered why he hadn't noticed how beautiful she was until the previous weekend, less than three weeks before their marriage. Probably, he hadn't noticed her at all. He had been busy with more pressing matters like his estates, his shadowy birth, his three constantly demanding former mistresses, and his half-sister's impending return from Australia.

"I missed you," Victoria said, planting a kiss on his cheek as soon as the coach moved.

Alexander slipped his arm around her shoulder and drew her close to his body, so close that he inhaled her vanilla scent. He said nothing. In truth, he wasn't sure if she was sincere or practicing her wiles on him. He had missed her, too, but had no intention of telling her that and letting her get the upper hand. No woman was ever getting the upper hand with him again. Especially not his eighteen-year-old bride.

Victoria felt disappointed. She had hoped that he had missed her, too. Perhaps her expectations had been too high. Alexander didn't love her, after all. He hadn't sought a union with her, merely accepted her aunt's proposed match because he wanted to clear his conscience about what Charles Emerson had done to her family.

Would Alexander ever love her or harbor a fondness for her? Probably not. Who could love a stupid woman? True, no man looked for intelligence in a prospective mate, but no man would want to become known as the husband of the village idiot. How long would it be before Alexander realized his mistake in marrying her and sought comfort in the arms of another, smarter woman?

"I always attend the opera on Thursday evenings because it relaxes me," Alexander told her. "Later, Rudolf and Samantha will meet us at the Wilmingtons' ball. I must warn you that society will be curious about whom I have chosen as my countess. Do not let their stares bother you."

"I wish you hadn't told me that," Victoria said. "I dislike attention on me and will worry about doing something wrong."

"You don't like surprises either," Alexander reminded her. "The surprises this week have all been pleasant."

"You are correct, my lord," Victoria replied. "Especially if I discount being threatened, seduced, and almost spanked."

"Are you fluent in Italian?" Alexander asked, changing the subject.

Good God, Victoria thought, she wasn't even fluent in English. Was she required to speak a foreign language?

"I am unfamiliar with Italian," Victoria admitted, giving him a worried look.

"Then I will translate for you," Alexander said. "I know you have attended the opera with your aunt and uncle. You did know that opera is sung in Italian?"

"I never gave the matter my attention," Victoria told him.

"To what did you give your attention?"

"Intermission."

Alexander shouted with laughter just as their coach halted in front of the Royal Opera House on Bow Street. Which is why, when a smiling Alexander climbed out of the coach, the crowd of aristocrats stared at the usually somber Earl of Winchester. Whispers swept through the theater's lobby that the Earl of Winchester and Lady Victoria Douglas, his betrothed, appeared very much in love.

Victoria kept her gaze on Alexander as they walked through the crowded lobby and up the stairs to his box. He nodded greetings to many aristocrats he knew but didn't stop to speak to anyone, for which Victoria was exceedingly grateful. She needed to accustom herself to the curious stares.

"People are watching us through their lorgnettes," Victoria whispered, feeling uncomfortable. She despised being the center of attention as much as she hated surprises and church services.

"Intermission will be worse," Alexander said, moving his chair close to her. He lifted her hand to his lips, murmuring, "Most will want an introduction."

"People are watching you hold my hand," Victoria whispered.

"I am performing for their scintillating edification," Alexander said, his eyes bright with amusement.

"And what the blue blazes is that?" Victoria asked, turning to look at him.

"I am demonstrating our loving relationship for our audience. Now then, sweetheart, tonight's opera is *The Marriage of Figaro,* by Mozart," Alexander said resting his arm on the back of her chair.

"He is the composer?"

Alexander nodded. "Mozart's opera is the sequel to *The Barber of Seville,*" he explained, as the orchestra began the overture. "Count Almaviva married Rosina, a young heiress, in spite of her guardian's intentions to marry her. A man named Figaro assisted the Count in his intrigue.

"When tonight's opera opens, three years have passed. The Count and Countess are bored in their marriage. The Count spends his days touring his estates and bedding as many pretty girls as possible."

"The Count is unfaithful to his wife?" Victoria asked. "Is that a proper subject?"

"We don't see the Count making love to those women," Alexander whispered against her ear, his hand dropping to her bare shoulder and beginning a slow caress.

Victoria felt hot and cold all at the same time. How could she follow the opera when his hand on her flesh distracted her concentration?

"The day before the story begins, the Count called on Barbarina, the twelve-year-old daughter of his chief gardener," Alexander said, his warm breath on the side of her neck making her nerves tingle. "He found his young page Cherubino there and dismissed him from his service. Cherubino loves all women, especially Countess Almaviva, to whom he appeals to intercede for him with the Count."

Victoria's breath caught raggedly when Alexander's fingers left her shoulder and stroked the side of her neck. When she turned her head to look at him, he said, "Until recently, the Count has enjoyed the ancient custom of *le droit de seigneur.*"

"What is that?" Victoria asked, fixing her gaze on the stage. She sensed rather than saw his smile.

"*Le droit de seigneur* gives the lord the right to bed any of his dependents on her wedding night," Alexander said. He grinned when she whirled toward him in surprise.

"You mean that—?"

"The lord has the right to deflower any woman he desires on her wedding night," Alexander said.

Again, Victoria gave her attention to the singers on stage.

"The lord expects obedience when he orders the woman to disrobe and lie on the bed," Alexander whispered, leaning close. "Naked, he would join her there and kiss every inch of her flesh from her neck"—Alexander flicked his tongue along her ear—"to her breasts and the inside of her thighs. The lord would suckle her pink-tipped breasts—licking and nipping her aroused nipples."

Victoria felt her breasts swelling. Her nipples ached for his mouth.

"The folds of flesh between her thighs would be wet," Alexander continued, his voice husky. "She would spread her legs and invite the lord's hardness into her body. Thrusting himself deep inside her, the lord would ride her until she melted and cried out her pleasure and he flooded her with his juices."

Victoria closed her eyes and made a whimpering sound in her throat. Pressing his lips to her ear, Alexander asked, "Are you wet for me, Tory?"

"Yes."

"Later," he promised.

Victoria stared at the stage without seeing and heard the music without listening. Instead, in her mind's eye she watched the previous Sunday's amorous tryst. She became aware of where she was when the curtain closed, signaling intermission.

"You will charm everyone who begs an introduction," Alexander said, drawing her attention.

Victoria flashed him a smile filled with confidence, a confidence she didn't feel. The only reason Alexander considered her charming was he hadn't realized how stupid she was.

And then society descended upon their box. Victoria decided the best course of action was to smile and say little. She managed to do that until she sensed a change in the atmosphere around her. Aristocrats in other boxes were turning to stare. Several had their opera glasses fixed on them.

Victoria saw two gentlemen and a dark-haired beauty of about twenty-five greeting Alexander.

She felt his discomfort and glanced at his tense expression. Something was happening that she didn't understand.

"Is this the child?" the woman asked, an insincere smile pasted on her face.

"Victoria, I present Lydia Stanley, the Marchioness of Tewksbury," Alexander said, breaking etiquette which required him to present her to the marchioness. He gestured to the two gentlemen, adding, "Lord Russell and Lord Somerset."

"A pleasure to meet the young lady who has captured the earl's hand in marriage," Lord Russell said.

"The earl captured *my* hand in marriage," Victoria corrected him. She glanced at the woman who appeared distinctly unhappy.

Though she said nothing impolite, Lydia Stanley let Victoria know by nuance of expression that Alexander and she were close friends. Intimately close.

"So, Alex, is this taste for redheads a passing phase?" Lydia Stanley purred. Before he could reply, she looked at Victoria and said, "Alex and I have known each other forever."

"We must return to our seats now," Lord Somerset announced, sounding nervous.

"I'll see you soon," Lydia Stanley said to Alexander, and then flicked an insincere smile at Victoria.

"Meeting Alexander's *older* friends is a pleasure," Victoria said with a sunny smile.

With a decidedly irritated expression on her face, the Marchioness of Tewksbury turned away and left the box with her escorts. Victoria looked at Alexander, who was grinning.

"Your tongue draws blood," he said.

"She insulted me first," Victoria replied, and gave him a mischievous smile.

Victoria wasn't smiling inside, though. Something important had passed here, and she disliked the sensation of feeling her way in the darkness. Her sisters would know the gossip, and Victoria intended to ask them at first opportunity.

The remainder of the opera passed uneventfully, though Victoria felt more gazes directed at her than the stage. Alexander's proximity, his hand on her shoulder, and his whispered translations added to her distractions.

Reaching the Wilmingtons' mansion on Upper Brook Street, Alexander slipped her hand through the crook of his arm and gave it a soothing pat. "Are you prepared for more scrutiny?" he asked, climbing the stairs to the second floor ballroom.

"You certainly know how to calm a lady's nerves," Victoria teased.

Alexander leaned close to the majordomo and spoke in a low voice. Then the man announced in a clear, strong voice, "The Earl of Winchester and Lady Victoria Douglas."

"If you look at me, Tory," Alexander said, starting down the stairs, "you won't see the hundreds of curious gazes on you."

"How exceedingly conceited of you to believe that hundreds of people are interested in whom you are escorting," Victoria said, and then glanced at the crowd. "Oh, they *are* watching."

"I told you so," Alexander whispered against her ear, looking to all the world like a man in love.

Victoria cast him a sidelong smile and crooked her finger at him. When he leaned close again, she whispered, "I dislike the words *I-told-you-so* unless I am the one using them."

At the bottom of the stairs, well-wishers surrounded them, all of whom were Alexander's acquaintances. Lord and Lady Wilmington, their host and hostess, stood in front of them.

"Congratulations," Lord Wilmington said to Alexander, his gaze fixed on Victoria.

"Best wishes," Lady Wilmington said to Victoria, *her* gaze fixed on Alexander.

"Rupert and Miriam, I present Victoria Douglas, my fiancée," Alexander introduced them.

Victoria inclined her head, saying, "I am pleased to meet you."

"You must save a waltz for me," Lord Wilmington said to her.

"While you waltz with my husband," Lady Wilmington added, tipping her head toward Alexander, "I will guard your interests."

Victoria recognized the same look in Lady Wilmington's gaze that Lydia Stanley wore when she looked at Alexander. "I must greet my sister and brother-in-law," she said, wanting to escape these two as quickly as possible. "One must never keep royalty waiting, even if they are family."

"Miriam and I will talk with you later," Lord Wilmington said.

"That was well done," Alexander whispered, escorting her through the crowd. "Watch out for Rupert. The man is a known womanizer."

"His wife appears to be a manizer," Victoria replied. "Or is it only an Alexander-izer?"

"I dare say the Wilmingtons have an arrangement that allows them a certain degree of freedom," Alexander told her.

Victoria was shocked. "Do all married couples—?"

"*No.*"

Alexander led Victoria toward Samantha and

Rudolf. With them were Princes Viktor, Mikhail, and Stepan.

"How was the opera?" Samantha asked by way of a greeting.

"Quite enjoyable, but I believe more gazes were fixed on me than the stage," Victoria answered. "I should have taken a bow when the curtain closed."

"Lady Victoria, I believe this dance belongs to me," Alexander said, as the orchestra began playing a waltz.

With a shy smile, Victoria placed her hand in his. This was the first time they danced together.

With his hand at the small of her back, Alexander drew her close against his body, and they swirled around and around the ballroom. Comfortable in his arms, Victoria followed his lead. The world and all its people faded away. Intoxicating her senses, only the man and the music existed for her. Victoria felt buoyant, happier than she had ever expected to be, until the Marchioness of Tewksbury and her group walked down the stairs to the ballroom.

"A passing cloud has cast a shadow over your sunny smile," Alexander remarked, drawing her attention.

Victoria managed a bright smile for him. "How is that?" she asked.

"Much better."

The waltz ended, and Alexander escorted her back to their group.

"Lady Victoria, may I have this dance with my favorite, red-haired sister-in-law?" Rudolf asked, offering his hand.

"I would love to dance with my favorite, Russian brother-in-law," Victoria answered, placing her hand in his.

Rudolf and Victoria stepped onto the dance

floor. He held her somewhat less close than her fiancé.

Swirling around the ballroom in the prince's arms, Victoria saw Samantha dancing with Prince Viktor. Her heart sank when she spied Alexander step onto the dance floor with Lydia Stanley.

"What is wrong, Tory?" Prince Rudolf asked.

"Alexander is dancing with Lydia Stanley," Victoria answered. "She visited our opera box. What is between them?"

"Nothing."

Victoria arched a copper brow at him. "Let me rephrase that. What *was* between them?"

"Why don't you ask Alexander?" Rudolf countered, his dark gaze skittering away from hers.

"I am asking you," she replied. "As his bride-to-be, I have a right to know."

Prince Rudolf inclined his head and escorted her off the dance floor. Instead of returning to their group, he strolled with her in the opposite direction.

"Alexander and Lydia were involved three or four years ago," Rudolf told her. "Then Reginald Stanley, the Marquess of Tewksbury, a man old enough to be her father, offered for her. Lydia chose to become a marchioness rather than a countess."

"Where is her husband now?" Victoria asked.

"Reginald Stanley did Lydia the favor of dying after she had given birth to his only son," Rudolf answered. "Which left her free to marry Alexander."

"Why didn't they marry?"

"Alexander is a proud, unforgiving man who would never take another man's leavings," Rudolf told her. "Lydia Stanley has thrown herself in his path since coming out of mourning."

Victoria worried her lower lip. "Do you think Alexander still cares for her?"

"I think it is time for us to return to our group," Rudolf said with a smile.

Rudolf and Victoria reached their group just as Duke Magnus and Aunt Roxie arrived. Her aunt and uncle greeted everyone and then stepped onto the dance floor together.

Lord and Lady Wilmington had also joined their group. Lydia Stanley and Miriam Wilmington eyed each other with cool politeness. Victoria wondered how she could ever hope to compete against two sophisticated and beautiful women for Alexander's affection? How many other women in this ballroom were angling to capture Alexander's eye?

"Lady Victoria, you must be excited about your impending nuptials," Miriam Wilmington said.

"Alex is more excited than I am," Victoria answered. "He promised to cover me in diamonds and, as you can see, has made an excellent start."

Victoria glanced at Alexander, who appeared to be struggling against laughter. Rudolf and he turned away as if in deep conversation.

"His proposal was so romantic," Samantha entered the conversation. "In front of the entire family, Alexander knelt on bended knee and asked her to marry him."

"That does sound romantic," Miriam Wilmington agreed.

"How did you like tonight's opera?" Lydia Stanley asked.

"*The Marriage of Figaro*, wasn't it?" Miriam Wilmington asked.

"I adore opera," Victoria drawled, trying to sound sophisticated. "Mo created a remarkable composition."

"Mo?" Lydia Stanley echoed in obvious confusion.

"Mo Sart is the composer," Victoria told her, feeling smart for once.

Everyone stared at Victoria as if she had turned purple. She realized she had blundered somehow, but what she had done wrong eluded her.

"Lady Victoria, you promised me this dance," Prince Viktor said, offering his hand.

Glad to escape whatever she had done, Victoria accepted his hand and stepped onto the dance floor. As they waltzed, Victoria refused to meet the prince's gaze but kept a watchful eye on Alexander. Ladies Wilmington and Stanley appeared to be vying for his attention. When Lydia won and stepped onto the dance floor with Alexander, Victoria felt her heart sinking to her stomach.

Alexander and Lydia made a striking couple and waltzed as if they had been made for each other. They were smiling, too. At her expense, no doubt.

"Generally speaking, people make small talk while they dance," Prince Viktor said.

"I'm sorry," Victoria said, lifting her gaze to his. "I'm not feeling very well at the moment."

"Can I help?" the prince asked.

"Only if you can remove my foot from my mouth," she answered, making him smile. "Alex told me Mo Sart was the composer."

"The man's name is Wolfgang Amadeus Mozart," Prince Viktor told her. "Mozart is one word. Trust me, everyone makes mistakes."

"Some of us make more mistakes than others," Victoria replied, as the music ended.

"You are much too hard on yourself," the prince told her.

"I would like to freshen up," Victoria said, unable to face the others. "Please, tell Alex I will be along in a few minutes."

Victoria retreated to the ladies' withdrawing room. She needed to compose herself before facing the others, especially women who wanted Alexander for themselves.

Unseen by others, Victoria sat in a dark corner and tried to calm herself. The more she appeared in public, the more mistakes she would make. Soon, Alexander would regret marrying someone as stupid as she.

All her problems stemmed from her word blindness. If only she could read, she would have known that Mo Sart was Mozart, Napoleon was at Elba, and the apprentice law had been repealed. Her only hope was the Philbin brothers.

"The twit actually called Mozart *Mo Sart,*" Lydia Stanley said, walking into the withdrawing room with another woman.

"So?" the other woman said. "She didn't mispronounce it."

"My God, Sarah, you are almost as stupid as she is," Lydia Stanley exclaimed. "Anyway, I doubt winning him back will be difficult. Blushing innocence is merely a novelty."

"There you are, darling," Aunt Roxie said, marching into the room. "Alexander is looking for you."

"Lady Victoria, I didn't see you there," Lydia Stanley said in surprise.

"Apparently not." Victoria rose from the chair and started to leave.

Obviously flustered, Lydia kept speaking, "May I present my dear friend Sarah—"

"No, you may not present anyone to me," Victoria snapped, and brushed past the two women.

"I love your gown, Lydia," Aunt Roxie drawled, "but that color makes you look sallow."

With his arms folded across his chest, Alexander stood a few feet away from the entrance to the withdrawing room. He straightened when he saw her.

Victoria walked toward him. She tried to smile but could not banish the angry embarrassment staining her cheeks.

Alexander had loved Lydia Stanley kept pounding through her mind. And now Lydia Stanley wanted him back in her life, her heart, her bed.

"Anyone unfamiliar with opera could have made that mistake," Alexander said, taking her hand in his. "You should not feel—"

"Perhaps you should marry someone else," Victoria interrupted, thinking a little pain now would save her a lot of pain later.

"Why should I marry someone else when I want to marry you?" Alexander asked, his voice low and soothing.

Victoria tipped her head toward the withdrawing room. "Lydia Stanley intends to win your heart again. She's very beautiful and, probably, smart."

"Lydia and I were finished a long time ago," Alexander said, cupping her chin with one hand and waiting until she raised her gaze to his. "I want to marry *you*, Tory."

"You never wanted to marry me," Victoria said. "You agreed to the match my aunt proposed."

Alexander could have kicked himself for saying the words to her. She wouldn't feel this way if he had kept his mouth shut.

"No one twisted my arm to make me agree to marry you," Alexander told her.

"I would like to speak with my niece," the duchess

said, approaching them. She gestured with her hand and ordered, "Wait over there and give us privacy."

When Alexander walked out of earshot, Aunt Roxie turned on her. There was no mistaking the displeasure stamped across her features.

"I know more about men than you," Aunt Roxie told her. "Alex would never be tempted to resume his relationship with Lydia Stanley, and she is a fool to believe otherwise. No man will forgive his woman for betraying him. Now, about your little *faux pas*. I cannot understand how you carry my blood in your veins."

"You know I am hopelessly stupid," Victoria replied.

"It isn't that, darling," her aunt drawled. "No matter what you do or say, always stare your adversary out of countenance. Never cut and run, especially into the withdrawing room."

"Should I have stayed and listened to insults?" Victoria asked.

"Yes, and then returned the favor to whoever insulted you like I did to Lydia on your behalf," Aunt Roxie answered. "Never allow your emotions to show. Keeping a placid expression in the face of extreme provocation is required for social success."

"Thank you for your advice," Victoria said, a smile lifting the corners of her lips. "I shall bring no further disgrace to your reputation."

"Alex is waiting," her aunt dismissed her. "Run along."

"Are you all right?" Alexander asked when she approached him.

"I am fine," Victoria answered. "Will you walk with me?"

"I cannot think of anyone else with whom I would rather walk," Alexander told her.

Victoria slipped her hand in his. Alexander gave it a little squeeze and led her down the length of the ballroom toward an alcove where they could enjoy privacy but still be seen.

Alexander manuevered Victoria into standing against the wall. He turned his back on the ballroom, effectively blocking her from view.

"You are lovely, Miss Victoria Douglas," Alexander said in a low voice, tracing a finger down her silken cheek. "I wish the remaining days until our wedding could sprout wings and fly away so we could be alone all day, every day."

"Will you tell me about Lydia Stanley?" Victoria asked, and watched his expression become grim. "My aunt has instructed me to keep my expression placid, no matter the provocation. I imagine that unwritten rule applies to gentlemen, too."

Alexander inclined his head. "Lydia Stanley and I were friends a long time ago. You needn't concern yourself about her. I am flattered that you care enough to feel threatened but concerned that you do not trust me."

"I trust you," Victoria told him. "I was concerned because—" She never finished her thought.

"Alex," cried a woman behind him.

Alexander and Victoria stared at the brunette. Standing in front of them was Venetia Emerson, Alexander's sister, who was supposed to be in Australia. A tall, well built gentleman and a voluptuous, dark-haired beauty stood on either side of her.

Venetia threw herself into her brother's arms. "I told Harry and Diana you would be attending the Wilmingtons' ball."

Victoria peeked at Alexander. He did not appear to be pleased by the sight of his sister.

"Alex, I present my husband, Harry Gibbs," Venetia said.

The two men shook hands.

"Diana Drummond is Harry's widowed sister," Venetia said, gesturing to the dark-haired beauty. "I thought Diana and you would get along."

Victoria felt nauseated at the sight of the Widow Drummond. The last thing she needed was another woman competing for her fiancé's attention.

Alexander drew her forward. "You remember Victoria Douglas," he said to his sister. "Tory and I will be married in two weeks."

"How wonderful," Venetia said, but her smile did not reach her eyes.

"Best wishes," the Widow Drummond said, her voice low and seductive.

In that moment, Victoria compared herself to the widow and came out lacking. The widow was the ultimate sophisticate, beautiful, voluptuous, and self-assured. Compared to her, Victoria felt like a child. An illiterate child.

"Harry bought the town mansion only three doors down from Emerson House," Venetia told him.

"Charles?" Alexander asked.

"Father is dead," Venetia answered. "To the day he died, Father regretted those last angry words that passed between you."

"I'll bet he did," Alexander said.

Victoria noted the grim set to his jaw. Alexander was disappointed because Charles Emerson knew the secret of his birth and took that secret to his grave.

"Come to dinner tomorrow evening," Venetia invited him.

"Victoria and I planned to dine together," Alexander hedged, clearly uncomfortable with the invitation.

"Lady Victoria is welcome to join us," Venetia said.

Alexander nodded. "We'll be there at——?"

"Eight." At that, Venetia looped her arm through her husband's and walked away with the Widow Drummond in tow.

"How can you dine with a woman who once tried to kill you?" Victoria whispered, watching them walk away.

"Charles Emerson tried to kill me, not Venetia," Alexander told her.

"Well, Venetia tried to kill my sister Angelica," Victoria reminded him.

"Are you refusing to accompany me?" he asked.

Victoria had no intention of allowing Alexander to dine at the same table as the widow unless she was there. "I will accompany you," she said. "I intend to eat before I go lest the witch tries to poison me, and I urge you to do the same."

Alexander laughed and pulled her into his arms. "Victoria Douglas, you are an Original."

"I thought I was an Incomparable."

"You are that, too."

CHAPTER 7

"Good morning, Tinker."

"Good morning, Lady Victoria," the majordomo said.

Humming a waltz melody, Victoria walked across the dining room and tossed her bonnet onto the table. At the sideboard, she helped herself to plain black tea and a buttered roll.

"May I say how lovely you look this morning," Tinker said.

"Thank you."

Victoria wore a white, high-waisted muslin morning gown adorned with a petal pink ribbon below the bosom and pink embroidered rosettes along the hem. Her shawl and slippers were also petal pink as were the ribbons that fastened her white bonnet.

My aunt is a pain in the arse, Victoria thought, her gaze on the bonnet. She despised bonnets, but her aunt had insisted. A lady always wore a bonnet while riding in the park.

Alexander would arrive shortly to take her out,

and Victoria looked forward to being alone with him. If she could only contrive to be alone with him in a private place.

Sipping her tea, Victoria thought about the previous evening and all the women who were attracted to Alexander. Would their pursuit continue once he was married? Lydia Stanley, Miriam Wilmington, and Diana Drummond were beautiful, sophisticated, and intelligent. She'd bet her last shilling that each could read, too.

The *Times* lay on the table nearby. If Alexander arrived to see the newspaper opened in front of her, he would assume that she was reading it.

Victoria pulled the *Times* closer, stared at the headline for a moment, and then turned to the society page. Using her index finger, she pointed at each word and silently tried to read it. Love for the letters *O, T,* and *X* swelled within her. Those letters were more constant than true love and never misbehaved like the despicable *d* and *b.*

"Come here, please," Victoria called to the majordomo.

If Tinker read her a few tidbits from the gossip column, she could mention them to Alexander. He would believe she had read the newspaper.

"Yes, my lady?" Tinker said, standing beside her.

"I've forgotten my spectacles upstairs," Victoria lied. "Would you read me a few tidbits from the society page?"

"Of course, my lady." Tinker perused the page and then read, "London society is awaiting the Earl of Winchester's marriage to Lady Victoria Douglas.'

"Show me where it says that," Victoria said, smiling with pleasure at being mentioned.

When the majordomo pointed to the spot, Victoria placed a finger on the letters of her name

She recognized the *V, I, C, T,* and *O.* The other letters escaped her.

"Go on," she said.

"Society had a peek at the lovely bride-to-be when the earl and she attended the opera together," Tinker read.

"Tell me something more interesting," Victoria said.

"There is nothing more interesting than you," the majordomo drawled.

Victoria smiled. "Thank you, sir."

Tinker perused the column and chuckled as he neared the bottom of the article. "Listen to this juicy tidbit," he said. "A certain young lady about to marry a peer of the realm was overheard to say that she adored the composer Mo Sart. Hmmm. One wonders what criteria the gentleman used for choosing his bride."

I am the village idiot, Victoria thought, her eyes filling with tears.

"Thank you, Tinker," she said in a choked voice, pushing her plate away. "I have heard enough."

Victoria stared at the newspaper. Everyone at the Wilmingtons' ball would read the column and know the reporter referred to her. Those who hadn't attended would hear the story. Soon, all of London would know how stupid she was.

Though she held her sobs back, Victoria couldn't stop the tears streaming down her cheeks. She wiped them away with a napkin, but fresh droplets appeared and rolled down her flushed cheeks.

Alexander would cry off when he realized how stupid she was. If the deed were done, he would divorce her, and she couldn't fault him for that. No man of Alexander's stature would wish to be married to the village idiot.

"Is anything wrong?" Tinker asked.

"I am fine," Victoria lied, her expression grim.

"You are *not* fine," Tinker replied in an overly loud voice.

"What is wrong?" Alexander asked, walking into the dining room in time to hear the majordomo's words.

Her heart ached at the sight of the earl. She loved him, but he deserved better.

"I am quite well," Victoria lied, and then dropped her gaze.

Behind her back, Tinker shook his head. Alexander arched a questioning brow, but the majordomo shrugged.

"Tinker, I would love a cup of coffee," Alexander said.

"Yes, my lord."

Alexander sat beside Victoria at the table. She gave him a wobbly smile but said nothing.

Tinker set the cup of coffee down on the dining table. At a flick of the earl's wrist, the majordomo left the room and closed the doors.

"Why did Tinker leave?" Victoria asked.

"I told him to leave," Alexander answered.

"How did you do that without speaking?"

"Practice." Alexander lifted her hand to his lips and then turned it over to press a kiss on her palm. "Sweetheart, tell me what is bothering you."

"I can't marry you," Victoria told him, her bottom lip trembling as she fought back tears. She shifted her gaze to the table and pointed at the newspaper article.

Alexander read the offending words and then raised his gaze to hers. "Let me understand this," he said, leaning close to her. "You don't want to marry me because you thought Mozart was Mo Sart?"

"I *do* want to marry you," Victoria said. "I don't

want to ruin your life. People are already laughing at my ignorance. When they start laughing at you because you chose me, you will begin to hate me."

"Tory, I could never hate you," Alexander said, putting his arm around her and nuzzling her neck. "A husband and wife belong to each other, no matter what comes. I want to marry you."

"Do not try to make me feel better," she said.

"You don't want to feel better?" he asked.

Victoria heard the smile in his voice and turned her head to look at him. She smiled in spite of her misery.

"I will teach you whatever you need to know," Alexander promised, and then captured her lips in a lingering kiss.

Victoria slid her hand up his chest to entwine his neck and surrendered to his kiss. She parted her lips for him, allowing him entrance to her mouth, and let herself be carried along by his passion.

The dining room doors opened, drawing their attention. The duchess walked into the room, saying, "Tinker told me you weren't feeling well, but I see you have recovered." Her aunt looked pointedly at Alexander and then asked Victoria, "Were you feeling nauseated or dizzy?"

Victoria shook her head.

"As you were," her aunt said, and left the dining room.

"She keeps asking if I am nauseated," Victoria said in confusion, making him smile for some unfathomable reason.

Alexander stood and offered his hand. Victoria placed her hand in his. Reaching for her bonnet, she complained, "My aunt is forcing me to wear this. She insists that proper ladies wear bonnets when they go riding."

"Allow me," Alexander said, lifting the bonnet out of her hand. He placed it on her head and fastened the two ends of the ribbon beneath her chin.

Stepping outside, Victoria smiled to herself when she saw his phaeton in front of the duke's mansion. Apparently, he wanted to be alone with her, which matched her feelings for him.

Alexander helped her up and then climbed onto the phaeton, taking the reins in hand. Victoria looked up at the blue sky and then at him.

"What a perfect day for a ride," she said.

Off they went but not far. Hyde Park was located on the opposite side of Park Lane.

June had delivered summer's robust lushness to the park. Accentuated by the pastels of pink and lavender and peach, the primary colors of the red, blue, and yellow flowers abounded everywhere. Dark green shrubs and trees in bloom dotted the acres of lighter green grass.

Victoria suffered the urge to kick off her shoes and dance across the grass, letting each blade tickle her feet. The thought of what her aunt would say made her smile.

A parked carriage up ahead caught her attention, making her spirits plummet. Lydia Stanley, her friend Sarah, and two other women sat in a barouche, its hood down.

"Good morning, Alex," Lydia called, as they passed the barouche.

Alexander nodded curtly and stared straight ahead. Glancing over her shoulder, Victoria saw the women put their heads together and then burst into titters of laughter.

God, how she hated titters.

Victoria knew they were laughing at her stupidity of the previous evening. If only Alexander and she could live by themselves without society intruding.

And then trouble approached in the shape of two women on horseback. Alexander pulled the phaeton to the side of the road when he spied his sister and the widow.

"Good morning, Alex," Venetia said, reining her mount to a halt.

"Good morning, my lord," Diana Drummond said, her voice low and a trifle breathless.

"Good morning, ladies," Alexander returned the greeting.

Victoria forced herself to smile and inclined her head. Then she dropped her gaze to her hands folded in her lap. One of these witches had tried to murder her sister, and the other coveted her husband-to-be.

"Your impending marriage to Lady Victoria is mentioned in today's *Times*," Venetia said.

Diana Drummond chuckled throatily, and Victoria couldn't help thinking that even the witch's mirth was seductive. "I've been laughing all morning about the twit who thought Mozart was Mo Sart," the widow said. "How any gentleman could tie himself to so stupid a woman is beyond my ken. After all, a man must converse with his wife sometime."

Victoria froze, an embarrassed blush staining her cheeks. Insidious insecurity coiled itself around her heart and mind. Her *faux pas* must embarrass Alexander. How long would it be before he tired of her ignorance and set her aside?

"We'll expect you at eight," Venetia was saying.

Alexander started the phaeton moving. "What's wrong?"

"That woman insulted me purposely," Victoria said, without looking at him.

"Diana wasn't there, Tory," Alexander said. "The insult was inadvertent."

Victoria snapped her gaze to him. And she thought *she* was stupid? When it came to beautiful women, men were such simpletons.

"How can you defend her?" Victoria asked. "I am your betrothed."

"I'm not defending her," Alexander replied. "You should give other people the benefit of the doubt."

"Those who give others the benefit of the doubt usually end by losing everything," Victoria told him, a bitter edge to her voice.

"So cynical, my love?"

"My family has experience in being duped," she said flatly.

Alexander made no reply. Victoria glanced at him and noted his lips tightened into a grim line.

"I'm sorry, Alex," Victoria said, touching his arm. "I did not mean to imply—Please, don't be angry with me."

"I should be apologizing to you," Alexander said, steering the phaeton toward the Cumberland Gate.

"I intend to remind you of those words some day," Victoria returned, making him smile. "Where are we going now?"

"I want to see where you lived before His Grace sent for you," he told her.

"I don't think that is a good idea," she said.

"I insist."

"Alex—"

"I need to see it."

Alexander turned the phaeton onto Edgeware Road. From there, they drove down Marylebone Road to Park Road, which brought them to Primrose Hill.

"Turn the phaeton around," Victoria said, when they reached the two hundred and sixteen foot summit of Primrose Hill.

Alexander gave her a puzzled smile but did as she ordered. And then he knew why she had wanted to turn around. Beyond the sloping meadow lay London, its tallest landmarks—Westminster Abbey, Saint Paul's Cathedral, the Tower of London—easily visible.

"What an outstanding view," he said.

"I used to stand here and pretend that I was a princess looking over my domain," she told him, a smile touching her lips. "On New Year's Eve, I watched the fireworks from this spot. Did you know that giant oaks covered the hill two hundred years ago?"

"Where did you read that?" Alexander asked, enchanted by her beauty, her charm, her artless innocence.

"Mister Lewis told me."

"Poor Mister Lewis?"

Victoria nodded. "The very same man."

Pulling the reins, Alexander turned the horses around and down the western slope of Primrose Hill. Below lay a tiny hamlet of cottages with their pale pink, lemon, and sage stucco fronts trimmed with white, like frosted cakes.

"Which one is yours?" Alexander asked when the phaeton reached the bottom of the hill.

"The last cottage at the end of the lane," she answered, beginning to feel uncomfortable.

Victoria bit her bottom lip at the thought that Alexander was about to see where she grew up. Knowing she had been poor wasn't as graphic as actually seeing the poverty. She hoped he wouldn't feel too guilty because of what his father had done.

Alexander halted the phaeton in front of the

pale pink cottage with white trim. He sat in silence for a time, staring at it, and then asked, "Can we go inside?"

When she inclined her head, Alexander climbed out of the phaeton and then helped her down. Together, they walked up the the tiny path to the front door.

Victoria unlocked the door with the key hidden under the flower pot. Alexander followed her and stood just inside the doorway. The cottage consisted of one large room that served as kitchen and parlor with a hearth at either end, one for cooking and one for warmth. The kitchen had a table with four chairs while the parlor had a settee and small table. Three doors stood along the back wall of the room.

"My sisters and I slept here," Victoria said, opening the first door.

Alexander crossed the cottage and peered inside at the three cots. "This closet isn't big enough for one person," he said. "I suppose the other two rooms were for your aunt and your father."

"Please, Alex, do not torment yourself," Victoria said, noting the grim set to his jaw. She touched his arm, adding, "I didn't know I was poor and spoke truthfully when I told you I was happy here."

"I cannot credit that," Alexander said.

"Whatever troubled me here would have troubled me on Park Lane or Grosvenor Square," Victoria told him.

"How did you manage to live once your aunt's funds were depleted?" Alexander asked, putting his arm around her shoulder and pulling her close.

"Angelica was an expert cheat at dice and cards," Victoria answered, her face flaming with her embarrassment. In a mumble, she added, "Samantha and I picked pockets."

Alexander closed his eyes against the injustice

Charles Emerson had wrought. Three young girls had lost the security of a home, their mother in childbirth, and their father to drunkenness. Lady Roxanne—*God bless her*—had kept the girls alive.

"Come here," Victoria said, sitting on the cot. When he sat beside her, she said, "Life was good. My sisters and I had fun."

"How can you possibly have enjoyed life in this hovel?" Alexander asked, putting his arm around her.

"This is my home," Victoria corrected him, her voice choked with emotion.

"I'm sorry," Alexander apologized, gently forcing her to look at him. He touched his lips to hers. "Tell me about the fun."

Victoria shrugged. "We had fun the usual way, by playing with the hamlet's other children. Except—" She broke off and shrugged again.

"Except what?" Alexander asked, a smile tugging at the corners of his lips.

"Samantha and I prayed each night for our heart's desire," Victoria answered. "We never did get it."

"What was your heart's desire?"

"Samantha wanted a tiara because the other children wouldn't make fun of her limp if she was a princess," Victoria told him, her smile jaunty. "I wanted a magic wand."

"What would you have done with a magic wand?" he asked.

"Point, circle, point," she answered.

Victoria pretended to hold a wand in her hand and demonstrated. She pointed at an invisible object, made an invisible circle, and pointed at the unseen object again.

Alexander laughed. "Why did you want to do that?"

"I wanted to turn the other children to stone," she admitted.

Alexander smiled. "What a naughty chit."

"I wanted to stop the other children from making fun of Samantha and me," Victoria explained. "Whenever I had trouble with directions, like the day we played croquet, the other children called me *stupid.*"

Alexander lost his smile. The poignancy of her story tugged at his heart, and he regretted calling her *stupid.* If he could get his hands on the insensitive urchins—

"As you see, I survived," Victoria said, rising from her perch on the cot. She gazed into his hazel eyes and added, "I hope that isn't pity I see. I prefer stupidity to pity."

"You aren't stupid," Alexander told her, standing when she did. "You accepted my marriage proposal, didn't you?"

"My lord, you are conceited."

Determined to slay the dragons hiding in the shadows of her memory, Alexander pulled her against the hard, muscular planes of his body and imprisoned her within the protective circle of his embrace. He dipped his head and captured her lips in a slow, breath-stealing kiss that seemed to last forever.

Victoria sighed. "I thought we'd never be alone again."

"This could be the last time we are alone until the wedding," Alexander told her.

Victoria groaned with disappointment.

"Thank you, my love," Alexander said. "Since we are alone, I would like to tutor you on right and left."

"You are doomed to failure," she told him.

"Darling, cooperate with me," he said.

Without giving her a chance to reply, Alexander captured her lips again. His kiss was long and langorous.

"This is your left ear," he whispered, sliding his lips across her cheek to nibble on her earlobe. "And this is the left side of your throat." His lips followed his words.

"I never knew learning could be such fun," Victoria whispered, reveling in the sensations he was creating.

Alexander captured her lips again. Flicking his tongue across the crease in between her lips, he sought and gained access to the sweetness within. She was soft, and her delicate scent of vanilla and jasmine inflamed his senses.

Surprisingly, her gown fluttered to the floor when he stepped back. She stood in chemise, stockings, garters, and slippers.

"Left shoulder," Alexander said, unfastening the chemise's ribbons. "Right shoulder now."

Her chemise fell to the floor and pooled at her feet with her gown. Without shame, Victoria stood in her stockings and garters only, enjoying his perusal.

Alexander unpinned her hair, letting the curly mane of fire cascade almost to her waist. Then he stepped back to admire her nakedness. With a smile on his lips, Alexander studied her lovely face with its alabaster skin and pink lips, her breasts with their pink-tipped nipples, her slender waist, her curvaceous hips . . .

Victoria knew the instant he spied the small dagger inside the leather garter strapped to her calf.

"What is that?" Alexander asked, losing his smile.

"I think it's my leg," Victoria answered.

Clearly unamused, Alexander snapped his gaze to hers. "Tory, I am serious."

"Old habits die hard," she said.

His expression softened on her. "You look like a pagan princess with your red curls and that dagger."

"Please, continue with my lessons," Victoria said.

With a groan, Alexander lifted her into his arms and placed her across the cot. He spread her thighs and stepped between them, running a finger along her moist crease, eliciting a gasp from her.

"Left breast," he whispered, leaning over her to suckle upon one pink nipple.

"Right breast," he said thickly, flicking his tongue across her chest to capture her nipple.

Victoria moaned and wrapped her legs around his waist, trying to pull him closer. Closer. Closer.

Alexander freed his manhood and rubbed its tip against her nub. "I want to see you swell with my seed and suckle our baby at your breast," he said, gazing down at her.

"Yes, Alex," she breathed. "I want—"

Alexander thrust forward and pushed himself deep inside her until their groins touched. Then he moved . . . slowly, enticingly, inviting her to move with him.

Catching his rhythm, Victoria kept her legs wrapped tightly around him. She moved with him, hands clutching his back, his powerful muscles flexing beneath her silken touch.

Her throaty, whimpering moans incited him to thrust harder, deeper. Victoria cried out as her body shuddered with contractions of pleasure. Only then did Alexander join her, flooding her womb, collapsing upon her.

Long, silent moments passed. The only sound each heard was the life blood singing through their bodies, the rhythm of their heartbeats.

Finally, Alexander lifted his weight off her. Supporting himself on his elbows, he gazed down at her.

"What direction was that?" Victoria asked in a breathless whisper.

Alexander smiled. "That, my love, was dead center."

Victoria dressed with special care that evening, wanting Alexander's attention fixed on her, not the voluptuous widow. She chose a midnight blue silk gown, its bodice cut in a low *V* both in front and in back. Highwaisted, the gossamer silk clung to every curve. The only jewelry she wore was her diamond betrothal ring. Her aunt's maid had styled her fiery mane in an upswept fashion, the better to display her cleavage.

"Darling, you are more dazzling than the noonday sun and more enchanting than the silvery moon," Aunt Roxie drawled, walking into her bedchamber. "Come, Alexander is waiting."

After one final peek at herself in the cheval mirror, Victoria turned to her aunt. Her smile was sunny, but worry clouded her eyes.

"You aren't queasy, are you?" her aunt asked.

Victoria shook her head. Together, they left the bedchamber and walked the length of the corridor to the stairs.

"I can see that you're worried," Aunt Roxie remarked. "I have some advice."

"Thank you, Aunt," Victoria said, for the first time in her life appreciative of her aunt's experience. "I need all the advice you can give."

"First of all, there is nothing to worry about," Aunt Roxie said, taking her hand in hers. "If either of those two witches insults you, return the insult sweetly, putting them on the defensive. Look them in the eye as if you were superior to them in every way. Which you are, darling. Do *not* disagree with Alex in any way. If he does or says something you don't like, wait until you are alone to criticize him."

"What if the widow flirts with Alex?" Victoria asked, wishing she knew all that her aunt knew.

"If you aren't in close proximity to cling to him physically," her aunt answered, "then you must flirt with Venetia's husband. That will bring Alex scurrying to your side."

"How do I flirt with Mr. Gibbs?" Victoria asked, beginning to panic. Alexander was the only man she had ever flirted with.

"Trust your instincts, darling," Aunt Roxie said, cupping her niece's cheek. "You do carry my blood in your veins; flirting will come naturally once you start. Imagine you are the greatest actress in the world performing before an audience of four. Throw yourself into the role with aplomb."

"I love you, Aunt Roxie."

"I love you, too, darling."

Walking down the stairs to the foyer, Victoria caught Alexander's first glimpse of her. She smiled at his admiring expression and crossed the foyer to stand before him.

Alexander brought her hand to his lips. His gaze, however, was fixed on the alluring, alabaster cleavage above the low cut neckline of her gown.

"I know you prefer my hair down," Victoria purred, practicing her aplomb, "but if I wore it down, you would be unable to peek down my bosom."

Alexander smiled. "What are you planning, Tory?"

"I am planning an enjoyable evening with you," Victoria answered.

A short time later, the Gibbs's majordomo greeted them at the door. After taking Victoria's silk cape, the man escorted them upstairs to the drawing room where the others had already gathered.

"Welcome to our home." Harry Gibbs met them midway across the drawing room and shook Alexander's hand. Then he lifted Victoria's hand to his lips before escorting them across the room.

Venetia and Diana sat together on the settee. Alexander bent to kiss his sister's cheek and then lifted the widow's hand to his lips.

Victoria felt disheartened when she looked at the widow. Diana Drummond wore a black gown even more low cut than her own.

Insecurity welled within her breast, and Victoria wondered how she could compete with the widow's voluptuous sophistication. Then she thought of her aunt and gave herself a mental shake, telling herself she was just as good as the widow. Especially if reading was not required.

Think aplomb, Victoria told herself.

"How delightful to see you again," Victoria said to the women, an insincere smile pasted on her face.

She glanced at Alexander. His lips quirked as if he wanted to laugh.

"Is that your betrothal ring?" Diana asked, her gaze on the enormous diamond.

Victoria held her hand out for their inspection. "My devoted husband-to-be has vowed to drench me in diamonds," she told them. "I do believe he has made a good beginning."

"Alexander always did have excellent taste," Venetia said.

"Especially in my choice of a bride," Alexander added.

"Well said." Harry Gibbs gestured to the doorway. "Shall we go down to dinner?"

Venetia and Diana rose from the settee. As if they had planned their moves, the two women slipped an arm through Alexander's, trapping him between them, and escorted him out of the drawing room.

Victoria narrowed her blue gaze on their backs. Harry Gibbs offered her his arm. Walking beside him, Victoria noted the widow was unacceptably close to Alexander, close enough to press her breast against his arm.

"Is something wrong?" Harry Gibbs asked, his voice low.

Victoria managed a smile for him and thought *aplomb.* "Whatever could be wrong when I am escorted to dinner by such a handsome man as you?"

"Don't let my sister bother you," he whispered. "Diana is an incorrigible flirt."

Beneath the majordomo's supervision, two footmen served dinner. They dined on French cucumber soup, dandelion salad with sharp vinaigrette, stuffed meadow mushrooms, and roasted chicken with potatoes. There were lemon barley water and wine.

"Would you prefer warmed milk?" Venetia asked, eliciting a smile from her sister-in-law, when Victoria declined the wine.

There was nothing subtle about the woman's insult. In her mind's eye, Victoria pictured her aunt gesturing dramatically and saying, "Think aplomb."

"Lemon barley water will suffice," Victoria said, her smile sweet. She flicked a glance at Harry Gibbs, adding, "I admit I have not acquired a taste for wine or spirits. I'm certain my appreciation will grow with advancing age like Ladies Venetia and Diana."

Harry Gibbs grinned. "My dear, you need never acquire such a taste in order to be delightful."

"Thank you, sir." Victoria willed herself to blush and dropped her gaze as if shy. She slanted a glance at Alexander, who was smiling as if he knew her ploy.

"I adore opera," Diana Drummond said to Alexander. "Would you be amenable to my using your box one evening?"

"You are welcome to use it whenever you wish," Alexander answered.

"Do you still attend the opera every Thursday?" Venetia asked.

"Yes, I do."

Diana Drummond laughed throatily. "I am still tickled by the chit who thought Mozart was Mo Sart."

"I am the chit who said that," Victoria announced, grimacing inwardly though her expression remained placid.

Aplomb. Aplomb. Aplomb.

Their surprised expressions told her that she had caught them all—including Alexander—off balance. She could have kissed her aunt for the sound advice.

Harry Gibbs was the first to recover. "I dare say, Lady Victoria hasn't the experience of you older ladies," he said, coming to her defense.

With a come-hither expression, Victoria turned to him. She leaned close, giving him an excellent view of the tops of her flawless breasts.

"Did you know that Beethoven was a woman?" she asked, her smile conspiratorial. "Her name was actually Bea Toven."

Harry Gibbs burst out laughing. "Lady Victoria, you're a breath of fresh air after an evening in a smoky tavern."

"Call me Tory," she said. "All my friends do."

"Tory, then."

"Are you implying that *I* am a smoky tavern?" Venetia asked, her irritation apparent.

"Dearest, a compliment to one lady isn't necessarily an insult to another," Harry Gibbs told his wife.

"Diana loves to read," Venetia said, turning to her brother. She looked at her sister-in-law, saying, "Alexander has an extensive library."

"I would dearly love to see this library and, perhaps, borrow a few books," Diana said.

"A beautiful widow entering a bachelor's home is not done in England," Victoria said, before Alexander could reply. "You will be most welcome to browse in our library after we marry. Until then, London boasts numerous bookstores and lending libraries."

"I'm certain Diana could come to the library if I accompany her," Venetia spoke up. "After all, Alex and I are siblings."

"Estranged siblings," Victoria corrected, glancing at Alexander. She couldn't imagine why he was letting her do all the talking. His expression was pleasantly surprised rather than placid.

"They aren't estranged any longer," Diana said.

"That remains to be seen," Victoria drawled. "Your behavior may be as innocent as a babe, but vicious rumors are certain to spread if anyone sees you entering his house. Besides, Alex and I will be busy between now and the wedding. Won't we, darling?"

"We do have a full social schedule until then," Alexander agreed, amusement lighting his eyes.

Victoria smiled at Diana. With her hands in her lap, Victoria pointed her index finger at the widow, made a circle with it, and then pointed it toward her again as if she had a magic wand. In her mind, she had just turned the widow to stone.

Beside her, Alexander chuckled. Victoria glanced at him. Lifting his gaze from her lap, he leaned close and whispered, "Bravo, Tory."

"What is so amusing?" Venetia asked.

"I apologize for my rudeness," Alexander said to his sister, while he lifted Victoria's hand to his lips. "It's a private joke between my bride-to-be and me."

Victoria knew Alexander didn't trust her to be alone with the two women when he said, "Harry, there are only the two of us. Why don't we have our brandy in the drawing room?"

"I'm amenable," the other man said, and rose from his chair.

Alexander pulled Victoria close as they climbed the stairs to the drawing room. "You naughty minx," he whispered against her ear. "You are beginning to remind me of your aunt."

"I thank you, darling, on behalf of my aunt," Victoria drawled, making him smile.

Alexander and Victoria sat together on the settee as brandy, coffee, and tea were served. "Oh, drat, no warmed milk," she said, making both men smile.

When Alexander put his arm on the settee in back of her, Victoria cuddled close to his body. She ignored the two women and feigned attention to his conversation with Harry Gibbs concerning shipping lines, the wool trade, and other subjects.

"How did Charles die?" Alexander asked, during a lull in the conversation.

"It was his heart," Venetia answered. "There was nothing we could do."

"Did Charles say anything important before he died?" Alexander asked.

Victoria heard the hopeful note in his voice and knew what he wanted. Only Charles Emerson knew the secret of Alexander's birth. His death could signal the end of Alexander's search for the identity of his natural father.

"Father always regretted the angry words that passed between you," Venetia was saying. "Other than that—" She shrugged. "The end came too quickly for any deathbed sentiments."

The evening ended soon after that. Harry, Venetia, and Diana escorted them downstairs to the foyer.

"You must have dinner at my house," Alexander invited them. "Once she's settled, Victoria will send you a note."

"We'll be looking forward to it," Venetia said, her smile obviously forced.

The door closed behind them. Alexander leaned close and said, "I'm proud of the way you weathered the storm."

"Darling, I appreciate the praise." Victoria planted a kiss on his cheek.

When the door closed on their guests, Harry Gibbs turned on his sister. "Diana, that look bodes ill for Lady Victoria. If you cause trouble for them, I promise to send you back to Australia. Set your sights on an *available* gentleman. Do you understand?"

"Perfectly."

He kissed his wife's cheek, saying, "I have some papers to look over. I'll be along shortly."

The two women watched him walk upstairs and then disappear from sight. "I thought your brother was unattached," Diana said.

"Don't worry," Venetia said. "You will be his countess. We will need to lie low until after their wedding."

"After their wedding will be too late," Diana said.

"Marriages can be broken," Venetia assured her. "I have a plan that will send that redhaired twit running home to auntie, and no one will suspect our involvement."

"You are so deliciously wicked," Diana said, looping her arm through her sister-in-law's as they headed for the stairs. "Tell me about this scheme."

CHAPTER 8

"I'm so excited I could swoon," Victoria ex
claimed.

Hearing giggles behind her, Victoria turned
around and smiled at her sisters. Angelica and
Samantha, along with the duke and the duchess
stood in the nave of Audley Chapel. Both sister
had agreed to stand as her matrons of honor. The
duke would escort her down the aisle to the altar
where Alexander would be waiting with his two
groomsmen, Robert and Rudolf.

With the pre-nuptial social schedule, the days to
her wedding had passed faster than the blink of an
eye. Thankfully, her rivals for Alexander's atten
tion had backed away as the wedding approached
but Victoria felt certain the unrequited would gather
at a later date.

"You aren't queasy?" Aunt Roxie asked, drawing
her attention.

Victoria shook her head. "How do I look?" she
asked, turning in a circle.

"Exquisitely beautiful," Aunt Roxie answered

daintily dabbing at her tear-filled eyes. "I wish your mother could see you."

Like her sisters before her, Victoria wore her mother's wedding gown. Embroidered with hundreds of seed pearls, the white silk gown had a squared neckline, long sleeves shaped like bells, and a fitted bodice with a dropped waist.

Victoria wore her diamond betrothal ring, which had been moved to her right hand. Diamond florets glittered in her fiery hair, and she carried a bouquet of orange blossoms.

"I cannot believe my darling Tory is about to become a countess," Aunt Roxie gushed.

"Well, my dear, she won't become a countess unless you take your seat," Duke Magnus told his wife.

Aunt Roxie nodded and began to turn away. Victoria threw herself into her aunt's arms and hugged her.

"Thank you for all you've done for me," Victoria said. "I love you."

"Be happy, my darling," her aunt said, touching her cheek. She left the nave to find her seat at the front of the church.

When the violinists and organist began playing, Victoria hugged each sister in turn. "I love you," she told them. "I hope we will always remain as close as we are today."

"Be happy," Angelica said.

"Make that a double dose of happiness," Samantha added.

Victoria turned to the duke. She crooked her finger at him and, when he leaned close, planted a kiss on his cheek.

"Uncle, I thank you for taking me into your home and caring for me," Victoria said. "I apolo-

gize for being difficult. If justice does exist, I wil
have a daughter exactly like me."

"Thank you, child. My home will be especiall
boring without *your* gaiety," Duke Magnus said.

"You will live longer without me," she said.

"Are you ready, my dear?" the duke asked, offer
ing his arm.

Victoria shook her head. "I thank you for find
ing a wonderful man to be my husband an
promise to be the best wife ever. I intend to mak
Alex and you proud of me." She kissed his chee
again and said, "Now I am ready, Your Grace."

"Now *I* am not ready," the duke said, his eyes fil
ing with unshed tears. He took a deep breath
placed her hand on his arm, and moved to th
head of the aisle.

Samantha started down the aisle. Behind he
walked Angelica.

"I have a message from your aunt," Duk
Magnus whispered, leaning close. "Remember t
walk through life with *aplomb.*"

Victoria giggled, drawing curious looks fron
the guests. "Tell Aunt Roxie that I will honor he
considerable reputation, and society will kno
that I learned from the best."

Duke Magnus stepped forward. With her han
on his arm, Victoria glided down the aisle.

Hundreds of candles lit Audley Chapel, castin
eerie shadows on the walls. White roses and blu
forget-me-nots adorned the altar. A hundre
guests, garbed in a rainbow of colors, filled th
pews.

Victoria saw none of it. Her gaze and her smil
were only for her bridegroom.

At the altar, Alexander took her hands in his an
raised them to his lips. "Thank you for agreeing t
become my wife, my countess, and the mother o

my children," Alexander said, eliciting sighs from their feminine guests.

Surprising everyone, including her bridegroom, Victoria dropped him a curtsey fit for a king. "You honor me with your proposal," she said, her voice breathless with excitement.

The wedding ceremony was surprisingly short. Within fifteen minutes, the bishop pronounced them husband and wife.

Alexander drew her into his arms. They kissed as if no one was watching.

Victoria settled herself into the coach for the short ride to Campbell Mansion. She smiled when her husband put his arm around her, drawing her close, his lips touching hers.

"I have never seen a more beautiful bride," Alexander said, raising her hands to his lips. "My heart swelled with pride when you curtseyed and spoke those unforgettable words."

Victoria touched his cheek. "I am happy you chose me," she said. Her eyes gleamed with merriment when she added, "Though, at first, I did think you were a tad elderly and boring."

"What do you think now?"

"I think I married the most wonderful man in the world."

Alexander smiled. "Tory, I want to thank you for allowing me to invite Venetia and her relations," he said, growing serious.

"Your family is now my family," Victoria said.

"Life would be so much simpler if Venetia had remained in Australia," Alexander said.

"Will she be returning to Australia?" Victoria asked. If Venetia and Harry went home, the Widow Drummond would go with them.

Alexander shrugged. "Only God knows what my sister will do next."

The Duke of Inverary had spared no expense on the wedding breakfast for his youngest ward. There was an endless supply of tempting dishes from spinach nettle soufflé to baked salmon steaks and grilled Manx kippers to veal escalopes with mushrooms, cream, and sherry. Champagne and wines flowed from bottomless bottles, and a wedding cake fit for a queen was dessert along with fruits, nuts, and cheeses.

"I can't decide if His Grace is celebrating my marriage or my departure from his guardianship," Victoria whispered, making her husband smile.

Relaxing back in his chair, Alexander studied his wife's hauntingly lovely face. She was beautiful, enchanting, and passionate. Now she belonged to him. He could hardly wait until they took their leave of the wedding guests and secluded themselves in his Grosvenor Square mansion. He had already informed his majordomo that they were not receiving visitors for the next five days. No exceptions.

"What is this?" Alexander asked when the majordomo set a covered, silver tray down in front of them.

"Her Grace wants both of you to place your hands on the top and remove the cover together," Tinker informed them, and moved to the side.

Alexander put his hand on the knob, and Victoria placed her hand on top of his. Together, they lifted the silver cover. Hundreds of butterflies in every hue imaginable escaped their temporary confinement and flew upward, eliciting gasps of smiling astonishment from the wedding guests.

"I always wanted to do that," Lady Roxanne said.

"Damn it, Roxie," Duke Magnus exclaimed. "How will we get these blasted butterflies out of the house?"

The duchess gave her husband a feline smile. "Darling, the servants will use nets."

The duke gave her a sour look. "You'll need to pay a forfeit for my aggravation."

"I can hardly wait," the duchess drawled, making him smile.

Alexander stood and offered his wife his hand. Victoria rose from her chair. They made the rounds of their guests, and while Alexander played the smiling besotted groom, Victoria played the blushing bride. And then they reached his sister's table.

"You made the loveliest June bride I ever saw," Harry Gibbs said, standing to kiss Victoria's cheek.

"We thank all of you for attending our wedding," Victoria said, forcing herself to smile.

"I wouldn't have missed my only brother's marriage to such a sweet child," Venetia replied.

"Alex, last night's opera performance was simply superb," Diana said. "Didn't you think so?"

Victoria kept her expression placid. Her husband had accompanied another woman to the opera on the evening before their wedding? She hoped it wasn't mentioned in the *Times*. Oh, she could hardly wait to learn to read. Then she would know the gossip when everyone else knew.

"My mind was fixed on other things last night," Alexander was saying to the widow. He raised his wife's hands to his lips, adding, "I believe Tory and I can leave now without raising any eyebrows."

"You didn't mention you were going to the opera," Victoria said, as they walked away. Keeping her temper in control sapped her strength, though. She hoped she wouldn't behave badly and succumb to one of her "fits."

"I attend the opera every Thursday," Alexander reminded her. "You were busy preparing for today, and I didn't know what to do with myself."

"So, you escorted the widow?"

"I went alone," Alexander told her. "Diana showed up later. I gave her permission to use the box any time she wished."

"You should have stipulated any evening but Thursday," Victoria said, casting him a flirtatious smile. "I wouldn't wish to surprise her one evening when your hands have gone exploring."

Alexander laughed at that. Drawing her close against his body, he planted a kiss on her temple, murmuring, "You smell delicious, like vanilla and jasmine."

Though her expression was placid, Victoria's thoughts were disturbed. Apparently, Diana Drummond had set her amorous sights on Alexander even though he was now a married man. Was that what Rudolf had meant when he said that men wanted experienced women as their mistresses? She prayed her husband would prove as true to her as she would be to him.

And therein lay the problem. Alexander hadn't married her for love but merely accepted her aunt's proposed match as a way to make amends for Charles Emerson's crimes against her family.

After they had spoken to each of their guests, Alexander and Victoria left the wedding breakfast for his Grosvenor Square mansion. Victoria could hardly wait to be alone with her husband, who had awakened passion in her. That he hadn't wanted to linger with their guests heartened her beyond measure. She felt certain there was a good chance she could make him love her.

A tall, dignified-looking man opened the door of the mansion. Unexpectedly, Alexander scooped her into his arms and carried her across the threshold, making her giggle. Flicking an embarrassed glance at the majordomo, Alexander set her on her feet and said, "Your aunt made me promise to do that for luck."

"One can never have too much luck," Victoria said, and then realized that all of her husband's servants were lined up in the foyer to greet their new mistress.

"Victoria, I present Bundles, my majordomo, and Meade, my valet," Alexander said, and then gestured to an older woman. "Mrs. Hull, my cook and housekeeper, and her daughter Polly, who will be your lady's maid."

"I am pleased to make your acquaintances," Victoria said.

Alexander turned her to the line of footmen, maids, and coachmen. "This is Lady Victoria, the Countess of Winchester." His announcement met with polite applause. He nodded at the majordomo.

"Return to your duties," Bundles instructed them. Everyone except the majordomo and the cook hurried away. The man turned to Victoria, saying, "I am especially glad to welcome you to your new home. Mrs. Hull and I have served here since your father's time. We recall you as a child and were saddened to learn of his lordship's and his lady's passings."

"Though I cannot remember living here, you make me feel as if I've come home," Victoria said, unshed tears glistening in her blue eyes.

"Come, my love," Alexander said, putting his arm around her, guiding her toward the stairs. "Let's make ourselves more comfortable. I'll take you on a tour of the house later."

Suddenly, Victoria felt overwhelmed by the fact

that she was the mistress of this mansion and others outside London. She bit her bottom lip with her teeth and thought how much she needed to learn. Living in the cottage hadn't prepared her for this responsibility, and her inability to read could only make the situation worse.

"What's wrong, Tory?" Alexander asked, escorting her down the third floor corridor to their bedchamber.

"I have no experience running a household," Victoria admitted, her voice no louder than a whisper. "I feel stupid."

Alexander pulled her against the side of his body and dropped a kiss on the crown of her head. "Mrs. Hull will help with whatever you don't know," he assured her. "You will be fabulous."

Her bedchamber was bigger than the whole cottage where she grew up. On the far side of the room near an enormous bed was the hearth. Two arched windows overlooked the rear gardens. Chippendale furniture had been painted white and gold, and the canopied bed fitted with red, gold, and cream coverlet and bedcurtains. A cheval mirror stood in one corner near the bed; various occasional tables, chairs, a highboy, and an upholstered settee were positioned around the chamber.

"That door leads to your dressing room where Polly is finishing unpacking your gowns," Alexander told her. "This door connects to my chamber."

Victoria peered inside. His bedchamber was similarly appointed, but the furnishings were a dark mahogany and the bed gigantic.

"Polly will help you with your wedding gown," Alexander said, and dropped a kiss on her lips. "I'll see you in a few minutes."

When he disappeared into his bedchamber, Victoria turned toward the dressing room. With Polly's assistance, she removed the wedding gown and then dismissed the girl.

Victoria chose the sheerest ivory nightshift, a gown fashioned for enticement rather than sleep. The gown fastened at the shoulders with ribbons of lace, making it easy to remove.

Returning to the bedchamber, Victoria removed the diamond florets from her hair. Then she moved to the cheval mirror to check her appearance, a rueful smile touching her lips when she saw how immodest the gown was. A moment of insecurity assailed her, and she lifted her hand to look at her gold and diamond wedding band.

"Victoria?"

She looked up to see her husband, dressed in a black silk bedrobe, standing behind her.

"I missed you," he whispered.

Victoria turned in his embrace, their bodies touching from breast to thigh, and entwined her arms around his neck. "I missed you, too," she whispered, as his lips descended to hers.

Their kiss was long and languorous, leaving her breathless. He surprised her by lifting her into his arms and carrying her into his chamber.

"I want our son conceived in my bed," Alexander said, setting her down on her feet.

Victoria felt a melting sensation in her lower regions, his intimate wishes touching her physically, emotionally, spiritually. A yearning grew within her to become one with her husband and nurture his seed in the warm safety of her body, and deliver a son or daughter, the proof of their joining.

Was it only a few weeks since she had asked her sisters to teach her to flirt? The days seemed like years, the weeks like decades.

Victoria knew she loved her husband.

Alexander reached out and gently pulled one of

the lace ribbons on her gown. The gossamer silk dropped away from her body, revealing one plump white breast with a temptingly pink nipple. It hardened into arousal beneath his gaze.

Tugging at the other lace ribbon, Alexander let the silk pool at her feet and then studied his bride from her fiery mane of curls, cascading to her waist, to her hauntingly lovely face with her flawless alabaster complexion. Her neck was delicate and her shoulders finely boned. She was slender without being thin. Her breasts were full and ripe, swelling proudly beneath his intense gaze, and her hips curvaceous.

Boldly, Victoria reached out and tugged the sash of his black bedrobe. It opened slightly to tease her with the well-muscled body hidden beneath. When her husband shrugged it off, revealing himself, she caressed his chest with the palm of her hand.

With a low growl of arousal, Alexander pulled her against the hardness of his body and lowered his mouth to hers. Their kiss was long, wet, and slow. He slipped his tongue between her lips and stroked the sweet softness of her mouth. She leaned heavily against him in response, eager to surrender her body, her heart, her soul. His for the taking.

Alexander scooped her into his arms and placed her on the bed. He paused for a moment to admire what now belonged to him.

"My husband," she whispered, and opened her arms to him.

Alexander could not resist. He went into her arms, the weight of his body covering hers. She was so wonderfully soft. Arousal hardened him and softened her, until she melted into him, his to mold however he wanted.

Their lips met in a passionate kiss. A soft sigh escaped her.

Leaving her mouth, Alexander slid his lips down the slender column of her throat. And then lower. He cupped a ripe breast in each hand and placed dozens of kisses on each before his lips captured a nipple to suck upon it.

"I love your nipples," he said thickly, when she moaned with the pleasure. "Your nipples were made for me, my love, made for my pleasure."

Alexander knelt between her legs. He lifted one and ran his tongue down and then up the sensitive inside until he reached her upper thigh. Setting it down on the bed, he gave her other leg the same loving attention.

"Take me, my husband," she moaned. "I want to feel you inside me."

Alexander laughed huskily. "I see you haven't learned patience," he said. "Today I will not be rushed. I intend to savor every inch of your sweet flesh."

Refusing to be denied, Victoria cupped her breasts in her hands and held them up in offering. Her beaded peaks tempted him, and he leaned down to sample their taste—his lips sucking, his tongue licking, his teeth nipping in a gentle torment.

Victoria wrapped her legs around him, but Alexander slid down her body until his face was at the juncture of her thighs. He caressed her folds of flesh, his tongue sliding up and down, making her moan. Slipping between her pink folds of flesh, he thrust his tongue inside her and stroked her velvety flesh before flicking his tongue back and forth across her swollen nub.

"Alex," she cried, and clasped his head against

her. She melted into his tongue, her body shaking with spasms of pleasure.

The instant she stilled, Alexander rose up between her legs and lifted them over his shoulders. He pressed his hardened shaft against her and slipped inside her trembling body. Then he stilled, savoring the incredible feeling of her wet velvet drawing upon his manhood, enticing him to spill his seed deep within her.

With her fiery mane fanning the pillows. Victoria wore an expression of ecstasy. Never in her virginal daydreams had she ever imagined the fullness of a man inside her, the power and the strength of his dominating force, the pleasure to be had in surrender.

"Ride me, Alex," she pleaded in a whisper.

Alexander pulled the extra pillows beneath her head. "Open your eyes, and watch me take you," he ordered, his voice thick with passion. "I want us to watch our son being conceived."

Victoria opened her eyes and looked down to where his manhood joined her body. And then he moved. Slowly, he pulled himself out until only the head of his shaft was inside her. The he watched her face as he inched himself deeper and deeper until their groins touched.

Alexander smiled when she mewled low in her throat. He stroked her rhythmically, drawing himself almost out of her trembling body and then dipping, thrusting forward, letting her wet velvet surround him, caress him.

The tempo of his strokes quickened. Harder and harder he thrust until she shrieked and melted around him.

Alexander ground himself against her and shuddered with a groan, flooding her with his hot seed. He lay on top of her as they floated back to earth from their shared paradise.

Finally, Alexander moved to the side and pulled her with him, leaving their bodies intimately joined. And then they slept.

Victoria awakened later when someone rapped lightly on the bedchamber door, and she felt her husband move to rise from the bed.

"Don't leave me," she said drowsily.

"I'll be right back," Alexander told her, slipping into his bedrobe. He crossed the chamber to open the door a crack and then spoke in a low voice to someone. Closing the door again, he returned to their bed and lay down on top of the coverlet.

"Who was that?" she asked.

"Bundles wanted to know if we required supper."

"I don't need food," Victoria told him. "I have you. Take off that robe."

"I think I have created a monster," Alexander said, planting a kiss on her lips.

"I'm a dutiful wife," she corrected him.

Alexander laughed. "You certainly relish your duty."

Victoria pushed several wisps of fire away from her face. "Don't deny me, husband," she said, reaching for his sash. "Take off your robe."

"You can perform your duty later," Alexander said, covering her hand with his. "Bundles is setting a table for supper in your chamber."

Victoria sat up and, smiling coyly at him, drew the coverlet up to cover her bare breasts. Alexander put his arm around her shoulder, keeping her imprisoned against his body.

"Don't hide your charms from me," Alexander said, drawing the coverlet down to cup a ripe breast. Lowering his head, he kissed her while his thumb caressed the sensitive tip of her nipple.

Victoria moaned and arched her body toward his hand, the secret spot between her thighs throbbing for him. Slipping her hand between the sides of the robe's opening, she caressed the long length of him. He felt like hot silk covering steel.

"What a naughty chit," he murmured against her lips, which parted for his tongue.

A light rapping on the connecting door interrupted their love play. "Thank you, Bundles," Alexander called, rising from the bed. "Come, love," he said, offering his hand. "The food will be cold later, but you will still be hot."

"I'll eat without dressing," Victoria said, rising from the bed, unashamed of her nudity.

"You will do no such thing," Alexander said, picking her nightgown off the floor. "I won't be able to eat if you do that."

Reluctantly, Victoria drew the gown over her head. Alexander tied the lace shoulder ribbons that kept it from falling.

"The gown doesn't cover much," he said, his gaze traveling the length of her body.

A small table for two had been set before one of the open windows. The June evening was warm and alive with the garden's intoxicating perfume.

A light supper had been left for them. Alexander ate everything but Victoria only nibbled at her food. Her nerves still trembled from their lovemaking, stealing her appetite.

"I can't believe we are married and can spend every minute of the rest of our lives making love," Victoria said.

Alexander choked on his wine. "Though I do appreciate your enthusiasm," he said with a grin,

"I don't believe I have the stamina for that. Besides, once you get with child, I doubt you will want to make love as often as every minute of every day."

"I meant that as a figure of speech," Victoria explained. If her husband was making love to her, he wouldn't be warming another woman's bed. It wasn't that she didn't trust him; she simply didn't trust other women.

"I have instructed Bundles not to allow any visitors into our home for the next five days," Alexander told her. "I am at your disposal until then, Madame."

Victoria sighed. "I've gone from being a girl to a madame in less than a month."

"You were only a girl in your mind, sweet," Alexander said, covering her hand with his. "Your delectable body positively screamed your womanhood." He rose from his chair, saying, "Wait here. I have a gift for you in the other chamber."

When he returned, Alexander carried two boxes, one was rectangular and the other was long. He set the rectangular box down in front of her.

"I hate surprises," Victoria said, her blue eyes sparkling with excitement, "but yours have all been pleasant."

Lifting the box's lid, Victoria dropped her mouth open in surprise. On a bed of black velvet lay a dazzling diamond collar. More than sixty carats of white diamonds had been attached to a delicate, gold collar framework highlighted by a centerpiece diamond drop shaped like a pear.

Victoria knew the necklace had to be worth an obscene amount of money. She lifted her gaze from the necklace to her husband.

"Is this real?"

"I designed it myself," Alexander said, smiling at the question.

Victoria glanced at the necklace again. "Can we afford this?"

Alexander laughed out loud. "Darling, I am a very wealthy man."

"Thank you, but its real worth is that *you* gave it to me," Victoria said. "I want to give you your gift."

She set a small, square box down in front of him. Alexander opened the box. Inside sat a heavy gold ring set with an enormous star ruby.

"This is magnificent," he said.

"This ruby is special," Victoria told him. "A spirit lives within the star ruby and protects its owner. It darkens to the color of oxblood whenever danger threatens its owner."

"I will cherish it always," Alexander said, slipping it onto the third finger of his right hand. He set the long box in front of her, saying, "You may as well open this before you try on your necklace."

Victoria opened the box and smiled. Inside was a magic wand, which she immediately lifted to point, circle, point.

"The wand is made from pussy willow and the pentacle on top is crystal," Alexander told her.

While Victoria pointed, circled, and pointed, Alexander walked around the table and lifted the diamond collar from its box. He pushed her hair aside and fastened it around her neck.

"Come and see yourself in the mirror," Alexander said.

Victoria set the wand down and rose from the chair. They crossed the chamber to the cheval mirror.

Alexander stood behind her and unfastened the lace shoulder ribbons, letting her gown drop to the floor. Then he fanned her fiery mane around her.

Victoria stood naked, her only adornment the

diamond collar. Alexander shrugged out of his robe and stood, naked, behind her.

"You are a goddess sprung to life," Alexander whispered against her ear.

Victoria sighed and leaned back, the back of her head nestled against his chest. She watched in fascination as he slipped his arms beneath hers, his hands cupping and lifting her breasts. His thumbs slid across her nipples, and he smiled at her in the mirror when her breath caught in her throat.

"You belong to me," Alexander told her. He dropped one hand to the juncture of her thighs and one long finger caressed her dewy pearl. "I long to see you swell with my seed and give him suckle on your beautiful nipples."

Her breathing grew ragged, her breasts rising and falling with each breath. When she closed her eyes, he stopped her.

"Open your eyes," Alexander ordered. "I want you to watch what I am doing to you."

Victoria watched him in the mirror. One large hand squeezed and rolled a pink nipple while his other hand stroked the wetness between her thighs. She moved her hips and rubbed herself against his fingers. Feeling his hardness pressing against her, she felt surrounded by his strength.

"Let yourself go," Alexander whispered, his voice hoarse with desire. "Watch me bring you to paradise."

His husky words sent Victoria crashing over the edge of control. Struggling to keep her eyes open, she screamed and exploded with pleasure. Her body fell against his as waves of contractions shook her, and she closed her eyes in a near swoon.

Alexander carried her to his bed and lay down on top of her. "Wrap your legs around my waist," he said thickly. When she did, he pounded himself into her, rousing her to meet him thrust for thrust. They cried out together as he spilled himself inside her.

They lay still for long moments. Then Alexander rolled to the side, taking her with him, and unfastened the diamond collar to place on the bedside table.

"Sleeping in it could prove uncomfortable," Alexander told her. He drew her back into his embrace, and she cuddled against him.

"Where do I sleep each night?" she asked.

"Where do you want to sleep, love?"

"Beside you."

"I was hoping you would say that." Alexander tightened his embrace and planted a kiss on the crown of her head.

He loved her.

That thought startled Alexander. He'd only agreed to the match to make amends for Charles Emerson.

Love was for fools. Lydia Stanley's betrayal had taught him that.

Yes, he loved the woman in his arms, but she would never know. That was the only way to protect himself.

CHAPTER 9

"I wish we could have remained in Winchester," Victoria said, as their coach picked up speed on the last leg of their journey to London. She looked at her husband and sighed with disappointment.

"Like plants, my businesses need tending lest they wither and die," Alexander told her. He put his arm around her and drew her against his body. "You don't want to live in the poorhouse."

"Living in the poorhouse doesn't bother me as long as you're there," Victoria said, dropping her hand to his groin. She heard his sharp intake of breath and murmured, "Some of life's luxuries cost nothing."

Alexander tilted her face up, and his lips captured hers in a passionate kiss. That melted into another. And then another . . .

Desperate to escape the deluge of uninvited guests who descended on them the day after their wedding, Alexander had changed his plan to remain secluded at the Grosvenor Square mansion. The newlyweds had packed their bags and hidden at his country estate along the Itchen River in Winchester.

Alexander and Victoria had passed a gloriously sensual two weeks. They made love, strolled about the grounds, picnicked near the river, and shopped in the village. On the only rainy day, Victoria had entertained her husband with a flute concert; and Alexander had tried unsuccessfully to teach her the game of chess . . .

The sun's afternoon descent was casting long shadows by the time they reached Grosvenor Square. Victoria prayed that her husband's sister, living three doors down, was not looking out the window to see their return.

"The Randolphs expect us at their ball tonight," Alexander reminded her, as their coach halted in front of their mansion.

"I plan to wear my wedding gift and become the envy of all the ladies," Victoria told him.

"I'll never understand the female mind," Alexander said, and gave her a quick kiss. "You are adorable, though."

Several hours later, Victoria stared at her image in the cheval mirror. She had chosen a black evening gown with a daringly low cut neckline. Her maid had brushed her red mane back and plaited it into a knot at the nape of her neck, but several errant wisps of fire had escaped and framed her face. The stark color and alluring simplicity of the gown accentuated her diamond collar, her alabaster skin, and her youth.

Victoria could hardly believe the sophisticated reflection in the mirror was herself. She felt like a different person from the naive girl who had flirted and fought with Alexander only a month earlier.

Snatching up a lacy shawl, Victoria hurried downstairs to her husband's office adjoining the library. Alexander stood near the windows and turned when he heard her enter.

Victoria gave him a flirtatious smile as she crossed the room. She enjoyed his surprised stare when his hazel gaze dropped to her cleavage.

"I missed you," Victoria said, standing on tiptoes to plant a kiss on his cheek. Inhaling his bay scent, she suffered the urge to disrobe and make love to him right there.

"Sweetheart, did I mention that you needed to wear clothing to the Randolphs' ball?" Alexander asked, his lips quirking into a smile at her generous display of cleavage. "That gown borders on indecent, and I dislike the idea of other men ogling what belongs to me."

"Lydia Stanley and Diana Drummond wear gowns cut lower than this," she told him.

"What Lydia Stanley and Diana Drummond wear is not my concern," he replied. "Darling, your breasts look beautiful, but the gown reveals too much of your charms."

"I'll change the gown," Victoria relented. "Selecting another gown with accessories will take time, though. Why don't you go ahead without me?"

"Wear the gown," Alexander said, accepting defeat. "The need to guard you from a legion of admirers precludes an enjoyable evening."

"You will be the envy of all the other gentlemen," Victoria told him. "I wonder who will protect me from you, my lord."

"Your husband is allowed to fondle as much as he desires," Alexander said, draping the shawl around her.

A short time later, they stood at the top of the

ballroom stairs at Lord Randolph's mansion. The majordomo announced their arrival, "The Earl and Countess of Winchester."

Alexander lifted her hand to his lips. "That ballroom is filled with wolves waiting to gobble you up."

"The wolves have always kept their distance from me," Victoria said.

"Those wolves behave differently toward experienced wives," Alexander said. "Promise me you won't waltz with anyone but me."

"I promise," Victoria said, her love for him shining in her eyes.

After greeting their host and hostess, Alexander escorted Victoria to her family. Her aunt and her uncle stood with Prince Rudolf and Samantha.

"You gave all of London the slip," Duke Magnus said, shaking Alexander's hand and kissing Victoria's cheek.

"Leaving town proved easier than avoiding unwanted guests," Alexander said.

"What a lovely trinket," Aunt Roxie said, her gaze on the diamond collar.

"Alex gave me this for a wedding gift," Victoria told her.

"Well done, my lord," her aunt praised the earl. "You could not have done better even if I had instructed you."

"Marriage seems to agree with you, Tory," Duke Magnus remarked.

"Yes, it does." Victoria blushed when she glanced at her husband.

"Good, now the only problem is your lack of clothing," the duke replied, making everyone laugh. He turned to the earl, asking, "How could you let her out of the house with that much flesh showing?"

Alexander shrugged. "I didn't think making her change was worth the argument."

"A man does need to pick his fights with his wife carefully," Duke Magnus said.

"Dance with me," Alexander said, taking his wife's hand.

The orchestra was playing a waltz. Victoria stepped into her husband's arms, and they swirled around the ballroom with the other couples.

Victoria couldn't help but admire her husband, who cut an imposing figure. He waltzed with sophisticated grace and held her close, more closely than the dance required.

"What do you think about Diana Drummond?" Victoria asked, noting her husband's relatives' arrival. She hadn't considered that they would be invited.

"I don't think about her at all," Alexander answered, giving her a curious look.

"Do you think she's a good reader?" Victoria asked.

"A good reader?" Alexander echoed, obviously confused by the question.

Victoria nodded.

"I suppose if she's interested in my library," he answered, "she must like reading."

Or you, Victoria thought.

"In general terms, what is your opinion of women who cannot read," she asked, her blue gaze fixed on his, her heartbeat quickening.

"All women should learn to read," Alexander answered. "If a woman lacked the necessary intelligence, then I would feel sorry for her."

Pity.

Victoria despised pity more than stupidity. His answer disheartened her. She had considered confessing her handicap, but that was impossible now.

She could never live with a man who pitied her. Too bad her disability hadn't been physical instead of intellectual.

"What's wrong?" Alexander asked.

Victoria gave him a bright smile. "Traveling all day has wearied me."

"We should have stayed home," Alexander said, escorting her from the dance floor. "We'll leave early."

Lady Lydia Stanley and her friends paused to greet everyone just as Alexander and Victoria returned to their group. "Have you seen any good operas lately?" Lydia asked Victoria, making her friends smile behind their fans.

Aplomb, Victoria thought, aware that her aunt was listening.

"Actually, my husband has kept me busy day and night since our marriage," Victoria told the dark-haired beauty.

Lydia Stanley lost her smile.

Aunt Roxie stepped closer to Victoria and admired the diamond collar. "I love your taste in jewels," she said to the earl. "That looks about fifty carats?"

"Sixty carats," Alexander answered, unable to hide the laughter in his voice.

"If you will excuse us?" Lydia said, and walked away with her entourage.

"Tory, may I have this dance?" Prince Rudolf asked, offering his hand.

The orchestra was playing a waltz. Victoria glanced at her husband, who nodded, and then accepted her brother-in-law's hand.

"Do you need your husband's permission to dance?" Rudolf asked, obviously amused by her meek demeanor.

"I promised to waltz only with him," Victoria explained, her blue eyes sparkling with merriment. "I suppose he considered you safe."

Prince Rudolf laughed. "You aren't in danger of falling out of that gown, are you?"

"Other ladies wear necklines lower than mine," Victoria said.

"Other ladies are not Alex's wife or my young sister-in-law," Rudolf replied.

"You sound like my husband."

"Alex is a brilliant man."

"Yes, he chose me for his wife," Victoria said, her smile dazzling.

Prince Rudolf laughed. "If you don't behave yourself," he said, "we will banish you to the Island of Elbow."

"Very funny."

Victoria danced, in turn, with Princes Viktor, Mikhail, and Stepan. She kept a sharp eye on her husband, though, who danced with his sister.

Harry Gibbs asked Victoria to dance next. A troubled expression appeared on her face when she noted Diana Drummond stepping onto the dance floor with Alexander.

"Don't let my sister bother you," Harry Gibbs said, his gaze following hers. "Diana is an incorrigible flirt who enjoys the chase."

Aplomb, Victoria told herself, and managed a sunny smile. "I would prefer she chase someone else's husband."

When the music ended, Harry Gibbs escorted her from the dance floor, but Lord Wilmington intercepted them before they could return to their group. "Lady Victoria, how pleased I am to meet you again," Rupert Wilmington greeted her, lifting her hand to his lips. He nodded at Harry Gibbs, who drifted away, and gave his full attention to Victoria.

"A pleasure to see you again," Victoria said, as the orchestra began another dance.

"Will you honor me with this dance?" Lord Wilmington asked.

Victoria had no desire to dance with Rupert Wilmington. She wanted to find her husband before he fell prey to the widow, but she felt uncertain how to refuse the gentleman without appearing rude.

"I have decided to sit this one out," Victoria said, scanning the crowd for her husband. "Alexander and I have been traveling all day, and my weariness has finally caught up with me."

"I understand," Lord Wilmington said, catching her hand in his. "Stroll with me, and do call me Rupert."

Victoria inclined her head. She could look for her husband as they strolled.

Nearing an alcove isolated from the dance floor by statuary, Lord Wilmington maneuvered her against the wall. He stepped in front of her, effectively hiding her from the view of the other guests.

"I think this may afford us a small degree of privacy," Lord Wilmington said, inching closer.

Instinctively, Victoria tried to step back but was trapped against the wall.

"Do you know how beautiful you are," he said, towering over her.

"Actually, my husband tells me that every day," Victoria said. Her expression remained placid, but the man's nearness and height intimidated her.

"I would like us to become better acquainted." Lifting his hand, Lord Wilmington reached to touch the exposed swell of her breasts.

A hand materialized from nowhere and caught the lord's hand before it made contact with her skin.

"I dislike anyone touching my property," Alexander said, his smile not quite reaching his eyes.

"Alex, I've been looking for you," Victoria cried, a tremulous note in her voice. "I want to go home now."

"Of course, sweetheart, you've had a long day," Alexander said, grasping her hand. He nodded at Lord Wilmington before escorting his wife out of harm's way.

"Thank God, you found me," Victoria said, clinging to his arm. "Rupert Wilmington is much too bold."

"I warned you about wolves lying in wait for a succulent morsel like you," Alexander said, steering her toward the door. He nodded at acquaintances but didn't pause to speak.

"Why would he believe I wanted an association with him?" Victoria asked.

Alexander glanced sidelong at her as they walked outside to await their carriage. "Darling, if you display your wares, you will certainly need to deal with prospective buyers."

"What are you talking about?" Victoria asked in confusion.

"I told you the gown bordered on indecent," Alexander answered. "Rupert Wilmington mistakenly believed your display was meant to attract gentlemen."

"That is the most preposterous statement I have ever heard," Victoria said, climbing into the coach. "You are blaming the victim instead of the perpetrator."

"Do not wear that gown again in public," Alexander ordered, sitting beside her. "I dislike other men pawing my property."

"I am your wife, not your property," Victoria

whispered against his ear, and flicked her tongue around it.

Tugging the bodice of her gown down to free her breasts, Alexander said, "These belong to me." He cupped a plump breast, rubbing his thumb across the tip of her nipple, and lowered his head to kiss her.

Victoria grabbed her gloves, her reticule, and her parasol as soon as Alexander left the house to lunch with business associates at White's the next afternoon. Passing her in-laws' town mansion, she walked down Brook Street to New Bond Street which brought her to Oxford Street. Soho Square and the Philbin brothers' home lay two miles down the road.

Though the day was warm, Victoria's step was sprightly. Perfumed scents from myriad gardens intoxicated her senses. Her excitement grew as she neared her destination.

Victoria could hardly wait to read. Oh, how she wished the tutors had a real magic wand to wave at her and make her smart.

"Good afternoon, my lady," Phineas Philbin greeted her at the door. "Come this way." He led her into the front room where she had met them before.

"Good day to you," Victoria greeted Barnaby, the younger brother.

"And a good day to you, my lady," Barnaby said. "Sit here at the table. The light from the window will suffice."

Victoria sat down and opened her reticule to produce a wad of notes, her entire monthly allowance from her husband. She set it on the table, saying, "This is the agreed-upon amount for the next month."

"Thank you, my lady," Phineas said, taking the notes from the table and setting them on a shelf.

"We must warn you that our strategies will take much time and effort on your part," Barnaby told her. "You may suffer some frustration as there is no timetable we can give you for mastering each of these strategies."

"I am grateful for your help," Victoria said.

"Only hard work will improve your skills," Phineas told her.

Victoria nodded. "I am ready to begin."

"We would like you to read this paper to the best of your ability," Barnaby said.

Victoria took the paper out of his hand and placed it on the table. With one finger pointed on each word, she read haltingly as if each syllable was an individual word. "At nine in the morn-ing, the dark-ing bog saw in the bark dog." She looked up and said, "This makes no sense."

"Listen to our first strategy," Phineas said. "Whenever you see the letter *b,* pronounce it like the *d* in *did.* Try it."

"At nine in the morn-ing, the dark-ing dog saw in the dark dog," Victoria read again. "It still makes no sense."

Barnaby Philbin smiled. "That is because we can only teach you only one strategy at a time. Three strategies are needed to read the sentence correctly."

"What are the other three?" she asked.

"We cannot tell you until you learn the first strategy," Phineas told her. "*B is d* as in *did* must become as natural and involuntary as breathing."

"What do you mean?" she asked.

"Involuntary is something you do without thinking about how to do it," Barnaby told her.

Victoria stared at him blankly.

"You breathe in and out every second of your life," Phineas explained, "but you never actually think about breathing."

"You breathe without thinking about how to do it," Barnaby added.

"You must read *b* as *d* in *did* without thinking to do it," Phineas told her. "When you do, we will progress to the next strategy."

"How do I make it involuntary?" Victoria asked.

"By practicing," Barnaby told her. "Your homework is to sit with the newspaper every day and translate *b's* into *d's* as in *did.*"

"We will test your progress when you come next," Phineas said.

"*B* is *d* as in *did,*" Victoria said, rising from her chair.

Both Philbin brothers nodded with enthusiasm.

Victoria gave them a worried look. "Do you think I will be able to write my husband a love letter for Christmas?"

"Don't worry about that, my lady," Barnaby told her. "When the time comes, you will make the earl a proud man."

"I will see you next Thursday or the week after that," Victoria said, shaking their hands. "Until then, *b* is *d* as in *did.*"

Waving goodbye, Victoria left the Philbin home and started down Oxford Street. "*B* is *d* as in *did,*" she chanted to herself, her lips moving silently.

"Lady Victoria?"

Whirling around at the sound of her name, Victoria smiled at Barnaby Philbin. "Did I forget something?"

The tutor nodded and gestured down Oxford

Street. "You forgot that Grosvenor Square lies in the opposite direction."

Victoria was still chanting when she arrived home. Bundles opened the front door for her when she reached the top step.

"Is my husband home?" Victoria asked, passing him her parasol.

"No, my lady."

"Please bring the *Times* and a glass of lemonade to the drawing room," Victoria said, walking toward the stairs. She lowered her voice, chanting, *"B is d as in did."*

"My lady, did you say something?"

Victoria turned around and gave him a smile filled with sunshine. "I said, *b* is *d* as in *did."* Then she continued up the stairs.

A few minutes later, Bundles arrived with a tray containing a pitcher of lemonade, a crystal goblet, and the morning's *Times*. He set the tray on the table in front of the settee and then paused as if in indecision.

"Is something wrong?" Victoria asked, noting his troubled expression.

"There is a woman—*not a lady*—in the foyer who is demanding to speak to you in His Lordship's absence," the majordomo told her.

"Who is it?" Victoria asked.

"She is a bad woman," Bundles answered. "I explained that you couldn't possibly speak with her, but she said she'd wait for His Lordship."

"A bad woman?" Victoria echoed, giving him a puzzled smile.

The majordomo nodded.

"I will see her." Victoria rose from the settee and, followed by Bundles, walked downstairs to the foyer.

There were three females waiting to see her husband. A beautiful, ebony-haired woman paced the foyer and turned toward the stairs when she heard Victoria approaching. The woman wore a low cut gown that displayed generous breasts, though she was petite without being thin.

An ebony-haired girl, about five years old, sat on the bench and was quite obviously the woman's daughter. With her was an older woman, of perhaps forty years.

"Are you the Countess of Winchester?" the woman asked.

"I'm sorry," Victoria said, her smile apologetic. "Either my husband or Mr. Bundles hires the household staff."

"I have not come for a job," the woman said, her tone haughty. "I am a dancer with the ballet."

Victoria felt confused. "Then, how may I help you?"

"Tell His Lordship that Suzette is returning one of his gifts," the woman said. "His daughter, Darcy. Her bags are on the sidewalk outside." At that, Suzette fled the mansion.

After a moment of frozen shock, Victoria recovered herself. She raced after the woman, only to see the dancer climbing into a coach at the corner.

Returning inside, Victoria saw the girl weeping while the older woman offered what comfort she could. Bundles stood there, apparently at a loss what to do.

"Nanny Pinky, I want my mother," the girl sobbed, burying her face on the woman's lap.

"Shall I send for His Lordship?" Bundles asked.

"Do not send for him," Victoria said. She knelt in front of the weeping child. "Darcy?"

The girl looked up at her through hazel eyes blurred with tears. *Alexander's eyes.*

"Your mother needed to go out for a while," Victoria lied, producing a handkerchief and gently wiping the girl's tears. "She brought you to visit us. Did you know your father lives here?"

"No."

"Have you ever met your father?" Victoria asked, hoping the hazel eyes were only a coincidence.

"My daddy is very tall," Darcy said, perking up. "He has yellow hair."

Victoria felt her heart sinking to her stomach, but she managed a warm smile for her husband's daughter. "How old are you?" she asked.

"Five." Darcy held out her hand to wiggle her fingers and thumb, emphasizing her age.

"I was just going to tell Bundles to bring me lemonade and walnut pudding," Victoria told the girl. "Would you like to join me?"

"I love walnut pudding and lemonade," Darcy exclaimed, clapping her hands together. "Can Pinky come, too?"

"Pinky is also invited." Victoria stood and held out her hand. The girl stood, too, and accepted the offered hand.

"Send a footman for their bags," Victoria instructed the majordomo. "Then serve us walnut pudding and lemonade in the dining room."

"But, my lady—"

"Do it now."

Followed by the nanny, Victoria led the little girl into the dining room and helped her to sit down. Then she turned to the nanny and gestured to a chair.

"Oh, I could not sit down at the table with a countess," the woman said, obviously flustered.

"Sit down," Victoria ordered. "Now."

"Sit, Pinky," Darcy said, imitating her new friend.

Bundles returned and set the tray on the table. He set a dish of walnut pudding in front of each of them and poured lemonade into crystal glasses.

"Ask my husband to come here when he returns," Victoria told the majordomo.

"Yes, my lady." Bundles left the dining room.

"Did you know that your name, Darcy, means dark hair?" Victoria asked the five year old.

"You have red hair," Darcy said.

Victoria nodded. "That is correct."

"Who are you?" Darcy asked.

"I am your daddy's wife," Victoria told her. "That means I am your fairy godmother. I own a magic wand and fairy dust."

"Can I see them?" Darcy asked, her enormous dark eyes even larger with her excitement.

"I'll let you hold them if you want," Victoria promised, staring into hazel eyes so much like her husband's. "Do you like playing games?"

"I love games," Darcy cried.

Victoria felt an insistent tugging on her heartstrings. She leaned close and said, "I know lots of games we can play."

Darcy clapped her hands together in excitement.

Sensing a movement near the doorway, Victoria turned her head and saw her husband standing there. The nanny followed her gaze and leaped out of the chair to drop him a curtsey.

"Do you know who this is?" Victoria called to her husband.

Wearing a grim expression, Alexander walked across the dining room. "Darcy is my daughter."

"You've met?"

Alexander nodded. "Several times."

Several times? Victoria wondered in surprise.

How could he sire a child and then only see her several times? What kind of man had she married?

"Do you have a kiss for me?" Alexander asked, leaning down to the little girl.

Darcy threw her arms around his neck. Then she planted a smacking kiss on his lips.

"You taste very sweet," he said.

Darcy laughed. "It's the walnut pudding."

Alexander stood then and looked at Victoria. "I want an explanation."

"So do I, darling," Victoria drawled, sounding like her aunt. "Mister Bundles, escort our guests upstairs and help them settle into one of the bed-chambers."

"Have you gone mad?" Alexander asked, his irritation all too evident in his voice.

Victoria ignored him. When the majordomo hesitated, she said, "Do it now, Bundles."

"Why didn't you tell me about Darcy?" Victoria asked when they were alone.

"My daughter is none of your business," Alexander said. "I'll make arrangements to send her home."

"Darcy is home," Victoria told him. "I cannot in good conscience return the child to the mother who abandoned her."

"Don't be naive," Alexander said. "Harboring a gentleman's bastard is unacceptable and unseemly."

"Unseemly is begetting her in the first place," Victoria told him.

There was no mistaking the fury in her glittering blue gaze. Alexander opened his mouth to speak, but Victoria was faster. "If you ever use the word *bastard* in this house again, I'll—I'll wash your mouth with soap."

Her threat brought a smile to his lips. "I do appreciate your concern for my daughter," Alexander said, his tone softening. "However, you cannot keep another woman's child."

"That dancer surrendered her rights when she abandoned Darcy," Victoria told him.

"I have provided handsomely for Darcy," Alexander said. "Her mother is merely trying to get more money."

"Look at the silver lining," Victoria said. "Since Darcy now lives here, you need not send the dancer any money. We will take tea in the library and discuss this further. Now I must see to our guests' comfort."

Victoria stood and breezed out of the dining room, leaving her husband staring after her in amazement.

What a damn mess, Alexander thought, watching his bride. He sat at the table and, staring into space, wondered what to do about Darcy.

That his bride of less than a month would champion his illegitimate daughter surprised Alexander. He had never seen Victoria the way she had faced him—mature, determined, in command of herself and others. She behaved as kindly to his daughter as any man would wish.

He loved her but trusted her no more than any other woman.

Fickle and flighty creatures, women suffered no qualms about betrayal when it suited their purpose. Lydia Stanley had taught him that hard lesson.

Alexander noticed his daughter had eaten only half of her walnut pudding. Dragging the dish in front of him, he finished her pudding and then rose wearily from the chair.

The situation could have been worse, Alexander

decided, leaving the dining room. He found his majordomo waiting for him in the foyer.

"My lord, what should I do about these?" Bundles asked, gesturing to the bags.

Shoving his hands in his trouser pockets, Alexander looked from the majordomo to the bags and then back again. "My wife insists that Darcy stays a while," he told his retainer. "Have a footman carry their bags upstairs."

Bundles smiled. "Very good, my lord."

Alexander went directly to his office, located in the section of the library nearest the windows overlooking the garden. He sat down at his desk, intending to work, and opened one of his ledgers.

When he realized he'd read the same figures for the fifth time, Alexander closed the ledger and poured himself a whiskey. Then he relaxed back in his chair to ponder his domestic situation.

The *ton*'s gossipmongers would have a party with this juicy tidbit. Even worse, his daughter's arrival could have ended his marriage before it had begun.

Surprisingly, Victoria had not responded to the problem like a typical society wife. His bride had behaved with infinite charity and kindness.

Now what was he to do? He would need to call upon Suzette. No, he would send his solicitor to discover what the woman wanted.

Alexander smiled to himself when he recalled Victoria threatening to wash his mouth out with soap. His bride was full of surprises. Not only had he discovered she was a creature of passion but possessed an abundance of the maternal instinct. He ought to get down on his knees and thank God for this blessing.

Intending to see what was happening upstairs, Alexander rose from his chair and walked through the library. Venetia and Diana Drummond walked into the room just as he reached the doorway.

Good God, this was all he needed to make the day complete.

"Good afternoon, Alex," Venetia greeted him, planting a sisterly kiss on his cheek.

"Good afternoon, my lord," Diana greeted him, her voice sultry.

Alexander smiled at his uninvited guests and wished he had not given them *carte blanche* to his library. The lovely widow had been making not-so-subtle overtures to him. He only hoped his wife's innocence blinded her to the widow's amorous bent. Though he had no intention of becoming involved with the widow, Alexander did not want his wife bothered by uncertainty.

"Diana wanted to browse in your library and, perhaps, borrow a few books," Venetia told him.

While the widow began looking at the books, Venetia made herself comfortable on the settee. "Is anything wrong?" she asked. "You appear a bit distracted."

"All is well with the world," Alexander lied, and decided to leave the library before his wife arrived. "If you will excuse—"

Too late.

Victoria marched into the library like Napoleon advancing on Moscow. She stopped short when she saw their guests.

Both women greeted Victoria with a "Good afternoon".

Victoria ignored them. "We need to speak," she said to her husband.

"We'll discuss that matter when our guests leave," Alexander told her.

"I'm certain your guests don't mind leaving immediately," Victoria said, purposely rude. She did not want his sister and the widow visiting without an invitation.

"Victoria." Alexander sounded surprised.

"Is there trouble?" Venetia asked, rising from the settee.

"Suzette abandoned her daughter here today," Alexander told her.

"That ballet dancer with whom—" Venetia glanced at Victoria.

"Why would a ballet dancer leave her daughter here?" Diana asked.

"Alexander is the father," Venetia answered. She turned to Alexander, saying, "Send the girl home at once."

"That would be best for all," Diana agreed.

"My wife refuses to part with the child," Alexander told them, smiling.

Her husband should have been the one refusing to part with the girl, Victoria thought. The situation seemed like a twisted coil.

Venetia and Diana threw surprised looks at each other. Victoria caught their silent exchange but had no idea what it meant.

"Lady Victoria, please accept this advice in the spirit it is given," Diana Drummond said. "Housing your husband's by-blow is unacceptable. The gossips will chew on this for years."

"Mind your own business," Victoria snapped.

"Alexander," Venetia whined.

"Tory, you are speaking to my sister and her sister-in-law," Alexander reminded his wife, a warning note in his voice.

"I know to whom I am speaking," Victoria said. "I'm not blind."

"You should consider Alex's reputation," Venetia scolded her.

"If Alex did not consider his own reputation before, then why should I consider it now?" Victoria countered, her anger rising to a dangerous level. How dare these two interfere in her marriage? "As a matter of fact, I find your company offensive. Get out of my house and do not return without an invitation."

"*My* house," Alexander corrected her.

"I thought this was *our* house," Victoria said, stung by his sentiment.

"You are behaving badly," Alexander told her.

"And so are you," Victoria returned, furious that he was speaking to her in that manner in front of the other two. "Your sister and the widow wouldn't recognize morality if it jumped up and bit their arses."

"This is outrageous," Venetia complained. "She's taking her anger over your daughter out on us."

"Venetia and Diana are merely trying to help by getting you to think about the repercussions of gossip," Alexander told her. "Apologize at once."

"I wouldn't apologize to save my soul," Victoria said. Muttering to herself about disloyalty, she stormed out of the library.

With a troubled expression, Alexander watched her leave and knew he could have handled the situation differently. In his efforts to show politeness, he had insulted his wife. Now she would make him pay for it. If he had known marriage was this difficult, he might have remained a bachelor.

"I can see that Victoria has upset you," Venetia said, rising from the settee. "Really, Alex, you should have married an older, more experienced woman. Perhaps even someone who'd been married before."

"With all due respect, my lord," Diana Drummond said, "Lady Victoria's lack of common sense is appalling."

"The twit is stupid," Venetia said.

"My wife is far from stupid," Alexander said, a hard edge to his voice as he came to her defense. "I cannot fault her for an opinion, only her lack of tact in giving voice to it. Tory has good reason to dislike you."

"Come, Diana," Venetia said. "Let's leave Alex to deal with this."

After they'd gone, Alexander sat down on the settee and stretched his long legs out. His wife was magnificent in her fury, but she had better direct that anger at someone else. Unlike her uncle, he would not tolerate her temperamental fits or her rudeness to others.

Leaving the library to dress for the evening, Alexander walked through the connecting door into his wife's chamber. Victoria sat on the chaise and stared into the darkened hearth.

Was she angry or hurt? Or both?

Alexander knew that Victoria knew he was there. She refused to acknowledge his presence.

Crossing the bedchamber, Alexander stood beside the chaise and stared down at her. Several moments passed before he realized that she would not look at him no matter how long he stood there. Her petulance irritated him.

"Will you be accompanying me to the opera?" Alexander asked, breaking the silence.

Victoria turned her head, her gaze on him frosty. "I do not wish to intrude on *your* opera box," she said.

"As you wish."

After eating a lonely dinner at the forty foot dining table, Alexander left the house and climbed into his carriage. He had planned to attend the opera, but the widow would most likely show up there. He had no interest in encouraging her pursuit of him, especially since the gossip columnist from the *Times* would comment on his wife's absence and the widow's presence. Reading that in the *Times* would hardly help to douse the flames of their argument.

"Drive to White's," Alexander called to his coachman, taking himself out of harm's way.

A short time later, Alexander walked into White's Gentleman's Club. What he needed was a drink. Several, in fact. Spying his brothers-in-law sitting together at a table, he crossed the room and dropped into a chair at their table.

"Whiskey," Alexander growled when a waiter appeared beside him. He looked at Prince Rudolf, adding, "I wish they served your vodka here."

Prince Rudolf and Robert Campbell looked at each other and smiled. "I believe His Lordship has argued with his wife," the prince said to the marquess.

"It certainly appears that way," the marquess agreed.

Alexander gulped his whiskey and grimaced at his brothers-in-law. "My former mistress abandoned my daughter at my home today," he told them.

"Which one?"

"Suzette."

"Ah, the ballet dancer," Robert said.

"Tory is upset?" Rudolf asked, obviously struggling against a smile.

"My wife wants to keep the girl," Alexander complained, eliciting their laughter.

"That makes three for three," Robert said to the prince.

"What do you mean?" Alexander asked.

"The Douglas sisters have big hearts," Prince

Rudolf told him. "They never met a stray they didn't want to keep. Take my advice and surrender to the inevitable. Make a place for your daughter in your home."

"Society will frown upon this," Alexander said.

"You are bedding down with Tory at night, not society," Rudolf said.

"My six-year-old Daisy is mine by a former mistress," Robert admitted. "Angelica abducted the girl from her negligent mother. Of course, I had to part with a small fortune in order to keep her, but the peace in my domestic life was worth every pound."

"My adopted sons, Grant and Drake, are orphans that Samantha and I found on a road in Scotland," Prince Rudolf told him. "Go home to your wife, and do not argue again until she is pregnant."

"There's more to the situation than Darcy," Alexander confessed. "In the midst of the afternoon's turmoil, in walked Venetia and Diana Drummond who urged me to return the girl to her mother."

"So?" the prince and the marquess said simultaneously.

"Their meddling incited Victoria to rudeness," Alexander explained. "Her rudeness incited me to reprimand her which, in turn, incited her to anger. Only Venetia and Diana enjoyed good moods."

"Apologize to Tory and tell her that your daughter stays," Prince Rudolf advised him. "She will forgive you."

"What if she doesn't?"

Prince Rudolf grinned. "I have a spare bedchamber at my house."

"Very funny." Alexander started to rise from his chair, but the marquess gestured to him to remain seated.

"I know Venetia is your sister, but she may not have your best interests at heart," Robert said. "I do believe the widow is angling to make you her lover. Beware of those two plotting to destroy your marriage."

"You are right about the widow," Alexander said, rising from his chair, "but I cannot credit their plotting against Victoria and me."

Thirty minutes later, Alexander returned to Grosvenor Square. Wearily, he climbed the stairs to his third-floor chamber and wondered if his wife's anger had kept her in her own chamber that night. Sleeping alone was out of the question, and he intended to lay down the law about that. No matter what passed between them, he wanted his wife beside him at night.

Alexander walked into his chamber and stopped short. His wife was sleeping in his bed.

Stripping down, Alexander slid into the bed and drew his wife into his arms. She wore nothing, too.

"How was the opera?" Victoria asked, her eyes opening when he touched her.

"I passed the evening with Robert and Rudolf at White's," Alexander answered, as her eyes closed again in sleep. "Tory?"

"Yes?"

"I apologize for my behavior," Alexander said, his lips hovering above hers. "Darcy can stay."

He pressed a kiss on her lips. Sighing, she entwined her arms around his neck and returned his kiss. Their naked bodies melted together from breast to thigh.

"What made you change your mind?" she whispered.

"I realized you were exhibiting the quality I most wanted in a wife," he answered.

"What is that?"

"An abundance of maternal instinct to nurture my children."

"Alex?"

"Yes, sweetheart?"

"I need money to take Darcy shopping tomorrow," Victoria told him.

Alexander drew his head back to look at her beautiful face. "What about your allowance?"

"Gone."

"Good God, Tory," Alexander exclaimed. "Today is only the eighth day of July. Twenty-three days remain before your next allowance. How could you have squandered that money in only eight days?"

"I spent it on your Christmas present," she told him.

"Christmas present?" he echoed. "It's only July."

"This present will take months to finish," Victoria said.

"What is it?"

"A surprise."

"I refuse to give you another shilling until the first day of August," Alexander said. "You must learn to manage your money."

"Very well, I'll tell the shopkeepers to send you the bills," Victoria replied.

Alexander laughed. Just before his lips claimed hers, he whispered, "You are an incorrigible brat."

"My aunt should have mentioned that before you married me."

"She did."

CHAPTER 10

"Please teach me the other two strategies," Victoria begged the Philbin brothers.

"Lady Victoria, you have not progressed enough with the first strategy," Phineas Philbin told her.

"I may never progress to your satisfaction," Victoria snapped, her frustration rising.

Two weeks had passed since she had last seen her tutors. Her new daughter, Darcy, had kept her busy, but Victoria had taken an hour each day to practice the first strategy, *b* is *d* as in *did*.

"I apologize for my waspishness," Victoria said, fanning herself. "This heat has darkened my mood."

"There's no need to apologize," Phineas assured her.

"We understand your frustration," Barnaby added.

"You are the hardest worker we've ever seen," Phineas told her, "but we warned you the progress could be slow."

"My head aches with defeat," Victoria said with a dejected sigh. "If you teach me the other two strategies, I will practice two hours a day instead of one."

The Philbin brothers looked at each other. Barnaby shrugged, and Phineas nodded.

"We will give you three more strategies," Phineas said.

"You will need to master all the strategies before we can progress to others," Barnaby warned her. "Your pleading will not change our minds."

Victoria smiled, eager to learn. "I promise not to press you for others."

"The first strategy was *b* is *d* as in *did*," Phineas said. "The second strategy is the reverse; *d* is *b* as in *baby boy*."

"*D* is *b* as in *baby boy*," Victoria repeated.

Phineas handed her the parchment with the now-familiar sentence on it. "Read this, my lady."

Victoria placed the parchment on the table near the window. With her index finger pointing the way, she read haltingly, each syllable becoming a separate word.

"At nine in the morn-ing, the bark-ing dog saw in the dark bog," Victoria read. With tears in her eyes, she exclaimed, "The sentence makes sense. I really did it."

The Philbin brothers smiled at each other. "The sentence makes sense," Phineas said, "but that is not precisely what is written."

Victoria lost her smile.

"Here are two more strategies," Barnaby said. "When you see *saw*, read *was*; when you see *was*, read *saw*."

"*Saw* is *was* and *was* is *saw*?" Victoria echoed.

Barnaby nodded. "Six is nine and nine is six."

"Forget about the numbers for now, my lady," Phineas advised her. "Too much at once will only confuse you."

"*B* is *d* as in *did*," Victoria chirped. "*D* is *b* as in *baby boy*."

Both Philbin brothers smiled and nodded.

Victoria looked down at the parchment. Again, with her index finger pointing the way, she read aloud. "At six in the morn-ing, the bark-ing dog was in the dark bog."

"Bravo!" The Philbin brothers clapped with approval.

"I read," Victoria said, her voice filled with awe. Tears welled up in her eyes and brimmed over to roll slowly down her cheeks. "I'm so happy." She rose from her chair, asking, "Do you think I'll soon be able to read a bedtime story to my husband's daughter?"

"Not soon, my lady," Phineas said.

"Some day, perhaps," Barnaby added.

"I will dwell on today's victory and remain optimistic," Victoria told them. "I'll see you in a week or two."

Victoria stepped outside into the bright sunlight and opened her parasol. She hadn't walked far down Oxford Street when she felt a tap on her arm.

Turning around, Victoria saw Barnaby Philbin and asked, "Am I going the wrong way?"

Barnaby nodded. "Grosvenor Square is in the other direction."

"Thank you, sir."

The afternoon was unusually warm. As she walked down Oxford Street, Victoria regretted not taking the carriage, but she didn't want anyone to know where she went on Thursdays. Her only consolation for walking in the heat was the mingling flower fragrances that permeated the air.

"Is my husband at home?" Victoria asked, entering the foyer almost an hour later.

"His Lordship had an appointment," Bundles answered.

"Where is my daughter?" she asked.

"Mistress Darcy is in the garden with Mrs. Pinky," Bundles answered.

Victoria walked upstairs to her bedchamber to freshen up and change her gown. Then she took her magic wand off her dresser and crossed the chamber to the window.

Darcy and Pinky sat together on a bench shaded by a silver birch tree. Pinky looked hot and Darcy looked bored.

Turning away, Victoria left her bedchamber and hurried downstairs. "Darcy," she called, stepping into the garden.

The little girl smiled and waved. When she reached the bench, Victoria said, "Pinky, you appear wilted. The house is cooler than the garden. Go inside and rest."

"Thank you, my lady," the nanny said, and returned to the house.

"I've brought my magic wand," Victoria said, holding it up.

"Are we going to use it?" Darcy asked, her hazel eyes gleaming with excitement.

"I will teach you how to use it."

Darcy clapped her hands together. Victoria felt an insistent tugging on her heartstrings as she gazed into hazel eyes that resembled her husband's.

Lord, but she loved Alexander. Victoria didn't think that any woman could love any man as much as she loved her husband. Too bad her husband didn't love her.

"What's wrong, Mama Tory?" Darcy asked.

"Like you, everything is perfection," Victoria told her. "Do you want to learn to use the magic wand?"

The lttle girl nodded.

"Point the wand at what you wish, make a circle, and then point it again," Victoria explained. "Point, circle, point. While you do that, you must think of your wish."

"What if I want something that can't be seen?" Darcy asked.

"Point the wand at the sky, make a circle, and then point at the sky again," Victoria said, rising from the bench to demonstrate. "Recite these magic words: 'Fairies and pixies, come to me. Fairies and pixies, hear my plea. Send a—blank—straight to me. Fairies and pixies, thankee, thankee.'"

"Mama Tory, what's a blank?"

Victoria burst out laughing and hugged the five-year-old. "Blank is the word I used to fill the space where you say your wish. Do you want to try?"

Darcy stood and accepted the wand as if it was the king's scepter. Looking skyward, she pointed and circled and pointed.

"Fairies and pixies, come to me," Darcy called. "Fairies and pixies, hear my plea. Send a *sister* straight to me. Fairies and pixies, thankee, thankee."

Victoria clapped in approval for a job well done.

"How long will the fairies and pixies take to grant my wish?" Darcy asked, passing her the wand.

"A sister is a very big wish that might take some time," Victoria answered.

"Lady Victoria," Bundles called, drawing her attention as he hurried across the garden. "There is a woman in the foyer demanding to speak to you."

"Who is it?"

Bundles shook his head. "The woman brought an older woman and a girl with her."

"That's my sister," Darcy cried. "Those fairies and pixies do fast work."

Victoria glanced at the five-year-old and refused

to believe what her instincts were screaming. It could not be what she was thinking.

"Come, Darcy," Victoria said, taking the girl's hand. "Let's see who has come to visit."

With the majordomo following in their wake, Victoria and Darcy returned to the house. Walking into the foyer, Victoria knew she would be replaying the scene she had with Suzette.

The woman was blonde and exceptionally beautiful. In an instant, Victoria compared herself to the woman and found herself lacking. She shifted her gaze to the child, a blonde girl who appeared around five years, and an older woman, who perched on the bench where Pinky and Darcy had sat.

"Are you the Countess of Winchester?" the woman asked.

"Yes."

The woman dropped her gaze, boldly inspecting Victoria. When she lifted her gaze again, the blonde smiled as if she also found her lacking.

Victoria stiffened at the unspoken insult. Assuming a deceptively sweet smile, she said, "Mister Bundles hires the scullery maids."

"I am an opera dancer, not a maid," the woman said, her voice haughty.

"How may I help you?" Victoria asked, knowing she had hit her mark.

"Tell His Lordship that Maeve is returning one of his gifts," the opera dancer said, gesturing to the girl. "His daughter, Fiona." At that, the woman quit the foyer.

Victoria didn't bother to chase after her. Instead, she crossed the foyer to the girl, who clung with fright to her nanny. Crouching down to be at eye level with the child, she said, "Your name is Fiona."

The girl nodded.

"Fiona means light hair," Victoria said, gazing into hazel eyes that resembled her husband's. "How old are you?"

"Five."

Victoria flicked a glance at Bundles, who appeared scandalized. "And who is this woman holding your hand?"

"Nanny Hartwell."

"Do you know who lives in this house?" Victoria asked.

Fiona shook her head.

"Your daddy lives here," Victoria said. "I am your daddy's wife, and that girl is your sister."

"My wish came true," Darcy cried. She began to dance around the foyer, chanting, "Fairies and pixies, I love you."

"Come here," Victoria ordered. When Darcy approached, she said, "Fiona, I present your sister Darcy, who is also five-years-old."

Fiona smiled at her sister. Encouraged, Darcy hugged the other girl and kissed her cheek.

"Do you like vanilla pudding with strawberries?" Victoria asked.

"Yes, she does," Darcy answered for her sister.

Victoria stood then and offered her hand to the older woman, saying, "Welcome to our home." She turned to the majordomo and instructed him, "Send a footman to bring their bags upstairs. Then serve us vanilla pudding with strawberries in the dining room. Tell Pinky to help Hartwell settle in."

Victoria and Darcy sat on either side of Fiona. Darcy kept up a steady stream of chatter.

"Mama Tory is daddy's wife," Darcy told her sister. "She is our fairy godmother and even has a magic wand that makes wishes come true. I wished for a sister, and then you came. If you are a good girl, Mama Tory will teach you how to use the magic wand. Isn't that exciting?"

Darcy stopped eating her pudding to give her sister a sideways hug. "I am very happy you've come to live with us."

Fiona gave her sister a shy smile.

Victoria wiped a stray tear from her cheek. Feeling another presence, she looked over her shoulder toward the doorway.

Alexander stood there. His expression said he was trying to gauge her reaction to Fiona.

"My lord, come and see who has joined our domestic tranquility," Victoria called, a sarcastic edge to her voice.

Alexander crossed the dining room but paused to greet his daughters. "Welcome home, Fiona," he said, and kissed the crown of her blonde head. Next he kissed Darcy, saying, "I am glad that you have met, at last."

Flicking a glance toward the majordomo, Alexander instructed, "Deliver the girls to their nannies and close the door when you leave." He sat down beside Victoria, gave her a sidelong glance, and then ate the remains of his daughters' pudding.

"You have nothing to say?" Victoria asked, surprised by his nonchalance.

"I'm eating pudding because I don't know what to say," Alexander admitted. "Except, those affairs happened long before I met you."

"Alex, two women gave birth to your children in the same year," Victoria said. "How do you explain that?"

"Virility?"

"This is no joking matter."

"You are correct, but what has been done cannot be undone," Alexander said. "I cannot fault you for being upset." He lifted her hand to his lips and planted a kiss on it. "I had a wild year when I was twenty-three. Two mistresses informing me of my impending fatherhood was a bucket of cold water tossed in my face. I amended my ways and never took a mistress again.

"I support them financially, of course. When I learned Charles Emerson wasn't my father, I understood how heartbreaking it was never to know your own father. So, I began to visit my daughters a few times a year . . . I hope you will forgive me."

"You owe your daughters an apology, not me," Victoria said.

He nodded in agreement. "I will apologize when they are older."

Victoria stared at him for a long moment. "Are there any more?"

"No, of course not," Alexander answered, sounding offended by the question. Then he added, "Darcy seemed rather pleased with her sister."

"Darcy believes the magic wand worked a miracle," Victoria said, rolling her eyes.

"Perhaps it did."

"The only wand that works is your you-know-what," she snapped.

"You *are* angry."

"As you said, a husband and wife belong to each other, no matter what troubles may come," Victoria reminded him, her blue gaze softening on him. "I have enough love for Darcy and Fiona as well as for any children we make."

"Thank you, Victoria." Alexander drew her out of her chair and onto his lap. Cupping her chin, he brought her hauntingly lovely face close and pressed a tender kiss on her lips. "You are the most forgiving, understanding woman I have ever met and as beautiful inside as you are outside."

* * *

Two weeks of domestic tranquility, Victoria thought as she walked downstairs to breakfast on the fourteenth morning after Fiona's arrival. Even Venetia and Diana had kept their distance, though Alexander and she had seen them at various functions. And the opera, of course.

Victoria smiled at the sight that greeted her in the dining room. Alexander sat at the table with his breakfast and the morning *Times* in front of him, a daughter on either side.

"Good morning," Victoria called, heading for the sideboard where Bundles stood at attention.

"Good morning," the three at the table returned her greeting.

"Good morning, Bundles."

"Good morning, my lady."

Victoria helped herself to a plain scone and a cup of black tea. Then she sat across the table from her husband and stepdaughters.

Alexander looked up from his newspaper, gave her a smile, and dropped his gaze to her plate. "Why aren't you eating?"

"I'm not hungry."

Alexander returned his attention to the *Times*.

"Daddy, will you butter my scone?" Darcy asked, apparently unhappy with his inattention.

"Of course, sweetness." Alexander cut the scone and buttered each half.

"Thank you, Daddy."

"You are welcome, sweetness." Alexander resumed reading.

"Daddy?"

"Yes, Fiona?"

"Will you butter my scone?"

"Of course, precious." Alexander cut her scone and buttered each half.

"Thank you, Daddy."

"You are welcome, precious." Again, Alexander resumed reading.

"Daddy?" Victoria said in a sultry drawl. "Will you butter my scone, too?"

"I've been looking forward to buttering *your* scone," Alexander said with a devastatingly wicked smile. He smothered the scone with butter and pushed the plate toward her.

Keeping his gaze captive to hers, Victoria lifted the scone to her lips. She flicked her tongue out and slowly licked the butter off the scone.

"Daddy, Mama Tory is playing with her food," Darcy told him.

"Mama Tory is naughty," Fiona agreed.

"If you are naughty, Mama Tory," Alexander said, "I will need to take you upstairs."

Victoria laughed at that. Darcy and Fiona giggled, making their father smile.

"Breakfast was always a peaceful affair, but I can see that has changed forever," Alexander said, and resumed reading the paper. A moment later, he pushed the paper toward Victoria and said, "Read that."

Caught off guard, Victoria felt her stomach lurch sickeningly and stared at the paper as if it was a poisonous snake. "I—I don't have my spectacles with me."

"You never have your spectacles handy when you need them," Alexander said. "Listen to this: *A recently married peer of the realm has had two of his past indiscretions dropped on his doorstep.*"

"How could the reporter know that?" Victoria asked, her expression mirroring her surprise.

Alexander shrugged, his gaze on the article. "I suppose servants gossip with other servants who, in turn, gossip with other servants."

"What is *indiscretion*?" Darcy asked.

"*Indiscretion* is getting caught doing something you shouldn't," Victoria answered.

"Like stealing a cookie and having crumbs on your mouth?" Fiona asked.

Flicking a glance at her husband, Victoria smiled at the girl and said, "Yes, dear, that is correct."

Later that afternoon, Victoria sat on the stone bench in the garden, shaded by the silver birch tree, and watched her husband's daughters. Darcy and Fiona, happy to have found a friend in each other, gamboled around, though the August afternoon was warm.

The shrill cries of blue jays and the buzz of insects had replaced the nesting robins and wrens. High in trees, cicadas called to each other while crickets, hiding in the shade, gave voice to creaky songs.

Victoria closed her eyes and inhaled the mingling flower scents. She could hardly believe she had been married for nearly two months and was the stepmother of two girls. Only a few weeks earlier, she had never even kissed a man, but then her husband had introduced her to the delightful world of sensuality.

She loved him.

Victoria knew that as surely as the heat made her queasy and her studies made her dizzy.

Too bad Alexander didn't love her. She could have confessed her stupidity if he had. Hiding her problem from him wearied her, and practicing those *b*'s and *d*'s made her dizzy.

"Mama Tory, what are you thinking?" Darcy asked.

Victoria opened her eyes to find both girls standing in front of her. "See a *b* and say a *d*," she answered. "See a *d* and say a *b*."

"Is that magic?" Fiona asked in a hushed voice, her hazel eyes gleaming with excitement.

"Would you like to play magic?" Victoria asked, producing a small cloth pouch containing powder mixed with tiny, glittering particles.

"What is that?" Fiona asked.

"Pixie dust," Victoria answered, handing her the pouch. "Turn slowly in a circle, tossing pixie dust into the air as you do, and say: 'Pixie dust here, pixie dust there, pixie dust is everywhere. Send me—*blank*—and this I swear, for pixies I shall always care.' "

"Blank is where you name what you want," Darcy informed her sister.

With a nervous smile, Fiona took the pouch and, turning in a circle, tossed the pixie dust into the air. "Pixie dust here, pixie dust there, pixie dust everywhere. Send me a *brother* and this I swear, for pixies I shall always care."

"Very good, Sister," Darcy praised her. Then she asked, "May I use the magic wand?"

"Be careful what you wish for," Victoria said, passing her the wand.

Darcy pointed the wand at the sky, made a circle with it, and pointed it at the sky again. "Fairies and pixies, come to me. Fairies and pixies, hear my plea. Send a *brother* straight to me. Fairies and pixies, thankee, thankee."

"Lady Victoria."

Victoria spied Bundles hurrying across the garden. The majordomo wore an anxious expression, filling her with a sense of foreboding.

"His Lordship left the house for a meeting with the Duke of Inverary," Bundles told her. "There is a woman in the foyer demanding to speak to you in His Lordship's absence."

"That must be our brother," Darcy exclaimed.

Victoria rose from the bench. She couldn't credit what she was thinking. Her husband would not have lied to her.

Followed by the majordomo, Victoria guided the girls back to the house and went directly to the foyer. Her fear took the shape of a beautiful, buxom, flame-haired woman who paced back and forth. As before, a young girl and an older woman sat on the bench.

"Are you the Countess of Winchester?" the red-head asked.

Victoria stiffened when the other woman smiled as if she found her lacking. Anger, instead of insecurity, swelled within her. How many tarts in England had given birth to her husband's children?

"Are you looking for employment?" Victoria asked. "If so, I must tell you this is not a brothel."

"I am an actress," the woman informed her, and then gestured to the girl. "Tell His Lordship that Nell is returning one of his gifts. His daughter, Aidan." At that, the woman left the house.

Before greeting her newest daughter, Victoria instructed the majordomo, "Send a footman to carry their bags upstairs. Tell Pinky and Hartwell to help—" She looked at the older woman.

"Juniper," the woman supplied.

"Juniper," Victoria said to Bundles. "Serve us chocolate pudding in the dining room, and send a message to His Lordship asking that he come home immediately."

"Yes, my lady." Bundles hurried away.

Victoria gave her attention to the little girl. She crouched down to be at eye level with the child. "I am your daddy's wife," she introduced herself. "Welcome home, Aidan. I bet that you are five-years-old."

Aidan's hazel eyes, so much like her father's, widened with her surprise. "How did you know?"

"These are your sisters, Darcy and Fiona," Victoria said, gesturing them closer.

"The fairies and pixies made a big mistake," Darcy said.

"We wished for a brother," Fiona added.

"We'll take you," Darcy told Aidan. She wrapped her arms around her new sister and hugged her. Fiona followed her lead, making Aidan smile.

While Victoria waited for his return, Alexander sat in the Duke of Inverary's study. With them were Prince Rudolf and Robert Campbell.

"Married life agrees with you, Alex," Duke Magnus was saying.

Alexander smiled. "I am more than pleased with my choice of a wife."

"How is Tory adjusting to being a stepmother?" Robert asked.

"A stepmother twice," Rudolf teased, and shared a chuckle with the marquess.

"Tory adores the girls," Alexander told them. "I know how lucky I am to have married a forgiving woman."

"Has Victoria suffered any emotional outbursts?" the duke asked.

"No fits and no tantrums," Alexander answered.

"You can imagine how Tory could irritate me," Duke Magnus said, a smile touching his lips.

A knock on the door drew their attention. Tinker entered at the duke's call.

"Excuse me, Your Grace," the majordomo said. He looked at the earl, saying, "One of your footmen is here with a message."

"Send him in," Alexander replied, a puzzled expression etched across his features.

A moment later, the footman appeared. "My lord, the countess needs you at home immediately."

"Is she ill?" Alexander asked in alarm, rising from the chair.

"No, my lord."

Alexander snapped his brows together in consternation. "My daughters?"

"Healthy, my lord."

"Is anyone bleeding, convulsing, or unconscious?" Alexander asked, irritated at being summoned home for less than emergency.

"No, my lord."

"What the bloody hell is so urgent I need to be disturbed?" Alexander asked.

The footman glanced uncomfortably at the others and then cleared his throat. "Another indiscretion has dropped onto your doorstep, my lord." The man's words echoed the *Times* article of two weeks earlier.

Alexander had the good grace to blush. Rudolf and Robert burst into laughter while the duke shook his head in disbelief.

"Tell the countess I will return shortly," Alexander instructed the footman. He sat down again, asking, "Do you have any vodka?"

Grinning, Rudolf rose from his chair and poured his brother-in-law a vodka. "This will help," the prince said, passing him the glass.

Alexander downed the vodka in one gulp, grimaced, and shuddered. "I don't understand how you can drink that poison."

"Three indiscretions?" Duke Magnus said.

Alexander inclined his head. "I sired three daughters by three women."

"Are there any more?" Robert asked.

"No."

"Tory forgave you for the other indiscretions," Rudolf said. "Why should the third be any different?"

Alexander picked a piece of imaginary lint off his trousers. "I told her there were only two," he mumbled.

The prince and the marquess looked at each other and winced. "Tory must be furious," Rudolf said.

"You are a braver man than I," Robert remarked. "I wouldn't dare lie to Angelica."

"Tory had no need to interrupt my meeting," Alexander said, rising from his chair. "This was no emergency."

"Be sure you tell her that," Rudolf said, and then looked at the marquess and laughed.

"Why do you think three mothers would abandon their daughters on your doorstep within weeks of each other?" Duke Magnus asked.

"I had assumed it was an unlucky coincidence," Alexander said.

"Three is no coincidence," Robert said, agreeing with his father's implication.

"Who wants to ruin your marriage?" Prince Rudolf asked. "Lydia Stanley?"

"Why would anyone want to destroy my marriage?" Alexander asked, unable to credit what they were suggesting.

"I'd wager my last shilling on Venetia," Robert said.

"What could Venetia gain by doing that?" Alexander asked.

"She gains the satisfaction of making you unhappy," Robert answered.

"Marrying Harry Gibbs has changed her," Alexander told them. "She favored returning the girls to their mothers."

"Still, your sister bears watching," Prince Rudolf said. "I would question the veracity of whatever she said."

"She could harbor a grudge against you," Duke Magnus said.

"Why don't you ask the mothers involved?" the prince suggested.

"I sent my solicitor to speak with Suzette and Maeve," Alexander told them. "Both had left London for a few weeks."

"I guarantee this third mother has left London by now," Robert said. "Which proves someone is behind their actions."

"I cannot believe any of them would abandon their daughters for money," Alexander said. "However, I will consider what you've said."

Ten minutes later Alexander arrived home. "Where's my wife?" he asked, marching past the majordomo.

"The countess is in the dining room, my lord."

Pausing in the dining room doorway, Alexander saw his three daughters sitting together and thought they made a fetching picture. Victoria sat across the table and spoke to them in a low, soothing voice.

"Welcome home, Aidan," Alexander said, drawing their attention as he crossed the room. He gave each little girl a kiss and then gestured Bundles to take them to their nannies.

"Close the door on your way out," he instructed the majordomo.

After they had left, Alexander stuck his hands in his trouser pockets and watched his wife, who avoided his gaze. "Are you going to look at me?" he asked.

Victoria said nothing. She raised her gaze to his.

"I was in the middle of an important business meeting," Alexander said, trying to put her on the defensive.

Victoria couldn't credit what she was hearing. The man had illegitmate children appearing on his doorstep and had lied about the third's existence. And he was concerned about business?

"Why did you lie to me?" Victoria asked.

"I felt too humiliated to admit to the truth," Alexander told her, and sat down in the chair directly across from her.

"You should feel humiliated," Victoria said. "You should have considered the consequences before you made the rounds of London."

Alexander said nothing. What could he say? He ate the remains of his daughters' puddings and then pointed to his wife's untouched dish. "Are you going to eat that?"

His question broke the dam of her control.

"You son-of-a bitch," Victoria exploded, leaping out of her chair so quickly it fell over. She grabbed her dish of pudding and smashed it on the table.

"Tory, control yourself," Alexander ordered, his voice stern.

"Why should I?" she asked. "You have never controlled yourself."

"I will not countenance one of your emotional fits," he said.

"I don't have fits," Victoria shouted, her blue gaze hurling daggers of anger at him. "If I did, I would be entitled."

"Sit down, Victoria."

"You lied to me."

"I was wrong," Alexander admitted. "I apologize and swear never to lie again."

His words lowered her boiling rage to a slow simmer. "Are there any others?"

"No."

"Are you certain?"

"Yes."

Victoria nodded, accepting his words as truth. "I forgive you, but I want to get away from London," she said, her voice coolly civil. "The girls and I will leave in the morning for my uncle's estate."

"I don't have anything pressing," Alexander said. "I'll go with you."

"No, thank you."

"You want to get away from me?" he asked, without bothering to hide his hurt.

"I need a few days alone," Victoria told him, her heart aching but her mind settled. "I hope you understand."

Alexander inclined his head. "I understand perfectly."

That night Victoria slept alone for the first time since her wedding. She had never felt more miserable in her life.

CHAPTER 11

How long would Alexander mourn her? Victoria wondered in misery. Would he marry Lydia Stanley, his first love, or Diana Drummond, the widow who lusted for him?

Almost a week after leaving London, Victoria lay in her bed in her old bedchamber at her aunt's and uncle's country estate and stared at the ceiling. She had been unwell since before leaving London, and the illness had worsened during the past week.

Tears welled up in her eyes as she recalled the last time she had used this chamber. Alexander had taken her virginity in this bed, and now she would end her life in it.

Living without her husband for almost a week had shown her how intensely she loved him. With time and space separating them, Victoria had realized the reason her husband had hidden his indescretions. After all, she was hiding her stupidity from him. Where was the difference?

If only she had understood before leaving London, Victoria thought, her heart swelling with regret. She would have the comfort of her husband's presence during her final hours.

Alexander was in London and so were Diana Drummond, Lydia Stanley, and Miriam Wilmington. That unsettling thought sent her stomach into a rolling turmoil as if she sailed on storm-tossed seas.

Leaping out of the bed, Victoria dashed across the chamber. She dropped to her knees beside the chamber pot and retched dryly.

Aunt Roxie appeared like an angel sent from God and hurried across the bedchamber. With her spasms ended, Victoria leaned heavily against her aunt's legs.

"Send Alex a message," Victoria sobbed. "Tell him I am dying."

"Let's get you back to bed," Aunt Roxie said, helping her to rise.

With her aunt's arms supporting her, Victoria hobbled across the chamber to the bed. She lay down and closed her eyes in misery.

"I should never have left Alex," she moaned. "The thought of all those women with him in London has sickened me."

"Eat this," Aunt Roxie said.

Victoria opened her eyes a crack and saw the piece of bread her aunt held out to her. "I couldn't possibly—"

"Eat the damn bread," her aunt ordered, "or I'll cram it down your throat."

"Why are you tormenting me?" Victoria asked, a sob catching in her voice. She lifted the bread from her aunt's hand and took a bite.

"Darling, you aren't dying," Aunt Roxie told her. "You are carrying Alex's heir."

"I'm pregnant?" Victoria asked, surprised.

Aunt Roxie gave her a knowing smile. "When did you last have your menses?"

Closing her eyes, Victoria thought for a long moment and then said, "I can't remember."

"Have you bled since marrying Alex?" her aunt asked.

"No, I don't think so."

"Have you been queasy in the morning?"

"I have been queasy the whole damn day," Victoria complained. "Certain smells also sicken me."

"Queasiness without menstruation means pregnancy," Aunt Roxie said. She gave her a dimpled smile, adding, "Consider this another excuse to avoid Sunday church services."

Victoria closed her eyes and slid her hand to her belly. *A baby,* she thought. *Alexander's baby.*

"I suggest you return to London and inform your husband of his impending fatherhood," Aunt Roxie said, patting her hand.

"Alexander lied about Aidan," Victoria reminded her.

"Your husband was protecting you from the truth," Aunt Roxie replied. "God created men imperfect, darling, which benefits womankind. Caught in a lie, a man will do anything to regain his place in his wife's good graces. Instead of insisting you needed to be alone, you should have told Alex that a fur or diamond bracelet would make you feel better."

Victoria couldn't credit the cynicism of what her aunt was saying. "Do you mean I should allow my husband to bribe me to forgive him?"

"Darling, you cannot erase what has already been done so you may as well take advantage of his guilt," Aunt Roxie said. "Your husband is alone in

London with all those female sharks swimming around him. If you don't go home, one will soon sink her teeth into him."

"Alexander is a married man. He would never—"

"Oh, dear God, where did I falter in your up-bringing?" Aunt Roxie cried, throwing her arms up in surprised horror. "You sound like the village idiot."

"I'm not stupid."

"Listen, darling. Men will always take what is of-fered," Aunt Roxie told her. "Your pregnancy gives you an advantage. Hurry home and rescue your husband from those circling sharks."

Victoria smiled at the image her aunt's words conjured. "Very well, Aunt Roxie, I trust your judg-ment and vast experience."

"Leave the girls and their nannies here," Aunt Roxie said. "Magnus and I will bring them home in a few days."

"I love you," Victoria said.

"Thank you, darling. Now go home and seduce your husband," Aunt Roxie said, rising from her perch on the edge of the bed. "Remember to eat some bread every morning before rising."

Worried that her stepdaughters would feel aban-doned again, Victoria ate a leisurely lunch with them. She wanted to explain her reasons for leav-ing them behind and make them understand the separation was temporary.

"I am returning to London to speak with Daddy about getting you a baby brother," Victoria told them.

"Hooray!" the three little girls clapped their hands with excitement.

"Aunt Roxie and Uncle Magnus want you to stay with them a few more days," Victoria said, smiling into three pairs of hazel eyes that resembled her husband's. "Aunt Roxie wants to take you on a picnic, to wade in the stream, and to give you pony rides. Won't that be fun?"

"I love pony rides," Darcy cried, clapping her hands.

"I love picnics," Fiona said.

"I love wading in the stream," Aidan added.

"I should have guessed the redhead would love wading in the stream," Aunt Roxie said dryly.

Victoria hugged her aunt. "Don't drive too fast," she instructed the coachman. "I don't want to be jostled over the bumps."

Without the girls to entertain her, the ride to London seemed never ending. Though she didn't want the babe jostled, Victoria could hardly wait to tell her husband the good news.

Afternoon's long shadows had faded into twilight by the time the coach halted in front of the Grosvenor Square mansion. Victoria alighted from the coach and hurried up the front stairs. Bundles opened the door just as she reached it.

"Welcome home, my lady," the majordomo greeted her.

"Thank you, Bundles." Victoria smiled at the man. "Is my husband home?"

"His Lordship has left for the evening," Bundles told her. "He planned to dine at White's before the opera."

His words disappointed Victoria. She was bursting with the need to tell her husband the joyful news. "Send Polly to me. I'll need to change my gown for the opera."

"Yes, my lady."

An hour later, Victoria sat impatiently while her maid put the finishing touches on her upswept coiffeur. She wore an ice-blue silk gown with low

V-neck and a hemline short enough to expose her ankles.

Finally reaching the opera house, Victoria stepped down from the coach and hurried into the lobby. The music and the singers' voices reached her there.

Uncertain what to do, Victoria looked around. An usher materialized to escort her up the stairs to her husband's opera box.

Stepping inside just as the curtain fell for intermission, Victoria stopped short. Her smile of greeting died on her lips. Alone in the box, Alexander and Diana Drummond sat together, their heads close as they spoke in low voices.

Victoria felt as though she'd been kicked in the stomach. Shock and pain made her queasy as if the babe she carried protested his father's desertion. Her husband hadn't waited long to replace her.

Transfixed by the sight, Victoria stood statue-still. In some part of her mind, she realized that people in other boxes were watching. Her husband glanced over his shoulder and saw her there.

"Victoria—" With a smile of greeting, Alexander rose from his chair. The sound of his voice broke her paralysis.

"Don't let me interrupt your evening," Victoria said, her voice filled with scathing contempt.

Alexander grabbed her wrist. "What is—?"

"Unhand me, you philanderer," Victoria ordered, her voice rising with her anger. She yanked her hand out of his and added in a voice loud enough for others to hear, "If she drops an indiscretion on our doorstep, I swear I will drown this one."

Victoria watched as her husband's complexion

mottled with anger. She didn't stay to listen to his tirade, but whirled away and left the opera house.

Hearing her husband calling her name, Victoria quickened her pace. Her head pounded, her stomach rolled, and her heart ached.

Too insecure to attend a ball without her husband, Victoria searched her mind for a way to upset him in a like manner. She refused to go directly home. Let him wonder about *her* fidelity.

Victoria ordered the driver to take her to Montague House, her sister's home. Somewhere between the opera house and Montague House, her angry pain fanned into raging fury.

How dare Alexander humiliate her by carrying on in front of society. His having a mistress would be painful enough, but flaunting the affair passed beyond the bounds of discretion.

An inner voice insisted that his sitting with the widow did not prove unfaithfulness. He could have gone to the opera where the widow descended upon him. Purposely, no doubt.

Be quiet, Victoria snapped at her inner voice. Alexander appeared smitten with the widow, which humiliated her in front of society. She intended to even the score.

If he wanted to regain her favor, Alexander would need to rescind his open invitation for the widow to use the opera box. There were six other nights in the week. Let her attend the opera on one of those nights or purchase her own damn opera box.

Fortunately, Rudolf and Samantha had stayed home that evening. Victoria walked into the drawing room and burst into tears. In an instant, her sister had enfolded her within a comforting embrace and led her to the settee.

"What happened?" Samantha asked her.

Before she could answer, Rudolf asked, "Is this about the third daughter?"

"You know about that?" When he inclined his head, Victoria told them, "His lies angered me so much I passed this week at His Grace's estate. I left the girls there and—"

Rudolf chuckled. "You took Alexander's daughters and left him?"

"They are *my* daughters, too," Victoria told him. "When I arrived at the opera this evening, Alexander and Diana were sitting close together."

"And then what happened?" Rudolf asked.

"I called him a philanderer and left," Victoria answered. In a small voice, she added, "Unfortunately, I arrived at intermission and people were watching. May I stay here for a while?"

"You may stay as long as you like," her sister told her.

"No, Samantha, she may *not* stay here," Rudolf said. "Tory, you need to go home and make peace with your husband. Alex will worry if you don't return."

"I *want* him to worry," Victoria said. "I need to stay until two or three in the morning so he'll believe I continued with my evening."

"Why didn't you go to one of the balls?" Rudolf asked.

"I would never do that without Alex," Victoria said, making him smile. "Please, let me stay until midnight."

"Very well, but you are leaving at midnight," Rudolf relented. He rose from the settee and returned with a snifter of brandy. "Drink this, Tory. You will feel better."

"I don't think spirits will agree with the baby," Victoria said in refusal. "May I have a cup of tea or some warm milk?"

"To what baby are you referring?" Samantha asked, her expression bewildered.

"I'm pregnant," Victoria said, and burst into tears.

"What wonderful news," Samantha said. "Aren't you happy about it?"

"I've never been happier in my life," Victoria sobbed, and then hiccupped.

"Alex never mentioned it," Rudolf said.

"He doesn't know," Victoria said. "I didn't know until Aunt Roxie told me. I thought I had caught a dreadful disease."

Prince Rudolf laughed and her sister smiled. "I'll get you a mug of warm milk," the prince said, and left the drawing room.

Victoria leaned back against the settee and closed her eyes. She fell asleep before the prince returned with the milk.

"Wake up, Tory."

Victoria opened her eyes and saw her brother-in-law. She yawned and stretched, asking, "Where's Samantha?"

"She went upstairs an hour ago," Rudolf answered, helping her rise from the settee. "You need to go home now."

"I'm sorry I kept you awake," Victoria said, as he escorted her to her waiting coach.

"Tell Alex about the baby," Rudolf advised her. "Then accept his apology for upsetting you."

"Thank you, Rudolf."

The prince smiled. "How could I refuse to help my favorite red-haired sister-in-law?"

"I'm your only red-haired sister-in-law."

"I know."

Twenty minutes later, Victoria climbed the stairs to her third-floor bedchamber. She wondered where Alexander was. Had he accompanied the widow to any of that evening's social gatherings? What was he thinking and feeling?

At that precise moment, Alexander sat in a darkened corner of his wife's bedchamber. Worry and anger warred with his emotions. He had returned home, sorted through the invitations, and gone to each of those balls. Victoria was nowhere to be found. Where the bloody hell had she disappeared to? When she decided to come home, he intended to kiss her with relief and then paddle her backside for worrying him, not to mention creating that embarrassing scene at the opera.

The door opened slowly, and Victoria walked into the room. She set a plate down on the bedside table and glanced at the connecting door for a long moment. With a sigh, she turned away and took a step toward her dressing room.

"Where have you been?"

Victoria stopped short and turned around.

Alexander rose from the chair and sauntered across the chamber to tower over her. He noted her swollen, tear-reddened eyes and steeled himself against the remorse welling up in his chest.

"Answer my question," he ordered.

His eighteen-year-old wife had the audacity to lift her nose in the air. "I went out."

"That is no answer."

"That is the only answer you will get."

"Where were you?" Alexander repeated, a hard edge to his voice. "Whom were you with? What were you doing until midnight?"

"I went to the Templetons' ball and danced with whoever asked," she lied.

Victoria noticed his right cheek muscle begin to twitch. That was a bad sign. She wet her lips, gone dry from nervousness.

"You did not attend the Templetons' ball," Alexander said. "Neither did you go to the Richards, the Murrays, or the Carletons."

"I lied."

"Where were you?"

"That is none of your business," she told him.

"Your whereabouts is my business," he told her. "You answer to me." *Or else* was left unspoken.

"I went to Montague House and fell asleep on the settee," Victoria admitted. "If you don't believe me, ask Rudolf. He woke me up and sent me home."

The twitching in his cheek muscle subsided. "Where did you put my daughters?"

"*Our* daughters are extending their visit with my aunt," Victoria told him. "His Grace and my aunt will return with them in a few days."

"Why did you create that scene at the opera?" Alexander asked. "That was a stupid stunt."

"I am not stupid." Then Victoria demanded, "What is between you and the widow?"

"Tory, I have no interest in the widow," Alexander told her.

"The widow has an interest in you," Victoria said. "Your actions encourage her."

"I went to the opera alone," he said. "She appeared just before the curtain went up. Should I have left?"

"Revoke your opera invitation," Victoria said, "or stipulate that she is not to attend on Thursdays."

"What reason could I give for changing my mind?" Alexander asked, his irritation apparent in his voice. "Tory, the woman is my sister's sister-in-law. She's practically family."

"Do what you want," Victoria said, walking toward the dressing room.

"Are you coming to bed?" he asked.

Victoria halted and, without turning around, said, "I am going to *my* bed."

"I forbid you to go out in the evenings unless I accompany you," Alexander ordered.

Victoria turned around slowly. Anger blazed at him from the depths of her blue eyes. "Why?"

"I dislike the feeling of wondering where my wife is," he told her.

"You don't own me."

"I *do* own you," Alexander countered. "A wife belongs to her husband. That is the law."

"I don't give a fig about the law," she snapped.

"You will obey me," Alexander warned, "or you will regret it." At that, he disappeared into his chamber.

Victoria awakened late the following morning. Making a mental note to tell her maid to leave some bread on her bedside table early each morning, she sat up and leaned against the headboard while she ate the bread she had placed there the previous night.

Why couldn't Alexander see Venetia and Diana for the cunning manipulators they were? Unless he rescinded the open invitation, Diana Drummond would appear at the opera every Thursday. Why would the widow seek to become Alexander's mistress when a woman as beautiful as she could have any man for a husband?

Divorce was not an option. The widow could not be harboring any hope to become Alexander's wife.

Once the bread calmed her queasiness, Victoria dressed and went to the dining room for a late breakfast.

"Good morning, Bundles," Victoria greeted the majordomo.

His lips twitched. "Good afternoon, my lady."

"Is there any food left?" she asked. "Or has my husband eaten everything?"

"We always have food for you, my lady."

Victoria looked over the morning's fare and felt the nausea returning. She chose a dry roll and a cup of black tea and then sat down at the table.

"Wouldn't you care for eggs or ham?" Bundles asked, standing beside her chair. "Mrs. Hull will cook something fresh."

Putting a hand to her throat, Victoria gulped back the nausea his words provoked. She closed her eyes as beads of sweat broke out over her upper lip and the crevice between her breasts.

"I'll wait for lunch," she said in a small voice.

"Are you ill, my lady?"

"I am perfectly well." Victoria managed a faint, reassuring smile.

Bundles returned to the sideboard.

Thinking the house seemed empty without the girls, Victoria sipped her tea and glanced at the *Times* on the table near her. She turned to the society news and wished she could read it. Had her scene at the opera been mentioned?

"Bundles, would you do me a favor?" she called.

The majordomo was at her side in an instant.

"I forgot my spectacles upstairs," Victoria lied. "Would you read me the society news and tell me if the reporter mentioned the earl or me?"

Bundles didn't bother to look at the newspaper. "Intermission at the opera last night entertained the audience more than the performance," he quoted. "A certain countess arrived late to discover her husband huddled with a beautiful widow."

Victoria felt her heart sink to her stomach. "Did my husband read the article?"

"I believe so, my lady."

"That bad?"

"I'm afraid so."

"Is he at home?" she asked.

"His Lordship is working in his study," Bundles told her.

"Thank you." Victoria sat at the table for a few minutes more while she summoned her courage. Alexander was furious with her. She had better go to his study and make peace as Rudolf had advised.

Victoria walked upstairs but hesitated outside his study. Pasting a bright smile onto her face, she breezed into the study, calling, "Good afternoon, my lord."

Wearing a grim expression, Alexander watched her cross the room. His implacable expression boded ill for making peace.

Victoria sat down in the chair in front of his desk and fidgeted for a moment, settling herself. Glancing up, she saw her husband watching her closely.

"I returned to London to tell you that I understand why you lied about Aidan," Victoria said.

"Do you?" Alexander cocked a brow at her. "How generous."

"Are we attending the Cavendish affair tonight?" Victoria asked, her smile forced and overly bright. "My sisters and brothers-in-law will be attending."

"I am engaged for the evening at White's," Alexander replied, watching her expression droop. "You will be staying home where you belong."

"Reading a Jane Austen novel sounds wonderful," she said, rising from the chair. "Will we be dining together?"

"I'm afraid not."

"I see." Without another word, Victoria breezed out of his study as if she had not a care in the world.

Watching her, Alexander gave her high marks for bravery for facing the lion in his den. She must have read the *Times* gossip column. His wife would be passing many evenings alone at home until she learned who gave the orders and who obeyed.

"Victoria never actually refuses to do anything. She agrees to whatever you want and then does what she wants." The duchess's words slammed into his consciousness.

Alexander sat up straight. Would Victoria attend the Cavendish affair without him? Was she that brave? Or foolish?

Smiling to himself, Alexander decided that he would take himself to the Cavendish affair before the guests went down to supper. If his wife was there, he would drag her home and make sure she couldn't sit comfortably for a week.

Later that evening, Victoria sat on the settee in her chamber and practiced transposing her *b*'s and *d*'s while waiting for her husband to leave. Her thoughts were mutinous. She felt tired and didn't actually want to go to a ball, but her husband was forcing her to do this. He needed to be taught a lesson.

White's was for gentlemen only, but how could she be sure that was his real destination? Could he secretly be rendezvousing with Diana Drummond? Another woman?

Victoria heard the connecting door open but ignored his presence until she spied his shoes planted on the floor beside her. She looked up and noted his formal evening attire. Was that required at White's or was he going somewhere else?

"What were you mumbling?" Alexander asked.

"Incantations."

Alexander grinned. "I hope you aren't hexing me."

"I would never do that," Victoria said, a smile on her lips.

"I see you are comfortable in your bedrobe," he said. "Have you eaten?"

"I had a late lunch," she answered. "Mrs. Hull will send me a tray later."

Alexander shoved his hands in his trouser pockets. "Is there anything I can do for you before I leave?"

Love me, Victoria thought, looking at him with longing in her eyes. "I can't think of anything," she answered.

"Have yourself a good evening," Alexander said, and left the chamber.

Victoria felt tears welling up in her eyes as the door clicked quietly behind him. She forced her tears back and sat staring into space for a long time.

What if she went to the Cavendish affair and Alexander showed up there with another woman? Her husband would never be so cruel as to escort another woman to a ball, would he?

Thankfully, both Samantha and Angelica planned to attend the Cavendish affair. She need not worry about being alone.

Judging nearly an hour had passed since her husband's departure, Victoria rose from the settee and removed her bedrobe. Beneath it, she wore the revealing black gown her husband had forbidden her to wear in public. Leaving her fiery curls cascading around her, she donned her diamond collar and walked across the chamber to inspect herself in the cheval mirror.

Aplomb . . . aplomb . . . aplomb. Victoria thought, smiling at her image. Though her stomach was still flat, her breasts were swollen, which made the gown's neckline even more daring.

Planning her evening, Victoria decided to dance and flirt with Rudolf's three brothers. Then she would return home before her husband and hope the *Times* reporter would mention her being at the Cavendish affair. She would be declaring her independence without actually facing her husband. Her rebellion would tell Alexander that he could not issue edicts and expect obedience, especially when he held himself to another standard.

Thirty minutes later, Victoria arrived at the Cavendish mansion. She hoped her sisters had already arrived and had no idea what to do if they were late.

"The Countess of Winchester," the Cavendish majordomo announced.

Walking down the stairs into the ballroom, Victoria spied her sisters and brothers-in-law on the far side of the room. She also noticed several gentlemen giving her appreciative glances and wished that her husband could see that other men found her attractive.

Aplomb, Victoria reminded herself, wending her way through the crowd.

Spying Venetia and Diana made her feel better. At least, Alexander wasn't with the widow that evening. He wasn't with Lydia Stanley either, she noted with pleasure.

"Where's Alex?" Samantha asked, when she reached their group.

"We've gone our separate ways this evening," Victoria answered.

"I thought he forbade you to wear that gown in public," Angelica remarked.

Victoria gave her sisters a jaunty smile. "He did." She saw her brothers-in-law look at each other and smile, but then noticed Rupert Wilmington approaching, his gaze fixed on her breasts. Panicking, she grabbed the prince's hand and said, "Dance with me."

Prince Rudolf and Victoria stepped onto the dance floor together. They began the swirling steps of the waltz.

"Are you certain you won't fall out of that gown?" Rudolf teased her.

Victoria felt the heated blush rising on her cheeks. "Rupert Wilmington certainly had an anticipatory expression on his face."

That made Rudolf smile. "I'm surprised Alex and you went your separate ways tonight," he said. "I would have thought Alex so happy about the baby that he would remain by your side all evening."

"Alex doesn't know about the baby yet," Victoria told him. "We argued when I arrived home last night, and he forbade me to go out unless he escorted me. Just to be difficult, he insisted he had a prior engagement at White's tonight."

Gently but firmly, Rudolf waltzed her off the dance floor. "Tory, I suggest you leave immediately and pray that Alex doesn't get home before you."

"I am not ready to go home yet," Victoria said.

"Don't be stubborn," the prince said. "Your disobedience is not a good idea."

"If my husband can huddle with the widow," Victoria replied, "then I can take myself to a ball and dance with whomever . . . *oh, my God!*" Her horrified gaze fixed on the stairs as the Cavendish majordomo announced, "The Earl of Winchester."

"Tory, do not swoon," Prince Rudolf ordered.

"I need to hide," she cried in a panic, trying to yank her hand out of his.

"Tell Alex about the baby immediately," Rudolf advised, grasping her forearm before she could bolt. "He will forgive your disobedience."

"Yes, I'll tell him," Victoria agreed, her complexion pale. "I need to hide until I compose myself."

Rudolf dropped his hand. Victoria headed in the direction of the ladies' withdrawing room. How much harm could her husband do before she spilled the news of her pregnancy?

Victoria neared the the sanctuary of the withdrawing room, but a strong hand on her arm halted her progress. "I believe this is our dance," she heard her husband say.

Trembling, Victoria faced her husband. Panic quickened her heartbeat and incited her stomach to somersaults. Raising her gaze to his, she saw amusement tempered with anger gleaming at her from his hazel gaze.

"Tory, you are so wonderfully predictable," Alexander said.

"You're supposed to be at White's," Victoria said, and then realized how idiotic she sounded.

"What am I going to do with you, wife?" Alexander asked, running a long finger down the side of her cheek. "You disobeyed my order to remain at home." He dropped his gaze to her cleavage, adding, "Even worse, you are wearing that gown."

"Please, Alex, I must speak to you before you do anything," Victoria said, an urgent note in her voice.

Grasping her wrist, Alexander led her to an alcove where they could expect a measure of privacy. He maneuvered her into a position with her back against the wall and towered over her.

"Speak," he ordered.

"Did you come here tonight to see Diana Drummond or Lydia Stanley?" she asked.

"I came here to fetch you," Alexander told her.

"I came tonight because you ordered me to stay home," Victoria tried to explain. "If you had *preferred* I stay home, I would not have disobeyed."

"Are you telling me your disobedience is my fault?"

"No, but I don't know how to explain myself." With tears welling up in her eyes, Victoria blurted out, "Alex, we're going to have a baby."

"A baby?" he echoed, surprised.

"I didn't know until my aunt told me," Victoria said. "That's why I hurried back to London. Only I couldn't contain my news until you returned from the opera. When I saw you with the widow—"

"I understand," Alexander said, gently drawing her closer. He tilted her chin up and kissed her with tenderness. "I'm sorry for upsetting you."

"I'm sorry I disobeyed," Victoria apologized. "Why can't you see what Diana Drummond is doing?"

"I do see that Diana Drummond is throwing herself at me," Alexander admitted. "Because of my sister, I could not give her the cut. You need feel no jealousy over Diana or any other woman."

"Can we go home now?" Victoria asked, her blue gaze filled with love.

"If we leave now," Alexander said, "people will speculate about why we are leaving so early." He tipped his head toward the dance floor. "Let's dance and speak to your relations. Then we'll go home."

Taking her hand in his, Alexander led her onto the dance floor. He drew her into his arms, and they joined the other couples in the waltz around the ballroom.

I love you, Victoria thought, her heart shining in her eyes.

Unexpectedly, Alexander stopped dancing. "What did you say?"

Victoria blushed, realizing that she'd spoken aloud. "I—I love you, Alex."

"You are the best thing that ever happened to me," Alexander said, lifting her hand to his lips, disregarding the curious looks they were drawing. Then he ushered her off the dance floor and led her in the direction of her relations.

Did his words mean he loved her? If so, why couldn't he say the words?

He doesn't love you, Victoria told herself. He agreed to Aunt Roxie's proposal to clear his conscience about Charles Emerson's transgressions.

"We have an announcement," Alexander said to her family. "Victoria and I are expecting a baby."

Thankfully, Rudolf and Samantha pretended surprise. Her sisters hugged her while Robert and Rudolf shook her husband's hand.

"Are you ready to leave?" Alexander asked her.

"Yes, I feel tired tonight," Victoria answered. Seeing the disappointment in his gaze, she amended herself, "Not *that* tired."

Everyone laughed, which made Victoria blush. That made her husband smile.

"Will you join Robert and me for lunch at White's tomorrow?" Rudolf asked.

Alexander nodded. Taking his wife's hand, he escorted her across the ballroom. As they neared the stairs, Rupert and Miriam Wilmington blocked their path.

"You aren't leaving?" Miriam asked, her gaze on Alexander.

"We haven't danced yet," Rupert said, his gaze on Victoria's cleavage.

"Victoria feels tired tonight," Alexander answered. "Expectant mothers tire easily."

"What wonderful news," Miriam gushed, turning to Victoria. "I am certain your sisters are a wealth of knowledge, but if you need advice, don't hesitate to call upon me."

Victoria blushed. "Thank you, Lady Miriam."

"I hope you get your heir," Rupert said.

"We hope so, too." Taking his wife's hand, Alexander escorted her to the stairs where Venetia and Diana blocked their path. "I left Harry at White's," he said to his sister before she could speak.

"You aren't leaving, my lord?" Diana asked.

"My expectant wife feels tired tonight," Alexander said.

Victoria could see their smiles did not quite reach their eyes. "Congratulations," both women said, ignoring her.

"Don't let us keep you," Venetia said.

Alexander started to turn away and then paused. In a low voice, he told them, "I dislike being rude, but I would prefer privacy at the opera on Thursday evenings. You are welcome to use the box any other evening. Please, send us a note before you stop by to visit our home. Tory hasn't been feeling well. I know you'll undersatand."

Both women inclined their heads.

Victoria felt her spirits rise. Her husband had done what she had asked. Perhaps, he did harbor more than a little fondness for her.

Venetia and Diana watched them leave. "I doubt Lady Victoria will leave your brother now," Diana remarked.

"If Victoria Douglas won't leave Alexander," Venetia said, "then he will leave her, and you will be his countess. I will hire an investigator to watch her and find us some dirt."

"What if there is none?" Diana asked.

Venetia smiled. "Then we'll manufacture dirt to throw at her and hope it sticks."

CHAPTER 12

"Mama Tory, let's play magic wand," Darcy called.

"And pixie dust," Fiona added.

"Hooray for fairies and pixies," Aidan shouted, tossing a handful of leaves into the air.

"No more wishes until your baby brother arrives," Victoria told them, and then smiled at the three nannies sitting on a nearby bench in the earl's garden.

Autumn wore its most serene expression on that first day of November. The humid days of August had faded into the morning mists and warm afternoons of September. Michaelmas daisies had come and gone, the season melting into October's golden afternoons, crisp nights, and carpets of brilliantly colored leaves in red and orange and gold.

My belly bulges, Victoria thought, placing the palm of her hand against it. She prayed the next six months would be as peaceful as the last few weeks.

Thankfully, Venetia and Diana had respected her husband's request. Neither had attended the opera on Thursday evenings and never visited without permission. Still, Victoria suffered the uncomfortable feeling that they were planning her demise.

"Lady Victoria, His Lordship wishes to speak to you in the library," Bundles said, drawing her attention.

"Thank you, Bundles."

Victoria stopped short when she stepped into the library. On the settee sat Suzette, Maeve, and Nell, her husband's former mistresses. Alexander stood with his back to the hearth and faced the three women.

Panic swelled in Victoria. The women could only be there to retrieve their daughters. She loved the little girls and could not bear to part with them now.

"No," Victoria moaned, grabbing the doorjamb as dizziness washed over her.

"Please, excuse me," Alexander said to the women. "I must speak with my wife before—"

Alexander broke off. Crossing the library, he took his wife's hand in his and led her down the corridor to the drawing room.

"Sit here," Alexander ordered, gently pushing her into a chair. He knelt on one bended knee in front of her and said, "They want their daughters."

"Send them away," Victoria cried. Tears welled up in her eyes and rolled down her cheeks.

"I know you are hurting," Alexander said, "but you can't keep another woman's child. You know that, Tory."

"The girls belong to you, too," Victoria sobbed. "Offer money and visitation if they will assign guardianship to you."

Alexander held her in his arms and stroked her back in an effort to soothe. "I know you love them," he said, "but their mothers' demands will be never ending."

"The girls will believe that we abandoned them," Victoria argued through her sobs.

"The girls love their mothers, too," Alexander said.

"I can't bear to part with them," Victoria said, her voice muffled against his chest.

"I'll ask the girls with whom they would prefer to live," Alexander offered.

"Don't make them choose," Victoria said, lifting her gaze to his. "The girls will always feel guilty about hurting the unchosen parent. Will their mothers let them visit us?"

"Yes, I'm sure of that," Alexander answered. "I never imagined this would happen."

Victoria looked at him, asking, "Shall I pack their belongings?"

"Stay here until I send for you." With his fingertips, Alexander brushed the tears from her face and then stood to return to the library.

His wife did not deserve to suffer this pain, Alexander thought. She had opened her heart and their home to the girls and hurt herself in the doing. Her pain was his fault.

Suzette and Maeve and Nell didn't deserve their daughters. Someone had paid them to cause trouble. He was certain of that. Three ex-mistresses abandoning their daughters was too much of a coincidence.

Alexander stepped into the library and nearly laughed out loud. A hostile silence pervaded the chamber. His mistresses' dislike of each other was almost tangible.

"Someone paid you to abandon your daughters on my doorstep," Alexander said. "I want to know that person's identity."

"I don't know what you are talking about," Suzette said.

"No one paid me a shilling," Maeve insisted.

"I went out of town unexpectedly," Nell told him.

Undecided about how to handle the situation, Alexander wandered across the room to stare out the window into the garden below where his daughters played in the leaves. The girls had been so happy here. Sending them off with their mothers seemed almost criminal. He needed to persuade his former lovers to let their daughters remain in residence with him.

"I know you love your daughters," Alexander said, turning around to find them watching him. "Victoria—my wife—loves them, too, and defied society's rules to welcome them into her heart and our home. She even made excuses to the girls for your leaving them here. And now she's suffering for it. Tory would never have abandoned any child of hers, no matter how much money was offered."

"Your wife never felt the need for money," Suzette said. The others nodded their agreement.

"Until two years ago, my wife lived in poverty in a small cottage on the far side of Primrose Hill," Alexander informed them.

"But she's an earl's daughter," Maeve said.

"A bankrupt, alcoholic earl," Alexander qualified, and noted the uncomfortable glances the women gave each other.

"Naturally, Victoria doesn't want to part with the girls but understands they belong to you," Alexander continued. "When I suggested that the girls choose where to live, she refused to put your daughters in the position of choosing between parents."

Alexander tipped his head toward the window. "If you look outside, you'll see how happy they are together."

The three women rose from their seats and crossed the library. In silence, they watched their daughters romping in the leaves. When Aidan tripped and fell, Darcy helped her up and hugged her. Refusing to be left out, Fiona rushed across the garden and hugged her sisters. Then the three girls giggled and jumped into a pile of leaves.

Alexander gave his former mistresses a sidelong glance. All three were smiling at the sight of the three half-sisters playing happily together.

"I'll return them to you if you want," Alexander said. "If you leave them with me, I'll support you at the rate of one thousand pounds per month, a one percent holding in my businesses, and visitation rights. The offer is generous. My wife only receives two hundred and fifty pounds per month."

"I accept your offer," Maeve spoke first.

"So do I," Suzette said.

"I also agree," Nell said, her gaze on the girls, "but I want you to know that I love my daughter."

"All three of us love our daughters," Maeve said.

"I think the sisters should grow up together," Suzette added.

"I understand how difficult this is for you," Alexander said, and crossed the library to the doorway. "Bundles, fetch the girls and their nannies."

Meanwhile, Victoria sat in the drawing room and stared into space. She felt bereft of hope, her whole life of eighteen years nothing more than a series of heartwrenching good-byes. Why did she always lose the people she loved? Was she also fated to lose her husband and baby?

"My lady, the earl requests your presence in the library," the majordomo said, standing beside her.

"Thank you, Bundles."

When she walked into the library and saw the

girls sitting on their mothers' laps, Victoria felt her heart breaking. She struggled against tears and tried to swallow the lump of raw emotion rising in her throat.

"Mama Tory, look who's here," Darcy called.

"Yes, sweetie, I see." Victoria managed a bright smile. "Didn't I promise your mother would return?"

Alexander crossed the library and put his arm around her. "The girls will be staying with us," he said.

The unexpected relief nearly felled Victoria. Sagging against her husband, she hid her face against his chest and wept openly.

Victoria felt an insistent tugging on her skirt and looked down. Wearing worried expressions, the three girls stood there.

"Mama Tory, what's wrong?" Darcy asked, her face pale with fright.

"Don't cry, Mama Tory," Fiona said, her bottom lip trembling.

Aidan couldn't speak. She burst into tears of sympathy.

Victoria knelt and pulled all three into her arms. "I am weeping with happiness," she said.

"I never cry when I'm happy," Darcy said.

Fiona nodded, agreeing with her sister. "I laugh when I'm happy."

"Me, too," Aidan whispered.

"Kiss your mothers," Victoria said, standing. "Then your nannies will take you downstairs for gingerbread and—?"

"Whipped cream," the three girls shouted with enthusiasm.

Victoria watched the girls run back to their mothers. After kissing and hugging them, the girls left the library with their nannies.

"My solicitor will contact you about the arrangements," Alexander said, when the women stood to leave.

"I promise to take good care of your daughters," Victoria said, with tears streaming down her face.

"Thank you for loving my daughter," Suzette said.

"Breeding women are always emotional," Nell told her.

"You'll feel better once you've delivered your baby," Maeve added.

"How did you know?" Victoria asked.

Nell smiled. "You've grown since the last time we saw you."

Victoria blushed and dropped her hand to her belly.

"Don't worry," Suzette said.

"You'll flatten out again," Maeve added.

Alexander escorted the three women downstairs. When he returned a few minutes later, Victoria walked into his arms and rested her head against his chest, murmuring, "Thank you."

"I admire your ability to love," Alexander said, tilting her face up to gaze into her eyes, "but life hurts you too easily."

"I cannot change what I am," Victoria said.

"I would never want you to change," Alexander told her, lowering his head to capture her lips in a long, healing kiss . . .

The second day of November appeared a replica of the first, a rarity of bright sunshine and blue skies and warm breezes. Ideal for keeping the girls romping in the leaves, Victoria thought, walking around the perimeter of the garden in an effort to get some exercise. She watched almost longingly as the five-year-olds rolled in the colored leaves. If she hadn't been pregnant, Victoria would have joined them.

Spying her husband walking across the garden in her direction, Victoria gave him a smile filled with sunshine. "Are you joining our play?" she asked.

"I wish I could," Alexander said, his gaze on his daughters. "They are certainly enjoying themselves."

"A year from now, our son will be romping with his sisters," Victoria said.

Alexander grinned. "A year from now, our son will be too small to romp with his sisters. Don't wait tea for me. I'm taking Harry Gibbs to White's to meet several gentlemen. I could be late if they start talking business, and I gave Venetia and Diana permission to use the library while I'm gone."

Victoria grimaced with displeasure.

"Be careful, Tory," he teased her. "Your face could freeze with that look upon it."

"Are they here now?"

"They'll be along once I fetch Harry."

Victoria gestured the nannies to supervise the girls and looped her arm through her husband's. "I'll walk inside with you," she said. "I don't want them near the girls."

Thirty minutes later, Victoria sat on the settee in the library and knitted a blue blanket for her baby. She knew her husband could purchase hundreds of blankets, but wanted to make one with love.

"Good afternoon, Victoria," Venetia called, breezing into the library.

"You're looking well," Diana said with a smile.

"Bundles, serve us tea," Victoria instructed the majordomo. She looked at the widow, saying, "Use the library to your heart's content."

"Could you recommend a book?" Diana asked.

Victoria gave her a sharp look. There was something in the widow's tone that made her uneasy, but these two couldn't possibly know of her inability to read. Even her husband didn't know about that.

"Jane Austen?" Victoria suggested.

"I've already devoured her books," Diana said.

Victoria shrugged. "I'm certain I couldn't possibly know what you would like. Look for yourself."

"How are the girls?" Venetia asked, sitting beside her on the settee.

"The girls are enjoying the afternoon in the garden," Victoria answered, feeling uncomfortably disoriented. Her sister-in-law had never asked about the girls before.

"Has your morning sickness passed?" Diana asked.

"I still become queasy at times."

"You look wonderfully radiant."

Victoria dropped her gaze to her knitting. Something wicked was afoot. These two had never been so kind to her. She wondered what they wanted.

"I do hope we can get together for Christmas dinner," Venetia was saying. "Come the spring, we'll be returning to Australia."

Though heartened by the news of their departure, Victoria asked, in a disappointed tone, "You won't be in England when our baby is born?"

"That depends on what Harry thinks best," Venetia answered. "When spring comes to England, autumn arrives in Australia."

"I didn't know that," Victoria said.

Bundles returned to the library, followed by two footmen carrying silver trays with coffee and tea service. "My lady, this arrived by courier," the majordomo said, passing her a sealed missive.

"Thank you, Bundles." Victoria couldn't imagine who would send her a message.

"Aren't you going to open your letter?" Diana asked, once the servants had gone.

"Actually, I broke my spectacles and haven't replaced them yet," Victoria lied. "I'll need to wait for Alex to come home." She looked at the message and, acting on impulse, asked, "Would you be kind enough to read it to me?"

"You don't mind?" the widow asked.

"No, of course not." Victoria opened the missive and passed it to the widow.

"Tory, meet me at the Philbin brothers' house at five o'clock. Alex," Diana read, and then handed her the note.

Her Christmas surprise was ruined, Victoria thought in disappointment. Somehow, Alexander had discovered her disability, probably one of her sisters inadvertently mentioning it to Robert or Rudolf who, in turn, remarked upon it to her husband.

"I must go out," Victoria said, pocketing the note. "I'll leave you to browse."

Victoria left the library and fetched her cloak and reticule from her chamber. Then she walked downstairs. Finding the foyer deserted, Victoria decided to walk instead of ordering a coach.

Thirty minutes later, Victoria arrived at the Philbin house and banged on the door. A moment later the door opened to reveal Barnaby Philbin.

"Lady Victoria, what a surprise," Barnaby exclaimed. "Please, come inside."

"The earl learned about my reading lessons," Victoria told him, entering the house. "He's meeting me here shortly. Could we possibly work on my love letter to him while we wait?"

"Of course, my lady, but I must warn you that Phineas is not home," Barnaby replied. "You and I will be alone."

Victoria sat down at the table. "I am certain you will act the gentleman."

Barnaby set ink and parchment down on the table, saying, "You write the letter while I make us tea. Then I'll help you with corrections."

Victoria looked up when Barnaby set the steaming teacup on the table beside her. "I'm almost finished," she said, fixing her name and her title at the bottom of the note. "Do you want to read it?"

"I'll read it while you drink your tea," Barnaby said.

Victoria sipped the tea and watched him perusing her note. "How bad is it?" she asked.

Barnaby looked at her and smiled. "I can see improvement in your ability."

"Really?" Victoria yawned. Lord, but she felt so tired. "Your tea has relaxed me so much I can hardly keep my eyes open."

"The baby tires you," Barnaby replied, blushing at the intimacy of his comment. "There's a daybed in the next room. Why don't you lie down while you await the earl?"

"Yes, I think I will." After sanding the note, she slipped it into her reticule and then walked unsteadily into the adjoining room.

"Welcome home, my lord," Bundles said.

"Good afternoon, Bundles," Alexander replied, walking past the majordomo into the foyer. "Where are my wife and daughters?"

"The young misses are enjoying a mug of cider," Bundles told him. "The ladies are in the library."

"Do you mean our visitors are still here?" Alexander asked.

"I'm afraid so," Bundles drawled, his dislike of the visitors all too evident.

Almost reluctantly, Alexander walked up the stairs to the library. He had felt certain his sister and the widow would have gone home by now. His wife was probably furious with him for leaving her to contend with them. If the truth were told, he couldn't blame her.

Pasting a smile onto his face, Alexander walked into the library. "Good afternoon, ladies," he greeted them. "Where is Victoria?"

Venetia and Diana exchanged worried glances. "Victoria went out shortly after we arrived," Venetia answered.

"She went out?" Alexander echoed, confused.

"I'm sorry, my lord," Diana murmured, passing him a note with the seal broken. "Your wife received this, made her excuses to us, and left. She dropped the note in her rush to leave."

Alexander stared at the note in his hand, a feeling of foreboding overwhelming his senses. Slowly, he unfolded the note and read:

> *Meet me at the Philbin brothers' house on the corner of Oxford and Soho Streets. No one will suspect a visit to the tutors. I am counting the moments until we are together again.*
>
> *R.W.*

R.W. Alexander thought in shock, *Rupert Wilmington.* Victoria and Rupert were engaged in an affair.

Without a word to either woman, Alexander folded the note and left the library. "Did my wife receive this today?" he asked the majordomo, holding the note up.

"Yes, my lord."

"And then she went out?"

"I never saw Lady Victoria leave," Bundles answered, sounding confused.

"I want the coach brought around again," Alexander ordered, and stormed out the door.

Reaching the corner of Oxford and Soho Streets, Alexander bounded out of the coach before it came to a complete stop. He pounded on the door but no one answered. Twisting the knob, he realized the door was unlocked and walked into the quiet house.

"Victoria," Alexander called.

No one answered.

Fearing what he would find, Alexander entered the room on his right, a study. She wasn't there.

Alexander saw an open door across the room. He walked toward it and slipped into the adjoining room.

His heart broke at the sight that greeted him. On a daybed lay his sleeping wife, still naked from her amorous tryst.

Caught between fury and pain, Alexander crossed the room and stared at his faithless wife. Why did every woman he love betray him? Only, this was worse than Lydia Stanley. Much worse.

A solitary tear ran down each cheek, but he wiped them away. His head pounded with the thought that his pregnant wife had made love to another man.

Even if he needed to drag her through the courts for an adultery conviction, Alexander determined to set her aside. Banish her from his heart, his mind, his life. He prayed she carried his heir because once she delivered, the babe would belong to him.

Then Victoria Douglas could go wherever she wanted, do whatever she desired, to whoever suited her fancy. He and his son would take no part in her life.

"Wake up, Victoria."

No answer.

The thought of touching her revolted him, but he had no choice. Alexander reached out and shook her shoulder.

"Wake up, Tory."

Her fabulous blue eyes opened. The smile he'd grown to love appeared on her face.

"Come to bed, husband," she murmured, her eyes closing in sleep again.

She's drunk, Alexander concluded. *His faithless wife was drunk.*

"Wake up."

Victoria heard the voice as if from a great distance. Reluctantly, she opened her eyes and then instantly closed them again. The brilliant sunlight streaming through the window blinded her.

"Wake up, I said."

The insistent voice spoke again. Definitely irritated.

Victoria rolled over, opened her eyes, and saw Alexander. She gave him a drowsy smile and said, "Good morning, husband."

Alexander stared at her. His grim expression registered in her sleep-befuddled brain.

Victoria sat up and stared back at him. Her husband looked furious. She had no memory of him arriving at the Philbin house, but he must have been there because she was home in her own bed.

Her own bed. Not her husband's bed, where she always slept.

Was Alexander angry because he had discovered her embarrassing secret? Would he still want her now that he knew she was hopelessly stupid? Did he fear their baby would inherit her disability?

"Get dressed and come to my study," Alexander ordered.

"Are you angry because you've discovered my secret?" Victoria asked, her bottom lip trembling as she struggled against tears.

His right cheek muscle began twitching.

"I can't help what I am," Victoria said in her own defense.

His left cheek muscle began twitching.

"Bring your cloak and your reticule," Alexander said, turning to leave.

"Are we going out before breakfast?" she asked, confused.

"*You* are going out before breakfast," he answered, and stalked out of the chamber.

Her husband's behavior frightened Victoria. Was Alexander infuriated by her stupidity? Yes, she should have confessed it before the wedding, but he needn't fear being embarrassed by her. She hadn't told anyone about her need for reading lessons. No one but her aunt and her sisters knew of her handicap.

With a sigh, Victoria rose from the bed and dressed. As instructed, she grabbed her reticule and cloak. She had better get this interview over so they could make peace and resume their lives.

Victoria walked into the study and stopped short. Her male relations—Duke Magnus, Robert, and Rudolf—stood there. All three had censure stamped across their features.

"What is happening?" Victoria asked, giving her husband a confused smile.

Why had Alexander sent for her relations? What did he expect they could do about her problem?

"Your family has come to take you away," Alexander announced. "You are no longer welcome in my home."

Stunned, Victoria stumbled back. She felt as if he had kicked her stomach and knocked the breath from her body.

"You are making me leave my own home?" Victoria asked, her complexion a deathly white.

"*My* home," Alexander corrected her. "I am suing you for divorce, and if you have the sense of a flea, you will not contest it."

"Divorce me on what grounds—stupidity?" Victoria asked, her whole body trembling.

"Adultery."

Victoria gasped and, her hand flying to her breast, fell back two paces. She couldn't credit what he'd said.

"I never did *that*," she cried. "How could you think—?"

"I found you naked in another man's bed," Alexander said, cocking a brow at her. Then he turned away, adding, "I read your lover's note making the arrangements."

"*You* sent me a note to meet you at the Philbin house," Victoria said, grasping his forearm.

Alexander looked down at her hand and raised his gaze to hers. Victoria read the revulsion in his expression and dropped her trembling hand.

"You met your lover there," Alexander said. "You carry my child in your body, yet you willingly—" He broke off as if unable to speak the words.

"Listen to me," Victoria said.

"Enough!" Alexander shouted, cutting her words off.

"Please, Alex, I beg you to listen to me," Victoria pleaded, with tears streaming down her face. She dropped to her knees in front of him, sobbing, "Don't do this . . . I love you."

"Get her out of my sight," Alexander said to the others, though his voice cracked with emotion.

"What about the girls?" Victoria cried, clutching his legs.

"You, my lady, are unfit to be anyone's mother."

A shriek of unspeakable pain escaped Victoria, doubling her over, sending her brothers-in-law rushing forward. Prince Rudolf reached her first.

"Let me help you," the prince said, lifting her into his arms.

"Venetia is behind this," Robert said to the earl. "I told you—"

"My sister had nothing to do with my pregnant wife giving herself to another man," Alexander said. "You speak about Venetia as if she were Satan's handmaiden."

"Perhaps she is," Robert snapped, and walked out of the room.

"I intend to get to the bottom of this," Duke Magnus told the earl. "If Victoria is guilty, I'll lock her away on my estate until the day she dies. If not, I'll call you out myself." Then he quit the study.

"Emerson, you are a very great fool," Prince Rudolf said, and carried his weeping sister-in-law out of the room.

Hours later, Victoria lay on her bed in her old chamber at the duke's mansion on Park Lane. She had lost Alexander and the girls. All she had left was her unborn child.

Would the babe bring Alexander back to her? Or, at least, make him listen to her explanation?

Wearily, Victoria rose from the bed and donned her robe. She took the note she had received and the note she had written from her reticule. The time had come to face her uncle and her brothers-in-law. They were waiting for an explanation.

Victoria walked down one flight of stairs to her

uncle's office and took a deep, calming breath before knocking. For the first time in her life, she would reveal her stupidity to others. What she had tried to hide had brought her to this sorry moment.

Victoria knocked on the door and, hearing the duke's call, walked into his office. The prince rushed across the room and helped her to the chair in front of her uncle's desk.

Thankfully, Aunt Roxie sat there, too. Her aunt could verify her stupidity.

"Uncle, you must make Alexander listen to me," Victoria said, fresh tears welling up in her eyes. "I never did what he said."

"Alexander is too angry to listen. Perhaps when time passes, he will be thinking more clearly," Duke Magnus told her. "Why don't you tell me what happened?"

"I don't know what happened," she said, stifling a sob.

"Were you at the Philbin house?"

"Yes."

"Why did you go there?"

Victoria glanced at her aunt, who nodded at her to tell them everything. A sob escaped her at the thought of confessing what she had hidden her whole life. But what else could she do? She would rather lose her pride than her husband and stepdaughters.

"I went to the Philbin house because I am . . . *stupid,*" Victoria admitted, her voice barely louder than a whisper. "Aunt Roxie can verify this. I cannot read, write, or cipher very well. The letters and numbers get jumbled inside my head. I can't even tell left from right."

Victoria removed her shoes and held them up.

An *L* had been marked on the bottom of the left shoe.

"You see," Victoria said, "Angelica and Samantha mark my shoes for me. I felt ashamed to admit my problem to Alexander and wanted to improve myself before I told him. I begged the Philbin brothers to teach me secretly. Both brothers were there for each lesson except yesterday."

"I'm sorry, child. Revealing your problem must be difficult," Duke Magnus said. "However, your problem does not explain your nakedness in another man's bed."

"I received this note but couldn't read it," Victoria told him, passing it to him to peruse. "I asked Diana Drummond to read—"

"I knew Venetia was behind this," Robert said.

"Let Tory finish," Duke Magnus said to his son.

"I thought Alexander had somehow learned about my problem," Victoria continued, watching the duke pass the note to the marquess and the prince.

Victoria gave her uncle a second note. "I wrote this for Alexander while Barnaby made me tea."

She couldn't control a sob when the duke winced at her writing. Even worse, he handed the note to the prince and the marquess.

"Go on," the duke said.

"The tea made me drowsy," Victoria said. "Barnaby suggested I lie down in the next room, and he would call me when Alexander arrived. If you don't believe me, ask Barnaby."

"The Philbin brothers have left town," Duke Magnus told her.

Victoria wrapped her arms around her middle, hung her head in defeat, and wept. She had never felt more miserable in her life.

"Alexander will listen to reason once he calms," Duke Magnus assured her. "Besides, I have more influence than your husband. My friends at King's Bench could delay a divorce proceeding for months. I think I can persuade them to give us an informal hearing before they consider adultery charges. That would give you a chance to explain yourself to Alexander."

"Someone set a trap to make Tory appear unfaithful," Prince Rudolf said. "Apparently, Barnaby Philbin helped whoever it was."

"Venetia and her sister-in-law conspired against Tory," Robert said. "No one will ever convince me otherwise."

"The widow wants Alex for herself," Victoria said. "Venetia and she will use this time to poison my husband against me even more. What will happen if he won't listen or doesn't believe me?"

"I'm sorry, Tory, but I believe being prepared for the worst is wise," Duke Magnus warned her. "According to the law, your baby belongs to his father. No doubt, Alexander will take the baby away, and society will shun you for the rest of your life."

Victoria burst into tears again and needed her aunt to help her upstairs.

CHAPTER 13

There was a hole in her world where Alexander had stood.

Bereft of hope, Victoria passed the first miserable week in bed, unable to face the world or her empty existence. She alternated between sleeping, weeping, and wondering what her husband and stepdaughters were doing.

During the second week, Victoria roused herself enough to dress. She walked like a sleepwalker through lonely days, her mind traveling through space to journey from Park Lane to Grosvenor Square.

Several times she had almost asked Tinker, the majordomo, to read her the *Times* gossip column. Fear of learning her husband had Diana Drummond by his side had kept her from making the request.

On the fourteenth morning after being banished from her husband's life, Victoria decided to visit Alexander. Sufficient time had elapsed for him to calm himself. Her husband might be more amenable to listening to her explanation.

Victoria donned her black woollen cloak. After pulling the hood up to cover her red hair, she left her uncle's house.

The chill in the air announced the end of autumn and the beginning of winter. A brisk wind blew dead leaves across her path, and branches showed as stark silhouettes against a dark gray sky.

The gloominess of the November day drained the optimism out of her. The closer Victoria got to Grosvenor Square, the more pessimistic her outlook grew.

Was seeking out her husband the correct course of action? Perhaps she should wait until he asked for an explanation. If she waited, would he ever ask for one? Or would he divorce her and take her baby?

Alexander had never cared for her, after all. He only agreed to her aunt's proposed match to make up for Charles Emerson's crimes against her family.

Victoria stared at the mansion as she neared it. When she reached the front stairs, she lost her nerve and decided that appearing nervous would not help her credibility. Trying to calm herself, Victoria walked down the alley that bordered the rear garden.

And then she heard the sound of little girls giggling. Darcy, Fiona, and Aidan were playing in the garden.

The irresistible sound of their laughter drew Victoria like a magnet. She entered the garden through the rear gate and stood in silence watching them. The three nannies sat together on a stone bench and stared at her, apparently uncertain of what to do.

"Mama Tory," Darcy shrieked suddenly, and

dashed across the garden. Fiona and Aidan ran two steps behind her.

Victoria knelt to receive their hugs. She drew all three girls close within the circle of her arms.

"I missed you," Darcy said.

"I missed you, too," Victoria told her. "I missed all three of you."

"Where did you go?" Darcy asked.

"I'm staying with Aunt Roxie because she's been ill," Victoria lied.

"Will she die?" Fiona asked.

"No, Aunt Roxie will soon recover."

"I'm happy," Aidan whispered. "I love Aunt Roxie, but I love you more."

Again, Victoria clutched all three protectively to her breast. Wondering if she should enter the mansion by the garden door, Victoria raised her gaze to the window of her husband's study, and her heart sank to her stomach.

Diana Drummond stared down at her.

The garden door crashed open, drawing her attention. Wearing a grim expression, Alexander marched in her direction.

Victoria stood to face him and knew that coming here had been a mistake. She forced herself to smile, saying, "Alex, I—"

"Come, girls." Ignoring her, Alexander ushered the three little girls away from her. "Your nannies will take you inside for cider."

Her husband didn't want her near his daughters, Victoria realized, her heart breaking. She was carrying his child, and he acted as if she were a leper. He had treated his three former mistresses with more respect.

"Alex, you said a husband and wife belong to each other, no matter what," Victoria said, following him across the garden. "I must speak with you."

After his daughters disappeared inside, Alexander turned the full force of his displeasure on her. "You are trespassing on private property," he warned her. "The nannies will be instructed to take my daughters inside if you show yourself here again."

"Please, Alex, I beg you to listen to me," Victoria pleaded, beginning to weep.

"Speak to me through my barrister," Alexander said, and slammed the door in her face.

Stunned by his vehemence, Victoria stared at the door for a long time. Finally, she turned away, her shoulders slumped and her head bent, and left the garden.

Five excruciatingly long weeks passed. Five months pregnant, Victoria had begun to feel her baby's movement, especially at night when she lay in bed. Each time she felt that fluttering, the baby banished the loneliness from her heart for just a little while, and she wished her husband could share the moment with her.

Christmas Day, Victoria thought, peering out her bedchamber window at the dusting of new-fallen snow. She thought of her stepdaughters and wished she could see their excitement at the season's first snowflakes.

Though she despised attending church services, Victoria determined to attend that morning's service at Audley Chapel. She felt certain that Alexander would take the girls to the Christmas service.

Victoria promised herself that she would not approach them. In fact, she planned to arrive late and to sit in the back of the chapel to feast her eyes on her family.

An hour later, Victoria slipped into the chapel and sat in the last pew. Alexander and his daughters sat in the front of the chapel. With them were Harry, Venetia, and Diana.

Victoria noted the girls sat between Alexander and Diana like a real family would, only she had been replaced by the widow. Her heart ached at the sight. She should have been sitting there, not Diana Drummond.

The service neared its conclusion. Wanting to remain unseen, Victoria left the pew and stood in the shadows. Her bottom lip trembled as they passed by, and she heard Darcy saying, "I asked God to bring Mama Tory home."

"So did I," Fiona told her sister.

"Me, too," Aidan said.

Giving them a chance to climb into their coach, Victoria waited several long moments and then left the chapel. She pulled the hood of her fur-lined cloak up to cover her hair lest its brilliant color draw their attention.

Too late.

"Mama Tory," Darcy cried, and dashed toward her.

Alexander caught Darcy, lifted her into his arms, and put her in the coach. Then he turned around and walked toward her.

Victoria stood her ground.

"Why are you here?" Alexander demanded.

"I wanted to see you again," Victoria answered. "And the girls, too. I never intended them to see me."

"Why would you want to see me?" he asked.

"I love you," she told him, her blue gaze fixed on his.

Alexander seemed to falter. He hesitated, his expression softening.

"Alex, are you coming?" Diana Drummond called.

Victoria tipped her head in the direction of the coach. "Is Diana my replacement?"

Alexander shrugged. "Perhaps."

"The girls are cold," the widow called, drawing his attention.

Victoria saw Alexander visibly steel himself against her, his expression hardening. "Stay away from my family," he ordered.

"Merry Christmas, Alex," Victoria said, her vision blurred by tears, her voice aching with raw pain. She turned and started walking down the street.

"Victoria."

She turned around.

"Where is your coach?" he asked.

"I walked from Park Lane."

"Your aunt allowed you to walk here in the cold in your condition?" Alexander asked in obvious surprise.

"My aunt and uncle are passing the holidays in the country," Victoria said.

Alexander snapped his brows together. "What about your sisters?"

"My sisters and their families are with my aunt and uncle," Victoria answered.

"You're alone today?"

"I'm alone every day."

"Why did you remain alone in the city for Christmas?" Alexander asked.

"I told you, I wanted to see you again." Victoria gave him a wobbly smile and said, "Goodbye, Alex." At that, she walked in the direction of Park Lane.

Weeks slipped by. The cold days of winter kept

Victoria inside, giving her hours of quiet contemplation. The lengthening days of January drew to a close, and the gray skies of February arrived.

Victoria prayed that her uncle could persuade his contacts at King's Bench to insist on an informal hearing before they accepted her husband's divorce petition.

If he won his divorce, Alexander would demand custody of their baby, and Victoria had no intention of parting with her child. She would run away if need be. Depriving her child of his father would sadden her, but depriving her baby of his mother is what her husband planned.

Almost two months after Christmas, a seven-month-pregnant Victoria stood in front of the cheval mirror in her bedchamber. Her high-waisted, black velvet gown pulled tightly across her belly.

Victoria decided she didn't look too misshapen. And then she turned for the side view and grimaced.

Reluctantly, Victoria had surrendered to her sister's and brother-in-law's nagging to get out of the house. Both believed she needed a change of scene, if only for an evening.

Victoria would never have agreed to the opera on a Thursday, but they had asked her for a Wednesday evening performance and refused to take *no* for an answer.

"Don't worry," Samantha whispered, on the ride to the opera house.

"Relax and enjoy yourself," Prince Rudolf added.

Victoria harbored misgivings about attending the opera, and the first—becoming a spectacle—seemed to come true the moment she entered the crowded lobby. She felt society's disapproving gazes upon her and wished she had remained home.

Aplomb. Victoria recalled her aunt's advice. She

lifted her chin, squared her shoulders, and walked through the lobby with her head held high.

Apparently, all of society knew her husband was divorcing her on grounds of adultery. She should have known Venetia and Diana would act quickly to discredit her.

Walking between her sister and brother-in-law, Victoria reached the base of the stairs that led to the balcony boxes when a familiar voice said, "The Douglas slut is bolder than brass to show her face in polite society."

Miriam Wilmington, Victoria thought without turning her head.

"Poor Emerson, I heard the brat belongs to her lover," another woman replied.

Victoria stiffened at the slur on her baby. She could suffer the poisonous arrows of gossip, but her baby was another matter.

"Keep walking," Rudolf whispered, leaning close.

"Your condition precludes bashing her brainless head," Samantha said, making her smile.

Victoria nodded and climbed the stairs. Entering the prince's opera box, she sensed people turning to stare at her and felt like crawling under the chair to hide. Instead, she stared without seeing at the stage's closed curtain.

"Oh, dear," her sister murmured.

"Damn," her brother-in-law muttered.

Victoria followed their gazes to the opera box on the right, her husband's, and her stomach flip-flopped from surprise. Alexander, Diana, Venetia, and Harry had just entered the opera box and sat down.

"Diana is wearing my husband's wedding gift to me," Victoria whispered to her sister.

"Bastard," Samantha swore.

"What did you say?" Rudolf asked his wife in obvious surprise.

"Baskets," Samantha lied, making her sister smile.

Rudolf gave Victoria's hand an encouraging squeeze. "I'm sorry, Tory, but leaving now would be worse than staying."

Victoria inclined her head, but her bottom lip quivered from her struggle to keep from weeping. God, she wished she was anywhere else but here.

Pretending that Alexander and his new lover weren't sitting only a few feet away proved impossible. Victoria couldn't keep from glancing in their direction, but each time she did, she saw her husband's gaze on her.

Thankfully, the opera began, but Victoria still felt the cold stares of the opera-goers. And Alexander. Which, she supposed, was better than remembering the tender, loving moments she and her husband had shared at the opera.

She only needed to survive until intermission. No one would notice if she left during the second act.

Victoria wondered idly why society accepted her husband's obvious moral transgressions while they crucified her because of gossip. Lord, but she wished she lived in the old cottage. Her only worry then was where her next meal was coming from.

The curtain closed on the stage, signaling intermission, a time when society socialized. The object in attending the opera was to see and to be seen. Only a few, like her husband, attended because they loved the opera.

Feeling a presence in the opera box, Victoria turned to see Lord Russell who started to talk business with Rudolf. Lydia Stanley was with him. This was all she needed to complete her miserable evening.

"Good evening, Princess Samantha," Lydia Stanley greeted her sister. "How fares your family?"

"The children enjoy excellent health," Samantha answered, her smile polite but not overly warm. "You remember my sister, Victoria?"

Lydia Stanley looked at Victoria as if she was a replusive bug. Turning her back on Victoria, she said, "Excuse me, Princess, I see some friends with whom I must speak." The voluptuous beauty looked directly at Alexander and smiled before leaving the opera box.

Victoria paled. She had just received the cut direct from one of her husband's former lovers.

Making her public humiliation even worse, someone watching from a nearby opera box applauded Lydia Stanley's performance and said in a loud voice, "Bravo." Venetia and Diana burst out laughing as did several other opera-goers.

Victoria looked directly at her husband, her gaze fixed on his, accusing him as the source of this humiliation. Alexander appeared stricken, but Victoria could feel no sympathy for his regret. He had encouraged the spread of gossip about the mother of his unborn child and inadvertently cast a shadow over his own son's paternity. She would never forgive him for that.

"I appreciate your efforts to cheer me," Victoria said, rising from her chair. "I cannot remain here."

"I'll escort you to the coach," Prince Rudolf said, his expression grim.

"I would prefer to leave alone," Victoria said, gesturing for him to sit. With her head held high, she left the opera box and started down the corridor.

"Victoria."

Halting at the sound of her husband's voice, Victoria watched him advancing toward her. She didn't feel strong enough at the moment to withstand his anger, but as pregnant as she was, bolting down the stairs was not an option.

"I'm sorry, Tory," Alexander said, surprising her with his apology.

Victoria arched a copper brow at him. "Are you?"

Alexander nodded and then spoiled his apology by saying, "You should have known better than to attend a social event."

"Thank you for enlightening me about that," Victoria replied, and started to brush past him.

"I'll escort you to your coach," Alexander said, reaching for her hand.

"I can find my own way out," Victoria said, snatching her hand back, noting the surprise registering on his face as she did so. "You had better return to your seat. Diana will be wondering why you deserted her."

"You are carrying my child, Tory," Alexander said, dropping his gaze to the mound of her belly. He gestured toward the stairs but refrained from reaching for her hand again. "I *insist* on escorting you to your coach."

Victoria inclined her head. In silence, they descended the stairs to the lobby. Those members of the *ton* who still milled about cast curious gazes in their direction.

Outside the theater, Alexander called for his own coach to be brought around. "I received notice from King's Bench," he said while they waited. "They have scheduled an informal hearing for the first of April."

"Yes, I know." Victoria slanted a glance at him and asked, "How are the girls?"

"The girls are well," Alexander said. An expression of hesitation crossed his face and then he added, "The girls miss you, of course. In spite of our troubles, I want you to know that I am grateful for your bringing them into my home."

Victoria swallowed the lump of emotion rising in her throat. "Does Diana love them?"

"Not especially," Alexander answered, drawing her attention. He smiled, adding, "The girls dislike Venetia and Diana, who never play with them like you did."

His coach halting in front of the theater saved Victoria from replying. Alexander opened the door, helped her climb inside, and then called instructions to his driver.

"Victoria—"

Whatever he intended to say was lost as the coach moved into the road. Victoria stared straight ahead, willing herself to suppress the urge to look back and catch a final glimpse of the man she loved.

Winter bowed to spring, and February faded into March. Soon, March waned toward April.

Victoria had refused to leave the house since the evening at the opera. She waited for her husband to visit and to listen to her explanation, but he never appeared. Victoria persuaded herself to try again and, possibly, save themselves from a humiliating hearing on the first day of April.

Her marriage had been damaged beyond repair, but she wanted her husband to know that she had never been unfaithful. Perhaps, if he believed her, Alexander would allow her custody of their child. She would retire to her uncle's country estate, and Alexander could enjoy generous visitation rights. Perhaps he would let her renew her relationship with his daughters.

Getting into the Grosvenor Square mansion

without Venetia's and Diana's presence was difficult. She needed to pick her time carefully. When Alexander was dressing for the opera seemed best because Venetia and Diana would be home dressing for the opera, too.

The Thursday before the hearing dawned bone-chillingly wet. Wearing her black woolen cloak, Victoria pulled its hood up and slipped out of the house.

With her more-than-eight-months-pregnant belly leading the way, Victoria felt like a ship sailing down the street. Thankfully, the inclement weather kept people indoors.

Victoria felt optimistic that her husband would finally give her the opportunity to explain what had happened all those long months ago. She had grown even larger since that night at the opera. How could he be cruel to the woman who swelled with his child?

Victoria climbed the front stairs of the Grosvenor Square mansion. The front door opened before she could knock.

"Welcome home, my lady," Bundles greeted her, wearing a broad smile. "His Lordship is upstairs dressing for the opera."

"Thank you, Bundles." Victoria removed her wet cloak and passed it to him. Victoria waddled across the foyer and climbed the stairs to the third-floor bedchamber. She hadn't been inside the house since the previous November. If she had only known last autumn how futile those reading lessons would be, she could have saved herself a great deal of heartache.

Victoria hesitated outside her husband's bedchamber door. Her old friend insecurity stepped from the shadows of her mind, making her heartbeat quicken.

Without knocking, Victoria opened the door silently and stepped inside. Alexander stood with his back to her and was tying his cravat. Her heart ached at the familiar sight of him dressing for the opera.

Victoria was about to make her presence known when the connecting door to her old bedchamber opened. The widow walked into the room.

"Alex, darling, are we going to the Websters' ball after the opera?" Diana asked, fastening the diamond collar around her neck.

Victoria stood frozen in shock. Her husband was divorcing her for alleged adultery but had his whore ensconced in the bedchamber reserved for his countess.

Turning toward the widow, Alexander saw Victoria standing there. His gaze dropped to her enormously distended belly.

"How could you do this?" she asked brokenly.

Without waiting for a reply, Victoria ran from the bedchamber and hurried, as best as her bulk would allow, down the stairs to the foyer. She heard her husband calling her name but didn't pause in her flight.

"Give these to the earl for my replacement," Victoria said, dropping her betrothal and wedding rings into the majordomo's hand. Without breaking stride, she flew out the front door and hurried in the direction of Park Lane. Raindrops mingled with teardrops on her cheeks.

A moment later, Alexander bounded down the stairs to find his majordomo holding a cloak and staring stupidly at the open front door.

"Where is my wife?" Alexander demanded.

"She left, my lord," Bundles answered.

"Without her cloak?"

"Without her cloak and without a coach."

"Do you mean my pregnant wife walked here in the rain?" Alexander asked, looking in surprise at the older man.

"Apparently."

"Has she left?" Diana Drummond asked, walking down the stairs to the foyer, her smile decidedly feline. "You won't need to go through the trouble of divorcing her if she catches a chill."

Alexander snapped his gaze to the widow. If she hadn't detained him, he would have caught his wife before she escaped out the door. For months, he had wanted to visit his wife at Park Lane and listen to what she had to say, but his pride had kept him at Grosvenor Square. Instead, he had waited for her to approach him. He knew one thing for sure; his wife would not come to see him again.

"Lady Victoria asked me to give you these for her replacement," Bundles said, passing him the rings.

Alexander stared at the wedding and betrothal rings he had given Victoria. Unspeakable loss surged through him, depleting him of hope.

"Shame on you," Bundles said in a scathing voice, drawing his attention. "Find yourself another majordomo—*I quit.*"

CHAPTER 14

"Are certain you want to go through with this?" Duke Magnus asked, his dark gaze on her.

"I refuse to admit guilt for something I didn't do," Victoria answered, meeting his gaze across the coach. "If Alexander wants Diana Drummond, he'll need to find another way."

"Good for you," Robert said, sitting beside his father.

"Be strong, Tory," Prince Rudolf said, beside her.

The first day of April had come quickly, Victoria thought. For five months, the moments had seemed like hours and the hours like days. And then, suddenly, she had awakened on the morning of the hearing.

"Where is Mr. Howell?" Victoria asked.

"Percy will meet us at court," Duke Magnus answered.

A few minutes later, the ducal coach halted in front of the Old Bailey Sessions House. A noisy crowd loitered outside the building.

"Who are those people?" Victoria asked, her

panic level rising at the thought of making her way through the crush.

"Though the hearing is informal," Duke Magnus answered, "the rabble wants to see a countess accused of adultery."

"The sins of the wealthy sell newspapers," Robert said.

"We will protect you," Rudolf promised, giving her hand an encouraging squeeze.

The driver appeared and opened the coach door. Duke Magnus climbed down first and then Robert. Rudolf alighted next and turned to assist Victoria.

"That's her," someone in the crowd called.

"Douglas slut," shouted another.

Victoria shrank back in fright. Rudolf put his arm around her and drew her forward.

"Whore!"

Victoria cried out as a stone hit her cheek. Robert yanked the hood of her cloak up to shield her face from view. Rudolf and he huddled around her protectively as Duke Magnus cleared a path through the angry throng.

Victoria shook visibly by the time they reached the safety of the courthouse. Without taking his supporting arm away from her, Rudolf examined her cheek.

"You will live," the prince said. "We will need to wipe the blood."

"Let's get her inside the courtroom first," Percy Howell said. "Being pregnant and stoned by an angry mob will win her instant sympathy."

"Excellent idea," the duke agreed.

Entering the courtroom, Rudolf and Robert ushered her to the tables at the front. Victoria saw Alexander and his barrister, Charles Burrows, on the opposite side of the aisle. Sitting in the gallery behind her husband's table were Venetia, Diana, and Harry.

Victoria ignored them and slowly lowered her bulk into a chair. Rudolf dipped his handkerchief in a glass of water and wiped the blood off her cheek, making her wince. Then he folded it and placed it on her face again.

"Hold it there to reduce the bruising," Rudolf instructed her.

Victoria kept her eyes downcast while she held the cloth against her cheek. She didn't want to see her husband, knowing that today was the first step toward dissolution of their marriage. Victoria harbored no illusions about the outcome of the hearing. If her husband wanted to be rid of her, the judges would find in his favor.

"If this is informal," Duke Magnus was asking the barrister, "why are there so many spectators?"

"Informal does not mean private, Your Grace," Percy Howell answered. "Dozens of the curious, as well as reporters looking for the big story, fill the gallery."

Victoria cringed inwardly at the thought of revealing her stupidity to the crowded courtroom. She had no choice, though. She was either stupid or an adulteress.

"*What happened?*" The voice belonged to her husband.

"The crowd outside stoned her for being an adulteress," Rudolf answered.

"Tory, I am sorry," Alexander apologized.

Victoria refused to look at him. Without speaking, she turned her body away.

"Why pretend what you don't feel?" Robert said, challenging his sincerity. "You hired people to incite that crowd to violence."

"I had nothing to do with that," Alexander defended himself.

"Oh, then I see the fine work of Satan's handmaiden and her charming sister-in-law, the black widow," Robert shot back.

"Venetia and Diana would never—"

"Go back where you belong," Victoria cried, refusing to listen to his defense of the two who had destroyed her. "I should have known Charles Emerson's son would hurt a Douglas."

"We should never have married," Alexander said, his expression grim.

"That is the first correct statement you've made in five months," Victoria told him. "When you learn the real truth today, do *not* come near me. I will never forgive you for this."

"I doubt I'll be apologizing at the end of this day," Alexander said.

"You will beg for my forgiveness the way I begged you to listen to me," Victoria said, her voice cracking with emotion.

"Alex, Victoria is more than eight months pregnant," Duke Magnus reminded the earl. "Refrain from upsetting her more than you already have."

Alexander returned to his own table. He sat down, but Victoria felt his gaze upon her.

"Let me take your cloak," Rudolf said. Then he smiled, adding, "A virginal white gown tight across your enormous belly . . . an excellent choice of apparel."

"Aunt Roxie thought the Madonna look would suit," Victoria said, a little smile playing over her lips.

"All rise," the bailiff called.

Everyone stood when the three judges entered and took their seats. The one in the middle seemed to be in charge.

"The barristers will approach the bench," the Chief Justice ordered. "This is an informal hearing, *not* a trial. Both of you will conduct yourselves appropriately. Mr. Burrows, present your client's evidence."

"I call Alexander Emerson, the Earl of Winchester," Burrows said.

Alexander rose and crossed the courtroom. Then he took his place, standing inside the witness box.

"My lord, please tell the court the events of the evening in question," Burrows said.

"I arrived home from White's sometime after five o'clock," Alexander said in a clear, strong voice. "My sister and her sister-in-law happened to be in my library. When I asked the whereabouts of my wife, my sister told me the countess had gone out after receiving a note by courier."

"Here is the note, my lords," Burrows said, passing the parchment to the judges. "My client prefers not to have it read out loud since it would cause the gentleman in question a great deal of embarrassment. As you said, this is not a divorce trial. Yet."

The Chief Justice looked at Percy Howell and asked, "Do you wish to see this?"

"No, thank you, my lord," Howell answered, drawing surprised looks from everyone except the family he represented.

"Are you certain?" the Chief Justice asked.

"My lord, that note has no bearing on the truth of what transpired that night," Howell answered.

An audible ripple of excitement raced through the spectators in the gallery.

"Are you implying the note is a fraud manufactured by my client?" Burrows demanded.

"No, Mr. Burrows." Howell smiled at his colleague. "We contend that the note is a fraud manufactured by a third party."

"Please, continue," the Chief Justice said to the earl.

"I immediately went to the Philbin house as the note said," Alexander went on. "The door was unlocked so I went inside. I found my wife naked and asleep on a daybed. I tried to awaken her, but she was quite drunk."

Titillated murmurs raced through the crowd of spectators.

Embarrassed, Victoria dropped her gaze to the mound of her belly. Her husband had just ripped her reputation to shreds. Again.

"Do you claim her baby as yours?" Burrows asked.

"Oh, God," Victoria gasped in surprise, drawing her husband's attention. Her complexion paled and her head spun dizzingly.

"I acknowledge the baby is mine," Alexander said. "Victoria became pregnant within a relatively short period after the wedding."

"What a pity such a good breeder proves unfaithful," Burrows said, shaking his head.

"My lords," Percy Howell called, rising from his chair.

"Burrows, stifle the editorial comment," the Chief Justice reprimanded the barrister.

"I apologize, my lord," Burrows said. "No further questions."

The Chief Justice gestured to Percy Howell. The barrister walked toward the witness box.

"I am pleased to meet the man about whom I've been hearing so much," Howell said, his smile affable.

"I am pleased that my in-laws hold me in esteem," Alexander replied, making all but his in-laws smile.

"Quite so. My lord, I and my client have no reason to disbelieve what you have stated except, of course, her alleged drunkenness," Percy Howell said. "We contend that you are ignorant of the whole truth." The barrister paused for a moment. "I need to ask you a few questions of a personal nature."

"I have nothing to hide," Alexander said, looking perfectly relaxed.

"My lords, I object," Burrows called, rising from his chair. "My learned colleague cannot ask—"

"Burrows, sit down," the Chief Justice interrupted. "This is an informal hearing, not a trial. Continue, Mr. Howell."

"Thank you, my lord." Howell looked at the earl and said, "Describe in a few words your relationship with your sister."

"Until recently, we've always been at odds," Alexander said. "We've become close since she returned from Australia with her husband and her sister-in-law."

"How would you describe the relationship between your sister and her sister-in-law?" Howell asked.

Rudolf leaned close to Victoria and whispered, "Partners in crime." Then, "I knew I could make you smile."

"Venetia and Diana are the best of friends," Alexander was saying.

"Friendly enough to want her sister-in-law to become a countess?" Howell asked.

"If you are implying—"

"I imply nothing," Howell interrupted. "I ask merely for your opinion."

"In that case, I would guess that Venetia wishes the best for her sister-in-law," Alexander answered.

"Why did you marry Victoria Douglas?"

Victoria raised her gaze to her husband, who glanced in her direction. The words he spoke, though wholly truthful, brought tears to her eyes and heartache to her breast.

"The Duchess of Inverary, her aunt, proposed the match," Alexander answered. "I accepted in order to make amends for my late father's transgressions against the Douglas family."

"This was no love match?" Howell asked, and tears rolled slowly down his client's cheeks.

Alexander hesitated and glanced at Victoria. "We did not marry for love. There was no love."

"Do you speak for yourself or do you include Lady Emerson in the pronouncement?" Howell asked.

"I wouldn't presume to speak for Lady Emerson," Alexander replied.

"There is a history of bad blood between the Emersons and the Douglases, which you sought to correct?"

"Yes."

"Who are the three girls in residence with you?" Howell asked.

Victoria dropped her gaze. She had specifically asked the barrister not to mention the girls. There was no good reason they should be hurt, too.

"The girls are my daughters by my former mistresses," Alexander answered.

"How old are they?"

"Five."

Howell grinned. "Three five-year-old daughters by three mistresses?"

"Yes."

"Gawd, if he ain't a struttin' cock," called one of the spectators, drawing ribald laughter.

The Chief Justice banged the gavel.

"How did your daughters come to live with you?" Howell asked.

"Their mothers abandoned them in my foyer," Alexander answered.

"Before or after you married Victoria Douglas?"

"After."

"Did you ever wonder why three mothers would abandon their daughters?" Howell asked.

"I assumed someone paid them in order to cause trouble between me and my wife," Alexander said.

"And did it cause trouble?"

Surprising Victoria, Alexander looked at her and smiled. "My bride welcomed the girls into our home and her heart. Victoria insisted the girls remain with us permanently."

"Very commendable of Lady Emerson, wouldn't you say?"

Alexander glanced in her direction again. "Yes, I would say that."

"By the way, did your sister return from Australia before or after you married Lady Emerson?" Percy Howell asked.

"I believe it was a couple of weeks before the wedding," Alexander answered.

"So the marriage contract had been signed and the wedding plans finalized?" Howell asked.

"Yes."

"And when did the first daughter arrive at your home?"

"I can't remember exactly," Alexander said. "Perhaps, two or three weeks after Victoria and I married."

"Thank you, my lord." Percy Howell turned to the judges and said, "No further questions, my lords."

"Mr. Burrows?" the Chief Justice asked.

"No more witnesses," the barrister answered.

"Mr. Howell, you may present your client's evidence," the Chief Justice said.

"I call to the witness box Victoria Emerson, the Countess of Winchester," Percy Howell said.

A collective gasp shot through the crowded courtroom. Silence followed, all gazes focusing on the young woman rising from her chair.

Victoria felt every gaze on her. With the prince's help, she rose from her chair and, one hand on the mound of her belly, moved toward the witness box.

Her virginal white, highwaisted gown accentuated her youth, but her face was pale and drawn. Dark smudges of fatigue lay beneath her eyes. So many months of heartbreak and worry had taken their toll.

"My lords, I beg a chair for Lady Emerson," Percy Howell said.

"Yes, of course." The Chief Justice gestured to the bailiff who set a chair in the witness box.

"Lady Emerson, I want you to relax," Percy Howell said. With a smile, he added, "We prefer to finish these proceedings today and *not* wait for you to recover from childbirth."

Victoria blushed and gave him a wobbly smile. She didn't know what to do with her hands, though, and felt that everyone could see them shaking.

"Lady Emerson, please tell the court how you know the Philbin brothers," Howell said.

"Phineas and Barnaby tutor my nieces and nephews," Victoria answered, her gaze downcast.

"Other than that, what is your association with them?" Howell asked.

Victoria raised her gaze to her barrister and

took a deep breath. Her moment of truth had arrived.

"The Philbin brothers tutor me." Victoria glanced at her husband, who stared at her with an expression of curious disbelief.

"When, how, and why did you hire tutors for yourself?"

"Last June, before I married the earl, I visited the Philbin brothers and asked them to tutor me," Victoria said. "They accepted my offer and stipulation."

"What stipulation?"

"I wanted no one to know they were tutoring me," Victoria said. "We met on Thursday afternoons because both could be present. Being alone with only one would have been improper."

Her statement elicited chuckles from the spectators. Victoria cast a nervous glance toward the gallery and then focused on her barrister.

Percy Howell cocked his head to one side. "Why didn't you want anyone to know?"

"My—*inability*—embarrassed me," Victoria said, choosing her words carefully. "I wanted to improve myself for the earl so—"

"What is your inability?" Howell snapped, startling her.

Victoria remained silent for several long moments. The signs of her inner struggle played across her lovely, care-worn face.

"What is your inability?" Howell repeated, a hard edge to his voice.

"I am *stupid,*" Victoria exclaimed, and burst into tears.

The spectators in the gallery laughed, which added to her humiliation. She couldn't bring herself to peek at her husband.

"In what way, specifically, are you stupid?" Howell asked in a gentler tone, offering her a handkerchief.

Victoria accepted the handkerchief and wiped the tears from her cheeks. "I cannot read. Letters and numbers become jumbled in my mind," she answered. "You see a *b*, but I see a *d*. *P's* become *q's*, *was* becomes *saw*, *sixes* become *nines* . . . I can't even tell left from right.

"My aunt and my sisters tried to teach me many times, but I could never learn. Finally, I stopped trying . . . until the earl and I became betrothed." She looked directly at Alexander as if speaking directly to him. "I didn't want him to know I was stupid because I feared he wouldn't marry a stupid woman. I did so want to marry him."

"How long have you suffered with this?" Howell asked.

Victoria lifted her chin a notch. "I've been stupid my whole life and—"

The spectators erupted into loud guffaws of laughter. The Chief Justice banged his gavel for order.

Victoria peeked at Alexander. He was smiling at her.

"And?" Percy Howell asked, when the courtroom quieted.

"And I expect to die stupid," she finished.

Another eruption of laughter resounded in the gallery. Victoria glanced at the judges, who were smiling, and her husband, who was still smiling. Even her relations were smiling.

"How did you travel from Grosvenor Square to the Philbin house?" Howell asked.

"I walked."

"Why didn't you take a carriage?"

"If I did that, the driver would have told the

earl," Victoria answered. "Then I would have had to tell the earl about my stupidity."

Muffled chuckles sounded in the gallery.

"Did you try to sneak in any way?" Percy Howell asked.

"I walked out the front door," Victoria said. "When I reached the bottom of the stairs, I turned left—no, right—left, I think . . . I can't remember which way I turned. Thinking about left and right gives me a headache."

The chuckles from the gallery were not quite so muffled this time.

"You walked *openly* from your home in Grosvenor Square to the Philbin house?" Howell said.

Victoria nodded. "Precisely."

"My lords, counsel is leading the witness," Burrows complained, rising from his chair.

"Burrows, sit down and be quiet," the Chief Justice ordered.

Percy Howell continued, "So, if someone wished to know where you went every Thursday, that person could have you followed and find out?"

"Yes, I suppose."

"Did the Philbins help you?"

"Phineas and Barnaby gave me strategies to cope with my problem and praised my enthusiasm," Victoria said, "but I suspect I was the least capable student they'd ever tutored."

"Then, the strategies did not help?"

"I practiced transposing letters two hours each day but only managed to give myself a headache," Victoria said, her tone mirroring the defeat she had felt.

"You said you cannot tell left from right?"

Victoria nodded. "My sisters mark the bottom of

my left shoes with an *L* so I'll know which shoe matches which foot."

Pockets of laughter sounded from the gallery again.

"Lady Emerson, kindly show the court the bottom of your shoes," Percy Howell said.

"I'm sorry," Victoria said, blushing. "I cannot reach or see my feet anymore."

More laughter sounded from the gallery. This laughter was more amused than derisive as if the spectators were warming to her.

"Since you're still married to the earl," Howell said, "would you mind if he stepped forward to remove your shoes?"

"That will be unnecessary," the Chief Justice said. "We'll accept the countess's word."

"Thank you, my lord." Howell turned to Victoria, asking, "How did you pay for tutoring?"

"I spent the pin money my husband gave me each month."

"Wouldn't you have preferred buying ribbons or such for yourself?"

"I needed to read more than I needed ribbons," Victoria answered.

"Why?" Howell asked.

"I wanted to read my children a bedtime story," Victoria cried. "I didn't want them to read one to me. And—"

Laughter interrupted her.

"And?"

"And I was tired of lying."

"Explain what you mean by *lying,*" Percy Howell said.

"I always told people that I forgot my spectacles or misplaced my spectacles or broke my spectacles," Victoria answered. "I don't own spectacles because there is nothing wrong with my eyesight, only my brain."

"Lady Emerson, kindly tell the court what happened on the night in question," Howell said.

"Alex—I mean, the earl—had gone to White's and left me to deal with his sister and her sister-in-law," Victoria began.

"You are not in accord with your in-laws?"

"Venetia despises me," she answered, "and I whole-heartedly return the feeling."

"Please continue."

"Venetia and Diana had supposedly come to browse in the library," Victoria went on. "They'd only been there a few minutes when Mister Bundles brought me a note that had been delivered."

"One moment, my lady." Percy Howell walked back to the table, lifted the parchment, and held it up. "My lords, this is the note Lady Emerson received. With your permission, I'll read it."

The Chief Justice nodded.

Percy Howell read aloud: "Tory, Meet me at the Philbin brothers' house at five o'clock. Alex." The barrister handed it to the judges.

"If you cannot read," Howell said, "then you had no idea this wasn't your husband's handwriting?"

"Correct."

"Well, how did you know the contents of the note?"

"Diana Drummond asked why I didn't read the note," Victoria answered. "I told her I'd lost my spectacles and would wait for the earl to return. Then"—her voice cracked with emotion—"I asked Diana if she would read it to me, which she did."

Victoria watched Alexander turn around to look at Diana Drummond. The widow shook her head in denial and said, "She's lying."

"What did you do next?" Percy Howell asked.

"I made my excuses and left the house," Victoria said, wondering whom her husband believed—her or the widow. "Bundles wasn't in the foyer when I came downstairs so I walked to the Philbins."

"Which way did ya turn?" someone yelled from the gallery. Laughter followed.

Victoria covered her face with her hands and began to weep. This was how the remainder of her life would be. Soon people would be calling her the "stupid adulteress". She heard the judge banging his gavel, and then all grew quiet.

"Lady Emerson, can you continue?" Percy Howell asked. When she nodded, he said, "Tell the court what happened at the Philbins."

"Phineas wasn't there. Barnaby made me tea, which I drank while writing my husband a note, which I intended to give him for Christmas," Victoria answered. "When the tea made me drowsy, Barnaby suggested I rest on the daybed in the next room until the earl arrived. I fell asleep and have no other memory until the earl awakened me the next morning."

Percy Howell walked to the table, lifted a parchment, and said to the Chief Justice, "My lord, this is the note Lady Emerson wrote her husband that night." The barrister crossed the courtroom and handed the note to the Chief Justice.

The three judges read the note. Their expressions registered surprise, and Victoria knew her stupidity astonished them.

"Lady Emerson, I believe you should read this out loud," the Chief Justice said, passing her the note.

Using her finger to point to each word, Victoria read in a halting voice and pronounced each syllable as if it was a separate word:

No-vim-deer 2, 1814. Mi Beer-est Lorb, the Erl of Winb-chess-tear, Mi bar-ling hus-danb. A-lix. I love U va-re moch. Wit hole hart and sol. A-lot. Ma-re Kriz-mas. Yor bee-vo-teb wif wit chil, Vic-to-ri-a, Cun-tess of Winb-chess-tear.

"Child, that is a beautiful note," the Chief Justice praised her. "However, the next time you write your title, add an *O* to countess."

Boisterous laughter echoed within the court-room. Victoria had no idea what was so funny. She glanced in her husband's direction and saw him watching her, a smile playing across his handsome features.

When the laughter ceased, Victoria turned to the Chief Justice and asked, "My lord, where shall I put the *O?*"

Again, the courtroom erupted into laughter.

"Put the *O* after the *C,*" the Chief Justice said.

"Thank you, my lord."

"You are very welcome," the Chief Justice said, passing the note to the bailiff. "I am certain the earl will wish to read this."

Worrying her bottom lip with her teeth, Victoria watched the bailiff cross the courtroom and hand her husband the note. He took several, excruciatingly long moments to peruse the note and then looked up at her.

Even from this distance, Victoria saw the tears rolling down his face. Her stupidity made him weep. Did he fear his son would be born with the same affliction? She worried about that, too.

"What do you think caused the events of that evening?" Percy Howell asked her.

"I *know* what caused the events of that night," Victoria told the court. "The Philbin brothers wrote my uncle a letter that explained everything. An anonymous woman bribed Barnaby, a gambler in debt, into putting sleeping herbs into my tea. Then Barnaby undressed me and left me there for my husband to find."

"My lords, where is this letter?" Burrows called. "Why aren't the Philbins here?"

"The Philbins are in hiding because they fear for their lives," Percy Howell answered. "If there is a divorce trial, they will testify. The letter is in a safe place in the event of a trial."

"How convenient," Burrows drawled.

"Lady Emerson, why didn't you tell the earl all of this?" Howell asked.

"My husband refused to listen to me."

"Did you ever try to speak to the earl between last November and today?"

"I tried twice," Victoria answered. She gave her husband a long look and said, "The first time the earl slammed the door in my face, and the second time—last week—I found the earl in his bed-chamber with Diana Drummond."

Chaos erupted in the courtroom. It seemed to Victoria that everyone was talking at the same time while the Chief Justice hammered the bench with his gavel like a shoemaker at work.

Victoria glanced toward her husband, who appeared irritated, and then beyond. Diana Drummond's face was bright red. Now the widow would also know how a tattered reputation felt. She hoped someone at the opera would give her the cut direct.

"Lady Emerson, were you ever unfaithful to the earl?" Percy Howell asked, when the courtroom quieted.

"No, I was not."

"You knew appearing at today's hearing would be a public humiliation, but you chose to come and tell your story," Percy Howell said. "Why?"

"I never committed adultery," Victoria answered. "I wanted to explain to the earl what had happened and"—she closed her eyes—"I love my husband."

"You love the earl in spite of the heartache he has caused you?" Howell asked.

"Yes."

"So, you feel the damage to your marriage can be repaired?"

"My marriage to the earl is beyond repair," Victoria answered, looking straight at her husband, "but he will not divorce me for something I did not do. If he desires the widow, my husband will need to find another way to get to her."

Howell looked at the Chief Justice. "No further questions, my lords."

Victoria rose unsteadily from the chair. She turned to step out of the witness box, but Mr. Burrows's voice stopped her.

"You're not going anywhere, my *lady*," Burrows said, placing sarcastic emphasis on the word *lady*.

Victoria looked at him in confusion. "I don't go home now?"

"Gawd, she *is* stupid," yelled a spectator from the gallery, making everyone laugh.

"Lady Emerson, the earl's barrister gets a chance to ask you questions," the Chief Justice said in a kind voice.

"Oh." Victoria sat down again.

"Lady Emerson, were you a virgin on your wedding night?" Burrows asked.

A lawyer's trick, Victoria thought. Technically, she hadn't been a virgin because she had already given herself to her husband.

"My wife was a virgin when she came to my bed," Alexander called out. "Ask her another question."

Everyone in the courtroom, including Victoria, looked in surprise at the earl. Her estranged husband was defending her against his own barrister?

"Why did you marry the earl?" Burrows asked.

"As the earl testified, my aunt arranged the marriage," Victoria answered.

"Did you want to marry him or merely agree to the arrangement?"

"As I testified, I wanted to marry the earl," Victoria said. A smile flirted with her lips when she added, "At first, I thought he was a tad elderly and quite boring."

"Then why did your aunt arrange a marriage with him?" Burrows asked.

Victoria smiled sweetly at the barrister. "I suppose my aunt wanted me to marry an old, boring gentleman."

The spectators in the gallery laughed. Even the judges smiled.

"When did you change your opinion of the earl?"

Blushing, Victoria smiled at the remembrance. "I changed my opinion of the earl the first time he kissed me."

"Why?" Burrows asked.

"The earl did *not* kiss like an old, boring gentleman," Victoria told him.

"How does an old, boring gentleman kiss?"

"Not like my husband."

The spectators in the gallery shouted with laughter. Even her husband was smiling.

"How do you know that?" Burrows countered. "How many men have you kissed?"

"Only my husband."

Nonchalantly, Burrows tossed his next question

at her, "And with how many men have you engaged in intercourse?"

"Damn him," Alexander muttered, banging his fist on the table, drawing her attention.

Victoria had no idea what was happening. She only knew that her husband was angry and the gallery had grown quiet.

"Well, Lady Emerson?"

"I can't answer that."

"Why?" Burrows asked, going in for the kill. "Have there been so many?"

"I don't know what *intercourse* means," she told him.

Howls of laughter echoed off the walls. Reporters scribbled furiously on their parchments.

"With how many men have you engaged in sexual relations?" the barrister asked. "You do understand *sexual relations?*"

"There's no need to be rude," Victoria said, drawing laughter from the gallery. "My husband is the only man with whom I have been intimate."

"Your husband?" the barrister echoed, his tone implying disbelief.

"How else could I be eight months pregnant?" Victoria countered, her tone exasperated.

Shrieks and howls of laughter erupted from every man inside the courtroom. Except Mr. Burrows. The Chief Justice was laughing so hard he couldn't bang his gavel.

Five minutes later, the only sounds in the courtroom were men gasping to catch their breath. In a nasty tone of voice, Burrows said, "You were found in another's man bed. Do you expect the court to believe this fiction?"

"I don't give a fig what this court believes," Victoria said, her voice rising with her anger. She rose from her chair and said, "I only care what my husband believes. Apparently, he believes I am the whore of Babylon and beyond redemption." Fighting back tears, Victoria stepped out of the witness box and moved awkwardly toward her barrister's table.

Burrows stepped in front of her, blocking her path. "I am not finished with you, my lady."

"*I* am finished with *you,*" Victoria told him.

"If you don't return to the witness box," Burrows warned, "this court will grant the earl's petition for a trial."

"My husband will get his trial and his divorce whether I stay or go," Victoria said, all the bitterness of the previous months evident in her voice. "Except for my relations and my barrister, there isn't a man in this courtroom who believes me."

"*I believe you.*"

Victoria whirled around and faced her husband. Alexander stood and, staring her straight in the eye, said, "I believe every word, Tory." He shifted his gaze to the judges. "My lords, I wish to withdraw my petition for a divorce trial and apologize for wasting your time."

"Young man, you have the unenviable task of opening doors that *you* slammed shut and locked," the Chief Justice said. "Next time save your anger until *after* you've given your wife the courtesy of an explanation."

"Thank you for the advice, my lord," Alexander said.

Victoria couldn't comprehend the abrupt end to the situation that had consumed her for months. She felt dizzy, five months of stress having taken its toll.

A powerful surge of relief sent her crashing to

her knees. Victoria bent her head, covered her face, and began to weep. She had won. And lost. Never again could she love her husband as unconditionally as she had. The pain he had caused was too great to set aside.

And then Alexander was kneeling beside her and drawing her into his embrace. "Tory, I'm sorry for doubting you."

"I begged you on my knees to listen to me," Victoria sobbed. "I begged you, Alex, and you turned your back on me."

What have I done? Alexander thought, holding her close as she wept. He had taken a vibrant, lively young woman, broken her spirit, and held her up to public ridicule. Good God, his wife was nineteen years old, eight months pregnant, and hurt almost beyond repair. He prayed he could make amends. Somehow.

"I'll do whatever I must to repair the damage," Alexander promised, his heart aching at what he had lost.

"I'm having your baby," Victoria said, "and you never even inquired about my health."

"Tell me what to do," Alexander said. "Whatever it is, I'll do it."

"Go away." Victoria looked at him through tear-blurred eyes. "And leave me in peace."

"Do as she says." Prince Rudolf stood beside them. The prince helped Victoria rise and then, lifting her into his arms, carried her out of the courtroom.

Alexander felt as if a dagger had pierced his heart. *A self-inflicted wound,* he thought, staring after his wife.

"Give her a day to rest," Duke Magnus said, standing beside him. "Victoria loves you and will feel differently after she has rested. Come to Park Lane tomorrow." The duke tipped his head in the direction of Alexander's relations, adding, "That will give you time to tie up some loose ends."

"Thank you, Your Grace," Alexander replied, and then headed in the direction of his loose ends.

"I'm sorry, Alex," Harry Gibbs said. "I had no idea what was happening beneath my nose."

Alexander nodded.

"This is a terrible misunderstanding," Venetia defended herself. "Diana and I—"

"Robert Campbell is correct," Alexander interrupted. "You *are* Satan's handmaiden." He looked at the widow, saying, "If I were you, Mrs. Drummond, I would return postehaste to Australia. After today, your reputation is as shredded as my wife's."

Without another word, Alexander walked out of the courtroom. He started down the corridor to the front door when someone called his name. Turning, he saw the society reporter from the *Times.*

"My lord, will you give me a statement?" the man asked.

Alexander started to turn away without speaking and then changed his mind. "My sister and her sister-in-law conspired against my countess and duped me into believing my wonderful wife was unfaithful. Lady Emerson has proved herself completely innocent. Now I add *courageous* to loving and loyal, which also describe her."

"Why courageous?" the reporter asked, without looking up from his scribbling.

"Only a woman of great courage would stand before the world to confess what she considers a serious flaw," Alexander said.

The reporter looked up from his notes and asked, "You mean, her stupidity?"

"My wife is *not* stupid," Alexander said. And then his fist connected with the reporter's jaw, sending the man sprawling to the floor.

CHAPTER 15

"Good morning, darling."

Victoria turned away from the window to see her aunt walking across her bedchamber. She had slept peacefully for the first time in five months and awakened early. After dressing in a pale pink gown, Victoria had paused to gaze out the window at a perfect spring morning—blue skies, bright sunshine, blossoming forsythia, chirping birds. So why didn't she feel perfectly happy?

"Alex will soon be here to take you home," her aunt told her.

"This is my home," Victoria replied.

"Now why did I know you would say that?" Aunt Roxie asked, taking her hand and leading her to the chaise to sit down. "Darling, listen to me. You have won. Be gracious in your victory."

"If I've won," Victoria asked, "then why do I feel as if I've lost?"

"You haven't made peace with Alexander," Aunt Roxie answered, patting her hand. "Life can never be as idyllic as we would wish. Nothing is ever black and white, but usually a shade in between."

"What are you talking about?" Victoria asked, confused.

"I am speaking about the facts of life," Aunt Roxie answered. "You are married to Alexander, whom you love, and will remain married to him until the day you die."

"If he doesn't try to divorce me again," Victoria qualified.

"After this, if you took ten men into your bed," her aunt disagreed, "Alexander would believe your denial. You have your husband where you want him. Take advantage of the opportunity."

"I begged him on my knees, but he refused to listen," Victoria said. "Alex slammed a door in my face, allowed that woman to wear my wedding gift, and set her in my chamber. I passed lonely days and nights, including Christmas, while Alex entertained himself with the widow."

"You can't know that for certain," Aunt Roxie argued. "As *you* should have learned from this experience, appearances can be deceiving."

"My reputation has been torn into shreds," Victoria went on, without really listening to her aunt. "Miriam Wilmington slandered my unborn child, and Lydia Stanley gave me the cut direct, which earned applause from someone watching. I can never show my face in society again. Worst of all, my husband's pigheadedness forced me to confess my stupidity to the world."

"What is done is past, darling," Aunt Roxie said. "Very soon, Alexander and you will share a child. Look to the future, Tory. Promise me you will listen to what Alexander says."

"Of course, I will listen to Alexander," Victoria said, rising from the chaise. "Then I'll tell him to leave."

"Alexander gave the *Times* a statement which

amounts to a public apology," Aunt Roxie told her, walking with her to the door. "He called you loving, loyal, and courageous."

Victoria smiled in surprise. "He did?"

Aunt Roxie nodded. "I left the *Times* in the dining room. Bundles is waiting to help you downstairs and will read you the words."

"Thank you, Aunt."

Her aunt smiled. "I'm glad you are the last," she said. "I'm too old for all of this excitement."

Victoria left the bedchamber. Bundles, whom she had hired, stood in the corridor and waited to escort her down the stairs to the dining room.

"Good morning, Bundles."

"Good morning, my lady." Bundles offered her his arm. "Are we feeling better this morning?"

"Much better. Thank you for asking."

"I saw an interesting article in the *Times* yesterday," Bundles told her, speaking as they walked down the third-floor corridor to the stairs. "An Irishman and a Scotsman went into a tavern to share a pint. When the tavernkeeper asked who would pay for it, the Scotsman said that he would. The next day, yesterday, the *Times* headline read: *Irish Ventriloquist Slain.*"

Victoria laughed out loud.

"May I say, my lady," Bundles remarked, "your laughter is sweeter and more welcome than springtime birdsong."

When they reached the dining room where Tinker stood in his usual position at the sideboard, Bundles escorted Victoria across the room. She chose scrambled eggs, three slices of bacon, and a hot roll with butter. Carrying her plate, Bundles escorted her to the table and helped her into a chair.

"I don't know what I would do without you,"

Victoria told him. "His Lordship must be missing your services."

"His Lordship is an arse," Bundles drawled.

Victoria smiled. "I agree. Will you bring me the *Times* and point out the compliments he gave me?"

Bundles flicked a pointed look at Tinker who said, "I'm sorry, my lady. We don't have the *Times* today."

"My aunt told me she read the earl's statement in this morning's paper," Victoria said.

"I didn't know we had the *Times,*" Tinker said to Bundles.

"Neither did I," Bundles replied. "I can't imagine where it could be."

Victoria realized something insulting had been written about her in the paper. These loyal retainers were trying to protect her.

"I see the paper at the other end of the table," Victoria said, pointing to it. "Bring it to me."

Victoria needed to know how badly the *Times* had insulted her. Steeling herself against slander, Victoria put the paper down on the table and read the headline.

Victoria recognized the words *countess* and *not,* but the other two words escaped her. "Read me this headline," she ordered.

Bundles hesitated. "I-I-I forgot my spectacles in my chamber."

Victoria raised her brows at him. "Bundles, do not use *that* lie on *me.*"

Bundles inclined his head. Then he read aloud: "*Countess Stupid, Not Guilty.*"

Victoria stared at the headline for long moments. Her bottom lip quivered as she struggled with her emotions. She almost won, too.

The thought of her baby some day being told about his mother's stupidity overwhelmed Victoria. She pushed her plate and the paper out of the way, put her head down, and wept. Her whole body shook with the force of her sobs.

"My lady," she heard Bundles say.

"You'll make yourself sick," Tinker told her.

"I don't care," she said, her voice muffled by her arms.

"I *do* care." The voice belonged to her husband.

Victoria felt his hands on her, gently drawing her out of the chair to sit on his lap. His arms around her felt strong, solid, comforting. She didn't struggle but rested her head against his chest until she had run out of tears.

"Everyone in England knows I'm stupid," Victoria said, her voice filled with anguish. She let him wipe the tears from her face.

"You are *not* stupid," Alexander told her. "Only someone exceedingly smart could have hidden such a disability from so many people for so long. Tory, please come home with me and make a new start. I swear I'll never accuse you of anything and always ask for an explanation before I become angry.

"God, I should have recognized the signs of your disability. I was too distracted by our physical relationship, my businesses, and other insignificant problems to see what was in front of my eyes. I'll hire the best tutors in England if that is what you want, but I think you are perfect the way you are."

Her husband hadn't said the word *love*, Victoria thought. At the trial, he testified that theirs was no love match. Yet, her aunt was right. What choice did she have but return to Grosvenor Square and go on with her marriage?

"Tutors can't help me," Victoria told him.

"I wanted to come and speak with you many

times during the past five months," Alexander said, holding her close. "My damned pride wouldn't let me. I want you to know I did not make love to anyone else, including Diana Drummond. That evening last week when you came to Grosvenor Square was not what it appeared. Diana had sent me a note saying that Harry and Venetia were arguing, and she needed to get away from them. She asked to dress for the opera at my house and accompany me for the evening."

"And did she?" Victoria asked.

"I sent her home after you left," Alexander answered. "Then I went to my study and drank myself into a stupor because I knew you wouldn't seek me out again."

"What about the night at the opera?" Victoria asked. "She was wearing my wedding gift."

"I overheard your brothers-in-law talking at White's and knew you would be attending the opera with Rudolf and Samantha," Alexander said. "I offered Diana the opportunity to wear the necklace but regretted it as soon as I saw you. I'm having the diamonds reset into another necklace."

"You knew I would never wear it again?"

"Your aunt suggested it," Alexander said. "I've learned that your aunt is the wisest of women."

They sat in silence for a long time. Victoria cuddled on his lap while Alexander held her close. Unexpectedly, her stomach shifted, and he looked at her in surprise.

Victoria guided his hand to her belly, asking, "Can you feel him? He's very active, especially at night when I lay in bed."

"I've missed so much these past months," Alexander said, his hand still on her belly. "I'll never forgive myself."

"Do you think he'll be smart like you or stupid like me?" Victoria asked, her expression worried.

"You are not stupid," Alexander insisted, tilting her face up to touch his lips to hers. "I only pray he has your heart and ability to love."

"We'll teach him that," she said.

"Please come home with me," Alexander said. "I and the girls need you."

"Can Bundles come home, too?"

"Why *is* Bundles here?"

"Bundles works for me," Victoria told him.

Alexander grinned. "What does he do?"

"Bundles helps me up and down the stairs," she answered. "He fetches things I need or want and acts as majordomo on Tinker's day off."

"Do you think Bundles would be interested in returning to work for me?" Alexander asked.

"I'm positive a pay increase will persuade him to accept," Victoria answered.

"You'll come home?"

Victoria nodded.

Alexander lifted her off his lap and rose from the chair. "I have something for you," he said, producing her wedding and betrothal rings. First, he slipped her diamond ring on the third finger of her right hand. Then, slipping the diamond and gold wedding band on the third finger of her left hand, he said, "With this ring I thee wed *again . . .*"

Three weeks later, Alexander sat with Duke Magnus, Robert, and Rudolf in the drawing room at Grosvenor Square. Upstairs, Victoria labored in childbirth, attended by her aunt, her sisters, and the physician.

"Why is it taking so long?" Alexander asked, his

brow creased with worry as he paced back and forth in front of the hearth. "Is this normal?"

"First babies can be slow," Duke Magnus said.

"Take a shot of vodka for your nerves," Prince Rudolf suggested.

"Lord Emerson?"

Alexander saw Dr. Smythe walking toward him. The physician did not look happy.

"My lord, I'm sorry," Dr. Smythe said. "I am losing mother and child."

Alexander stared in disbelief at the physician. "I don't under—"

"Your wife is fighting the birth," Dr. Smythe told him. "She's struggling to keep the baby from being born, and both are tiring. The child will come, but I fear too late."

"Why would Victoria fight it?" Alexander asked, panicking at the thought of losing her. "She's been anticipating the baby's arrival. Good God, she knitted twenty-three blankets."

"Lord Emerson, I think she fears losing the baby," Dr. Smythe said. "Your wife keeps mumbling about your taking her baby away from her."

"That is ridiculous," Alexander exclaimed. "Why would she think that?"

"You did intend to divorce her," Duke Magnus said.

"Do you love Victoria?" Robert asked.

"Well, of course, I love her," Alexander said, flushing. "She's my wife."

"Have you ever told her?" Prince Rudolf asked.

"A thousand times in a thousand different ways," Alexander answered.

"Unless one of those thousand was saying the words *I love you*, then you haven't told her," the prince said.

"Lord Emerson, you must go upstairs and convince your wife that you do not intend to take the baby from her," Dr. Smythe said. "If you can't do that, she and the baby may die."

Alexander bolted out of the room and took the stairs two at a time. He burst into the bedchamber, startling her aunt and her sisters, and approached the bed where his wife lay writhing in the midst of a contraction.

Leaning close to her, Alexander took her hand in his and brushed sweat-soaked wisps of fire off her forehead. She had the frightened look of a trapped, fatally injured animal.

"Tory, listen to me," Alexander said, his voice calm and gentle though his nerves were rioting crazily.

Victoria turned pain-glazed eyes on him.

"Tell her to push when the pain comes," the duchess said. "Then pant when it stops."

"Tory, please don't die and leave me alone," Alexander pleaded, his eyes brimming with tears. "I love you, Tory, and don't want to live without you."

"You love me?" Victoria echoed, her grasp on his hand tightening.

Alexander nodded. He didn't bother to wipe the tears streaming down his face.

"Why are you weeping?" she whispered.

"I'm afraid I'm going to lose you," Alexander told her. "Please, love, push when the contraction comes. I'll stay with you the whole time."

"I hurt, Alex."

"I know you do," he said, "but if you push when you feel the contraction, the pain will soon be over. If you love me, Tory, you'll push with the contraction."

"I hurt," she said, her voice mirroring her panic. Her hand tightened on his painfully.

"Tell her to push," Dr. Smythe said.

"Push, Tory," Alexander whispered against her ear. "Push, now."

Victoria cried out as she bore down. Alexander could see her whole body trembling with the strain.

"Tell her to stop."

"Pant, Tory," Alexander said against her ear. "Catch your breath."

"Again," the physician told him.

"Push, Tory," Alexander ordered. "Help our baby be born."

Victoria pushed, and the baby slipped from her body. Hearing the wail of a baby, she lay her head back against the pillow, and the physician set the squalling infant on her belly.

"We have a son," Alexander told her. "A big, strong boy. We did it."

"*I* did it," she said, her fatigue evident in her voice.

"Yes, you did." Alexander dropped a kiss on her brow. "I love you, Tory."

Victoria crooked her finger at him, beckoning him closer. Then she asked, "Does he look smart?"

"Victor Douglas Emerson looks like a genius," he answered.

"You want to name him after me?"

"I want to name him in honor of the woman I love . . ."

The next afternoon, Victoria sat in bed and leaned against the headboard. She held her sleeping son in her arms.

The door swung open, admitting her husband. Behind him walked Darcy, Fiona, and Aidan who stood beside the bed to catch their first glimpse of the baby.

"Do you like your brother?" Victoria asked.

"Those fairies and pixies know what they're doing," Darcy said.

"Why is Victor so small?" Fiona asked.

"And wrinkled," Aidan whispered.

"Victor will grow and his wrinkles will smooth," Victoria told them.

"All babies look like this," Alexander added, sitting on the edge of the bed.

"I never looked like that," Darcy said.

"Neither did I," Fiona said.

"Not me, either," Aidan agreed.

"Show Mama Tory what we've been doing all morning," Alexander said.

Darcy, Fiona, and Aidan lifted their left feet into the air. Marked on the bottom of their shoes was an *L*.

Victoria laughed.

Alexander removed his left shoe and held it up. An *L* marked the bottom of his shoe, too. "Every left shoe we own bears an *L*," he told his wife.

"We certainly have a very *L* family," Victoria said, unshed tears glistening in her eyes.

"Household," Alexander corrected her. "All the servants have marked their shoes with an *L*, too."

"Mama Tory and Victor need to rest," Alexander told his daughters. "Your nannies are waiting to take you downstairs for cider."

Each little girl kissed Victoria and then they left the room.

"I found this in an old trunk this morning when the girls persuaded me to help them look for dress-up clothes," Alexander said, producing an old, worn journal. "It belonged to my mother."

"Does it mention your natural father?" Victoria asked.

Alexander smiled and nodded. "My natural father is Prince Adolphus."

"You're the king's grandson?" Victoria exclaimed in surprise.

"Illegitimate and unacknowledged," Alexander qualified.

"What will you do about it?" she asked.

"Nothing, I am satisfied merely to know where I came from," Alexander said. "I'll pass this journal to Victor and our descendents."

"Aunt Roxie's vision was correct," Victoria said. "She told me I would marry an earl and a prince but not necessarily two different men."

"I told you Roxie is a wise woman," Alexander said, moving to sit beside her. He leaned back against the headboard and put his arm around her. "Now if Roxie could only predict something practical like the price of corn next year."

Victoria smiled at that. "I hope you don't inherit your royal grandfather's mental condition," she teased him. "I wouldn't wish to see you conversing with the elms in Hyde Park."

"You are incorrigible," Alexander said, and then turned her face toward him. "Have I said the words today?"

Victoria shook her head.

"I love you, Victoria Emerson."

"And I love you, Alexander Emerson."

"I love you more," he said, lowering his head to claim her lips in a lingering kiss.

It melted into another. And then another.

Until, Victor Douglas Emerson screeched for his mother.

Victoria bared her breasts and touched her nipple to her son's mouth. The infant quieted instantly.

"Victor is a lucky man," Alexander said, watching his son suckle. *"And so am I, my love."*

Bestselling author Patricia Grasso weaves intrigue, passion, and unforgettable romance into a captivating tale that proves when you follow your heart, anything is possible . . .

An illegitimate daughter of the Russian Czar, Amber Kazanov knows time is running out. Her stunning beauty has made her prey to nefarious schemers, and she flees to England to find a husband before her uncle can sell her to the highest bidder. Here she is introduced to the one gentleman who might help her. But Miles Montgomery is a man laid low by life's cruelty, a man who has given up on love and happiness. Fortunately, Amber has not given up on him . . .

Shrouded in darkness and tragedy, Miles Montgomery, the Earl of Stratford, bears the emotional and physical scars of the fire that killed his wife and shattered his world. Despite himself, he is intrigued by this exquisite beauty, and he asks her to remain as his houseguest. Yet he fights the attraction he feels, masking his deep longing behind harsh words and cold indifference . . . until a glorious night of passion seals his fate. And when a shocking turn of events threatens to steal Amber from him forever, he must choose either to dwell in the past or to embrace the future—before it's too late.

Look for *To Love a Princess* coming in November 2004!

Please turn the page for an exciting sneak peek of **To Love a Princess!**

CHAPTER 1

Stratford-upon-Avon, 1820

He hated days like this.

Trees colored themselves green, flowers bloomed in the sun's warmth, chirping birds flew across a cloudless sky.

The world was too damn happy.

Miles Montgomery, the fifteenth Earl of Stratford, turned away from the nauseatingly cheerful sight outside his study window. He shifted his gaze to the portrait over the hearth. Sweet Brenna, gone in the flash of a midnight fire.

Out of habit, Miles reached to close the drapes and shroud his study in comforting darkness. He stopped himself, though, remembering his guests. John Saint-Germain, the Duke of Avon and his brother-in-law, and Prince Rudolf Kazanov had several business ventures in the offing and wanted to include him.

Business ventures. Miles twisted his chiseled lips into the ghost of a smile. Since the fire, business ventures had filled his empty existence.

Miles touched the mask that covered the left side of his face. His love, his face, his life had died on that fateful night of the fire. Now he needed to wait for his heart to stop beating.

"My lord, His Grace and His Highness have arrived," the majordomo announced.

Miles touched his mask again. "Send them in, Pebbles."

"Come on inside," Pebbles called, his hands cupping his mouth.

Both the prince and the duke grinned at the majordomo as he passed them on the way out. Pebbles inclined his head as if he was aristocrat and they were the servants.

Miles met the two men in the middle of the room. With a smile of greeting, he shook the prince's hand first and then the duke's. Both men were as tall as he, a couple of inches over six feet.

Located on the second floor in the west wing of the manor, the earl's study sat at one end of the Long Library. Floor to ceiling windows bathed the room in afternoon sunlight when the draperies were open, as they were now. Thousands of volumes filled the bookcases, and a thick red Persian carpet covered the floor. Over the main fireplace mantel hung an enormous portrait of a woman.

"Brenna, my wife," Miles supplied, seeing where the prince's gaze had drifted.

"She was a beautiful woman," Prince Rudolf said.

"Shall we get down to business?" Miles gestured across the chamber. He sat behind his desk while the other two men took the chairs opposite him.

"Caroline misses you," John said.

"Tell Caroline I will visit her soon," Miles replied.

"I'm surprised to see the drapes open," his brother-in-law continued. "Normally, you sit in the dark. I was beginning to wonder if you were a vampire."

"I opened the drapes for you," Miles told him. "Normally, you comment on my sitting in the dark."

Prince Rudolf chuckled, drawing their attention. "You bicker like my brothers and me."

"We aren't bickering, Your Highness," Miles said. "His Grace prefers to mind *my* business instead of his own." Though he spoke with the hint of a smile, his tone held a hard edge.

"You need a wife," the duke said, undeterred by his brother-in-law's sarcasm. "If you die without an heir, Terrence the Weasel will inherit."

Miles wished he could be in his family's company without listening to their comments regarding his life. Why should he care if his cousin inherited his title?

"I finished with the wife business when Brenna died," Miles said, his weariness with the topic apparent. He glanced at the prince. "Do you see the nagging my sister and brother-in-law inflict upon me?"

"The nagging will cease if you remarry," Prince Rudolf said.

"No woman can ever replace Brenna." Miles touched the masked side of his face. "Besides, what woman would consider marrying a scarred beast?"

"Vanessa Stanton lost her husband," the duke told him. "She asked about you the last time I saw her."

Miles shrugged with indifference. "Vanessa enjoyed her pleasures when I had a whole face. I prefer living alone to wearing horns."

"What would you do if a virtuous woman did want to marry you?" Prince Rudolf asked.

"I would marry and plant a dozen sons inside her," Miles answered, hoping to drop the topic.

"Consecutively, I hope," John quipped, making the other two smile. "Come to London and look over the latest crop of hopefuls."

"I retired from society four years ago," Miles refused. "If you've seen one debutante, you've seen them all."

"Damn it, Miles," John snapped. "Brenna is dead but you still live. Do you think she would want you to live in shadows?"

Miles said nothing, and an uncomfortable silence descended on the three men. Why, in God's name, did John and Isabelle need to solve his problems? Why couldn't they leave him alone in his misery?

"I couldn't reach her in time and lost half my face for nothing," Miles told the prince.

"I am sorry for your loss," Rudolf said. "I cannot imagine the horror of losing the woman you love."

Miles inclined his head, accepting the prince's condolences.

"John is correct, though," the prince added. "You need to return to the living."

"Are you going to nag me, too?"

Prince Rudolf held his hands up in a gesture that he would say no more.

"I told you how pigheaded he is," John said. Before Miles could reply, he added, "Shall we get down to business?"

Miles lifted his gaze to his wife's portrait. He knew they were correct about living while he could, but his wife was gone. And the woman who equaled her had not been born . . .

Moscow

"Princess Amber, we will make beautiful babies together."

Amber laughed, a melodious sound that complimented her sweet expression. Looking at her companion, she became almost mesmerized by his piercing gray eyes. With his handsome features and midnight black hair, Count Sergei Pushkin stepped out of every maiden's dream. His heart belonged to her. For the moment.

"Sergei, you should not voice such thoughts," Amber scolded him, her expression flirtatious. "I do not think your mother would appreciate the sentiment."

"What about you, Amber?" Sergei asked, fingering a lock of her silver-blonde hair. "Would you appreciate my planting a child inside your body?"

Her alabaster complexion deepened into an embarrassed scarlet. "I refuse to continue this improper conversation. Tell your driver to take me home. Uncle Fedor will be annoyed if I am late."

Sergei lifted her chin and waited until she raised her disarming violet gaze to his. "Amber, I promise we will make babies together. I love you."

"I am fond of you, too, but look for another woman to be your wife," Amber said, her practical nature rising to the fore. She harbored no silly illusions about a future with the man beside her. "Your mother will never approve a union between us."

"My mother *will* approve," Sergei said. "You are the czar's daughter."

"I am the czar's unacknowledged bastard," Amber corrected him, her voice mirroring her weariness with the same old argument. Why did he refuse to understand? They had discussed this several dozen times.

"The czar sends you a gift each year, which is unofficial acknowledgement."

"I would appreciate the gift of a public acknowledgement."

Nobody understood how difficult life was for those born on the wrong side of the blanket. She supposed that particular heartache had brought Cousin Rudolf and her closer. Though a dozen years separated them, they had always been two of a kind. Only Rudolf understood her suffering.

Amber stared into space, her small white teeth worrying her bottom lip. Recently, Uncle Fedor had been making comments about her being a grown woman of twenty, an age to begin a loving relationship with a gentleman.

The important word was *loving*. Amber feared her uncle would force her into an illicit relationship with the wealthiest aristocrat who offered to take her. She didn't want to be a mistress. She wanted to be a wife and mother.

"Where have you gone, my princess?" Sergei teased her.

Amber focused on him. Too bad she'd been born a bastard. She would have enjoyed being Sergei's wife.

"I have returned to you," she said, forcing herself to smile.

Sergei drew her close before she could escape. "One kiss, my love."

Amber turned her face away and pressed the palm of her hands against his chest. "My kisses belong only to the man I marry."

"Surely, one kiss cannot hurt," Sergei coaxed.

"One kiss led to my being born a bastard," she

refused. "I will not be painted with the same brush as my mother."

"Very well, Princess." Sergei called instructions to his driver, who turned the coach around and headed in the opposite direction.

Reaching her uncle's home, Amber peeked into the deserted foyer. She paused to remove her shoes and, on silent feet, dashed up the stairs.

"I wish to discuss the princess . . ."

Amber heard her name spoken as she neared the second floor office, her uncle having neglected to close the door tightly. She didn't recognize the voice. The gentleman sounded older, sophisticated, cultured. Had someone decided to offer for her?

Curiosity getting the better of her, Amber leaned against the wall and listened to their conversation. The longer she listened, the faster her heart pounded, the sharper her panic grew.

"Do you wish to court my ward's affections, Count Gromeko?" Uncle Fedor was saying.

Count Gromeko? Amber had heard his name whispered somewhere.

"With her platinum blonde hair and violet eyes, Princess Amber is unusually beautiful," Gromeko said, ignoring her uncle's question. "Unfortunately, the princess is a bastard and unacceptable to the best families."

"My niece will marry a younger son or make a first-born's devoted mistress," Fedor replied.

"God forbid she should be wasted like that," Gromeko said. "Her beauty can bring us immense wealth."

His statement confused Amber. She had no money, no dowry. All had been spent on her living expenses since she'd come as a child to her uncle's home. How could she possibly bring them wealth?

"As you know, I deal in high quality slaves," Count Gromeko was saying. "The moment I saw the princess, I knew I must have her. Not for my pleasure, of course.

"I own a slave with the identical coloring. If the princess and he mate, their children will certainly be born with the same coloring, which commands the highest prices in the Ottoman markets. God willing, she could produce a child each year for the next fifteen or twenty years."

Shocked and revolted and frightened, Amber struggled against a swoon. Her knees warbled and her hands shook like she had the palsy.

Her uncle remained silent. He could not actually be considering the devil's offer.

"Princess Amber will live in relative luxury as befitting her station," Gromeko continued. "The princess is too rare a flower to be abused or neglected. I guarantee that, once breached, she will enjoy my stud. His member is large, his seed is potent, and he has sired a dozen babies in the past two years. He will, however, service the princess exclusively until she gets with child."

"I don't feel—"

"I will give you fifty thousand rubles for the girl and ten percent profit on each of the babies sold."

"Do you wish to take her tonight?" Fedor asked.

Amber couldn't believe it. Her uncle was selling her into sexual slavery, a brood mare for profit.

"Do or say nothing to alarm her. Frightened women do not easily conceive," Gromeko warned her uncle. "My business keeps me in Moscow another month. In a day or two or three, tell the princess you have had an offer for her hand in marriage. Then I will join you and your niece for dinner and charm her into feeling comfortable with me. As the month draws to a close, we will tell her that I am escorting her to her betrothed. I need the princess calm and content."

"When can I expect—"

"You will sign a bill of sale giving me the princess," Gromeko told him. "I will give you twenty-five thousand rubles and pay the remainder on the day I take her away."

"About that ten percent profit . . ."

Amber sneaked up the stairs to her bedchamber. With tears streaming down her face, she leaned back against the door for support. Her heart pounded, her legs trembled, her hands shook.

She needed to leave Russia.

Through sheer force of will, Amber wiped the tears from her cheeks. Her uncle was not easily duped. She must remain calm or all would be lost.

Should she ask Sergei for help? He had no legal authority to thwart her uncle. Besides, his mother would see this as a way to get rid of her permanently.

Perhaps she should appeal to the czar. No, she would never gain an audience. Her uncle would tell the czar she was a stubborn chit who was refusing a perfectly acceptable marriage offer. His lie would be more believable than her truth.

Cousin Rudolf would protect her. She needed enough money to get to England and a good disguise.

A black dress and widow's veil would allow her freedom of movement. No one would recognize her, and strangers would assume she was older than twenty.

A sob escaped her, and an involuntary shudder shook her body. Amber forced herself to take several calming breaths. There would be time enough to break down when she reached England. If she broke down now, Fedor and Gromeko would win.

London, Six Weeks Later

Amber looked at the brick town mansion and then glanced at the address on her cousin's last letter. She had finally arrived at Montague House, her cousin's English inheritance.

Lifting her valise, Amber climbed the front stairs. The door opened before she reached for the knocker, and the majordomo looked down his nose at her travel-bedraggled appearance.

"May I help you?"

"I must speak with Rudolf Kazanov," Amber answered. "Is the prince in residence?"

"Are you seeking employment?"

"No." Amber tried to move past the man, but he blocked her way.

"State your business with His Highness."

This last obstacle to safety brought tears to her eyes. With a strength fueled by desperation, Amber shoved the man out of the way and darted past him into the foyer.

"You are trespassing on private property," the majordomo warned her. "I will call the authorities if you do not leave immediately."

"Please announce Princess Amber," she said, ignoring his threat.

"Princess?" His tone implied disbelief.

Amber yanked the black widow's headdress off, her silver-blonde mane cascading down her back, and prepared to defend herself against the man. She had traveled too far to be turned away.

"Rudolf," Amber shouted, nearing hysteria.

"You are disturbing the peace of this household." The majordomo caught her arm and dragged her toward the door.

"Rudolf!"

Behind the struggling duo, someone cursed loudly in Russian and then switched to English. "Bottoms, what is happening?"

"Tell your man to release me."

"Cousin Amber?"

Bottoms dropped her arm as if she'd scorched him. Amber dashed across the foyer, threw herself into her cousin's arms, and wept uncontrollably. All the humiliation and fright poured from her in a flood of tears.

"Bottoms, prepare a bedchamber with a hot bath," Prince Rudolf instructed the majordomo. "Then serve my cousin a hot meal in my study."

The majordomo hurried away.

"Protect me from Fedor," Amber sobbed. "Please."

Prince Rudolf held her close. "Is Fedor with you?"

Amber shook her head. "I have run away."

"You traveled across Europe alone?"

"I dressed like a widow so no one would bother me," she said. "Fedor will come after me. You must hide me."

"I will protect you," Rudolf promised, guiding her across the foyer.

With his arm around her, Rudolf helped her up the stairs to his second floor office. He led her to the settee near the hearth and then poured a shot of vodka.

"Drink this," he ordered. "You will feel better."

Amber gulped the vodka, shuddered as it burned a path to her stomach, and then set the glass down. "I need a husband. Can you find me one?"

"Start at the beginning and leave nothing out," Rudolf said, putting his arm around her. "Then we will speak about husbands."

"I overheard a conversation between Fedor and Gromeko," she began.

"Count Gromeko?"

"Do you know the count?"

"I have heard of him."

"Gromeko persuaded Fedor to sell me to him," Amber said, her eyes blurring with tears, her complexion scarlet with embarrassment. "The count owns a slave with my coloring. He proposed to mate me like a brood mare with this slave and sell my babies."

"Sweet Jesus, I regret not taking you with me when I left," Rudolf said, his grip on her tightening. "You are safe now. My brothers will also protect you. Wait until I tell them—"

"Do not tell anyone," she cried. "I am too ashamed."

"The shame does not belong to you," Rudolf said, "but we will keep this our secret for the present."

"I will not feel safe until I am married and pregnant," Amber told him. "Can you find me a husband?"

Rudolf gave her an indulgent smile, as if she was still the little girl he pampered. "When you recover from your journey, my wife and I will take you into society, where you will find your own husband."

"I need a husband now," she insisted. "Fedor and Gromeko will come after me."

"I do know an earl who needs a wife," Rudolf

said, "but the gentleman's face was badly scarred in a fire."

Amber lifted her chin and looked him straight in the eye. "Scars do not frighten me. I will marry this earl if he will take me."

ABOUT THE AUTHOR

Patricia Grasso lives in Massachusetts. She is the author of eleven historical romances and is currently working on her twelfth, which will be published by Zebra Books in November 2004. Pat loves hearing from readers and you may write to her c/o Zebra Books. Please include a self-addressed stamped envelope if you wish a response. Readers can visit her website at www.patriciagrasso.com

BOOK YOUR PLACE ON OUR WEBSITE AND MAKE THE READING CONNECTION!

We've created a customized website just for our very special readers, where you can get the inside scoop on everything that's going on with Zebra, Pinnacle and Kensington books.

When you come online, you'll have the exciting opportunity to:

- View covers of upcoming books

- Read sample chapters

- Learn about our future publishing schedule (listed by publication month *and author*)

- Find out when your favorite authors will be visiting a city near you

- Search for and order backlist books from our online catalog

- Check out author bios and background information

- Send e-mail to your favorite authors

- Meet the Kensington staff online

- Join us in weekly chats with authors, readers and other guests

- Get writing guidelines

- AND MUCH MORE!

Visit our website at
http://www.kensingtonbooks.com

More Regency Romance
From Zebra